*For Peter – whose encouragement and belief in me has
never wavered, even when I dared to dream.*

DINEY COSTELOE

The
Girl who Dared to Dream

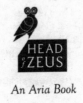

An Aria Book

First published in the UK in 2022 by Head of Zeus
This paperback edition first published in 2023 by Head of Zeus,
part of Bloomsbury Publishing Plc

9 7 5 3 1 2 4 6 8

A CIP catalogue record for this book is available from the British Library.

ISBN (PB): 9781801109826
ISBN (E): 9781801109789

Typeset by Divaddict Publishing Solutions Ltd

Printed and bound in Great Britain
by CPI Group (UK) Ltd, Croydon CR0 4YY

Head of Zeus
First Floor East
5–8 Hardwick Street
London EC1R 4RG

WWW.HEADOFZEUS.COM

1

'Mabel Oakley! Stay behind! I wish to speak to you.'
Miss Chapman, headmistress of Walton Street Elementary School, stood at the playground door, watching as the children streamed out into the yard, their voices loud as they were released at the end of afternoon school.

Mabel waited as directed, a shiver of excitement running through her. If Miss Chapman wanted to speak to her, it must mean she had received the letter from Dada.

Mabel's best friend Annie, worried for her, asked, 'D'you know why she wants you, Mabel? Are you in trouble? Shall I wait for you?'

'No,' Mabel replied, giving her friend a little push. 'You go on home. I'm not in trouble, I promise you, and I'll tell you all about it tomorrow.'

Mabel hoped she was right about the letter, but she wasn't prepared to explain, even to Annie, just in case she was wrong.

As she waited for the last of the pupils to leave the schoolyard, Mabel wondered what Dada had actually written. Had he asked if she could stay on for one more year, as she had begged him? It was what Mabel wanted above all things, but when she'd told him she wanted to stay at school after she turned sixteen, he'd been extremely sceptical.

'Why on earth would you want to do that?' he asked. 'Haven't you had enough of schooling? Don't you want to go to work and earn your own living?' He didn't mention the fact that they could do with another income coming into the household, but it was certainly on his mind. The premium for Eddie's carpenter's apprenticeship had to be found, and then there would be Stephen to consider. 'You'll be a grown-up!'

Mabel shook her head. 'No, Dada, really. I want to stay on, perhaps take some exams and go to secretarial school. I want to be a secretary like Miss Harper!'

'Like Miss Harper?' Her father sounded horrified. Hermione Harper, secretary to the senior partner at Sheridan, Sheridan and Morrell where he was a clerk, was the terror of the typing pool, and indeed, he thought wryly, of the whole office.

'She's the last person you want to be like,' he retorted. 'She's a dried up old stick of a woman, who enjoys bossing everyone around.'

'I might be quite good at bossing everyone around,' replied Mabel with a grin.

'Maybe,' her father answered darkly, 'but she's the last person I want you to be like. She hasn't an ounce of generosity in her.'

'All right then,' Mabel conceded, 'I won't be like her, not like that. But I do want to learn typewriting and work in an office, like you do. I don't want to go into service like Lizzie!'

'Your cousin has a good position and is doing very well,' pointed out her father. 'She's already a parlourmaid, and if she works hard she may move up through the household. You could do the same. You're a clever girl, you'd soon learn their ways and you'd have a job for life, in one household or another.'

'But I don't *want* that sort of job for life,' cried Mabel. 'I'd hate it. I do want to work for my living, Dada, but not cleaning someone else's house like poor Lizzie has to, just because they're too lazy to do it themselves.'

'Well,' her father had replied, 'I don't think Lizzie thinks of herself as "poor Lizzie" and that's not an attitude I should make known, if I was you. Remember, people who can afford to employ servants provide jobs and livings for hundreds of folk, who wouldn't otherwise have any work.' He looked his daughter firmly in the eye. 'Seriously, Mabel. Too many people rely on the monied classes for their livelihood. You won't make yourself popular with anyone if you start spouting remarks like that. I would hate to hear a daughter of mine openly expressing such ideas.'

'No, all right, Dada. I was only saying it to you.'

'So you were,' agreed her father. 'And that's the way it must stay.'

'So, can I stay on for another year?'

'I'll discuss it with your mother, and if she agrees, well maybe I'll write to your teacher and see what she says. All right?'

'All right.' Mabel knew it was the best she could do. She, too, was well aware it would mean that she wouldn't be adding to the family income for another year, but if she learned to type and even perhaps to take down shorthand, she could get a job in an office like where Dada worked and she would then contribute far more to the family income than if she were a live-in servant in some mansion. She would work office hours, not be at someone's beck and call all day, every day; her time outside the hours in the office would be her own. Dear Dada – she was the only person who called him that, her special name for him – dear Dada, surely he would say she could stay on. Wouldn't he?

Now, this afternoon, Miss Chapman wanted to speak to her after school, so she must have received Dada's letter.

'Come back into the classroom, Mabel,' Miss Chapman said, once the schoolyard was empty. 'Come and sit down. We should talk properly.' A chair had been set ready in front of Miss Chapman's desk, and Mabel did as she was told.

For a long moment, the teacher looked consideringly at the girl sitting in front of her. Mabel Oakley was one of the most intelligent of her pupils. Always well turned out, with her fair hair neatly plaited and her clothes clean and pressed, it was clear she came from a well-ordered home, where pride was taken in her appearance. Mabel had an inquisitive mind, and enjoyed learning for its own sake, not something Miss Chapman could say about most of her pupils, and when she had received the letter from the girl's father, suggesting she might stay at school for one more year, Miss Chapman had been delighted. But she knew she had to tread carefully in her response. It would be no good giving Mabel ideas above her station. Mr Oakley had said Mabel wanted to learn to type and work as a secretary.

Well, thought Miss Chapman, typing would only fit her for a typing pool, not to be a secretary. Miss Chapman thought Mabel would be far better off to train as a teacher and pass on her love of learning to the next generation. But whatever lay in the girl's future, the first thing was to convince her parents that it would be a waste of her potential to keep her in elementary school for only one more year, when she might be one of the lucky few who progressed to secondary education. Did it depend, she wondered, on the answers she gave the father? Was it purely a matter of whether they thought the extra year was worth it for a girl, or would the problem be a financial one? Simply, could the family afford to keep Mabel at school? One never knew. Pride would never allow such parents to admit they couldn't afford to be without the extra wage, and so they would give some other reason for her to leave as soon as she could.

'Now then, Mabel,' she began, 'I've received a letter from your father. Do you know anything about that?'

'Yes, Miss Chapman,' Mabel replied. 'I want to stay at school, so I can get an office job when I leave.'

'So, that was your idea, was it?'

'Yes, Miss Chapman. I don't want to go into service like my cousin Lizzie.'

'I see. And why's that?'

'I want a job where I can use my brain. I don't want to go into service and spend the day running around at someone else's bidding. I want a job with set hours, like a secretary, so that it isn't my whole life.'

'Or like a teacher?' suggested Miss Chapman mildly, and almost laughed aloud at the scandalised expression on Mabel's face.

'Oh no, Miss Chapman,' and then she felt the colour flooding her cheeks. 'Sorry, Miss Chapman... I didn't mean...'

Her words tailed away as Miss Chapman gave her a wry smile and said, 'Never mind, Mabel, maybe not teaching. But I do think it would be a waste for you not to continue your education, and what you do at the end of it, well, that's a decision for then, not now.' She smiled across at the embarrassed girl. 'Don't worry, teaching wouldn't suit everyone, but I will write back to your father and suggest you stay on for at least another year and see where we go from there. What do you think?'

Mabel was so surprised to be asked for her own thoughts that for a moment she said nothing, but then her face broke into a smile and she said, 'Oh, please write that to him. I'm sure he'll let me stay on. I know my mam wants me to.'

'You realise you'll have to work extremely hard if you want to pass the exams to be a secretary? You wouldn't be able to stay here, we'd have to get you into the new secondary school in Farringdon.'

Secondary school! Mabel had never considered that possibility, and she stared at Miss Chapman in amazement.

'Secondary school!' she breathed.

'As I said, it will take hard work. There's an entrance examination you'd have to take in June, but I'm sure you could pass that easily enough if you applied yourself. What do you think? Are you prepared for that?' Miss Chapman raised an interrogatory eyebrow.

'Oh yes!' Mabel was thrilled with the idea. 'Oh yes, I don't mind how hard I'd have to work.'

'All right, I'll write to your father, and we'll see what he says,' said Miss Chapman. 'But in the meantime I suggest we keep this between us.'

When Mabel left the schoolyard, she was walking on air.

She and Mam would get round Dada. She was going to be allowed to continue at school, maybe even secondary school, and whatever she did at the end of that extra year, she was not going to go into service.

As she walked along the road on her way home, she passed the station and, on impulse, she turned down the alley that ran to the covered bridge across the railway tracks. Just before the bridge, with its back against the wall of the station yard, was a tiny building with a small painted sign over the door: *Thomas Clarke, Printer*. Even before she reached it Mabel could hear the regular thump of the printing press and knew Mr Clarke was hard at work. It was a cold day, but the door had been left ajar for some fresh air, and Mabel, peeping through, saw him standing at his press, rhythmically feeding it with paper.

Without missing a beat, Mr Clarke smiled and called out, 'Mabel, my dear, come in. I've nearly finished this.'

Mabel had met Mr Clarke several months ago, when running an errand for her mother to her father's sister, Susan, who lived across the old railway bridge. Mabel had gone happily enough, carrying the bag of shoes she and her brothers had all outgrown.

'Just take these to Auntie Susan,' Mam had said. 'Tell her you're all too big for them now, but there's plenty of wear in them and they should serve a turn for Milly and David.'

As Mabel had been passing the little print shed, a man had emerged from the covered bridge and lurched towards her, his trousers adrift and his member sticking out.

'Hello, little girl,' he slurred. 'Would you like to stroke piggy?'

For a moment she stopped dead, staring at him

7

uncomprehending, and then, as he reached to take her hand, she gave an agonised shriek, and backed away.

At the sound of her scream, the man dropped his hand and shuffled back onto the bridge, but her cry had been heard by Mr Clarke. He hurried out to see the man lurching away, trying to button his trousers, and Mabel cowering with her back to his own door.

'My dear child,' he cried. 'He's gone! You're safe now. Come, come into my shop and sit down for a minute. What a fright he must have given you!'

Mabel allowed herself to be led into the tiny shop. Inside, the single, free-standing printing press took up half the space. The rest of the room was furnished with a small upright desk, an old armchair, an electric lamp, a gas ring on a shelf and a tiny sink with a cold water tap. Shelves ran round three of the walls stacked with small cardboard boxes, and behind the door was a small chest of drawers. It all looked very businesslike and Mabel, pausing on the threshold, liked it at once.

'Come in, come in and sit you down,' said Mr Clarke. 'You've had a fright. Why don't I make us a nice cup of tea? I've got some biscuits, too.'

When he had made the tea in a small brown pot, he handed her a mug. 'There you are, my dear, you drink that and you'll soon feel better.' He smiled across at her. He was a small man, with untidy black hair shot through with grey, and horn-rimmed glasses so large they seemed to cover the top half of his face, but she could see that when he smiled, his eyes crinkled at the corners.

'Now then, my dear, I'm Mr Clarke. Who are you?'

'Mabel Oakley.'

'Well, Mabel Oakley, what brings you to this footpath?' He looked at the carrier bag she still clutched in her hand. 'Are all your belongings safe?'

'Yes, thank you, Mr Clarke. I'm taking some shoes to my Auntie Susan for my cousins. Me and my brothers have grown out of them, but they've got smaller feet.' Mabel sipped the tea, full of sugar for the shock, and then she noticed he wasn't having a cup. 'Don't you like tea?' she asked.

'Yes, I do,' said Mr Clarke with a smile, 'but I've only got one mug!'

'Oh no!' cried Mabel in dismay. 'I'm sorry.'

'Don't be,' replied Mr Clarke. 'I had one just a while ago. Now then, when you've finished, I'll walk to your auntie's house with you and then you won't be bothered by anyone else along the way.'

As good as his word, when Mabel had finished her tea, Mr Clarke walked her across the bridge and down the street to Auntie Susan's house. When they reached the front door, he held out his hand.

'It's been a pleasure to meet you, Mabel Oakley. I don't think you'll be troubled by that man again.' I'll be making certain you aren't, he thought, but didn't say. He'd have a word with PC Darke, the beat copper. 'Do come to call on me again. I'm always in my shop and I don't get many visitors.'

'Yes, I will,' promised Mabel, as she took his hand. 'I want to see how you do printing on your machine.'

Mr Clarke smiled. 'I'll look forward to that, Miss Oakley.'

'Who was that with you, Mabel?' asked her aunt, as she opened the door.

'That's Mr Clarke, the printer,' Mabel replied, but she didn't tell Auntie Susan about the other man on the bridge.

When she had delivered the shoes with Mam's message, she set off back home again, but when she reached the printer's shop, it was closed up with blinds at the window and the large padlock on the door.

'But I will come and see you again,' she promised, under her breath.

She'd gone back several days later, taking with her an old mug from the kitchen at home. He was delighted to see her and tickled pink that she'd thought to bring her own mug.

'I'll leave it here, if that's all right,' she said before she left. 'Then we can always have tea.'

It had been the beginning of a strange but firm friendship. Mabel didn't tell them at home about Mr Clarke. She didn't quite know why. Was she afraid they wouldn't approve and forbid her to go and see him again? Or was it that this was a tiny, but entirely private part of her life? She was never quite sure, but she and Mr Clarke were comfortable in each other's company and gradually, over the weeks, had come to know a little about each other.

Mr Clarke had remembered she wanted to see him work at the press, and one day, a few weeks later, he said, 'Do you want to have a go?' And when she nodded excitedly, he began to show her how to work the treadle with her foot while he fed paper into the machine.

Today Mabel had rushed to tell him she was going to be able to stay at school for another year. While he put the final sheets of paper through the press, she sat on the chair and watched. As soon as he'd finished, Mr Clarke wiped his hands on a piece of rag and reached for the kettle.

'You're looking excited,' he said as he lit the gas ring. 'What's up?'

So Mabel told him, explaining how this single fact was going to shape her future.

'So, you see,' she finished, 'if I can pass the exam, I can go to secondary school in the autumn. Miss Chapman thinks I could pass, if I work hard. Secondary school! And after that I could go to typing college, and then I can get a job in an office.'

'I see you've got it all worked out,' Mr Clarke said admiringly. 'They teach typing and that at night school, you know, so maybe you could learn the typing there, in the evenings.'

Mabel had never thought of night school and she asked was he sure they taught typing there? He said he was almost certain they did, and they discussed this new idea as they drank their tea.

'Something to find out about, anyway, just in case your father says no to more school, eh?'

'Yes, if he does, but I'm sure he won't.' She sighed as she finished her tea. 'I'd better go,' she said reluctantly, 'or Mam'll be wondering where I am.'

'Well, I'm delighted you've got the chance of another year's schooling,' Mr Clarke said, as he took her mug from her. 'Education's never wasted, whatever you decide to do with it.'

'Most people think it's wasted on a girl. They say all she'll do is fill in time and then get married, so she doesn't need to know things, like a man does.'

'Don't you believe it, my dear,' said Mr Clarke. 'Behind every great man there's a clever woman. There'll come a time, I reckon, when women will be as important as men in this world. Not in my lifetime, probably, but quite possibly in yours. Just needs a few girls like you to make a stand and you'll be surprised. Now you'd better cut along home and tell them what the teacher said.'

2

'**M**r Oakley.'

Andrew Oakley looked up from the document he was reading and found Miss Harper, the senior partner's secretary, standing at the door to the tiny office he shared with Arthur Bevis, a new and junior clerk.

He got to his feet at once, saying 'Yes, Miss Harper?'

'Mr Sheridan would like to see you in his office… immediately.' Miss Harper, an angular woman in her early fifties, was dressed in her usual grey suit and white blouse, her hair scraped back into a bun at the nape of her neck. She worked for the senior partner, Mr Sheridan, just as she had for his father before him, and she ran the office with a rod of iron. Now she looked across at Andrew Oakley, her expression bleak. It did not bode well for the interview.

'Immediately, Mr Oakley,' she repeated, although he was already on his way.

John Sheridan answered the knock on his door with a sharp, 'Come!'

Andrew entered the room, where Mr Sheridan was seated behind his desk, reading through a document. The solicitor did not look up straight away, but signed the document at the bottom before he laid down his pen and gave his attention to his clerk.

'Well, Oakley,' he said, coming straight to the point. 'Am I right in thinking that it was you who dealt with the matter of Mr Peter Everette's business?'

'Yes, sir,' agreed Andrew, wondering where this was going. Obviously something was wrong. 'I made two copies of each document by hand, as instructed.'

He had wondered at the time why they had to be copied by hand instead of getting one of the typists to make the copies. They were of course private papers, Mr Everette's will, and the increase in his son Alfred's allowance when he came of age next month, a settlement on his daughter, Evadne, intended, Andrew Oakley supposed, to improve her chances of making a good marriage. Private papers. But also, to Andrew's mind most importantly, there was a list of various properties in the area that Mr Everette was interested in buying. Though it was no concern of his, the list had intrigued him at the time. He knew Everette Enterprises, Peter Everette's firm, had interests in all sorts of projects in the area, but he did wonder where Everette got all his information from.

'One copy of each for our own records,' agreed Andrew, 'and the others were sent to Mr Everette at his home address.'

'No, Oakley, they were not.'

Andrew looked confused. 'Not what, sir? I dealt with the matter myself.'

For a long moment, Mr Sheridan looked at his clerk, before he said, 'You are aware that Mr Everette of Everette Enterprises is a client of long standing?'

'Yes, sir.'

'Mr Peter Everette, of Myddelton Square.'

'Yes, sir.'

'And that his cousin, Mr Edwin Everette, is also a client of ours?'

'I believe he is, sir, though I myself have never been party to any of his business.'

Even as he said this, Andrew felt himself go cold as the most awful idea took hold in his mind. The envelope with the documents had been dispatched to Mr Peter Everette, but surely to an address in Lamb's Conduit Street, not Myddelton Square.

'It appears, Oakley, that the documents were sent, incorrectly, to Mr Everette's cousin, with all the personal and confidential information they contained.'

Andrew stared at his boss in consternation. The documents he had so painstakingly copied by hand to preserve their privacy, had been sent to the wrong address, and had possibly, probably, been read by Mr Edwin Everette who lived there.

'I have a letter here from Mr Peter Everette,' went on Sheridan. 'It appears his cousin called upon him yesterday and handed over the documents sent to him in error.' Sheridan paused and for a moment, Andrew thought that all was going to be well after all, but this faint hope was dashed when the solicitor went on. 'It was clear to Mr Peter Everette that the envelope had been opened and re-sealed. He is certain his cousin has made himself familiar with all his private dealings, perhaps even copying the documents, before returning them. Mr Edwin Everette, though a cousin, is from an estranged branch of the family.

Mr Peter Everette's family have had no contact with him these twenty years.' Another pause. 'As you can imagine, with the estrangement between them, the damage is incalculable. In the letter that came to me this morning Mr Peter Everette states, and I quote: '"There has been an unforgiveable breach of confidence, crass carelessness by someone in your office, and I must insist that this person is dismissed forthwith from your employ. I could not remain a client of Sheridan, Sheridan and Morrell, if the firm continued to employ such an incompetent man. I shall call upon you myself in due course and I look forward to hearing that the person concerned is no longer on your staff…"'

Mr Sheridan removed his glasses and laid the letter aside. 'What have you to say for yourself, Oakley? What excuse can you give for this appalling mistake?'

'None, sir,' Andrew said quietly. 'It was my job to ensure these documents were sent to Mr Peter Everette. He was expecting them the next day, and as I was finishing the final copy, I asked Mr Bevis to find the address. I did not check that he had addressed the envelope to the right Mr Everette, and thus, the responsibility is mine.'

'I'm afraid it is, Oakley, and since we deal with considerable business for Mr Peter Everette, I cannot risk losing him as a client.' Mr Sheridan paused. 'It was indeed a grave error and though perhaps not entirely your fault, you, as the senior man, must take the blame.' Andrew Oakley said nothing, simply stood, pale-faced, and waited. 'Therefore, Oakley, I am afraid I have to dismiss you, with immediate effect. Miss Harper will pay what you are owed to date and you will clear your desk and leave the building at once. You will speak to no one else before you leave, this must remain a private matter.'

Andrew drew a deep breath and then said, 'Mr Sheridan, sir, I have worked for this firm for nearly twenty years. I've owned to my mistake, I have not blamed Bevis for his, but I would request, sir, that you provide me with a reference so that I may obtain work elsewhere.'

Sheridan looked up with an expression of surprise on his face. 'A reference, Oakley? I hardly think that would be appropriate. You're being dismissed for incompetence. I can hardly put my name, and that of this firm, to a document praising you for your efficiency. The reason for your dismissal might leak out and then any other firm who had employed you on the strength of my reference would have ample cause to question my integrity. No, Oakley. I bid you good morning.'

And with that, the senior partner returned to his reading and Andrew Oakley had no option but to leave the room. When he got back to his office he found Miss Harper waiting for him, and Arthur Bevis sitting, head down, concentrating on the ledger in front of him, apparently entirely unaware of his colleague's return.

In silence, Andrew went across to his desk. Under Miss Harper's eagle eye, he removed the few items that were his: a propelling pencil Alice had given him for his birthday, an ironed and folded handkerchief in case of emergencies, his reading spectacles and a cloth folded round a cheese and pickle sandwich which was his lunch. Carefully he packed them into his briefcase and quietly he walked out of the office.

Once he was in the corridor, Miss Harper said, 'If you

will come into my office, Mr Oakley, I will give you what you are owed.'

'What I am owed!' Andrew almost shouted out loud, but he held his tongue and followed the woman to the cubbyhole of an office where she worked. It was Wednesday and he couldn't afford to lose three days' wages. He stood in the doorway and waited as she went to the desk under the window. On it were a rack of pens and pencils, a bottle of ink and a block of paper neatly arrayed beside her typewriter; not a thing out of place. She looked, to Andrew, as she stood thin and spare in her private lair, like an angular spider, he thought irrelevantly, in the centre of its web. He watched as she opened a drawer and took out a black cash box, from which she extracted two sovereigns.

'It is more than you're owed, Mr Oakley, but Mr Sheridan has insisted you should not have to return the five shilling change which would be due.'

If she's waiting for me to express thanks, Andrew thought as he put the coins in his pocket book, she'll be waiting for an eternity!

Without another word, he turned on his heel, took the steep stairs leading down to the square and stepped out onto the pavement. Though the day was chilly, the winter sun was bright, causing him to blink, after the gloom of the office. For a moment he paused, seeing the street in its workaday busyness as if for the first time. Ever since he was thirteen, he had been a part of that busyness, people going to and from work, out and about, earning their living, and now, suddenly it all seemed strange, unfamiliar, and he felt like an outsider looking in.

I'm nearly forty, he thought, as he stood on the pavement,

buffeted by those hurrying past. I've no job and without a reference, no prospect of getting one. I've a family to keep and no wages to keep them on.

He fought down the sudden burst of anger that threatened to overcome him. Two pounds! That was all he was considered to be worth, after twenty years' service. It wasn't even his error, and Mr Sheridan knew it. His mistake had been that he hadn't spotted the mistake Bevis had made. But to be sacked for it?

Mr Peter Everette had demanded his dismissal. Money spoke, and Mr Peter Everette had money, plenty of it.

Andrew thought of his wife, Alice, already struggling to manage the expenses of the household on his wages. What was she going to say when he came home in the middle of the day, unemployed, with only two pounds in his pocket?

He could do nothing about it and anger boiled inside him. He wanted to stride out to Myddelton Square and demand to see Mr Peter Everette, but he knew that would be a waste of time; he wouldn't even get through the front door. Blindly he turned on his heel and headed for home. Better tell poor Alice the dreadful news sooner, rather than later.

As he joined the throng of people in the street, and turned into busy Clerkenwell Road, he found himself rehearsing what he might have said to Mr Sheridan. He shouldn't have simply stood there and accepted his dismissal. He should have made more fuss. After all, he knew what was in those documents. They had been important enough for Mr Everette to insist they be hand copied, so their contents would be completely confidential, instead of typed by some girl in the typing pool, who might gossip. Suppose he had threatened to tell the world of the details in those documents? Suppose he made that threat even now? Once this idea had come to him, he began to consider it seriously; planning what he could do and how he could do it. They'd never take him back, of course, he knew that, but they might pay for his silence! Yes, Mr Peter Everette might do that! Unaware of the crowds around him, the traffic in the bustling street, and in a world of his own making, he stepped out in front of a brewer's dray.

3

John Sheridan left the office that Wednesday evening as usual and walked to the station. It was a chilly evening, but he wasn't aware of the weather, nor the streets through which he walked. It had been a dreadful day at the office, and he was the only one there to deal with it. His partner, elderly Hugh Morrell, seldom came into the office these days and when he did he was, as John used to say to his wife Anne, 'Neither use nor ornament!' Everything was left to John now, and he was seriously thinking of taking in another partner. The business was doing well, and if it continued as it was, it would be able to support one; there always used to be three of them until his father had died.

And let's face it, he thought, when something happened like today, and there was only him to deal with it, he could use another safe pair of hands.

The train swept into the station and John was glad to find a seat; he felt exhausted. He sat down gratefully, his briefcase clasped tightly onto his knee. As the train swished through an underground tunnel, he thought back over the day and wondered what he could have done differently. Quite a lot, if he were honest with himself. He had allowed himself to be manipulated; he should never have dismissed Andrew Oakley. Quite apart from the injustice of his dismissal, he could ill afford to lose his senior clerk. And then, Peter Everette, secure in his own importance, had arrived without an appointment demanding to see him. Sheridan had been half expecting him, but when Miss Harper had rapped on the door to announce him, Peter Everette, not a man to be kept waiting, had almost pushed her aside as he strode into the office, clearly on the warpath.

'Well, Sheridan,' Peter Everette said, taking the chair opposite the desk without invitation, 'this is a bad business, this sending my documents to the wrong address. Most embarrassing for me, with all my private affairs going to someone else... particularly my cousin Edwin. Haven't been on terms for years! What are you going to do about it, eh? What action will you be taking?'

'I have already taken action, Mr Everette,' Sheridan answered. 'As you required, the man concerned was sacked this morning.'

'So I should think,' replied Everette. 'Deserved it. His carelessness could cost me a pretty penny.'

'But the papers were returned to you,' pointed out Sheridan. 'From what you said in your letter, all present and correct.'

'That's as maybe, but Edwin Everette will certainly have made copies, I know his type. Now he will be a party to many of my business affairs. It's not good enough, I tell you.'

John Sheridan looked at his client, masking with difficulty his dislike. Peter Everette was a large man, large in every way – height, girth, neck and chins. His suit was clearly made in Savile Row, cut to disguise his protruding stomach, heavy gold cufflinks gleamed at his wrists, and a gold watch chain strained across his waistcoat, the watch discreetly hidden in its pocket. When he smiled, a smile that never reached his eyes, there were flashes of gold among his teeth. He was an unprepossessing man, and yet he had a presence that meant few people chose to argue with him, and those who did invariably came off worst.

John Sheridan had to concede, if only to himself, that the man did have a grievance, but he knew he should have done more to discover what had actually happened, before dismissing Oakley.

Lately it had become increasingly clear to John Sheridan that Everette was somehow profiting from advance notice of the local council's decisions and plans. He had no idea where Everette got his intelligence, but it was clear that he knew exactly which properties to buy and when.

Of course, Sheridan reassured himself, *he* had no financial interest in Everette's business in any form. He was simply the lawyer who drew up contracts and conveyancing documents. It wasn't for him to question what his client was spending his money on, or where he got his information.

This was something Peter Everette had come to rely on. He knew he was lucky to have a solicitor such as John Sheridan, who asked no awkward questions, but followed his instructions as necessary. But what about the now-dismissed clerk who'd made the copies of the documents? Did he realise the value of the information he had? If he did, he could prove troublesome.

Everette realised, now, he had been too hasty in demanding the man's dismissal; insisting he be sacked had been a mistake. He needed to regain control of the situation.

'So, what about this clerk? Will he know to hold his tongue?'

John Sheridan stared at him across the table, disliking him intensely, and in that moment, he came to a decision. He would not be browbeaten, not any more, and if Everette Enterprises removed their business, well, it might cause short-term problems, but so be it. He would not be dictated to. He was already regretting the loss of Andrew Oakley. Young Bevis, who made the actual mistake, was not only far less experienced, but also nothing like as conscientious as Oakley.

'Mr Everette,' Sheridan said firmly, 'I followed exactly the wishes expressed in your letter, and the man was summarily dismissed. So far, apart from Miss Harper, no one else in this office knows. The staff will hear of it tomorrow when I address them all on the matter. But he has gone and thus I'm afraid I have no hold over his tongue; if he chooses to speak of what was in those documents, I can't stop him.'

'But they were particularly confidential,' spluttered Peter Everette. 'My will...'

'Indeed,' Sheridan agreed. 'It was on your instruction that the documents were all hand copied, twice, which was time consuming; so it is probable that the man will have a good recollection of what they contained. As I say, I followed your instructions on both matters.' Sheridan paused and then went on, 'It would have been better to reprimand him for his mistake and then keep him with us, earning his gratitude. He would then have kept his mouth shut, knowing certain dismissal would occur if he did not.'

For a long moment Peter Everette stared at his solicitor, before saying, 'And what is his name, this careless employee of yours?'

'Ex-employee, sir, and,' Sheridan's voice hardened, 'I have no intention of telling you, sir; that is *my* business.'

For a moment, Peter Everette seemed dumbstruck, but then he rallied and said, 'If that is your attitude, Sheridan, I shall have to consider, very seriously consider, removing my business to another firm.'

'That, sir, is your prerogative,' Mr Sheridan replied smoothly, getting to his feet. Even as he did so, he wondered if he were being foolhardy calling his client's bluff, but his gaze remained steadfast.

'Your firm has served me well over the years,' said Peter Everette, backtracking a little. 'And we have ongoing business. I should not want to change horses midstream, as it were, but if there are any further errors, I would have no alternative.' He, too, got to his feet, so that they faced each other across the desk. 'I shall need some more documents prepared for signature, in the next week or so, on two of those properties,' he said. 'And in the meantime, I'll bid you good afternoon, Mr Sheridan.'

Sheridan rang the bell on his desk and immediately Miss Harper materialised at the door. Had she been eavesdropping? Sheridan wondered, but all he said was, 'Mr Everette is leaving, Miss Harper. Perhaps you'd show him out.'

The secretary stood aside to allow Mr Everette to precede her and then pulled the door closed behind them. That had been another mistake, for although John Sheridan had heard them talking as they walked along the corridor, he had not been able to hear what they were saying.

Had Everette been pumping his secretary for information about Oakley? he wondered. Surely she'd be loyal to the firm that had employed her for almost thirty years. She had idolised his father, and when he had retired, John had inherited her, but though she was ruthlessly efficient, there had never been the closeness between them that she'd enjoyed with Mr Sheridan senior.

The train drew into Highgate station, and John Sheridan wearily got to his feet. As he emerged from the station into the evening air and walked the half mile to his home in Collingwood Crescent, he tried to put all thoughts of the disastrous day behind him. Reaching his gate, he paused and looked at Costessy House, the fan light above the front door glowing with the welcoming warmth awaiting him indoors, a plume of smoke from the chimney promising an evening by the fire with Anne, and he was relieved to be home.

They had bought the house fifteen years ago with the aid of a legacy from his grandmother. Their children had been quite young at the time, and it had been their family home ever since. Charles was nearly twenty-one now and Lavinia rising eighteen. It made Sheridan feel quite old when he realised he and Anne had been about the ages the children were now when they'd become engaged to be married. If either Charlie or Lavinia suggested getting married now, he would forbid it; they were surely far too young.

Dorcas, the parlourmaid, was waiting for him in the hall as he let himself in.

'Good evening, Dorcas,' he said as he took off his coat

and hat and dropped his briefcase on the floor. 'Is my wife at home?'

'Good evening, sir,' she replied. 'Yes, madam is in the drawing room.'

Sheridan thanked her and went in to join Anne. The curtains were already drawn against the early February darkness, and a fire snapped and crackled in the grate, providing cheerful heat.

Anne took one look at his face, set aside her book and said, 'John, dearest, whatever is the matter? You look worn out. Bad day?'

He did feel exhausted, and crossing to the trolley in the corner of the room, he poured himself two fingers of whisky with a splash of soda before he answered. 'You could say that,' he said, adding, 'Do you want one of these?' When Anne shook her head, he carried his drink over to his usual chair and sat down heavily.

'So,' Anne asked, sitting back down on the sofa, 'what's happened?'

'I had to dismiss Oakley.'

'Oakley!' Anne was shocked. 'Oh, John, why? He's been with you for years!'

'He made a mistake that could cost us a great deal of money,' replied her husband. 'An error affecting one of our most important clients.'

'Goodness,' said Anne mildly, 'what on earth did the poor man do?'

John took a long pull at his whisky and felt himself relax a little, as he savoured its peaty flavour. Sitting back into his chair, he explained about the documents being sent to the wrong address.

'Is that all?' Anne asked. 'And you sacked him for that?'

'The client was extremely angry and demanded his dismissal.'

'And you simply sacked him... on the spot.'

'Well, my dear, if you're going to sack someone, it's the only way to do it. You can't have them staying on and creating discontent among the rest of the staff. No, that person has to go, immediately.'

'But you sacked him, at someone else's behest?'

'At the time it seemed the only thing to do. We can't really afford to lose Everette's account.'

'Ah, Everette,' said Anne. 'I've heard you mention him before. Is he really that important? For you to dismiss Oakley, who's been with you for years? For a simple mistake, like getting an address wrong?'

'The documents were sent to another Mr Everette, his estranged cousin. He has returned them, but Everette maintains his cousin will have made copies before sending them back, and so knows all his business.'

'Hmm, that does make things more difficult, I do see,' said Anne thoughtfully.

'Everette even marched into the office this afternoon, to see if I had carried out his instructions. He's that sort of man.'

'Is he? He doesn't sound like your kind of client; he sounds most unpleasant. What makes him so important?'

'He's a businessman. He has fingers in many pies, much of it property, and he puts a lot of work our way.'

'And what would happen if he did decide to take that business elsewhere? Would the firm collapse?'

'No, but it might make life difficult for a while.'

'Then perhaps you could reinstate Oakley. Does this Everette know his name?'

'Whose? Oakley's, you mean? No, I refused to tell him.'

'Well, there you are. You can take him on again.'

'He may not know Oakley's name, but I'm sure he'd recognise his face. He must have seen him in the office. And,' John went on with a sigh, 'I think Miss Harper may well have told Everette what he wanted to know.'

'Why on earth would she do that?'

'Because she could. She has an inflated idea of her own importance, and likes to prove it!'

'Well, even if she has, there's nothing to stop you re-employing him... that is if he's prepared to come back.'

'And Everette?'

'John, dear, you did what the man asked you to do. You dismissed Oakley. You didn't say he wouldn't be brought back, did you?'

'That's just semantics,' replied her husband.

'And that's what they are for, isn't it, to allow for shades of meaning?'

'If I did that, Miss Harper would go straight to Everette and tell him what I'd done.'

'Then sack Miss Harper.'

'Anne, really...'

'Yes, John, really. Don't tell me you're not regretting the whole affair! You should call on Oakley first thing in the morning and offer him his job back.'

'I can't do that!' cried John, horrified. 'Imagine the loss of face!'

'Imagine the courage to admit a wrong and put it right! You're a good man, John, and you know Oakley didn't deserve to be dismissed, certainly without you discovering exactly how the mistake was made.'

Her husband said nothing and she got to her feet. 'Now it's nearly time for dinner and we don't want to annoy Cook by not being ready when the gong goes.'

'Where are the children?' John asked.

'What children? They're both grown up now, you know. Charlie is dining with some friends, but Lavinia is upstairs in her room and she'll be eating with us. So, I suggest you put the events of today out of your mind, sleep on what you might do and see how things look in the morning.' She held out her hand to him and pulled him up out of his chair. 'Come on, my John.'

'I don't deserve you,' said John as he pulled her into his arms.

'No, you don't,' Anne agreed with a smile. 'But you're stuck with me just the same.'

4

Mabel ran the rest of the way home from school full of excitement. She knew Mam would be delighted that Miss Chapman had agreed she could stay on another year, and perhaps even move on to the secondary school. Dada still thought it would be better for her to leave at the end of the summer term.

'Education for education's sake is wasted on girls,' he maintained. 'Waste of time!'

If it had been left to him he wouldn't even have written to Miss Chapman, but Alice was determined her daughter should have the same opportunities as their sons, Eddie and Stephen, had.

'You'll be demanding the vote next,' grumbled Andrew, but as usually happened he'd given way to his beloved Alice and written the letter.

When Mabel got home, she rushed into the kitchen where her mother was chopping vegetables for the evening meal.

'Miss Chapman says yes!' she cried with glee, and grabbing her mother round the waist, danced her round the room. 'I'm going to stay at school and she said, if I can pass the entrance exam, I might even get a place in the new secondary school at Farringdon!'

'Careful, Mabel!' exclaimed her mother, disentangling herself. 'Let me put this knife down before it stabs one of us!'

'But can you imagine, Mam? Miss Chapman thinks I can pass the exam. Me at the secondary! What will Dada say to that?'

'He'll ask how much the uniform costs,' replied her mother, with a wry smile.

'But it's so exciting,' cried Mabel. 'What will the boys say, when they hear?'

'If they're honest,' her mother answered with a grin, 'they'll both say they're glad it isn't them!'

'Well, Stephen has to do another year, anyway,' pointed out Mabel. 'He's only coming up thirteen. He's not allowed to leave, is he?'

'No,' agreed her mother. 'Now then, my girl, you finish chopping these spuds and put them in the pot, and then go and do your homework. If you're going to secondary school, you'll have to get used to working in the evenings.'

Mabel picked up the knife and started on the potatoes. 'If I want to learn typing, I could do that at evening classes,' she said. 'They hold them for grown-ups who want to improve their chances of a better job. I could go to those, couldn't I, Mam? I could enrol in one of those, as well as go to secondary.'

'One step at a time, my girl,' warned her mother. 'Your father hasn't actually agreed to the first part yet, has he?'

Mabel's face fell. 'But he said, if Miss Chapman thought it was a good idea…'

'Don't you "Miss Chapman" him,' said her mother. 'Your dad said he'd think about it, and he will, but don't push him too far, or he'll change his mind and you'll have to get a job somewhere.'

Mabel finished the potatoes then went upstairs into her bedroom and shut the door. Her bedroom was her refuge. It was tiny, but her own; at least she didn't have to share, like her brothers did. She flopped down onto her bed and opened her schoolbag. It was English tonight and she had a piece of poetry to learn, ready for discussion the next day. *Tyger Tyger, burning bright...* She loved its rhythm and its imagery and she set to with a will. Once she had it by heart, she went back downstairs and found her mother standing at the front door, looking out into the street.

'Isn't Dada home yet?' Mabel said in surprise. 'He's late.'

'He must have got held up at the office,' answered her mother, turning back into the house. 'He had some work to finish last week that kept him late, perhaps it's the same again.' Her words were calm enough, but they didn't account for the worried look in her eyes.

Five minutes later, the door opened and they both looked up, expecting Andrew to walk in, but it was only Stephen. He was his usual scruffy self, his socks concertinaed about his ankles, his knees scratched and muddy. Smaller than most of his peers, he was nevertheless determined to keep up with them, and there was seldom an evening when he didn't come home looking the worse for wear.

Now he pushed his hair out of his eyes with a grubby hand and, flopping down at the table, asked, 'What's for tea, Ma? I'm starving. Where's Dad?'

'Not home yet,' replied his mother. 'Now go and wash

your hands, you're a disgrace. I can't think what you've been up to!'

'Nuffink,' Stephen replied, as he crossed to the sink and turned on the tap. 'Just playing football, that's all!'

'Did you see Eddie?'

'Yeah, he was with the 'prentices in the market. Thinks he's one already!'

'We'll give your father another ten minutes and then we'll eat without him,' said his mother. 'I'll heat his up when he gets home.'

Ten minutes later, as Alice was ladling the hotpot onto plates, the door suddenly crashed open and Eddie, her eldest, burst into the room.

'Ma!' he cried. 'Is Dad at home?'

'No, not yet.' Alice put down the plate and the ladle. 'Why, what's the matter?'

'I don't know, but I just saw Joe Parker on my way home and he asked how was my dad. An' I said what d'you mean? An' he said that his ma had been coming home from the market this morning when there was an accident in the street and she'd thought it was Dad.'

Alice sank down onto a chair, the colour fleeing her face, and taking a deep breath, said, 'Thought *what* was Dad? Start again, Eddie, from the beginning.'

'Joe Parker told me that there was an accident in the street this morning,' repeated Eddie. 'A brewer's dray lost its load of barrels, and someone was trapped underneath them. And his ma, who was coming home from Exmouth Market, thought it was our dad.'

'She only thought,' repeated Alice. 'She wasn't certain... that it was him?'

'It's what Joe said... she thought it was him. So I ran all the way home to make sure it wasn't.' Eddie looked round the kitchen. 'Where is he?'

'Not home yet,' replied Alice, taking off her apron and picking up her hat. 'Mabel, you go on with tea, I'm going round the Parkers'.'

'Can I come?' demanded Mabel, getting up from the table.

'No,' snapped her mother, before saying more gently, 'No, Mabel, you stay here and make sure the boys have their tea, I won't be long.' And with that Alice disappeared out into the street.

'But where *is* Dad?' asked Eddie, still looking round as if he thought his father might suddenly appear from upstairs.

'He's late home,' murmured Mabel, as she finished serving the hotpot. 'Mam was beginning to worry.'

'I don't 'spect it was him,' Eddie said. 'Not in the middle of the morning. He wouldn't be in the street then, would he? He'd be in the office, stands to reason. Old Ma Parker must have got it wrong. Must have been someone a bit like him.'

As the eldest, Eddie decided to take charge. 'Come on, you two. Eat up. Mam'll want to see clean plates when she gets back.'

When Winnie Parker opened her door and found a pale Alice Oakley on her step, she held out her hands and said, 'Oh, Alice. I'm so sorry. How is he? It looked bad.'

'Was it him?' cried Alice. 'This accident? Are you sure

it was him? Joe told Eddie you thought it was, but...' Her voice tailed off as she saw the look on Winnie's face.

'You mean you didn't know there'd been an accident?' Winnie stepped back. 'You'd better come in.'

Alice followed her into the house. 'Are you really sure it was Andrew?' Alice's eyes were begging Winnie to say no.

'I didn't see the accident happen.' Winnie led her into the front room, used only for best or solemn occasions. 'Better sit down,' she said, and perched on the sofa.

Alice sank onto an overstuffed armchair and said, 'So... tell me!'

'I was on my way home from the market. Mid-morning it were, and I come round the corner into Clerkenwell Road and the whole street was blocked. A brewer's dray was tilted on its side, and some of the barrels had rolled off. They'd managed to get the horses free, but several people had been injured. Lots of folk was trying to help, but it was all a bit chaotic.'

'But Andrew,' cried Alice. 'Was Andrew one of them?'

'It was difficult to tell, what with everyone crowding round,' admitted Winnie, 'but someone was on the ground, sort of under one of the barrels. They was trying to pull him clear, but it did look a bit like your Andrew. Then one of them new motor ambulances came and they loaded him into it and took him to the hospital.'

'But which hospital?'

Winnie shook her head. 'I don't know, but the London would be the nearest, wouldn't it? Only a mile or so.'

'You should have come to find me!' wailed Alice.

'Well, to be honest I wasn't sure it was your Andrew, but

I thought if it was, them at his office would come and tell you what happened. I mean, they must have missed him, mustn't they?'

Alice got to her feet. 'I must go,' she said. 'I must go to him.'

'But where are you going?'

'Home first,' replied Alice, 'and if he isn't back safe, we'll go round all the hospitals until we find him.'

When she got back home, hoping against hope Andrew would be there, she found only the children waiting for her.

'What did Mrs Parker say?' demanded Mabel, as her mother walked in the door.

'It sounds as if it might be Dad,' Alice replied. 'So, we have to try and find him.'

'Shall I run round to the office and see if he's there?' suggested Eddie.

'Yes, all right, but I think it'll be long closed now. If they'd known anything about Dad and an accident, someone would have come to tell us. After all, it happened this morning, not after work. Still, go through St John's Square first, just to be sure. Then the best thing to do is to go to all the local hospitals and see if he's been brought in. Winnie Parker said that the injured man was taken off in a motor ambulance, so he'll be in a hospital somewhere. Now,' at least Alice had something to focus on, 'I'll go to the London in Whitechapel, you boys try St Pancras and Charing Cross. We'll meet back here after that.'

'What about me?' cried Mabel. 'Where shall I go?'

'You must stay here, in case your dad comes home, or somebody brings news of him.'

'But Mam, that's not fair! I want to look for him too.'

Alice's voice softened. 'I know you do, me duck, but think how it would be if Dad came home and found no one here? Or if someone brought a message and there was no one to hear it, so they went away again? Someone has to stay, Mabel, and I think it should be you. If Dad comes in you can heat up his tea, and explain to him what we thought had happened. All right?'

'All right,' muttered Mabel mutinously. 'But how will I let you know that he's come home?'

'You can't, but we'll all come back when we've been to those hospitals and have a council of war about what to do next.'

It was almost three hours later when they all returned home, the two boys disappointed to have no news, but when Alice came back, she was able to tell them she'd found their father.

'He's in the London,' she told them. 'It was him in the accident. He's had a bang on the head and has broken his legs. So, he'll have to stay in the hospital for a few days, but he's in safe hands, I promise you. Now then, bed, everyone, and get some sleep.'

Alice saw the children into their rooms and then went into her own bedroom. The bed she shared with Andrew was far too big without him on the other side, and she tossed and turned, unable to sleep. She had told the children their father was in good hands, and indeed she knew he was, but she hadn't mentioned how badly he'd been injured. As she lay in bed trying to sleep, her brain remained wide awake, going over and over what the doctor had told her.

The ambulance had taken Andrew to the London

Hospital where poorer patients were treated for free. When Alice walked in through the main entrance, she crossed to the desk to make her enquiry.

'Well, there was a man brought in this morning, following a street accident,' answered the receptionist. 'It might be your husband, I suppose.'

The almoner appeared and when Alice had spoken to her, she was taken through to see a Dr Miller. It was he who finally allowed her into a ward to establish whether the man who'd been brought in after the accident was indeed Andrew.

Alice stared for a long moment at the figure on the bed. He lay motionless, only the covers rising and falling with his breath, a cage keeping the bedclothes clear of his legs. His head was bandaged, but even so, Alice could see straight away that it was her Andrew.

'Yes,' she whispered. 'That's him. Is he going to be all right, Doctor?'

'We need to talk, Mrs Oakley,' said Dr Miller gently. 'He's had something to help him sleep now, and we don't want to disturb him. Let's go and sit down somewhere quiet, and we'll have a chat.'

He led Alice out of the ward and into a tiny side room, simply furnished with a table and two chairs. As soon as they were seated, Alice said, 'It's bad, isn't it, Doctor? You must tell me. I need to know the worst.'

'It's not good,' agreed Dr Miller. 'Unfortunately your husband's legs were crushed by one of the barrels that fell off the dray, and he was also knocked unconscious; he must have banged his head as he hit the pavement. There is also substantial bruising to his back and ribs, probably caused by the same barrel. As far as we can tell, his head wound is not serious. Though he's probably concussed, there are no obvious signs that there is any internal bleeding. He was still unconscious when he arrived here, which was a good thing, it meant we could splint his broken legs without causing him any more pain.' The doctor paused and looked at the pale-faced woman sitting opposite him. She had asked to know the worst, so perhaps it was better to get it over with.

Seeing his hesitation, Alice said, 'Is he going to die, Doctor?'

'No,' replied the doctor, 'I think, despite his injuries, and with careful nursing, he won't die. The trouble is we don't know if there is any damage to his spine. As I said, there is bruising to his lower back, but if the spine itself is damaged, well, he may not be able to walk again, and I'm afraid that's something we won't know until he regains consciousness.

'If he can move his legs when he comes round, then it will just be a question of waiting until the bones knit together again and for the other bruises to dissipate. His ribs will be painful, but those have to heal themselves. Whatever happens, it will take some time for him to recover. He'll need to be in the hospital for several weeks, so I think you must be prepared for your lives to be different, for some time yet.' The doctor gave her a reassuring smile. 'Come back tomorrow afternoon and we should know something, one way or the other.'

'So there's nothing to do but wait and see,' Alice said miserably.

'And pray, Mrs Oakley, if that's something that you

believe in and it brings you hope and comfort. Pray for his recovery.'

Lying in her bed now, Alice did pray. She didn't know if she believed her prayer would be heard, but it was all she could do.

5

The following morning Mabel was angry with her mother because she insisted she should go to school. 'But Mam,' she moaned, 'I want to be here with you, in case there's any news of Dada.'

When she had returned from the hospital the night before, Alice had only told her children their dad had broken legs and concussion. There had been no need to worry them yet about anything worse. Now she said, 'There's nothing you can do here, Mabel. As I told you last night, he's in good hands, but we shan't know any more until I see him this afternoon.' Seeing her daughter's mutinous expression, she added, 'And if you're hoping to go on to the secondary school in the autumn, you can't afford to miss school now, so off you go, or you'll be late!'

Alice realised, as soon as she had mentioned the secondary school, that it had been a mistake. If Andrew was laid up for several weeks, they probably couldn't afford to keep Mabel at school for an extra year. Quickly she said, 'Anyway, I'm going to see Dad this afternoon. I'll be able to talk to the doctor and then we'll know where we go from here.'

'Go?' asked Stephen anxiously. 'Go where? Have we got to move?'

'No,' Alice reassured him. 'We haven't. What I meant was we'll see how Dad is, and then we'll know what preparations we need to make so that he can come home. Hurry up now, the pair of you, you're going to be very late if you don't get a move on.'

Five minutes later Mam had shooed them out of the house. 'No need to tell anyone at school about your father's accident, yet,' she said. 'Better not to talk about it until we know more. All right? We don't want gossip going round about us.' And then they were running down the road, Mabel with her schoolbag banging against her legs, trying to stay ahead of Stephen, who though younger by nearly two years, could run faster.

When they reached the playground, they split up, Stephen to go in through the boys' gate and Mabel through the girls'.

'Don't forget,' Mabel said, as he turned back to wave. 'No telling!'

'I *know*,' he said, and stuck his tongue out at her before disappearing into the playground.

Annie was waiting for her just inside the gate.

'Are you all right?' Annie asked.

'Yeah, 'course. Why?'

''Cos you're never late!'

'Well,' Mabel replied sharply, 'I'm not today, am I? The bell hasn't gone yet.'

'No,' conceded Annie, 'but something's up. I can tell.'

Mabel looked at her for a long moment and then said,

'If I tell you something, you have to promise you won't tell, not anyone!'

'Promise!' The two girls spat in their palms and then clasped hands, the promise sealed.

'Is it about last night?' Annie asked. 'What Miss Chapman wanted you for?'

Mabel was about to say no, it was about her dad, when she thought better of it. Mam had said not to tell anyone, and that probably included best friends. She would wait until tomorrow to tell Annie about Dada, when Mam had talked to the doctor again. So, needing something to tell now, she said, 'I'm going to stay on at school at the end of this term. Miss Chapman said she'll see if I can go to the new secondary school in Farringdon.'

'Is that what you *want* to do?' Annie sounded incredulous. 'Really?'

'Yes, I want to stay on and then learn to type, so I can be a secretary.'

'Well,' Annie shrugged, 'I can't wait to leave. I'll find a job and then I'll have some money of my own. You'll see,' she went on airily, 'you'll still be a schoolgirl and I shall be a woman of the world with a job and a wage packet!'

'What kind of job?' asked Mabel, wondering who would want to employ Annie. She was her best friend, of course, but she wasn't... well, she wasn't a *commonsensical* sort of person.

Before Annie could answer, the bell for the start of school rang out across the morning air, and they all hurried to line up in their classes, boys and girls still using separate entrances, and Annie, saved by the bell, didn't have to answer, which was a relief as she had absolutely no idea what she might do to earn her bread. All she knew was that she'd had enough of school. She could read and write and do simple arithmetic, what else could she possibly need?

They had no chance of further chat until the end of the morning, and by then Annie, no longer interested in Mabel's unusual plans for next year, did not mention them again. They sat in companionable silence on a bench in the pale winter sunshine, eating the sandwiches they'd brought for their midday meal. Annie sat back against the wall and, closing her eyes, turned her face to the sun.

Mabel was thinking of poor Dada, lying in bed in the hospital. How long do broken legs take to mend? she wondered. They must be very painful; Dada must be being very, very brave. Mam had told them he'd banged his head as well, but that had been bandaged and he'd been asleep, so she hadn't been able to talk to him.

Will he be awake when Mam gets there today? Mabel wondered. How she wished she could have gone to the hospital with Mam this afternoon. She was longing to tell him the exciting news about secondary school in the autumn. That would surely cheer him up; he'd be so proud of her.

At the end of the afternoon she didn't dawdle home with Annie as she sometimes did. When Annie suggested they go to the park, Mabel said, 'Sorry, Mam wants me to go straight home today.'

Annie accepted this. Mothers often had extra chores for their daughters after school. She knew her own mother did, and that knowledge often slowed her footsteps home. It was such a bright afternoon, she would put off her return home for as long as she reasonably could. Mabel sometimes did the same, but not today, and they parted at the school gates.

6

When Mabel and Stephen had finally set off for school, Alice sent Eddie to the office in St John's Square with a letter to Mr Sheridan, asking if she might come and see him on a matter of great urgency.

'Now you give that to Mr Sheridan and no one else,' she warned. 'Certainly not that Miss Harper, all right? If for any reason he's not there, you're to wait.'

'What happens if they don't let me?' asked Eddie. He'd met Miss Harper once and if he were honest, she terrified him. He certainly didn't want to be confronting her and refusing to give her the letter.

'If necessary, you wait for him in the street, but you tell them nothing about what's happened until you've given the letter to Mr Sheridan... and don't let them take that letter off you, all right?'

'Yeah,' Eddie replied reluctantly. 'All right.'

He set off with the envelope in his pocket, hoping against hope Mr Sheridan would be on time this morning. Whatever his mother said, Eddie knew everyone at the office would be wondering where his dad was, because in all the years he'd been there, Andrew Oakley had never been late.

As Eddie walked slowly the mile or so to St John's Square, John Sheridan was still at home, discussing with Anne exactly what he was going to do when he got to the office. He had not slept well. He was in a situation of his own making, but he didn't know how to escape. Anne, as usual, was his conscience. She thought he had allowed himself to be manipulated, that he should reinstate Oakley, even at the risk of losing Peter Everette's business. Perhaps she was right, but it would be a tremendous loss of face. First of all he needed to find out how such an error had occurred, but that would mean questioning young Arthur Bevis, and probably Miss Harper as well, and it would be all round the office in a brace of shakes, if it wasn't already.

Understanding his dilemma, Anne said, 'Why don't you go and see Oakley first? Go and see him at home, before going into the office and involving anyone else? Get him to explain exactly what he thought had happened.'

'But then if it's clearly not his fault, what do I do?'

'John,' Anne smiled at him, 'you're a good man. That's a decision only you can make.'

'The trouble is, I don't know exactly where he lives,' sighed John. 'I'll have to go into the office to get his address. Somewhere over towards Liverpool Street station, I think.'

'That is a pity,' Anne agreed. 'It would be better if no one knew you were going to speak to him until you'd made some sort of decision.'

'Can't be helped,' replied her husband as he began to gather up his things. 'I'll just have to ask Miss Harper and tell her she's to keep it confidential. You're quite right, of course. I need to talk to Oakley before I speak to anyone else.'

★

Eddie was frustrated Mr Sheridan wasn't yet in the office when he got there. The one day it was important, it seemed that the solicitor was going to be late.

'If you've got a letter for him, I'll make sure he gets it as soon as he comes in,' said Miss Harper as she barred the way at the top of the stairs. She held out her hand, but Eddie thrust the letter back into his pocket, clutching it tightly in his hand.

'No thank you, miss,' he said. 'I was told to put it into Mr Sheridan's hand. I'll come back later.' And before she could catch hold of him, he darted back down the stairs and out onto the pavement. He would wait here in the street until Mr Sheridan arrived, and only then would he part with his mother's letter.

It was nearly an hour before Eddie saw Mr Sheridan, briefcase in hand, hurrying into the square. Eddie recognised him at once and, peeling himself off the wall against which he'd been leaning, followed him across the square. He waited until he saw the solicitor actually go towards the office doorway before he called him by name.

Sheridan spun round.

'Mr Sheridan,' Eddie called again, afraid he was going to lose him into the building, 'I'm Eddie Oakley, sir. My father works for you.'

Sheridan waited. Oakley's son? What on earth did he want? To beg him to take his father back? That might make things even more complicated.

'Well,' replied Sheridan coolly, 'And what do you want?'

'I've got a letter for you, sir,' answered Eddie, stepping nearer and producing the envelope.

Sheridan didn't take it, but said, 'From your father, I suppose.'

'No, sir.' Eddie shook his head. 'From my mother!'

'Your mother!' exclaimed Sheridan. 'Why would your mother write to me?'

Eddie wasn't going to start to explain about his dad's accident. He knew his mother had asked if she might come to the office and speak to Mr Sheridan, and she would explain things far better than Eddie could. So he simply held out the letter, saying, 'She said I was to put it in your hands, sir. If you take it, I can tell her that I did.' He paused just before handing it over and added, 'I think she wants a reply.'

John Sheridan raised an eyebrow. 'Does she indeed? Oh well, give it to me and I'll see what she wants.' He held out his hand and Eddie solemnly placed the envelope into it.

'You'd better come up while I read it,' Sheridan said, turning again for the door.

Eddie hung back. 'Miss, upstairs, she told me to get lost.'

Sheridan couldn't help smiling. 'Did she indeed?'

'Well, not exactly in them words,' Eddie admitted. 'But it's what she meant.'

'Did she know who you were?'

'No, sir, I didn't let on my name.'

'Fair enough.' Sheridan was glad not to have to mention Oakley to his secretary yet, as he still wasn't sure what he was going to do, but he was intrigued it was Oakley's wife who'd written to him. 'I won't either, but I don't propose to open my mail in the street, so follow me.'

Reluctantly Eddie followed Mr Sheridan up the stairs. Miss Harper was waiting at the top, and when she saw Eddie, her face reddened angrily.

'You, boy,' she exclaimed. 'I told you to be off and not to be worrying Mr Sheridan with ill-written messages.'

'It's all right, Miss Harper, thank you,' said her boss firmly. 'I'll deal with him in my office. Follow me, young man.'

Eddie did as he was told, but he couldn't resist glancing back over his shoulder with a grin of triumph while the secretary glowered. A younger Eddie would have stuck his tongue out, but the sixteen-year-old Eddie recognised it wasn't worth the trouble it would cause.

'Shut the door,' instructed Sheridan as he hung his hat and coat on a stand in the corner. Still holding the unopened letter in his hand, he went round his desk and sat down. There was another chair by the window, but as the solicitor didn't offer it, Eddie remained standing. Sheridan took a paper knife from his drawer and slit the envelope open. Eddie watched him as he ran an eye over the contents, before starting to read it properly the second time. He looked up at the boy standing in front of him and said gruffly, 'Edward, isn't it? Pull up that chair and tell me what happened.'

Eddie fetched the chair and perched on it uncomfortably.

'Now what's all this about, young man?'

'We don't quite know,' Eddie began. 'My father was out in Clerkenwell Road yesterday morning. My mother guessed you'd sent him on an errand.'

He paused, but Sheridan just said, 'Go on.'

'There was a brewer's dray loaded with barrels, and as it come round the corner, some of its barrels fell off and one of them hit Dad. An ambulance came and took him to the hospital.' Eddie paused again and then added, 'Mam thought you'd know all about that, about the accident.'

Sheridan looked confused for a moment. 'Why would I know...?'

'Well, sir, my mother thought that you'd be wondering where Dad was, as he didn't come back to the office later on.'

'I see.' John Sheridan did see. He'd have to go at once to the Oakleys' house and see the wife. He couldn't let her come to the office.

'Is your mother at home now?' he asked.

'Yes, sir. She's waiting to hear if she can come and see you.'

'Right.' Sheridan got to his feet. 'Well, why don't I come and see her instead? You'd better take me to her straight away.' He collected his hat and coat. Opening the door he found Miss Harper standing in the passage outside her own little cubbyhole. Before she could speak he said, 'Ah, Miss Harper. I have to go out. I'm not sure when I'll be back. I'll talk to the staff then.'

'Just to remind you, sir,' she said stiffly, 'you do have appointments this afternoon.'

'Thank you, I should be back by then, but if I get held up, please present the clients with my apologies and make another appointment.'

As they went down the stairs, Eddie could feel Miss Harper's eyes boring into his back and was glad to be leaving.

Once out in the square Eddie led the way eastwards, through the tangle of streets towards Moorgate, before turning into a narrow cobbled side street, Cockspur Lane. John Sheridan looked around. He had never walked through this area before, and was unfamiliar with these particular streets. Cockspur Lane was lined with brick terraced houses, each much the same as its neighbour, each facing its opposite number across the cobbles of the lane. A small fenced yard separated each house from the street, and a step led up to a front door flanked by two windows, outlined in white. The first-floor windows matched the ones below and a skylight was set into the roof. One or two had a flight of steps leading down from the front yard to a basement or a coal cellar.

Family houses, John Sheridan thought, as he surveyed the narrow lane. So this was where Oakley lived. One cobbled street in a maze of cobbled streets, but the houses seemed reasonably well maintained, far better than some of the dwellings further east, in Shoreditch or Stepney. As Sheridan looked along the street he wondered who actually owned them. Surely not their inhabitants; there would be a landlord and rent to pay, but the families who lived there were unlikely to be labourers or unskilled workers. If he had ever thought about it at all, which until now he had not, Sheridan would have placed Andrew Oakley's home in just such a street. As he followed Eddie along the pavement he realised that the houses were not, in fact, all the same; their residents had tried to put their own stamp on their homes. Different-coloured front doors, whitened front steps, painted railings. Some had flower pots in the front yard, others had window boxes on the upper sills.

Definitely a street where they take pride in their homes, Sheridan thought. Certainly not a slum.

Eddie walked halfway along and then led him through an iron gate to a dark blue front door with the number 31 painted on its doorpost. The door was unlatched and Eddie pushed it open, calling as he did so, 'Mam! Mam! Mr Sheridan's here.'

Here! Mr Sheridan was here? Alice snatched off her apron and retied the scarf covering her hair before hurrying out of the kitchen.

Why on earth had Eddie brought the man here? At least he'd had the sense to take him into the parlour. With one quick glance at herself in the hall mirror, she followed them into the front room.

'Mr Sheridan!' Alice sounded flustered. 'Good morning, sir!'

Sheridan turned to face her, hat in hand, and said, 'Good morning to you, Mrs Oakley. I've come about your letter.'

'Oh, sir,' Alice sounded dismayed. 'I didn't mean you to be troubled to come here. I could easily have come to your office.'

'It is no trouble,' he replied, looking round for somewhere to lay his hat. Finding nowhere suitable, he sat down and kept it on his knee. 'Do sit down, Mrs Oakley.' He indicated one of the stuffed armchairs.

'Just as if it was *his* house and Mam was *his* guest,' Eddie reported to Mabel later. 'Like he owned the place! Arrogant bastard!'

'Having read your letter and thus learned of your husband's accident, I thought it would be better if we talked here, away from the office.' He glanced at Eddie who stood just inside the door. 'So I asked your son to bring me here

54

straight away. I am so sorry, I had no idea. What actually happened? Do you know?'

'We only learned of it ourselves yesterday evening,' said Alice. 'He didn't come home for his tea, and I was beginning to worry when he was so late.' She looked across at Sheridan. 'Not at first, because I know that recently he's had to work late to get something finished... but...' Alice felt tears threaten and determined not to cry in front of Andrew's boss, paused a moment, drawing a deep breath before she continued, 'We decided to eat without him, but then Eddie came in and said there'd been an accident in the Clerkenwell Road and a neighbour thought that it was Andrew she'd seen lying on the pavement.'

'And was she right?' Sheridan tried to curb his impatience. Was the woman ever going to get to the point?

'She wasn't certain, but she said a motor ambulance had taken him away, so if it was him, he'd be in hospital now. Me and the boys, we each went to a hospital where he might have been took, to try and find him... or whoever it was.'

'And did you find him?'

'Yes, sir, he was in the London.'

Now Alice couldn't keep back the tears as she remembered the silent, bandaged figure, lying on the bed.

'One of the barrels that fell off the dray had crushed his legs and he'd been knocked out, when he'd hit his head on the kerb.' Alice pulled a handkerchief from her sleeve and dabbed at her eyes. 'I'm sorry,' she murmured. 'It was seeing him like that, so injured.'

'Did you see a doctor?' asked Sheridan, feeling that at last he was getting somewhere.

'Yes, a Dr Miller. He was ever so kind. He explained they have splinted his broken legs, but—'

'And his head?' interrupted Sheridan.

'Dr Miller said he didn't think his skull was broken, that he was just badly concussed. He told me Andrew's ribs were bruised, maybe broken, and they'd know more once he'd come round again. I'm to go back this afternoon.'

'I see.' John Sheridan was thinking fast. Clearly Oakley wouldn't be fit to come back to work, not within the foreseeable future, if at all.

Maybe, he thought, this accident is a blessing in disguise, for me, anyway. The unfortunate error need not be mentioned. Oakley would recognise it was because of his accident that he was out of a job... Then he realised Alice Oakley was still speaking.

'It may take a while for his legs to heal properly,' she was saying, 'but you will keep his job open for him, won't you?' And then, seeing his expression change, she added forlornly, already knowing his answer, 'Just for a little while... just till they see how he goes on?'

'My dear Mrs Oakley,' Sheridan said smoothly, 'if I could, of course I would. But a business like mine can't function without a senior clerk in the office, you know. Clearly your husband won't be fit to work for some months yet, maybe longer. I have no alternative but to replace him as soon as possible. Of course, should he ever require one, I shall be happy to furnish him with a character.' He gave Alice a sympathetic smile. 'When you are able to visit him in the hospital, please do give him my best wishes and those of everyone in the office.' He reached into his inside pocket and took out his wallet. Abstracting a five pound note from its folds, he held it out to Alice.

'This should help tide you over for a few weeks, perhaps for your rent?' He looked across at Eddie still standing by the door and added, 'After all, you've got a good strong lad there, haven't you? He should bring you in a decent wage. People are always looking for a lad with broad shoulders.'

For a moment Alice just stared at the folded note and then slowly she stood up and took it from him.

'My Andrew worked for you faithfully for nigh on twenty years, Mr Sheridan. Don't you owe him a little more than five pounds?'

Sheridan's lips tightened with displeasure. 'I don't actually owe him anything, madam,' he replied calmly. 'It is hardly my fault that he walked out in front of a brewer's dray.'

'But why was he out of the office?' demanded Alice. 'I don't understand. Why wasn't he at his desk?'

'I really have no idea,' answered Sheridan.

'But you must have sent him out on business, on some errand!' Alice cried.

'No, I had not.' Sheridan put on his hat and moved to the door. 'I am, of course, extremely sorry to hear of his accident, and I wish him a speedy recovery, but now I must bid you good morning, Mrs Oakley, as I have appointments to keep at the office.' He paused as he was about to pass Eddie and said, 'And no doubt you will be around to look after your mother and...' there was the faintest hesitation before he added, 'And the younger children?' He was pretty sure there were two younger children, though he couldn't remember for certain.

As Sheridan went out through the iron gate into the lane, Alice sank back down onto her chair, her head in her hands. Eddie had never seen her cry. He looked down at her, feeling helpless, not knowing what to do or say. In the end he settled for, 'I'll put the kettle on, Mam, and make you some tea.'

7

Dr Miller had told Alice to come back in the afternoon, by which time they would have a better prognosis for Andrew. She decided to take Eddie with her for moral support. She dreaded facing Andrew alone if the news was bad. Mabel and Stephen would probably be back from school before they returned from the hospital, but they were well able to look after themselves.

Dr Miller was away from the ward, so they had to wait for him for a while, sitting side by side on a bench in the corridor as the busyness of the hospital went on round them. One of the nurses passed, carrying something on a tray. Alice caught her arm and said, 'Please, Nurse, may I speak to you? I want to know how my husband is. Mr Oakley. He was brought here yesterday after an accident in the street. Has he come round all right?'

The nurse looked down at her with sympathy and said, 'Sorry, I can't speak about one of the patients, you'll have to wait for the doctor. I don't expect he'll be long. Sister knows you're here and she'll tell him.' She gave what she hoped was a reassuring smile and went on her way. Alice was not at all reassured, but there was nothing they could do but sit and wait.

When Dr Miller finally came, he led them into the same little side room as the day before. Alice introduced Eddie and the doctor suggested they took the two chairs while he remained standing.

'Mrs Oakley,' he said when they were seated. 'The good news is that your husband regained consciousness during the night. He has no memory of what happened to him, indeed the last thing he says he remembers is leaving the house to go to his office yesterday morning. The rest is, at present anyway, a blank.'

Alice bit her lip. 'Will he get his memory back?' she asked in dismay.

'Probably a bit at a time. It's only the one day he can't remember.'

'And the bad news?' interjected Eddie. 'What's that?'

'I'm afraid your father has injured his back. We knew he had major bruising round his hips and pelvis, but it wasn't until he was conscious that we were able to assess the actual damage to his back.'

'And what is it?' Eddie demanded.

'I'm afraid the news we have for you isn't good.' Dr Miller looked at the two of them with compassion in his eyes. He hated breaking news like this to a patient's relatives, and he'd already had to break it to the man himself.

'I'm afraid there's no way to break this to you gently, Mrs Oakley. Your husband has no feeling in his legs. He is unable to move them, and I'm afraid you're all going to have to face the fact he'll never walk again. The barrel that crushed his legs, or another like it, must have ruptured his spinal cord and there is no communication between his brain and his legs.'

'Never?' whispered Alice. 'Not ever?'

'I'm sorry,' replied the doctor. 'But once that's happened, it can't be mended. We can mend the bones and muscles, but not the nerves that tell them what to do.'

'But there must be something you can do!' cried Eddie angrily. 'He can't stay in bed for ever!'

'No, he can't,' agreed Dr Miller. 'And hard as it is right now, we have to look to the positives. He will be able to use his upper body, his arms, his hands. He'll be able to sit up in a chair and you will be able to push him in a wheelchair, so he won't be housebound. In fact, in time, with the right chair, he should be able to propel himself on level ground.' He turned to Alice. 'The brunt of his care will fall on you, Mrs Oakley. Do you live in a house or a block?'

'We live in a house,' she murmured. 'With stairs.'

'There will be some things that he won't be able to do and stairs is one of them. Can you make him a room downstairs so that he's part of the household?' He paused and when neither of them spoke, he went on, 'There will be things he can do for himself, and he must be encouraged to. Then if you're able to look after him, there shouldn't be any reason why he can't live at home.'

For a moment a silence enveloped them, as Alice and Eddie tried to assimilate what the doctor had told them.

'Can I see him now?' asked Alice eventually.

'Yes,' replied the doctor, 'just for a few moments. He needs his rest, but I know he'd love to see you, both of you, but only one at a time, just five minutes each.'

He led Alice into the ward to the bed curtained off in the corner. He held the curtain aside and Alice slipped in past him. Andrew was lying with his eyes shut, the bandage still round his head.

'Andrew? Are you awake?' Alice's voice was a mere whisper, but it was enough to make him open his eyes. She took the bedside chair and reached for his hand.

'Alice,' he breathed. 'I can't move my legs. I can't even feel them.' As he spoke, a tear oozed from his unbandaged eye and slid down his cheek.

'I know, dearest,' murmured Alice. 'But you're alive! I was afraid you were going to die. I couldn't live without you, Andrew.'

'But I'm no good to you now, am I?' he said bitterly. 'A cripple? For the rest of my life? It would have been better if I had died. I wish I had. Dear God, I wish I had.'

Alice gripped his hand more tightly. 'Don't you ever say that again, Andrew,' she said fiercely. 'Never, you hear me. I need you, the children need you...'

'And I'll only be a burden... to all of you.'

'You're my husband, Andrew,' Alice spoke more gently, 'and I love you, as I have always loved you. "For better or worse, in sickness and in health", isn't that what we promised in church all those years ago? You're still the man I made that promise to.' She reached forward and stroked his cheek, wiping away his tears with her finger. 'The doctor said only a few minutes. Eddie's waiting outside to see you, just for a moment. He's as good as grown now, and we'll manage until we can get you home again.' She got to her feet and bent to kiss his face. 'I'll come back tomorrow and every day, I promise.' Then she turned away, slipping out between the curtains, before he could see the tears on her cheeks.

Eddie hesitated when he saw her distress. Should he go in?

'Just for a moment,' reminded the doctor.

'Dad?' Eddie looked down at the figure in the bed. Was it really his father? He looked so small under the bedclothes. 'Dad? It's me. Eddie. Just to tell you that I'll look after Mam until you can come home.'

The man in the bed had his eyes closed and even when Eddie spoke he did not open them. It was as if he hadn't heard him, and when he made no response, Eddie, not knowing what else to say or do, quietly left the cubicle to join his mother, waiting in the corridor outside the ward. The doctor had gone, the nurses were busy and so the two of them walked out into the street, where the world went on with its business as if Andrew Oakley were as fit and well as he had been yesterday.

'Mam,' Eddie said at last. 'How will Dad cope if his legs don't work?'

'Somehow,' replied his mother shortly. 'We'll all cope somehow. He's your dad, so we'll all cope.' But she wasn't sure how.

She had hoped for more from Mr Sheridan as Andrew had been with the firm for so long. Though she had seen him a few times, she had only really met him once. The partners rarely mixed with their staff in any social manner, but on Coronation Day back in the summer of 1911, the office had been closed for two whole days. On Coronation Day itself the staff had been able to join the cheering crowds in the street, and the following day Mrs Sheridan had organised a tea party for them all in her garden. On that occasion both Mr and Mrs Sheridan had spoken to Alice in the most courteous manner. Mrs Sheridan had asked after their children and Mr Sheridan praised Andrew as a valued member of staff. Alice had thought him a pleasant, outgoing man. He'd seemed approachable, which was why she had plucked up courage and asked to see him. She would have been happy to go to the office and thought it surprising that he should come to their home, especially as he didn't seem to have heard about the accident, but today she had seen a different side of him, dismissive and coldly businesslike. Admittedly he had given her the five pounds, but with little interest in how her family was going to manage with two children still at school and no regular wage coming in. She'd told Eddie they'd cope, but she wasn't at all sure how. All their lives were about to change.

Alice was right about John Sheridan's lack of interest in her family's fortunes. When he returned to the office, he called Miss Harper in to take dictation.

'Sad news, Miss Harper,' he said. 'Mr Oakley is in hospital after a traffic accident yesterday. He will not be returning to us after all. We need to advertise for another experienced clerk. Take this down.'

Miss Harper showed no surprise at the idea that Mr Oakley might have been coming back. She asked nothing about the accident, nor did she mention the fact that Oakley had already been sacked before it occurred. She simply said, 'Yes, sir.'

Once the advertisement had been drafted, Miss Harper was turning for the door when Mr Sheridan remarked, 'I will speak to the staff before they leave this evening and tell them about Mr Oakley's accident so they understand why he's unable to return to us... as I'm sure you do, Miss Harper.'

'Yes, sir. A very sad accident.'

'Indeed,' agreed her boss. 'Send Bevis in to me, will you?'

At the end of the day John Sheridan caught his usual train home. He had dealt with Bevis who now understood that he must forget anything he had seen or heard the previous day, and he had broken the sad news of Andrew Oakley's accident to the rest of the staff. All the loose ends seemed to him to have been tidied up, and once he had a new man to take Oakley's place, the office could continue as always.

Anne was sitting by the fire when he got home again.

'It's such a chilly evening,' she said as he reached down to kiss her cheek. 'I had the fire lit early so we'd have a cosy drink in here.'

'Good idea,' he said, and poured them each a whisky. Handing Anne her glass, he sat down with a sigh. 'It's been a bit of a day, one way and another.'

'Did you see Mr Oakley?' asked Anne once John was settled.

He took a swallow of his whisky. 'No, I didn't. I couldn't. He was in hospital.'

'In hospital!' echoed Anne. 'Why? What's the matter with him? Is he ill?'

'No,' John answered. 'He had an accident in the street on his way home yesterday.'

'An accident?' repeated Anne. 'What happened? Is he all right?'

John took another sip of whisky before he set his glass

down and told her about his visit to Cockspur Lane and what he knew about Andrew Oakley's predicament.

'Poor man!' she murmured. 'And his poor wife. She must be so worried.'

'She asked me to keep his job open for him...'

'And what did you say?'

'I told her it was impossible.'

'Oh, John...'

'Well, let's face it, Anne, it is. Heaven only knows how long he'll be in hospital with broken legs and ribs and a head injury, it could be months... and that's only if he is able to recover from those. It sounded to me as if he might have done more serious damage to his back. I can't be without a senior clerk for months on end. I need to replace him as soon as I can.'

'So what did you say?'

'I had to be honest with her. I had to say it would be impossible. But of course she has no idea about what happened yesterday at the office. She doesn't know he'd actually been dismissed.'

'But surely he'll tell her,' pointed out Anne. 'After all, it's hardly a thing he'll keep to himself.'

'Possibly, but we'll cross that bridge when we come to it. Whatever happens, he won't be working for us any more.' He looked across at Anne's anxious face. 'Don't worry about them, darling. I gave her something to help tide her over. The son who came to find me today, Eddie, he's a strong, hefty lad. He's almost certainly earning his crust.'

'But haven't they got two other children? A girl, isn't there? She must be about to leave school. And a younger boy?'

'Yes, you're right, darling,' replied John. 'Clever of you to remember. Well, no doubt the girl will go into service somewhere, which will help, and when the younger boy leaves school, which probably won't be long, there will be three wage earners in the family. They'll do all right, you don't have to worry about them. And who knows, Oakley himself may recover well enough to work again. I told Mrs Oakley, I'll be happy to give him a reference should he need one. After all, it will be clear to the world at large that he lost his job because of the accident. There'd be no need to mention the matter of Peter Everette's papers.'

Anne smiled at him, pleased that he had thought of all the things that might help the Oakley family. 'You're a good man, John.'

It's what she always thought, and what she always said when he made important decisions. And anxious for her approbation, it was what he allowed her to believe. There was no need to worry her with the minutiae of his business dealings.

8

Jane Birch was walking home from Holman's butcher's shop where she helped once a week with the accounts. On a Thursday, which was early closing, she would spend the afternoon going through the accounts with Robert Holman, sorting out the weekly takings and expenditure. Mr Holman was no good at figures and keeping on top of his finances was a weekly chore. When she had left today he had given her some scrag end of beef and she was hurrying home to have a meat pie ready for when George came in from the council offices where he worked as a clerk.

'I 'spect your George could fancy a bit of meat pie,' Mr Holman said and Jane had agreed. She thought there might be enough for two pies, if she were careful. As she rounded the corner into Wagg Street, she was almost floored by Winnie Parker. Jane's basket went flying and the brown paper parcel of meat landed in the gutter. She made a grab for it, before it could be spoiled, and pushed it back into her basket.

'Oh, I'm sorry,' Winnie cried, and then, seeing who it was that she'd almost knocked over, she said, 'Oh, Jane, are you all right?'

Having retrieved her meat, Jane said, 'Yes, no harm done.'

'Good,' said Winnie. 'Because you see, well, I'm glad it's you, cos I've just been round to see you, but you was out.'

'So I was,' agreed Jane wryly. 'What was it you wanted?'

'I just come round to ask how your brother was,' replied Winnie.

'My brother? He's fine as far as I know.' And then because Winnie Parker was a noted gossip, always anxious to be in the know, she added, 'Why?'

'Oh dear? Hasn't Alice told you?'

'Told me what?'

'Told you about poor Andrew's accident.'

Now she really had Jane's attention and she went on, 'Yesterday, he was knocked down in the Clerkenwell Road. A brewer's dray. He was took to hospital in an ambulance.' When Jane simply stared at her but said nothing, Winnie added, 'He didn't look good.'

'You saw him?' demanded Jane.

'Well yes, I'm pretty sure it was him. I told poor Alice last night. She hadn't heard. I told her he'd been took to hospital in one of them new motor ambulances, but I didn't know which one. So she said she'd go round them all, to see if she could find him.'

'And did she? Did she find him?'

'I don't rightly know,' admitted Winnie. 'She didn't come back and say.'

'I see,' replied Jane shortly. 'Thank you for letting me know.' She was about to hurry on home when she turned back.

'You're sure it was Andrew, Winnie?'

'Fairly sure,' Winnie replied. 'He was lying in the gutter. It was difficult to tell, but I think it was him.'

'I must get home,' Jane said, and with a brief nod, she turned and hurried along the road to her own front door. Once inside, all thoughts of meat pies dismissed, she stashed the beef in the meat safe and sat down at the kitchen table.

Andrew? Knocked down in the street? She didn't even take her coat off. She must go round to Cockspur Lane at once, and find out if Winnie had got things right. Jane would certainly take her to task, if she were wrong. She shouldn't spread rumours like that if she wasn't sure.

As she hurried to her brother's house her mind flipped from one thing to another. Perhaps Winnie had got it wrong. She probably had, knowing Winnie! Perhaps it hadn't been Andrew who was knocked down. If it was it might not be as bad as Winnie had thought. Surely Alice would have come and told her if Andrew was badly hurt. After all, they were only three streets away. No! Winnie must have got the wrong end of the stick... or she'd been mistaken. It must have been somebody else lying in the gutter.

When she reached the house in Cockspur Lane, she paused on the pavement before going up to the front door. Suppose it really was Andrew? Suppose he was dead?

Only one way to find out, she decided, and raised her hand to the knocker.

It was Mabel who came to the door. She looked pale and drawn, and tears had stained her cheeks.

'Hello, Auntie Jane,' she murmured. Not her usual ebullient welcome.

'Mabel?' her aunt said. 'Are you all right, duck?'

Mabel sniffed hard and, wiping her nose on her sleeve, replied, 'No, not really.'

'Is your mam at home?'

In answer Mabel stood aside and let her aunt into the house, calling, 'It's Auntie Jane, Mam.' Her relief at the arrival of another adult was immense. Someone grown up to take responsibility for what they should do. The burden of what had happened pressed down on her shoulders like a ton weight. Perhaps Auntie Jane would know what to do next. What Mam had been telling them was too much to take in, and again Mabel's tears began to fall.

She and Stephen had been waiting anxiously at home when Alice and Eddie got back from the hospital.

'How is he, Mam?' asked Mabel, the moment her mother was through the door. 'How's Dada? Is he getting better?'

'Let me get my coat off, girl,' replied Alice testily. 'And put the kettle on, I need a cup of tea.'

'It's just boiled,' Mabel said, picking up the pot that was warmed and ready.

Once they were all sitting round the kitchen table and Alice had taken a sip of her tea, Stephen ventured, 'Did you see Dad, Mam?'

Alice knew they had to talk about the news she had received that afternoon; that she had to explain, so they could all understand how different and difficult life was going to be. From today, nothing would ever be the same again. But how to begin? They were still children really, even Eddie, sixteen and about to start on his apprenticeship. She looked across the table at them, her and Andrew's children, and seeing their fearful faces brought tears to her own eyes.

Blinking them away, she took another mouthful of tea, grateful for its warmth before she began to explain.

'Yes,' she said at last. 'Yes, I saw him, Stephen.' She glanced at Eddie, saying, 'We both did.'

'Eddie did?' cried Mabel. 'That's not fair! I wanted to see him and you said I couldn't.'

'Mabel, love,' Alice said patiently, 'you have to understand that Dad is badly hurt. He's exhausted and in pain. We only had five minutes with him today,' adding, as she saw the disappointment on Mabel's face, 'Perhaps at the weekend he'll be up to having visitors.'

Mabel was about to protest further when Eddie cut her off. 'Mabel, Dad's very ill. The doctor told us he's never going to walk again!'

There, he'd said it. It was too blunt, Alice knew. She had been going to broach the subject gently, but it had been difficult finding the right words. Now Eddie had said it and perhaps it was the only way to break such dreadful news, to come straight out with it. His words were greeted with stunned silence and then Mabel burst into tears.

'But they've mended his legs,' she sobbed. 'You said so last night, Mam. When they're better, he'll be able to walk again, won't he?' She turned her tear-streaked face to her mother for reassurance. 'Maybe with a walking stick?'

'The doctors say that the bones in his legs will mend all right,' Alice said, 'but they say his back is broken; he can't feel his legs… and,' her voice a whisper now, 'he can't move them.'

Her words were greeted with an anguished silence, broken only by Mabel's sobs as she and Stephen stared at their mother in horror, trying to make sense of what they'd just heard; what the words actually meant. Dad couldn't move his legs.

Eddie thought of his apprenticeship, due to start on the first of next month with Carter's Cabinet and Furniture Manufacturers. His days would be long and hard; spent at the factory and with no real wages. He'd only be home to eat and sleep. How would Mam manage when Dad came home? If he came home.

Mabel realised she'd have to work extra hard at school to make sure she passed the exam, and then help Mam more when she got home. Evening classes would have to wait.

Stephen was thinking Dad wouldn't be able to play football with him in the park any more and wondered how he would be able to get to the office each day.

Alice knew none of them had understood the depth of the changes coming to their lives; how little they would have to live on, with no wages coming in. She had to give them time to adjust to their new lives... lives where sacrifices would have to be made. She would have to adjust to a whole new life herself; a new, caring routine with Andrew at its centre. She'd have to explain all this, but not yet, not until the dreadful truth of the situation had sunk in. She knew the best way to cope would be in practicalities.

However, before she could say more, there was a loud knock on the front door. For a moment nobody moved. Nobody wanted visitors, but at a nod from her mother, Mabel went to see who had called and Alice heard the familiar voice of Jane Birch, her sister-in-law.

Jane followed Mabel into the kitchen. She paused in the doorway, taking in Alice's strained expression, her pallor, the dark circles under her eyes, and said, 'So it's true, what Winnie Parker's just told me? That Andrew's had an accident?'

'Yes,' Alice replied. 'He'll be in hospital for some time.'

Jane's eyes widened. 'Is it that bad?' she said. 'What happened? Winnie said something about a brewer's dray.'

'I might have known Winnie Parker would be gossiping,' Alice said bitterly. 'Likes to be the centre of attention does Madam Know-all.'

'She came round to tell me,' Jane said. 'But I wasn't sure she'd got it right. Has she?'

'I've just come back from the hospital,' Alice said. 'Andrew's got broken legs, a cracked head and probably broken ribs.' And then she fell silent. Why couldn't she tell Jane the whole truth? But something held her back. She wasn't ready to tell anyone else the dreadful news, that her beloved Andrew was going to be paralysed from his waist down, paralysed for the rest of his life. The very word filled her with an aching emptiness.

None of the children spoke, no one wanted to tell Auntie Jane the whole story. But Jane wasn't stupid and the silence warned her that something far worse had *not* been told.

Eddie had got to his feet when she had come in and now she took his chair. Seeing the teapot on the table, she said casually, 'Any tea in that pot?'

Alice jerked her head and said, 'Of course. Mabel, top it up and get a cup for Auntie Jane.'

With tea poured and cup in hand, Jane said, 'So what did happen? Winnie was full of doom and gloom. Had I heard the dreadful news about Andrew? Did I know if he was still alive, and wondering how you were going to manage if he was left a cripple.'

'Winnie Parker has a big mouth on her,' retorted Alice. 'She saw an accident in the street and someone was taken to hospital. She thought it might be Andrew. She don't even know which hospital.'

'And which is it?' asked Jane gently.

'It's the London.'

'Well,' said Jane, 'if you have to be in hospital, I reckon that's as good as any. What does the doctor say?' She looked at the little family grouped round the table.

Alice drew a deep breath. Andrew's sister was entitled to know and so, fighting the tears that threatened to overwhelm her, she broke the news.

'They say he'll never walk again.'

As she heard the extent of his injuries, the colour fled from Jane's cheeks and she stared in horror at Alice.

'Is there nothing they can do?' she whispered, when Alice finally lapsed into silence.

Alice shook her head. 'Nothing. They say he's lucky to be alive.'

'Can he have visitors?' Jane asked softly. 'Can I go and see him?'

When Alice didn't answer, Mabel said, 'Mam says he's very tired. She and Eddie only saw him for five minutes today.'

'I see,' Jane said. 'Well, when he's a little stronger perhaps.' She placed her empty cup back on its saucer and, reaching for Alice's hand, asked, 'Alice, is there anything I can do to help?' She looked at the pale faces around the kitchen table and felt completely helpless. What could anyone do? But it was a family tragedy and at times like these, families must stick together. She suddenly thought of her sister, Susan.

'Does Susan know?' she asked. 'Would you like me to tell her?'

Until Jane asked, Alice hadn't even thought of Susan, Andrew's other sister. Of course she must be told.

'Will you? I – I haven't…' Her voice trailed off.

'No, of course you haven't,' Jane said at once. 'Don't worry about her, I'll go round there on my way home.' She got to her feet. 'I'd better go,' she said. 'I'll tell Susan and I'll come and see you again in the morning.' She sounded brisk and efficient, but she needed to get out of the house before her tears got the better of her. If she started to cry, she'd be no use to anyone. Mabel went to the front door with her and was surprised when Auntie Jane suddenly reached for her and gave her a long, hard hug.

'Look after your mam, now, won't you?' she said. 'Things are going to be difficult and you're all going to have to be very strong.'

Mabel nodded and Auntie Jane planted a kiss on her forehead and said, 'Good girl, I knew I could rely on you. Don't forget, if there is anything we can do, or if you need anything, you know where we are. Just come round and ask.'

9

It was with great relief that Mabel left for school the morning after Auntie Jane's visit. The previous evening had been horrible. Once Auntie Jane had gone, her mother had got to her feet and said, 'We'd better find something for supper.' And she had gone into the pantry and found some cheese and a rather tired-looking cauliflower and set about making cauliflower cheese. It was one of Mabel's least favourite meals.

'I like cauliflower,' she used to say, 'and I like cheese, but I loathe cauliflower cheese, they simply don't go!' But last night they had sat down to eat the cauliflower floating in runny cheese sauce and no one had said a word.

'Have you got homework?' Mam had asked her once the washing up was done.

Mabel said she had, maths, and she was sent upstairs to do it. She sat at the small table in her room and pulled her books out of her satchel, but when she opened her maths book and looked at the work she'd been set, none of it made any sense to her, and she pushed the book away. She thought of Dada, lying in his hospital bed, his broken legs all bound up... and useless. How would he manage for the rest of his life? For the first time she had an inkling of how things were going to be, and she flung herself onto her bed and began to weep. She wept for her father, only half a man now, and for herself, a girl with only half a dad. Mabel, with no tears left, lay on her bed and watched the moon sail out from behind a cloud, a silver disc hanging over the city. Was Dada looking at the same moon from his hospital bed? she wondered. Could he see the sky from where he lay? What would he be thinking about?

A little later she heard her mother and her brothers come up the stairs, the boys to the bedroom they shared and Mam pausing outside her bedroom door. Mabel lay still and quiet, hoping Mam wouldn't come in to see her. She didn't want to talk to anyone, not Mam, not the boys. After a long moment her mother must have decided not to disturb her again tonight for she did not knock, and Mabel heard her move along the landing to her bedroom, the sound of that door opening and closing and then silence. Sometime later, Mabel got off the bed and undressed. She switched off her light and, going to the window in her nightdress, looked across the tiny yard below to the back of the houses in the next street. Some still had light shining from uncurtained windows, others the warm glow of diffused light from inside, and a few were already shrouded in darkness. Even as she watched, one of the lights went out. Someone else going to bed, she thought, someone whose world is as it always has been, not turned topsy-turvy by a brewer's dray. Mabel turned away and got into bed, her final thought as she drifted off to sleep, I'll have to tell Miss Chapman in the morning.

Alice was pleased neither Mabel nor Stephen made any

fuss about being sent off to school in the usual way. Much better for them, she'd decided as she lay sleepless in her bed, for things to be as normal as possible until they had worked out exactly how they were going to manage. Jane had said she would come round again in the morning and perhaps they could discuss various possibilities.

At school, Miss Chapman listened as Mabel told her what had happened, and was pleased to hear Mabel say, 'It won't make any difference to me taking the exam next month. My mother's very keen for me to stay on at school for at least another year.'

'That's good,' she had replied. 'No doubt your mother will confirm that to me in due course. I quite understand that she has other things on her mind just now, so I will enter your name for the entrance exam, and we can take it from there.'

'Mam doesn't want us to talk about the accident,' Mabel told her. 'She doesn't want us to be the centre of gossip.'

'Of course,' said Miss Chapman sympathetically. The consequences of such an accident would be harsh and far-reaching, but she knew that the news would soon be common knowledge, the way that everything became common knowledge, as people passed it on and speculated. It would only be a couple of days at the most before everyone knew that Andrew Oakley would never walk again. She, Miss Chapman, would say nothing, but she was certain she would hear the news from someone, somewhere, before the day was out.

Mabel told no one else, not even Annie. She had promised Mam not to tell and she kept her word. All day she concentrated on her work, and was only pulled up twice for wool-gathering. At the end of the afternoon, she slipped quickly out of the playground, telling Annie that she had promised Mam to go straight home.

'She wasn't feeling well this morning,' Mabel improvised.

Annie watched as her friend hurried off round the corner.

That's the second day running she's gone straight home, she thought, and, seeing Stephen wandering across the schoolyard, she went over to him and asked, 'Is your mum all right?'

Surprised, Stephen said, 'Sort of. Why?'

Annie shrugged. 'Mabel said she wasn't feeling well.'

Stephen pulled himself together and mumbled, 'No, well she ain't. I got to go.' And he broke into a run, disappearing round the corner just as Mabel had done, and Annie was left feeling certain that something was badly wrong.

Mabel had no intention of going straight home, and once she was safely out of sight, she cut down towards the railway line and the bridge. She had to talk to someone, and the only person she could think of was Mr Clarke. He was her friend, he would listen to her. Telling Mr Clarke wasn't exactly breaking her promise to Mam. He would never gossip, and it was only gossip that was worrying Mam.

As she entered the alley leading to the bridge she listened for the regular clunk of the printing press, but heard nothing. Oh, please let him be there, she prayed. When she reached his little shed, she found the door ajar and the printing press silent. Mr Clarke himself was sitting in his chair, cradling a mug of tea in his hands. Mabel paused in the doorway and for a moment he didn't see her; the chair was turned to the small window that looked out across the railway lines below. Looking at him, he seemed to Mabel somehow smaller than usual, thinner, and because he had his back to her she could see that the hair on the back of his head was far whiter than the dark quiff that sprouted over his forehead. For a moment he looked suddenly much older.

'Hello?' she said, unexpectedly tentative.

He turned his head at once and, seeing who was there, his face broke into a wide smile.

'Mabel!' he cried, getting to his feet. 'My dear girl, come in and have some tea. I've only just stopped for mine and the kettle's still hot.' He picked up her mug and poured a dash of milk into the bottom of it before adding tea from the familiar little brown pot.

'Here,' he said, pulling out the stool he'd brought to the shed, especially for her. 'Sit you down and drink your tea. Tell me what you've been doing.'

Now he was facing her, he looked like himself again, his eyes shining with pleasure behind his spectacles. 'Did your father agree you should take the exam for the secondary school? I'm sure he did, because it would make him so proud of you if you passed that!'

At once he saw her expression change and he said, 'My dear girl. What's wrong? Did he say no?'

Mabel shook her head. 'No,' she whispered. 'He doesn't know.'

'Doesn't know? Doesn't know your teacher thinks that you should try?' He saw that she was trying not to cry and he said, 'Mabel? What's wrong? What's happened?'

For a long moment neither of them spoke, and Mr Clarke sat back in the chair and drank some more of his tea. He didn't ask anything else. If she wanted to tell him, she would, and if she didn't want to, he wasn't going to press her. The silence stretched between them, a bubble of peace enclosing them, and for a while they were content, neither of them wanting to break it.

'It's Dada,' she said at last, and then stopped again.

'Your father.'

'Yes. There's been an accident.'

'To your father?'

'Yes.' And then it all came pouring out, her words tumbling, at times almost incoherent, as she tried to explain what had happened. Mr Clarke listened without interruption, extracting the gist of what she was saying, so that when she finally fell silent he had a pretty good idea of what had occurred. She had been clutching her mug as she spoke and now she set it down. Her hands were shaking and she felt in her sleeve for her hankie, but somehow or somewhere it must have fallen out, and she dashed the tears from her eyes with the back of her hand.

Mr Clarke produced a crumpled handkerchief from his pocket and passed it over. 'Hasn't been ironed,' he said, 'but I assure you it's clean.'

Mabel took it, mopping her eyes and blowing her nose, before looking at it in surprise, as if she didn't know where it had come from.

'Keep it for now,' he said with a smile, 'you can bring it back another day.' There was a pause and then, knowing that now the news had been told, Mabel needed to talk about it, he asked, 'So, how is your poor mother?'

'Mam? She seems all right. She says everything will be different from now on.'

'I'm sure she's right,' agreed Mr Clarke. 'How could it not be... for all of you?' When she said nothing more, he asked, 'How long will he have to stay in hospital, do you know?'

Mabel shook her head. 'Till his legs have mended,' she said, adding on a sob, 'but even then they won't work. He won't be able to walk.'

'But he will come home again?'

'Yes, of course.' Mabel had never considered that he might not.

'That will be extremely difficult for your mother, he will probably need a lot of nursing, at least in the beginning.' He thought for a moment and then asked, 'Does she go out to work?'

'Mam? No. She looks after us all at home.'

'And your brothers?'

'Eddie's about to start his apprenticeship at Carter's and Stephen is still at school, he's not quite thirteen.'

'And you're at school. So your father is the only breadwinner.' He spoke matter-of-factly, so that at first Mabel didn't see what he was driving at.

'I suppose so,' she agreed. 'He's never allowed Mam to go out to work.'

'I think she'll have to now,' Mr Clarke said mildly, 'or you'll have nothing to live on.'

'But when I've trained as a secretary I shall be earning good money,' Mabel pointed out.

'So you will,' he conceded, 'but in the meantime?'

'Well, I don't know, I mean, well…'

Mr Clarke gave her a quizzical look. 'Your brother Eddie, he won't earn very much during his apprenticeship, will he? And Stephen? Nothing at all.' Another silence fell and then he said, 'And what about you?'

'I will be earning, just as soon as I've trained…'

'But you could leave school… and get a job now,' he suggested. 'You're fifteen, you can leave and find a job.'

'No!' Mabel jumped to her feet. 'No, I want to train as a secretary!'

'I know you do, my dear child—'

'I'm not a child!'

'No,' he agreed, 'you're not, which is why you have to consider what you can do to help your family.'

'I don't want to get just any old job,' Mabel said fiercely.

'I'm sure you don't, but then your father doesn't want to be without the use of his legs, and you have to consider which is the greater hardship.'

'That's not fair!' cried Mabel, sounding like the child she'd said she wasn't.

'No, my dear,' agreed Mr Clarke gently. 'But life isn't, and the sooner you learn that the better. You're an intelligent girl with great strength of character, but there are going to come times in your life when you have to make some hard decisions, and all I'm saying is that this could be one of them.'

'You don't know what it's like,' Mabel said truculently.

'Oh, I think I do. Life has a way of kicking you in the teeth, you know.'

'It's all right for you,' she growled.

'It is now,' he agreed amiably. She was staring at him angrily and he smiled at her. Her anger was because of the situation, not because of what he'd said to her, and when she'd had time to think it over he hoped she would see what had to be done.

'I'm going home now,' she said, defiance in her voice.

'And you needn't think I'm coming back. I don't need you to tell me what to do!'

'Of course you don't,' he allowed, 'but I'll always be here if you want to come and see me.'

When she had gone Mr Clarke squeezed another half cup from the pot and considered what Mabel had told him. It was a dreadful situation and he rather doubted that unless Mabel's mother was a really remarkable woman, she would not be able to have her husband to live at home. Mabel had clearly not taken on board the difficulties the family was going to face.

Was I too hard on the poor girl? he wondered. Maybe, but she's going to have to earn her keep, and not in two or three years' time, but now, when it truly matters.

10

Since Andrew's accident, Alice had started waking far earlier than usual. Sometimes, she awoke in the middle of the night and, unable to sleep, she would lie in bed, her mind churning with all the problems that threatened to overwhelm her. Often, she gave up trying to sleep and got up to make a cup of tea. How, she wondered as she sat in the kitchen in the grey light of dawn, were they going to survive without a regular wage coming in? Ideas came and went, were considered and discarded as impractical. It was clear to her that she, herself, must find some sort of employment, but she was qualified for nothing except for the most menial work – cooking, cleaning, laundry, mending. Going into service? Impossible! She was needed at home, and would be even more so when Andrew was eventually discharged from the hospital.

What would she do then? She had no real idea what it would entail, looking after him at home. It was something she would have to learn as they went along, but she knew she would need to be in the house with him, not going off to work, leaving him alone all day.

It was when lying awake in bed at three o'clock one

morning that she thought of Mr Moses. Saul Moses, the tailor from whom Andrew bought his office suit and shirts and his winter overcoat. The narrow shop, where the tailor designed and measured and cut out suits made to order, or more often off the peg, was among a jumble of crooked streets little more than half a mile away, and behind it was the overcrowded, stuffy workshop where apprentices and sewing maids actually produced the clothes. Alice had heard he also employed out-workers, those who worked at home. She wondered if he would take her on as one such and made up her mind to go and see him.

Saul Moses was working at the cutting table at the back of the shop when Alice entered, but looking up and recognising her as the wife of one of his customers, he put down his shears and came forward to greet her.

'Mrs Oakley,' he said. 'Good morning. How can I help you?'

Alice returned his greeting and he said, 'I heard about Mr Oakley's accident.'

Of course he had. Who had not?

'What a dreadful thing!' he continued. 'How is he, the poor gentleman? Still in the hospital?'

'For the time being,' Alice replied. 'We don't know how long for.'

'What a worry for you, my dear madam. What a worry.' He shook his head in sympathy.

'It is,' Alice said, 'and that's why I've come to see you.'

The tailor looked at her quizzically for a moment and then smiled encouragingly. 'You have come to see me... so tell me why. He needs pyjamas?'

'No, Mr Moses, not pyjamas.' There was no point in prevaricating. 'I've come because I need work,' she said.

Saul Moses raised his hands in dismay. 'My dear lady! Surely you cannot work here.' He waved a hand in the vague direction of the workshop in the outside yard. 'It would not do at all. Not at all!'

'Not in your workshop,' she agreed, and explained what she had hoped she might be able to do.

He heard her out in silence and then asked what experience she had.

'None,' she admitted, 'except that I've always made clothes for myself and my children.'

He looked at her, chin held high, as she waited for his response, and thought how brave she was, a woman of her class coming to ask him for work, the sort of work that was the province of the ill-educated girls in his overcrowded workroom.

Could he possibly employ her? She might work for him doing piecework, at home. Plain sewing at first, but if she proved more skilled, moving on to setting sleeves, and the delicate work on collars and cuffs.

'I could give you a trial,' he said at last. 'See how you get on.' And he laid out how it would work. She must collect the work before he closed up in the evening, and bring it back before closure the following evening. She would earn a few pence per article and be paid on Friday afternoons before the workshop closed for the Sabbath.

Alice found herself torn between relief that she might have some money coming in and worry that her work might not be good enough, but she managed a smile and thanked him.

'You are a neighbour,' he said, 'and you need my help, but,' he shook a finger at her, 'never doubt this is a business agreement. Either side may terminate it.'

This gave Alice a new routine, a framework for her life. She dealt with the usual household matters first thing in the morning, and then she sewed for the rest of the day, with only a short break in the afternoon to visit Andrew in the hospital. She never stayed with him very long because she knew her visits exhausted him; on more than one occasion he had fallen asleep as she sat beside him, holding his hand. When she left his bedside she went straight home, ready for the children's return, continuing to sew until the work was done.

Alice had not told Andrew about her job, or all the other things that were going on in the family. She always spoke very positively about when he would be home, and for a while, he allowed her to do so, not feeling able to face his future as bravely as she.

'It will take your husband some time to come to anything like terms with what has happened to him,' Dr Miller had told her one afternoon when she'd found Andrew angry and aggressive and she'd left the ward in tears. Once again the doctor had taken her aside and explained, as best he could, what was going on in Andrew's mind. 'You must be prepared for his morale to be low and accept that at present his future looks, to him at least, like an endless desert of nothingness and dependence. Mentally, things should improve, but only very slowly. He must learn not to look too far ahead, to take one day at a time; sometimes his frustration will turn to anger, and at others, to despair. The improvement will be very gradual and you will have to have strength and patience enough for both of you. He'll make better progress in his own home, provided you can manage his care.'

Alice thought he was right and was grateful for his help, but she knew that when it came down to it, it would be she who had to manage the change in all their lives and it added to the worries that kept her sleepless in the small hours.

After the confusion of the first days in the hospital, the blank in Andrew's mind had given way to flashes of memory; at first of the accident, the terrified neighing of the horses, the plunging hooves, rolling barrels and then darkness. It was several days before, piece by piece, the rest of that fateful day gradually returned to his memory, his arrival at the office, being called in to see Mr Sheridan, his summary dismissal. These memories added to his emotional turmoil; his moods swinging from rage, to misery, to self-pity, the depths of depression, bitterness, back to anger, blaming his accident on John Sheridan and Peter Everette. He should have been safe in the office, not out on the street.

All this made Alice's visits very difficult, never able to predict his mood from one day to the next. He longed to see her, but when she arrived he was consumed with misery. He couldn't talk to her, tell her the truth of what had happened that day, even when he finally remembered the events in the office quite clearly. Then one afternoon, when she was sitting down quietly beside his bed, he asked what his children were doing. So far he hadn't asked about them.

Alice said they were all well and working hard. It was then that she mentioned she was doing piecework at home for Mr Moses the tailor.

For a moment Andrew looked at her in horror, but she forestalled any comment by continuing quickly, 'We have to have an income, Andrew, and he's been very generous in allowing me to work at home.'

'What about Sheridan?' asked Andrew. 'Did he tell you that—'

'He came to see me at home,' she interrupted. 'He gave me some money to be going on with... until you can get back to work.'

'Get back to work!' Andrew gave a bitter laugh. 'What work? Didn't he tell you he already sacked me, before my accident?'

Alice stared at him in disbelief. 'He what?'

'Sacked me. I didn't remember at first, but it's all gradually coming back to me. There was a mistake made at the office; a fault made by a junior, but I should have noticed, so I was held responsible. Sheridan dismissed me on the spot.'

'I can't believe it. When he came round he seemed sympathetic, well, sort of, and when I asked him if he would hold the job open for you, he said he was very sorry but that was impossible. He said nothing about having sacked you. Try not to think about that now, Andrew, that's for another day; something we can talk about once we've got you home.'

'I can't think about coming home,' Andrew said. 'I'll be nothing but a burden to you all.'

'Andrew, listen to me.' Alice reached forward and took his hands in hers. 'Look at me, Andrew.'

Reluctantly, Andrew looked up and saw the tears of love in her eyes. 'You're never to say that,' she said softly. 'Where else would you go except home to your wife and family? I told you before we shall manage; one way or another we shall survive, I promise you. We can all work—'

'Except me!'

'That doesn't matter, not now at least. We want you home, with us. I've spoken to the doctor again and he says you'll adjust better at home than here in the hospital. Let's get you safely back and worry about the future as and when we need to. My dearest, all we want is for you to get well enough to come home.' She raised his hands to her lips and he felt the tears on her cheeks. 'As long as you're with us all, we'll be all right. Our lives will be different from what we planned, that's all.'

Andrew felt tears in his own eyes and forced himself to smile at her. 'You're so brave, Alice, so courageous, and me? I'm a miserable coward. I dread the rest of my life, being dependent on you, the children, on anyone but myself.'

11

It was a fortnight after the accident that Frank Taylor, Alice's brother, called a family conference.

'We all want to help you,' he said to Alice. 'We're all family and that's what family is for.'

Reluctantly, Alice agreed. The days had settled down a little, but the accident was now a permanent backdrop to life in Cockspur Lane. Mabel and Stephen still went to school, and Eddie hung about in the docks picking up any work he could. Mr Sheridan had been right. He was big and strong and the few shillings he was able to make had extended the family's income a little, but it was clear it wasn't going to be enough.

It was agreed that Andrew's sisters and their husbands and Alice's brother, Frank, with his wife, May, should come together and discuss the best way forward. They all crowded into the small front room, the women sitting on the sofa and armchairs, the men standing round behind them and the Oakley children sitting on the floor.

'Now then,' Frank said when they were all settled. 'We have to see what we can do to help Alice and her family, both now, while poor Andrew is still in hospital, and when he comes out, wherever he goes.'

'He's coming here,' Alice interrupted firmly. 'He's coming home.'

'That's one option,' agreed Frank.

'It's the only one,' stated Alice. 'Everything we do is to get him home here.' She looked round the crowded room and added, 'I'm not prepared to consider any other way forward.'

'I'm sure you don't want to,' Jane said, 'and I quite understand that, I'd feel the same, but you have to accept that it may be impossible.'

'I've talked it through with the doctor,' Alice said. 'He says we should be able to manage if we put a bed in here and convert this room into a bedroom for Andrew.'

Alice had told no one, certainly not the children and not even her own brother, about Andrew losing his job at Sheridan, Sheridan and Morrell. There was no need for anyone to learn of that, the shame that would attach to it, and eventually find its way into the public domain. If no one knew of his dismissal, people would assume that he could no longer work there because of his accident. Surely no one would query that? And if anyone presumed to do so, well, Alice would deal with it.

'He's coming home, here!'

'All right.' Frank knew his sister of old and knew once she had made up her mind, there was little anyone could do to change it. 'Let's go on from there. Suppose this room becomes Andrew's bedroom. If Alice says she's got all that sorted in her mind, let's assume she has and move on to some of the problems which may arise. First, and this is the major stumbling block, income. Andrew was the only wage-earner...'

Eddie started to speak, but Frank held up his hand. 'I know you've got an apprenticeship lined up, but that will bring almost nothing into the house. You will be eating and sleeping here, but contributing almost nothing for your board and lodging.' He turned to Alice and asked, 'Has Eddie's premium been paid to Carter's yet?'

'No, but it's been set aside,' replied his sister.

Eddie began to speak again and this time Frank did not cut him off. 'I've decided not to take up the apprenticeship,' he said. 'It's three years before I shall be earning a decent wage. Mam can have the premium money to use when necessary. I've been down to Smithfield market and I've got a job as a porter. I start tomorrow at four in the morning.'

'Oh, Eddie, you can't just decide that without telling us,' cried his mother. 'I won't allow you just to give up the chance of learning a good trade that will serve you well for the rest of your life.'

'I've already done it, Mam. I went to Carter's this morning and explained. I think they could have asked for the money anyway, but Old Mr Carter was very understanding. So my indentures won't be signed and the premium will stay with us.'

Frank reached over and shook his nephew's hand. 'Well done, lad,' he said. 'Your dad'll be proud of you.'

And after that there was little more Alice could say on the matter, and though she didn't say so in front of her brother and her in-laws, the twenty-five pounds' premium saved would be a godsend. But what would Andrew say about Eddie giving up his apprenticeship? Surely a meat porter at Smithfield market wouldn't earn very much. Dear Eddie, not a child any more, but a man, making his own decisions.

'Well,' said Frank, 'that's a step in the right direction. Now, what else can anyone suggest?'

For a moment there was silence and then Jane said, 'I've been talking to Lizzie. She was home for her afternoon off on Monday and she told me Lady McFarlane is looking for a tweeny. Lizzie suggested that Mabel might like to apply for the job. It would be nice if they were able to work for the same family, don't you think?' She looked around and her sister Susan nodded.

'I know you're at school until the end of this term, Mabel,' her aunt went on, 'but I'm sure you'd be allowed to leave straight away if you had a job to go to. I mean,' she smiled at her niece, 'what are you, fifteen? So there would be no problem if Lady McFarlane decided to take you on. In a household like that, you'd be trained up properly. That's why they're looking for a maid. The last tweeny moved to another family as a parlourmaid, which is definitely a step up, isn't it?'

Mabel didn't even look at her. She stared woodenly at the floor, and said nothing. 'Come on, Mabel,' Jane said with another encouraging smile. 'What d'you think?'

'I don't want to go into service,' Mabel mumbled.

'Oh come now, Mabel,' cried her Auntie Susan. 'Most girls would jump at an opportunity with such a prestigious family. Sir Keir McFarlane is a judge, you know.'

'I don't care if he's the Prince of Wales,' growled Mabel. 'I don't want to go into service. I'll get some other job.'

'Such as?' asked Auntie Susan sweetly. 'You don't know how to *do* any other job.'

'I can learn,' snapped Mabel.

'Mabel, please don't speak to your aunt like that,' said Alice severely.

Mabel didn't say anything else, but sat with a mutinous look on her face, and Alice knew the battle wasn't yet won.

'Shall I get Lizzie to speak to Lady McFarlane's housekeeper and ask if they are still looking?' suggested Jane. 'Of course, it may be too late, she may be already suited.'

I hope she is, Mabel thought fiercely, still staring at the floor. Please God let her have found someone already!

'And what about you, young man?' Anxious to take the heat off Mabel, Uncle Frank turned to look down at Stephen, who sat with his back against the side of his mother's armchair. 'How old are you now?'

'Thirteen,' he replied firmly. Well, almost, it would soon be true.

'Thirteen. So it won't be all that long before you're able to leave school as well, and in the meantime, I'm sure you could get a Saturday job. What do you think, eh?'

'I'll try, Uncle,' replied the boy. But as the adults looked at him, undersized and scruffy, no one thought he looked a very good prospect as a wage earner.

'Stephen must stay at school until he's at least fourteen,' said his mother. She looked at her brother with affection. 'It's very good of you, Frank, to suggest all these things to help us. I have already found myself a job.'

'A job!' exclaimed Susan in horror.

'Certainly a job,' replied Alice calmly. 'I went to see Mr Moses in Cuck Lane and he's giving me piecework to do at home; setting in sleeves, pockets and collars. It means when Andrew is home again, I can still earn some money without leaving the house.'

'Taking in sewing?' cried Andrew's sister in dismay. None of the wives in their family went out to work, their husbands priding themselves on being able to provide for their families. Their job was to keep the home. The nearest anyone came to it was Jane, helping Robert Holman one afternoon a week with his accounts, and she was paid very little and mostly in meat.

'I have to do something to support my family, Susan,' Alice said frostily. 'Would you prefer I let them starve?'

'But to work for the Jews,' Susan said in distaste. 'Slave labour.'

'Rubbish,' snapped Alice. 'It's a job I can do perfectly well, and one I can do at home when I'm looking after Andrew.'

'Well, I wouldn't want to,' sniffed Susan. 'James would hate it.' She turned to her husband. 'Wouldn't you, James?'

'It's a different situation, Susan,' replied her husband mildly.

'And I know my brother,' went on Susan, as if James had not spoken, 'and he won't like it!'

'Then he'll have to lump it,' retorted Alice. Typical Susan, she thought. Always thinking she was better than anyone else.

'I think we must let Alice make up her own mind about what she wants to do,' James said. And holding out his hand to his wife, he said, 'Come along, Susan, I think we've finished here for today.' He turned to Alice. 'You must do what you think necessary, and if there is anything we can do, please let us know.'

'Take no notice of her,' said Jane, when they'd heard the front door close behind them. 'I think you're very brave to make all these arrangements.' She glanced down at the rigid form of Mabel sitting on the floor and whispered, 'I'll find out about Lady McFarlane for you. It seems to me that it's the obvious solution. Don't worry about Mabel, she'll come round to the idea, you'll see.'

No more was said about it that evening, but Mabel continued racking her brains to think of something other than going into service. If she had to give up the idea of secondary school, an idea she still clung to, she would try and find a job, any job, to help with a wage. Perhaps, she thought, she could work for Mr Moses as well. She knew how to sew, Mam had seen to that, and mending the family's clothes had been part of her job at home for some time now, so she was sure she could learn to do pockets and collars like Mam. She would choose her moment and make the suggestion. In the meantime she would continue to prepare for the exam at school.

It was another week before Auntie Jane came round to Cockspur Lane again, and Mabel was beginning to hope that Lady McFarlane had already replaced her tweeny and there was no job available. She allowed Miss Chapman to believe she was still intending to take the secondary school entrance exam and prayed no other job would come up before that day. If she passed, she thought, surely they would let her go. Surely there would be no more mention of going into service, then.

But now, this afternoon when she had got home from school, she found Auntie Jane sitting in the kitchen, drinking a cup of tea with Mam, and her heart sank.

'Here you are, Mabel,' her mother said brightly as she came into the kitchen. 'Would you like a cuppa, love?'

For a moment Mabel paused in the doorway, tempted to say no, but then she nodded and sighed, 'Yes please.'

'Say hello to your auntie,' Mam said, as she reached for another cup and poured the tea. 'She's just come with some excellent news. Here's your tea.'

Mabel stood unmoving, her face set, her expression blank. She guessed only too well what the excellent news would be.

'I've just been telling your mother,' Auntie Jane said brightly. 'Lizzie has spoken to Mrs Kilby, Lady McFarlane's housekeeper, about the place for a maid, and she would like to meet you. She is still looking for a suitable girl to employ as a between-maid, and when she heard that you were looking for a place—'

'But I'm *not*!' Mabel interrupted, almost shouting. 'I'm *not* looking for a place, I'm taking the exam for secondary school next month.' Her voice broke as she fought against tears. 'I don't want to work for Lady McFarlane, or anybody else.' She turned on her mother. 'You *said* I could take the exam! You said I should go to secondary! Dada said I could!'

'Mabel, dearest, Dada said no such thing. You know he didn't.'

'Well, he would have,' Mabel said belligerently. 'He would have.'

'He might have,' agreed her mother gently. 'But that was before his accident. Everything has changed now and we have to change, too. Look at Eddie. He's given up his apprenticeship so that he's bringing home a wage packet.

We have only what he is earning and what little I get from Mr Moses. If you go to work for Lady McFarlane, you will earn a small wage, but you will have no living expenses. You will live-in and have three square meals a day. You will be trained to work in a gentleman's house. You may not want to stay in that household, but you will always be able to earn your own living.'

'Lizzie's very happy working there,' put in Auntie Jane. 'She gets a half-day every week, and one weekend each month, if she isn't needed for some special occasion.'

'But I don't *want* to be like Lizzie!' Mabel cried in frustration. 'I want to stay at school and then learn to be a secretary.'

'I know,' said her mother. 'I know that's what you want, but we have to be practical. We can't afford to keep you at school now. We're all having to do things we don't want to, and that's how it is. Mrs Kilby has asked me to bring you to meet her, and if she takes to you, she'll recommend Lady McFarlane employs you. We're to go tomorrow morning.'

'Tomorrow!'

'Yes, tomorrow.'

'But what about school? My exam?'

'You won't be taking the exam, Mabel,' Mam said patiently. 'I shall go and see Miss Chapman and explain the situation to her. She'll understand why you can't stay on, I'm sure.'

'But supposing this housekeeper doesn't take to me?'

'There's no reason she won't, if you speak when you're spoken to and answer up politely,' replied Mam. 'We need you to get this job, Mabel, you mustn't let us down.'

12

Following the careful instructions given by Lizzie's mother, Mabel and Alice arrived at the McFarlanes' house in Chanynge Place the following morning.

'You're to go to the tradesman's entrance in the mews at the back,' Jane had told them. 'Mrs Kilby is expecting you. If her ladyship wishes to see you, then of course you'll be taken to her, but Lizzie thinks she will almost certainly leave everything to Mrs Kilby.'

For a moment they paused outside in the road, looking at the grandeur of the street. Mabel stared up at the McFarlanes' house in awe. Could it really be just one family living in such an imposing house?

It was an impressive cream stucco building, with steps down to an area and basement, rising to five storeys above. Tall windows on the first floor, looking out on the street below, opened onto a narrow balcony which ran the width of the building and adjoined the houses on either side. She looked at the glossy black-painted front door beneath its grand portico, its polished brass accoutrements gleaming in the morning sun, and was relieved they would not be approaching the house from the front. She would never have dared walk up the steps and pull that bell.

'Come along, Mabel,' said her mother, taking her arm. 'Don't stand gawping.' Together they rounded the corner and turned into a narrow street at the back where there was a mews, stables converted into a garage and a way into the basement kitchen. A chauffeur who was polishing the bonnet of a large and gleaming blue car glanced up at them as they approached, but he said nothing, simply returned to his polishing as they knocked on the insignificant back door. It was answered by Lizzie who greeted them with a smile.

'Aunt Alice, Mabel,' she said. 'Come in. Mrs Kilby is expecting you.' She led the way inside, saying over her shoulder, 'I don't usually answer this door, but as you're my cousin, Mrs Kilby thought I should be the one to welcome you.' She took them through the servants' hall to a small room beyond, the door of which stood ajar.

'Good luck,' she whispered, and tapped on the door.

'Come.' The voice didn't sound very welcoming, but Lizzie pushed the door wider and said, 'Mrs Oakley and her daughter, Mrs Kilby.' Then she stood aside and allowed Alice and Mabel to go inside.

The room was clearly the housekeeper's private office and sitting room combined. She sat at a table with a sheaf of papers in front of her. Mrs Kilby was a thin woman, with shrewd dark eyes that looked at Mabel assessingly.

'Good morning, Mrs Kilby,' said Alice, and then when Mabel said nothing, her mother nudged her and she murmured, 'Good morning.'

Mrs Kilby gave a brief nod and then said, 'Your name, girl?'

'Mabel. Mabel Oakley.'

'Well, Mabel Oakley, I hope you're a hard worker,' she said. 'We've no time for passengers in this household. You understand?'

Mabel made no reply and Mrs Kilby went on, 'You address me as Mrs Kilby, and answer when I speak to you. Understand?'

Clearly an answer was required now, so Mabel murmured, 'Yes, Mrs Kilby.'

'Right, well, if you come to work here, it'll be me that's going to be telling you what to do and, very occasionally, Mr Felstead. He's the butler, who gets his orders direct from Sir Keir. It's her ladyship who I consult with, passing on her orders to the rest of you. Most of your work will be in the kitchen, helping Mrs Bellman, our cook. You'll live in with an afternoon off every two weeks, and a Saturday night each month if we don't need you. Your uniform will be provided and you will earn twenty-four pounds a year, paid monthly on the last day of the month.' Though she sounded as if she were speaking to Mabel, Mrs Kilby was actually looking at Alice. 'Do you understand all that?'

Mabel didn't answer at once. She couldn't believe how little she was going to earn. That wasn't going to help Mam pay the bills, was it? She glanced at her mother, about to protest, but Mam was nodding to the housekeeper… agreeing!

Mabel opened her mouth to speak, but a glare from her mother made her close it again. Mam's words the previous day echoed in her head. *We need you to get this job, Mabel. You mustn't let us down.*

Mrs Kilby got to her feet to show the conversation was

over. 'You'll do... on a month's trial. I'll expect you here at the same time tomorrow, to start work. I'm sure her ladyship will want to speak to you at some stage, but it will depend on her engagements. Come to the same door and Lizzie will show you where you're going to sleep; you'll be sharing a room with her. Good morning, Mrs Oakley.'

Alice took Mabel by the arm and together they left Mrs Kilby sitting at her table.

Lizzie was waiting for them in the servants' hall. 'Did she take you?' she asked.

Mabel nodded gloomily and her mother said, 'On a month's trial. She's to start tomorrow. Mrs Kilby said you'd let her in at the same time and show her where she'll be sleeping.' She smiled at her niece and said, 'I know you'll look after her, Lizzie. Show her the ropes and that.'

'Yes, of course, Auntie,' Lizzie replied. But Mabel, furious, turned on her mother. 'Don't treat me like a child!' she snapped. 'I'm not a child! Not any more. I've left school. Remember!'

Mother and daughter travelled back to Cockspur Lane in an uneasy silence. When they got there, they had some bread and cheese for lunch before Alice said she was going to the hospital to see her father.

'*I* want to see him,' Mabel said. 'Why can't I come, too?'

'That rather depends on you,' replied her mother. 'I'll take you with me if you like, but I don't want your dad upset. If I can't trust you not to make a fuss about going to work in Chanynge Place, then I'm not going to take you in to see him.' Alice fixed Mabel with an unblinking stare. 'I need your promise that you'll make no mention of the secondary school examination. If you want to tell him about going into service with the McFarlanes, well, you may, but not if you're going to complain about it. Understand?'

Mabel nodded.

'No, Mabel, I'm sorry, that's not good enough, I need your promise that you'll say nothing to upset him. Do you promise?'

'Yes,' muttered Mabel. 'I promise.'

'Then you can come with me this afternoon, but you'll only be able to see him for a couple of minutes, just to give him a kiss and say hello. I know it's not much, but he gets very tired.'

When they reached the hospital, Alice paused outside the gate and said, 'You must remember, Mabel, your dad has been badly injured. He's very weak, and he still has a lot of pain. If he happens to be asleep when we get in there, we shan't be waking him up. You may be shocked at how he seems, but you mustn't show it on your face. Just smile at him, take his hands, give him a kiss. See him as Dada. He's not the Dada he's always been, but he is still Dada; Dada doing his best to get well.'

'Yes, Mam,' murmured Mabel.

Alice ignored the desk in the hospital's main entrance hall and led the way upstairs and along a busy corridor to Andrew's ward. As they reached the door, a nurse put out a hand to halt them and said, 'No children at visiting times.'

'She's hardly a child, Nurse,' said Alice quietly. 'She just wants to see her father for a moment or two, before she takes up her position in service with Lady McFarlane.'

Was it Mam mentioning a well-known name in London society, or the promise that her visit would be a short one? Mabel didn't know, but with a curt nod the nurse let them both into the ward, saying, 'Just two minutes, then,' adding, as she turned to Mabel, 'but don't you go upsetting him. He's been very poorly today.'

Then I shall cheer him up, thought Mabel, as she followed her mother across the ward to his bed in a curtained alcove.

Despite Mam's warning, Mabel was horrified by the sight of him. If she hadn't been expecting to see her father, she might not have recognised him, so small and frail propped up against his pillows. His cheeks were unshaven, pale and drawn, his eyes sunk in their sockets; his hair had been shaved round the wound on his head, still covered with a square of white dressing, but the rest of his hair stuck out like an old bottlebrush.

'Dada!' she whispered. 'Dada, is that really you?'

'It is,' he replied in a husky whisper. 'Mabel! My dearest girl. Come here and let me have a look at you.' He held out his hand to her, more like a claw than Dada's normal hand with its long fingers and the habitual faint smudge of ink on its forefinger. For a fraction of a second Mabel hesitated, a fraction of a second too long, needing a nudge from her mother to urge her forward and grasp it in her own.

'Here I am, Dada,' she whispered. 'I wanted to see you today. I start my new job tomorrow, so it won't be easy for me to visit you again for a while.'

She felt his grip tighten a little on her hand as he said, 'What new job, Mabel?'

'I'm going to work with Lizzie at the McFarlanes'.'

'But your schoolwork? You were going to stay on and go to learn to be a secretary. What did your teacher say?'

Mabel took a deep breath. 'She said I'd be better finding

a job in service,' she lied. 'She didn't think an extra year would be any real help.'

'But you didn't want to go into service,' exclaimed her father, sounding more alert than Alice had yet seen him. 'Is it really what you want to do?'

'Yes, Dada, it really is,' she replied. 'It's time I was out in the world, cos I'm not a schoolgirl any more.' And as she said it, looking down onto her father's exhausted and pain-filled face, she realised with a rush of shame that it was true; she wasn't a schoolgirl any more and it was time she grew up. Her mother needed her to make her own way now, not be another unproductive mouth to feed. Seeing her father lying, a crumpled figure in the bed, far worse than she could have imagined, she knew she had to shoulder her share of the family burden.

'I've got to go, Dada,' she said, determined to keep the tears that burned the back of her eyes and the lump in her throat at bay. 'I've got things to do before I go tomorrow.' She bent forward to kiss him, her lips brushing his stubbled cheek, but he clung to her hand.

'Are you quite sure about this job, Mabel?' he asked. 'You don't have to take it if you don't want to.'

'Quite sure, Dada.' Gently she stood back, easing her hand free, and smiled down at him. 'You'll be home soon, and I'll be able to see you there on my afternoons off.'

Her parents watched her as she walked out of the ward without a backward glance, her head erect, but had they been able to see her face, they'd have seen the tears streaming down her cheeks.

13

Once outside the hospital Mabel paused in the street, pulled a hankie out of her sleeve, mopped her tears and blew her nose. How long would Mam be? she wondered. Should she wait for her, or go on home? She knew that Mam didn't usually stay very long, but with her new recognition of what they were all up against, Mabel wanted to be alone for a while. She hadn't told the truth when she'd said she was happy going into service. Of course she hadn't, she still hated the idea, but she knew now, having seen her father, that it was something she had to do and she must make the best of it.

She thought of Mr Clarke in his little printing shed by the bridge. That was what he had said to her last time she'd been there. Life wasn't fair and sometimes you had to make hard decisions. Remembering the rude, childish way she had spoken to him, her cheeks went hot with shame. How could she have spoken to him like that, he who had always been a friend to her? She didn't want him to think she had meant the stupid things that she'd said. His parting words to her had been gentle; that he would always be there if she wanted to come and see him. Now, suddenly, she did want to see him, to see him at once, to set things right between them. Once she was working in Chanynge Place, Mabel realised, she'd have no opportunity to drop in and visit him as she'd been doing for so long; this was her last afternoon of freedom and she must make the most of it.

She turned towards the railway alley, hurrying to find him. Suddenly, she was terrified he might not be there. Suppose he'd gone home for some reason, and his little shack was shut up?

Running fast now, she dodged in and out of other pedestrians on the pavement, gathering angry glances and muttered protests as she went. To the rhythm of her feet thudding on the pavement, she found she was chanting, 'Be there! Be there! Be there.'

When she finally reached the entrance to the alley, she paused a moment to catch her breath, and listened for the familiar rhythmical thump of the printing press. At first she couldn't hear it, because the sound of a train steaming out from the station below the bridge drowned all other sounds.

'Don't say you're not there!' she murmured as she walked towards the little shack. 'Please be there!' When she saw the door was open, a wave of relief flooded through her and with a lifting heart, she walked forward.

'Mr Clarke,' she said as she reached his door, 'can I come in?'

Without missing a beat of the press, the old man glanced across and his face broke into a smile. 'Mabel!' he cried. 'Yes, of course. Come on in. I've nearly finished these.'

She entered the room and watched as he fed the final sheets of card through the press, deftly replacing each printed sheet with a fresh piece.

'Put the kettle on again,' he said as he stacked the finished cards into a tidy bundle and tied them together with a piece of string. He had seen the reddened eyes and tear-streaked cheeks and decided normality should be the thing. Clearly she was upset about something and he guessed she would tell him in her own time, but if she didn't? Well, he wasn't going to ask awkward questions.

Mabel did as she was told and then turned to him. 'I'm very sorry, Mr Clarke,' she said.

'Sorry, Mabel? What are you sorry for?'

'I'm sorry I was rude to you last time I came,' she replied, 'when I shouted at you.' Her voice cracked and she gulped, trying not to cry again, 'And said I was never coming to see you again.'

'My dear girl,' Mr Clarke said in a comforting voice, 'don't give it another thought! You were upset, and I'm not surprised. Things are extremely difficult for you just now.'

'I know, but you were right and I was angry because I didn't *want* you to be.'

'Let's forget about all that,' he replied. 'Put it behind us. Time for a cuppa, don't you think?' He reached for the kettle as it began to sing, and made the pot of tea. 'Sit you down and tell me what's been going on.'

Mabel perched on the stool and sighed. 'I've just been to the hospital with Mam, to visit my father. It was dreadful. He looks so awful, all shrunken and pale. I didn't know how bad he was... is... always will be! Well, I did, but I didn't, not really; not till I actually saw him there, in the bed. I hardly recognised him... and he was trying to be so brave.' She looked at Mr Clarke in anguish. 'How could I have not realised how bad he is? I'm not stupid, but I just didn't know...'

'Of course you didn't, my dear,' said Mr Clarke gently. 'It's going to take some getting used to for all of you, but particularly for your poor mum and dad.'

Mabel drank a mouthful of tea, 'Well,' she said, 'I'm not going back to school again. I've got a job now. I start tomorrow, live-in, as a maid in the house where my cousin Lizzie is parlourmaid. Sir Keir and Lady McFarlane in Chanynge Place.'

'That's a smart address,' Mr Clarke replied carefully. 'Mayfair. If I'm not mistaken.'

'Yes. Mam's very pleased.'

'But you're not.' It was a statement, not a question.

'I only get one half day a fortnight and one weekend a month,' she said. 'So I shan't be able to come and see you very much.'

'I shall miss you,' he said with a smile, 'but on your half days, you must go home to your family.'

'I'll come on my weekend off,' she promised. 'I'll have more time then.'

'Will you? I shall look forward to that.'

'Oh!' Suddenly stricken. 'But you won't be here at weekends, will you?' she said.

'I'll make sure I am,' he promised. 'I am usually here on a Saturday, you know.'

An easy silence fell around them as they drank their tea and ate the biscuits he kept in his tin, but then he set his mug down on the desk and said, 'I'm very pleased you've come, Mabel, because I've had an idea.'

A moment of hope flashed into Mabel's mind, but instantly

vanished again; she knew whatever it was, it wouldn't get her out of going to Chanynge Place in the morning.

'I've got something that might be of help to your father when he comes home. My wife, Emma, spent her last days in a wheelchair, and when she died, I put it away and forgot about it. D'you think your father might like to have it? A help for your mother to move him about? Let him get out of the house when he's feeling stronger?'

Mabel stared at him. 'You mean,' she murmured, 'you mean you'd lend it to us?'

'I mean I'll give it to you. After all, it's no use to me any more. I got it out the other day and gave it the once-over. It's not in bad condition, and from my own experience with Emma, it makes all the difference to someone who wants to get out into the fresh air, go into town, or down the pub!' He cocked his head to see her reaction. 'It's a good sturdy chair, plenty of miles in it yet! What d'you think, young lady? Any good?'

'Oh, Mr Clarke! It would be wonderful. I know they'd be thrilled to have it. Poor Mam, she keeps on insisting Dad's coming home again, but now I've seen him, how bad he is, I can see that if he does, they're both going to have a very hard time of it.'

'That's settled then,' said the printer cheerfully. 'Now, we'd best be getting over to my place and collect that chair. We'll take it to your house straight away, so your mother's got it ready for when your dad comes home.'

Ten minutes later the shack was closed up and locked and they were walking the half mile to Mr Clarke's house in Barnbury Street. It was almost a sister to Cockspur Lane, cobbled, with deep gutters to carry away the water and detritus. A respectable area, home of clerical workers and shopkeepers. The only real difference was that the houses weren't terraced, but in pairs, semi-detached with a pathway down each unattached side, leading to tiny gardens or yards behind. Mr Clarke led her to the left-hand house of one of the pairs. Its front door had been recently painted and had a gleaming number 27 on the doorpost. The printer unlocked it with a latch key and, pushing the door open, he stood aside to let Mabel precede him indoors. She found herself in a long narrow hall with a steep staircase leading to the floor above. The hall passageway led to the back of the house, with two rooms opening off it to the left and a kitchen on the right at the far end.

'Do you live here alone?' Mabel turned round to ask him.

'I do now,' he replied. 'My wife died some years ago and my sister moved in to look after me. She's passed away now, so I'm on my own. I manage,' he added with a shrug and rueful grin. 'I'm a dab hand with a tin opener, and Mrs Frost next door, she keeps an eye on me!' He opened the second door and stepped inside. Following him, Mabel found herself in a small, neat room that smelled of stale air, stuffed furniture and disuse. Standing next to a window that looked out onto a square of garden was the wheelchair. Made of some sort of metal, it had four wheels, two large ones at the back and two much smaller at the front. Above the back wheels was the seat, and a bar for pushing the chair from behind; above the front wheels was a foot rest. It did not look at all comfortable to Mabel. She wondered if there were supposed to be cushions of some sort.

As if reading her mind, Mr Clarke said, 'I've given

the cushions a good scrub. I promise you it's not as uncomfortable as it looks!'

Anxious not to seem ungrateful for his offer of the chair, Mabel smiled at him. 'Can I sit in it?'

'Of course you can. Just let me fetch the cushions.' He disappeared and she heard his feet on the stairs. A few moments later, he came down again, carrying two cushions. He put one into the chair and when Mabel lowered herself gingerly onto the seat, tucked the second behind her. The foot plate wasn't the right distance away for her feet, but otherwise it was nothing like as uncomfortable as she'd been expecting.

'I've cleaned it all down,' Mr Clarke was saying. 'It has brakes and they work well enough.' He smiled across at her. 'So,' he said, 'what do you think? Any use to you?'

Mabel nodded. 'Oh, yes. Yes please,' she replied. 'I think it will be very helpful. If Dada has to stay in the house all the time, he'll go mad,' adding after a moment's thought, 'And so will Mam!'

'Shall we take it to her now?' suggested Mr Clarke.

'Yes, let's,' agreed Mabel, and together they set out for Cockspur Lane. Mr Clarke had offered her a ride in the chair, but despite the cushions making a difference, she wasn't keen on being pushed along the streets so close to her home, paraded like a freak at a funfair. Only time would tell if her father would feel the same.

When they reached the Oakleys' house, Mr Clarke stood back. 'You go and see if your mother's home yet.'

She was, and as soon as the front door opened, she was out on the step demanding where on earth Mabel had got to.

'I thought you'd be waiting outside the hospital for me,' she cried. 'I've been all round the streets looking for you. I even went to see if you'd gone back to the school, but no one there had seen you. I was really beginning to worry and…' Alice's voice tailed off as she realised Mabel wasn't alone. Standing at the gate was a small, elderly man with a shock of salt and pepper hair escaping from under his hat, the brim of which almost reached the frames of his oversized spectacles. This made him look a little furtive and Alice pulled her daughter by the hand, murmuring, 'Come inside at once, Mabel. There's a strange man looking in through the gate.'

'No, Mam, that's Mr Clarke. He's my friend. He's brought something for you, for us, to help Dada.' Turning back to Mr Clarke, she called, 'Come and meet my mother, Mr Clarke.'

Mr Clarke left the wheelchair at the gate and came to the front door, hand outstretched. 'Mrs Oakley!' he cried. 'I'm charmed to meet you. Thomas Clarke at your service! How do you do?'

Alice found her hand being gripped so firmly it tingled even after he'd let go.

'I'm sorry, Mr Clarke,' Alice said stiffly, 'but I have absolutely no idea who you are or what you want with my daughter.'

'I told you, Mam, he's my friend and he's brought you a present.'

'Don't worry, Mrs Oakley, I want nothing from your daughter. I'm a printer with a small business down by the railway bridge, and on occasion, Mabel pops in to see me. She's a lovely girl and we've become good friends.'

'She is a lovely girl,' agreed her mother coldly, 'and she should be having nothing to do with a man four times her age who, unknown to her parents, pretends to be her friend.'

Mr Clarke took a step back at this, to him, entirely unexpected attack.

'Mam!' Mabel's voice quivered with a mixture of anger and embarrassment. 'You've no right to speak to Mr Clarke like that.'

'I have every right,' retorted her mother. 'He's old enough to be your grandfather, and you shouldn't have been "popping in" alone to see him. It's not...' she searched for the word, 'it's not *suitable*.'

Mabel was about to protest when Mr Clarke said, 'Don't worry, Mabel. Your mother is quite right, and though there is nothing between us but our friendship and a few cups of tea, there might have been with someone less scrupulous.'

'You mean, like the man with his piggy?'

Mr Clarke glanced at Alice and nodded. 'Yes, I suppose I do. Your mother's right, it wasn't proper of me to encourage you to come and visit me alone in my workshop.'

'What man with a piggy?' Alice pounced. 'What has been going on behind our backs?'

'Absolutely nothing, madam,' replied Mr Clarke with quiet dignity. 'I bid you good afternoon.' And raising his hat to Alice he turned away, leaving the wheelchair standing on the pavement. He left without a backward glance at the girl he had come to love; the girl who had become the nearest thing he'd ever have to a beloved daughter.

Mabel pulled free of her mother and ran to the gate, but he'd disappeared round the corner. 'Oh, Mam!' she cried in dismay. 'How could you? How could you?'

'Mabel, you're too young to understand,' responded her mother, 'but a man like that is not a suitable companion for a girl of your age.' When Mabel simply glowered at her in mute fury, her mother continued, 'And what's this about his friend and "piggy"?'

'It wasn't a friend of his. It was a weird man on the bridge who tried to…' Mabel broke off, unable to explain exactly what the man had wanted, but thankful she'd never seen him again. She tried again. 'Mr Clarke came out of his little shop and chased the man away, and because I was frightened at the time, he took me into his printing shop and made me a cup of tea. Then he went with me all the way to Auntie Susan's, in case the man was waiting further on.' Tears were running down her face now. She dashed them away with an angry fist and almost shouted, 'So, you're wrong, Mr Clarke is my friend and he always will be.'

Grabbing the handles of the wheelchair she pushed it up the path towards her surprised mother. 'And what's more, he's given us this to use when Dada comes home. He had it for his wife, and now she's died he's given it to us, for Dada.' Alice stared at Mabel for a moment, not knowing what to say in answer to this outburst, and then looked at the wheelchair.

'Oh, Mabel,' she sighed. 'Where on earth are we going to put that great thing?'

14

Lizzie was waiting next morning when Mabel arrived in Chanynge Place, carrying an old canvas bag of her father's, containing her few belongings.

'You won't need much apart from your underwear and night things,' Mam had said. 'You'll be wearing your uniform when you're working.'

Even so, Mabel had chosen some of the second-hand books she had bought over the years from a market stall for the odd spare halfpenny, a couple of notebooks from school and her pencil case.

'What on earth are you taking all that for?' Eddie had asked when he brought the heavy bag downstairs. 'You won't have time for any of that.'

'I'm taking them because I want them.'

'I'd better come with you on the bus, then,' he said, but this suggestion was met with a point-blank refusal.

'No, I can manage by myself,' Mabel said firmly. 'I'm not going to arrive there with my big brother looking after me.'

'You know, I'm really going to miss you, Mabe.' His voice was unusually soft. 'We all are.'

'No you won't,' she answered shakily, fighting the lump

in her throat and determined not to cry. 'Once I've gone you won't give me a thought.'

She'd said goodbye to Stephen when he left for school that morning and then, with a quick hug to Mam and Eddie, she picked up her bag and stepped out into the lane. Only once did she look back, to see them both standing at the open front door watching her go, before she turned the corner and was out of sight. She was determined to arrive in Chanynge Place as an adult, out in the world earning her own money. She walked out of the lane and made her way to the bus stop to repeat the journey she had made with her mother yesterday.

At least I know how to get there, she thought. Which buses to take and where to change.

Her bag got heavier and heavier the further she walked, and she began to wish she had accepted Eddie's offer of help, but, she decided, the heavy bag was worth the effort; she would have all her favourite books with her.

When she knocked on the back door, Lizzie was there to open it.

'Right on time,' Lizzie said with a smile. 'That'll be noticed. Mrs Kilby hates anyone being late, whatever the reason. I'll take you through to her now.'

Mrs Kilby was in her little parlour. 'Ah, you've come,' she said. 'Lizzie will show you where you're to sleep. Your uniform is on your bed. I'll expect you down again in a quarter of an hour, ready for work. Off you go now.'

Lizzie led the way up the backstairs to the very top of the house where they were to share a room.

'I'm glad it's you who's come to take Ellen's place,' Lizzie said as she climbed the narrow staircase. 'I had to share a room with her and I didn't like her or trust her. I'm sure she used to go through my locker when I weren't there... I was really glad when she had to leave.'

'Had to leave?' echoed Mabel. 'Why? What did she do?'

'She was a flighty piece,' replied Lizzie. 'Flirt with anything in trousers, she would, but she made a mistake, batting her eyelashes at Mr Iain. Chalmers reported her and her ladyship gave her the sack. Good riddance, we all thought!'

Lizzie knew the episode hadn't been entirely Ellen's fault. Mr Iain enjoyed teasing the maids and he had encouraged her, lying in wait for her and stealing kisses in corners. Lizzie wondered if she should warn Mabel about Mr Iain, but decided her cousin was unlikely to come across him very much while working in the kitchen and there were other things she needed to know first.

'You want to watch out for Chalmers, Mabel,' she went on. 'Thinks she's a cut above the rest of us, she does.'

'Who is she?' asked Mabel.

'Miss Chalmers, we have to call her. She's her ladyship's personal maid. You don't want to get on the wrong side of her, I can tell you. She's got a tongue on her.'

It's a long way up these stairs, Mabel thought, as they finally reached the top. You wouldn't want to have forgotten something and have to come up and fetch it.

The stairs ended in the middle of a long narrow landing, which led off in opposite directions. Lizzie pointed to a door immediately opposite and said, 'The lavatory's in there, it's used by all of us, so make sure you lock the door when you're in there. You don't want one of the men walking in on you.' She pointed to her right, where the corridor stretched away. It was rather gloomy as all the doors were closed and the light there was had to squeeze its way in through three narrow skylights. 'The men sleep that end,' she said, 'we're this way.' Turning to the left, she opened the nearest door, saying, 'This is us,' and stood aside to let Mabel walk in. It was small, with two iron bedsteads, each with its own locker and one small chest of drawers, crammed into the room, leaving very little space for the two girls. Mabel crossed to the tiny casement window, the only source of light, and peered out. The sun beamed golden light onto the frosty roofs of the houses opposite and onto the street far below, but their tiny room remained gloomy and cold.

'You'd better get a move on,' advised Lizzie. 'We've got to get back downstairs, or we'll have Mrs Kilby after us. You can unpack your bag later.'

Mabel placed Dad's bag on top of her locker and picked up the black stuff dress that lay on her bed. Turning her back on Lizzie, she stripped off her blouse and skirt and pulled the uniform dress over her head. It wasn't a bad fit, but she noticed it wasn't quite as smart as the one Lizzie was wearing, and the apron and cap weren't stiffly starched.

'It's because I'm a parlourmaid now,' explained Lizzie when Mabel remarked on this. 'I have to be seen in the family's side of the house. Now,' she continued, 'you'll have to do something with your hair. You can't have it down your back like that. Here…' She stepped forward and, picking up a brush from her own locker, quickly brushed and plaited Mabel's hair then twisted the plait round her head, securing it with two long hairpins. She surveyed her handiwork and said, 'That'll have to do for now. Apron and cap and you're ready.'

There was no mirror in the room, so Mabel had no idea how she looked, but Lizzie gave her hand a squeeze and said, 'You'll do. Come on.'

As Lizzie led the way back down the stairs, she went on, 'Now, when you meet all the others, the best thing to do is say as little as possible, and of course, if you meet any of the family in their part of the house, just keep your mouth shut unless they actually address you. There's only the four of them most of the time. Sir Keir and Lady McFarlane, and their children Mr Iain and Miss Lucinda. They're grown up now, but of course they still live here.

'The servants that tell us what to do are Mr Felstead, the butler, and Mrs Kilby, the housekeeper. The other senior servants are Mr Blundell, that's Sir Keir's valet, and Miss Chalmers, who's Lady McFarlane's personal maid. You won't have much to do with them and we always address them as Mr Blundell and Miss Chalmers.'

'I'll try and remember who's who,' said Mabel obediently.

'Then there's Mrs Bellman the cook. She's all right, William the footman, he's nice, me, and Ada... she's the scullery maid. Paston the handyman and Croxton the chauffeur come in for their dinner with the rest of us.' She smiled encouragingly. 'Don't worry, Mabel, you'll meet everyone when we have our midday meal; that's after we've served luncheon in the dining room.'

As soon as she arrived in the kitchen, Mrs Bellman set Mabel to work with Ada, washing pots and pans stacked in the deep Belfast sink. After one glance, Mr Felstead ignored her entirely, before he went above stairs to supervise Lizzie and William serving in the dining room. As they came and went, the other servants cast surreptitious looks at Mabel, but she followed Lizzie's advice, kept her head down and spoke to nobody.

Once the family's luncheon had been served and cleared away, the servants were able to sit down to their own midday meal, the main meal of their day. The senior servants sat at the top of the table and the more junior towards the foot. Mabel cast a cautious glance at each of them. Mr Felstead she had seen before, but not Mr Blundell. He was a man of superior air, not tall but with a presence. He had a head of dark curly hair rippling outward from a centre parting, like sand left by the tide, and held in place with a generous serving of hair oil. He took his seat next to Mr Felstead and after casting one glance in Mabel's direction he paid her as little attention as the butler had, for which she was grateful.

William now gave her an appraising look and said, 'Well now, who've we got here?'

Mabel didn't reply and Lizzie answered for her. 'That's my cousin, Mabel. She's come instead of Ellen. You be nice to her.'

'I'm always nice to people,' William protested with a grin. 'How d'you do, Cousin Mabel,' he said, adding under his breath, 'I hope you ain't a flighty bit, like that Ellen was.'

'That'll do,' snapped Mrs Kilby, who took the chair at the centre of the table, opposite Mrs Bellman, thus uniting its two halves. 'Now then, Mabel,' she said. 'Make yourself useful. Fetch the pie out of the oven and set it here on the table.'

Mabel did as she was told and the housekeeper spooned shepherd's pie onto plates which Ada handed round before sitting down herself on the spare chair beside Mabel. Paston and Croxton had come in from outside; Paston also ignored

Mabel and didn't speak a word the whole time he was at the table. Croxton the chauffeur recognised Mabel from the day before. He nodded to her and said, 'Got the job, I see,' before returning his undivided attention to his plate.

Just as they had settled down to eat, the door opened and a middle-aged woman came in. She was not in uniform as such, but smartly dressed in a long, closely fitted, plain black dress. She had a small, thin-lipped mouth, and under the arch of her eyebrows, small, black eyes that reminded Mabel of the boot-button eyes of her old teddy bear. Her greying hair was swept up into the severity of a bun, and topped with a white lace cap. As she paused in the doorway and took in the scene, the room fell silent. She made no apology for being late, simply took the last empty chair between Mr Felstead and Mr Blundell and waited for Ada to get up and serve her.

Before beginning to eat, she looked across at Mabel and said, 'So you're the new girl! Couldn't be worse than the last one, I suppose.'

Mabel kept her eyes on her plate and said nothing. She guessed this must be Miss Chalmers, her ladyship's maid, clearly important enough to reduce the servants' hall to silence. 'Well, girl, speak up?'

After what seemed to be an endless silence, it was Mrs Kilby who answered. 'This is Mabel, our new between-maid, Miss Chalmers. Miss Chalmers is Lady McFarlane's personal maid.'

After that there was very little talk during the meal, everyone intent on the food, but Mabel kept her eyes down and her ears open. She knew these people would be part of her daily life here in Chanynge Place, and she was determined that she would be afraid of no one, not the organising Mrs Kilby, not poker-faced Mr Felstead, not the superior-looking Mr Blundell and certainly not the ramrod-backed Miss Chalmers, who seemed at odds with the servants' hall.

If necessary, she thought, I must hold my own among them.

After they had eaten their shepherd's pie, followed by jam roly-poly, Miss Chalmers pushed her chair back and left the room. Once she had gone, there was a distinct relaxation in the atmosphere about the table.

'You wanna steer clear of her,' murmured William, 'if you know what's good for you.'

But his comment was overheard by Mr Felstead who growled at him, 'Mind your manners!'

Mabel had heard William though; she thought it sounded good advice, and gave him a grateful smile.

'Ada, get this table cleared double quick,' said Mrs Bellman, 'there's vegetables to prepare for dining room dinner.'

Immediately everyone got up and the servants' hall moved easily back into its daily routine.

'Mabel, her ladyship wants to see you,' Mrs Kilby told her. 'Straighten your cap and I'll take you up now.' Moments later, Mabel was following Mrs Kilby up the stairs from the kitchen to a heavy baize-covered door. Here the housekeeper paused and said, 'You'll have to learn your way about, but unless I tell you to go into the main house, you don't go beyond this door. Understand?'

'Yes, Mrs Kilby.' Mabel's reply was dutiful, but having

seen the house from the outside, she was looking forward to seeing the family's quarters.

They emerged into a narrow passage which led into the spacious, marble-floored hallway. Several doors opened off this, and on the walls between them hung large paintings in ornate gilded frames; a portrait of a man seated at a desk looking up as if interrupted, another of a younger man on horseback, a third of a woman in a blue silk gown, hair piled high on her head, diamonds glittering about her neck and in her ears, and finally a more modern family group, the mother seated with a little girl on her knee, a boy at her side and, standing behind them, the tall figure of the father, his hand resting on the lady's shoulder.

Mabel stopped and stared at the pictures, causing Mrs Kilby to say, 'Her ladyship won't appreciate being kept waiting.'

A wide staircase curved up to a gallery on the floor above. 'You never use the front stairs,' Mrs Kilby warned her, as she led Mabel to one of the closed doors. 'And this is the morning room, where we meet with her ladyship if she wishes to speak to us.'

Mabel found herself in a pleasant, sunny room, with windows looking out into the street. It was furnished with a small dining table and chairs, several silk-upholstered armchairs and a golden brocade-covered sofa, set before a wide fireplace in which a fire glowed, and a large vase of white lilies stood on a corner table, breathing their scent into the room.

Lady McFarlane was sitting at a small writing desk near the window and standing beside her, straight-backed and still, was Miss Chalmers. Almost without looking at her, Lady McFarlane said, 'Thank you, Chalmers, that will be all for now.'

Miss Chalmers gave a tiny bob and said, 'Yes, my lady,' and left the room.

Looking at her employer, Mabel saw at once that she was the mother in the family group pictured in the hall. She was about forty, still beautiful, with smooth, dark hair that sprang from a widow's peak above elegantly arched brows and surprisingly deep blue eyes. It was an arresting face, but there was a certain determination in the set of her jaw that made Mabel decide she was not a woman to be crossed.

'Good afternoon, Mrs Kilby.' Lady McFarlane's tone was courteous, but she spoke without smiling. 'And who is this?'

'Good afternoon, my lady,' replied the housekeeper. 'This is Mabel Oakley, the new between-maid, to replace Ellen.'

Lady McFarlane turned her attention to Mabel and said, 'Good afternoon, Mabel.'

Primed by Mrs Kilby before they left the kitchen, Mabel gave a small bob and murmured, 'Good afternoon, my lady.'

For a moment the deep blue eyes scrutinised her before she nodded and said, 'I hope you'll be happy here, Mabel. How old are you?'

'Fifteen, my lady.'

'Good, old enough to be sensible. If you work hard and do as Mrs Kilby tells you, I'm sure you'll do very well.' She turned back to Mrs Kilby and said, 'Thank you, Mrs Kilby.'

And that was it. They were dismissed and at a nudge from the housekeeper, Mabel made another bob, and followed her out of the room.

As they were crossing the hall, a young man appeared at

the top of the stairs, and came leaping down them, two at a time.

'Well, well, Mrs K. Who do we have here?' He grinned at Mabel. 'I haven't seen you before, have I?'

He was tall, with dark hair a little longer than was strictly fashionable, swept back off his face, leaving him with a wide forehead, and a pair of dark brown eyes that surveyed Mabel quizzically from under thick, dark brows.

'A new girl! How exciting.' He laughed and gave her a broad wink.

'Now then, Mr Iain, that'll do,' Mrs Kilby scolded, but Mabel could see she wasn't really cross with him. 'This is Mabel, our new maid, come in place of Ellen.'

Ignoring the mention of Ellen, Iain McFarlane said, 'By the way, I won't be in for dinner tonight, Mrs K, did Mother tell you?'

'She did, sir.'

'Good, well. I must be off.' Iain spoke briskly, and then with another casual smile in Mabel's direction, turned and headed for the front door.

'Mr Iain likes his little jokes,' Mrs Kilby said as he disappeared into the street. 'The house is always more lively when he's down from Cambridge, but whatever he's up to, you pay him no mind.'

That night, when Lizzie and she climbed the stairs to their tiny attic room, Mabel felt exhausted. She had been on the go ever since she had come downstairs for the first time. As she finally fell into bed, Lizzie said, 'I'll wake you at six. You'll need to be downstairs to light the range and heat the water for upstairs.'

'Six?' Mabel cried in dismay.

'Don't worry, Mabel, you'll get used to it!' Lizzie said, and turned out the light.

Tired as she was, Mabel did not fall asleep immediately, but thought back over her day. She had met all the servants and tried to remember what each of them did.

The butler, Mr Felstead, was a tall man, with a narrow face thinning to a narrow, rather scrawny neck. He had a superior air, raising his aquiline nose when he looked at Mabel, as if avoiding an unpleasant smell, saying, 'Well, Mabel Oakley. I hope you're used to hard work.' After which he ignored her, which suited her very well because she had disliked him on sight. When William the footman heard Mabel and Lizzie were cousins, he began to tease her, calling her 'Cousin Mabel'. 'Now then, Cousin Mabel, you'd better make me a cuppa, that's part of your job.' To which Lizzie had said, 'Don't you pay him no mind, Mabel! He's too full of himself.'

Ada was the only one who was lower in the servants' hall than Mabel, and she crept round the scullery, afraid of her own shadow. There were Croxton and Paston from outside, but neither of them had been really interested in her. Miss Chalmers, however, was a woman apart, quite different from all the others. It was clear she considered herself superior to all of them, only one notch lower than 'family', and expected the others to wait on her.

Yes, Mabel thought as she lay there in bed, Croxton was right, she'd got the job and how she wished she hadn't. She had not enjoyed her first day in Chanynge Place, and the days that lay ahead stretched an endless procession into the future. She thought of Mam, back home in Cockspur Lane, of Dada lying in the hospital, of Eddie, going to Smithfield every day at four in the morning to carry sides of beef, of pork and whole sheep across his broad shoulders; portering in the meat market instead of learning the carpentry trade. Of Stephen, going to school each day and longing to leave and find some sort of job himself... and of Mr Clarke, whom Mam had sent away with harsh words.

At least, she thought as she was finally drifting off to sleep, I know where he lives now, so I can write to him. And with that thought to comfort her, she fell asleep.

15

The day came that Andrew Oakley was considered fit enough to be discharged from the hospital.

'There's nothing much more we can do for you here,' Dr Miller said. 'Your wife has prepared everything for your return home. She tells me she's found a nurse who's going to come in every morning for the first week or so while she learns exactly what she needs to do for you. You have a very strong woman there, Mr Oakley, and I'm sure you'll be more comfortable in your own home with your family round you.' He saw the look of dismay on his patient's face, and gave him a reassuring smile, which he could see did absolutely nothing to reassure him.

On the appointed day, the doctor accompanied Andrew to the main entrance of the hospital where a horse and cart, borrowed by Jane Birch from Mr Holman the butcher, awaited him. A mattress had been laid across the flat bed, and two hospital porters manoeuvred Andrew onto it, where he lay with his head on a pillow and covered by a thick blanket, for the journey home.

'Thank you for your care,' Alice said as the doctor shook

her hand. Her voice was tremulous. 'It's up to me to look after him now.'

'And he's lucky to have you,' Dr Miller replied. 'Try not to worry, you'll soon get into a routine; that, and being in his own place, are what will help him most.'

Alice nodded. There was nothing else to say, and with a last anxious glance at her husband, lying unable to move in the back of the cart, she climbed up beside Mr Holman's driver. He shook up the reins and the cart jolted forward and out into the traffic.

As it made its way slowly through the streets, Alice fought back the tears that threatened to overcome her. Glancing over her shoulder at the figure lying beneath the blanket, she wondered, as she had been wondering ever since she'd been told Andrew could leave the hospital, whether she was really going to be able to manage to look after a paralysed man for the rest of his life. She had been determined to try, but now as they clattered along the road on their way home through the noisy bustle of the city, the never-ending future stretching ahead seemed overwhelming.

The wheels of the cart rattled over the cobbles, and Andrew, lying on his back, looking up at a dull March sky framed by the upper floors and roofs of London's buildings, knew a wave of panic. He didn't want to go home, he wanted to be back in the security of the hospital ward. He had felt safe there, where everyone knew how to look after him; where his life had been governed by an unvarying routine. In the mornings he was washed and, as he got stronger, dressed. The doctor came round and was encouraging. They had got him out of bed and sat him in a chair. His food was set on a table before him and as he could still use his upper body, he had been expected to feed himself. Back to bed for a rest. Visiting time when Alice came to see him. Settling for the night. He knew exactly what was going to happen to him...

Now, suddenly, he was in a cart on his way back to Cockspur Lane, to the house which had been their home ever since he and Alice had married, a house which might now make him a prisoner, and he was terrified.

Alice had worked hard to prepare for his return, but though she'd longed to get him out of the hospital, she was at the same time dreading having him home; entirely her responsibility.

Eddie had brought Mabel's single bed downstairs and they had set it up in the front parlour, which would be Andrew's bedroom from now on.

'Mabel will have to sleep with me when she comes home on her weekends off,' his mother said. 'That won't be the problem. One of the main problems is going to be getting your dad in and out of the house. How will we get him up the front step?'

Eddie was ahead of her and had found a solution. 'I've been thinking about that, Mam,' he replied. 'There's a bloke down at Smithfield, Jack, who's got a brother works for a builder. I was telling him about Dad, and he said he'd get Bob to come and build a ramp over the step to the front door. Just a concrete slope, that we can push the wheelchair up.' So, to Alice's surprise, one Sunday morning Bob came, and the ramp was built.

The wheelchair had been a godsend. At first Alice was afraid they wouldn't be able to use it in the house, that it would be too wide to fit through the front door, but to her surprise it went in with half an inch to spare on either side. It didn't fit through the internal doors, but when they cleared all possible obstructions from the passage that ran to the kitchen it was just wide enough to accommodate it. Then one evening Eddie, ever resourceful, had come home with a set of four small casters.

'I went and saw Mr Carter, down the furniture factory,' he said. 'I explained the problem of the wheelchair being too wide for the doors and he let me have these, on tick. I'll fit them to the legs of a kitchen chair and then we can move Dad through any of the doors. Good, eh?'

'But how much did they cost?' asked Alice anxiously. 'We can't afford extras like that.'

'Mr Carter's let me have them at cost, which was five shillings the set, and I'm paying him back at ninepence a week. Come on, Mam, he's a good bloke.'

Thanks to the generosity of Mr Carter and Mabel's unlikely friend, Mr Clarke, they would now be able to move Andrew both around the ground floor of the house and outside in the street.

Mr Carter's generosity reminded Alice of Mr Clarke's, in giving them the wheelchair. She blushed when she remembered how she'd spoken to the printer. The recollection of how she had received his gift made Alice feel guilty and embarrassed. She tried to quieten her conscience with justification. How was she expected to know Mabel had struck up a friendship with a man old enough to be her grandfather? What would Andrew say if he knew of such a friendship? It was perfectly reasonable to be suspicious of such a strange old man. Wasn't it?

'If it's worrying you, Mam,' Eddie said one evening when she mentioned the printer yet again, 'for goodness' sake, go and see the man. Thank him for the wheelchair, it was very generous of him. We could never have afforded one on top of everything else.'

So, a few days before Andrew was due to come home, Alice had swallowed her pride and gone to the shack by the bridge to seek Tom Clarke out. His door was open, but before she tapped tentatively, she peeped inside and saw him hard at work, setting type onto a plate. As soon as he saw her, he stopped what he was doing and invited her in. Alice entered the shack, but stood awkwardly just inside the door.

'Come in, Mrs Oakley,' he said with a smile. 'I was about to stop for a cup of tea. Will you join me?'

She thanked him and perched on the stool that he set for her.

As he busied himself with the kettle and a small brown teapot, Alice drew a deep breath and said, 'Mr Clarke, I've come to apologise. I'm very sorry for the way I spoke to you when you so kindly brought us your wife's wheelchair. I said things that were inexcusable, and… well, I'm so sorry, I hope you can forgive me.'

'Please, Mrs Oakley,' the printer answered, 'no apology is necessary. There's nothing to forgive. My friendship with Mabel, well, it's become very special to me, but I do assure you, there is nothing improper about it.'

'No, I understand that now,' Alice said. 'But I should have at least given you a chance to explain.' She gave a rueful smile. 'Mabel was extremely angry with me, and she was right to be. Your generosity will make my husband's return from the hospital that much easier.'

'I'm glad,' he replied simply. 'That's what I hoped.'

He made the tea and, having left it to brew for a couple of minutes, poured some into Mabel's mug and handed it to her.

Seeing the familiar mug from home, Alice smiled and said, 'That's where it went! I thought Mabel must have broken it!'

Like her daughter, Alice found it very easy to talk to Mr Clarke. He was a good listener and she began to tell him her worries about having Andrew home, things she had said to no one else, not even close family.

'What if I find I can't manage?' she said, with an edge of panic in her voice. 'The doctor says he'll be better at home, but suppose I can't cope? He's a grown man. How will I be able to move him? I've got my son Eddie to help, but he's not going to be there all the time, is he? What will I do if he comes home and everything goes wrong?'

He could tell she was on the verge of tears.

'One bridge at a time,' he said soothingly. 'Why don't you tell me how far you've got?' So she did. When she'd described the plans they'd made, he said, 'How clever of Eddie to make an indoor wheelchair. He must be very good with his hands.' And so she told him about the proposed apprenticeship and how Eddie had given it up so he could earn proper money to help support the family.

'Eddie was so pleased when Carter's accepted him as an apprentice,' Alice explained. 'It would have been perfect for him. He loves making things. I'd have tried to talk him out of it, if I'd realised what he was going to do, but he made the decision without discussing it with anyone, and by the time he told us, he'd already spoken to Mr Carter and got himself a job as a porter down in Smithfield market.' She looked across at Mr Clarke, listening silently to her. 'I wish he hadn't,' she said. 'I don't know what Andrew will say when he knows.'

'I imagine he'll be very proud of him,' answered Mr Clarke. 'It must have made a difference.'

'And so am I,' responded Alice. 'But it seems such a waste of his abilities. He'd have made a first-rate carpenter, making furniture and that.'

'Nothing one does is really ever wasted,' said Mr Clarke. 'And your son realised helping you out in the immediate future was more important than anything he might do further down the road.'

'You're right, of course. I couldn't do without Eddie to help me make the house ready for Andrew.'

'Now,' he said, 'it sounds to me as if you're nearly there. There is just one thing...' He hesitated before continuing. 'If you won't consider me to be indelicate, there is the question of a lavatory.'

Alice did feel the colour rising in her cheeks, but she said softly, 'It's upstairs.'

'My wife and I found it convenient for her to have a commode in the corner of her room. Perhaps if you could send your son...?'

No more was said, but Alice went home again with another problem solved.

She hadn't told him about her money worries, that would have been a confidence too many, but he knew the family finances were going to be extremely tight. He offered her no advice on those, but it didn't stop him giving the problem some serious thought.

And now Andrew was on his way home.. When the horse and cart turned into Cockspur Lane, Eddie was waiting outside the house with two of his friends and the wheelchair.

'Welcome home, Dad,' Eddie said, fighting back the tears as he saw what his father had become; the husk of a man, his useless legs dangling. Drawing a deep breath he stepped forward. Very gently he lifted his father from the cart and carried him indoors. And so began the rest of their lives.

16

Mabel soon learned the routine of the Chanynge Place house, and before long it seemed to her that she'd been there for ever. The work she was set to do was tiring and for the first few days she fell into bed exhausted, knowing that her sleep would not have defeated her tiredness by the morning; that she would feel almost unable to struggle out of bed, even when it was her turn to make the first use of the water in the ewer. It was cold, whether you were first or second, but going second you had to put up with the soapy scum floating on its surface.

Their room never received direct sunlight through its tiny window and was both cold and stuffy. Even with the window closed against the weather, there was always a draught. However hard Mabel pulled at the casement, it screeched defiance and continued to leave a gap.

'Give up!' Lizzie advised. 'It's always been stiff and in the summer it only opens a few inches and the room is stifling.'

Mabel was expected downstairs by six o'clock in the morning to riddle the ashes in the kitchen range, bringing it back to life ready for Mrs Bellman to begin cooking the family breakfast an hour later. While Lizzie was cleaning the reception rooms ready for the family's use, Mabel was expected to clean the shoes, polish the brass on the front door and scrub the front steps. Breakfast for the staff was served in the servants' hall, though why it was called a hall, Mabel couldn't imagine. It was nothing more than an inner room off the kitchen with a large table down the middle, but at least the food was wholesome and filling.

As the between-maid, she seemed to be at the beck and call of everyone else; particularly Mrs Bellman, Mrs Kilby and Mr Felstead. Often this meant she was supposed to be doing three different things at once. On hearing her complain to Lizzie that she never had a moment's rest, Mrs Kilby said sharply, 'Count yourself lucky, my girl. If Sir Keir had not had the electricity installed, you would have had a lot more work with all the lamps to clean each day.'

Mrs Bellman was the easiest to work for, and Mabel was happy enough to join Ada in the security of the kitchen; she knew what was expected there. The work was tiring, but not difficult. Peeling vegetables, washing dishes, scouring pots and pans, were all things she'd done at home. Indeed sometimes, as she peeled potatoes or washed cabbages, she found herself blinking back tears as she thought of Mam at home, still doing those same things without her.

Most of the time she was too busy to be homesick, but occasionally, in an odd quiet moment, it hit her. She'd had no communication from home since she'd walked out of the door. How were Mam, Eddie and Stephen? What about Dada, lying in the hospital? And Mr Clarke? How was he? She had thought she would write to him when she was settled, telling him all about her life here in Chanynge Place, but come the end of the day she had no energy for anything, and her pencil case remained unopened, along with her notepad in the locker beside her bed.

Sometimes, Mrs Kilby sent her through the green baize door into the family's domain, and that was something that she dreaded. She might be sent to help Lizzie change the sheets on the beds, or to clear the table in the morning room after breakfast, or the dining room after luncheon. It was not so bad when Lizzie was with her, but on occasion she'd been sent on her own. She was not expected to answer a bell that rang below stairs, summoning the assistance of a servant, that was left to William or Lizzie, but a day came when Lizzie was upstairs cleaning the two bathrooms and William had been sent on an errand for her ladyship, so when the bell jangled, Mrs Kilby had told Mabel to wash her hands and answer it.

'That's the bell from the library,' Mrs Kilby said. 'It will be Sir Keir. Now, remember what I told you, a bob as you enter the room and only speak when you're spoken to.'

'Yes, Mrs Kilby, but what do I do next?' Mabel had not yet met Sir Keir and she was already afraid of him. After all, he was a judge!

'He will give you his orders, and either you simply carry them out, or bring them down here and pass them on to William or Mr Felstead.'

'But what if William's still out?' cried Mabel. 'Where is Mr Felstead?'

'He's busy,' replied Mrs Kilby shortly. 'Off you go! Don't keep the master waiting!'

When she reached the library, Mabel found that it wasn't the master who had rung, but Mr Iain. She had knocked on the door as she'd been told and then opened it and on entering the room bobbed a curtsy and waited. Iain McFarlane was sitting in a chair by the window, and lounging in the chair opposite was another young man. He was rather strange-looking, with a shock of carroty hair that had been smoothed down within an inch of its life with some sort of oil.

'Oh,' Mr Iain said, 'it's you.' He turned his head to the other man. 'This girl's new, Everette. Can't think of her name. Girl,' he snapped his fingers, 'what is your name?'

'Mabel, sir.'

'Mabel, oh yes, I remember now. Well, Mabel, we'd like a bottle of brandy with some of Mrs Bellman's savouries, quick as you like. She'll know what to send up. Don't know where the damned butler is,' he went on, turning back to his friend. Mabel stood waiting in case he had any further orders, but realising that she was still there, he said briskly, 'Off you go, girl. See to it.'

Mabel bobbed another curtsy and as she left the room she heard the other man, the one Mr Iain had addressed as Everette, say, 'Pretty little chit. Had any luck with her yet?' As she was shutting the door behind her, Mabel could not hear the answer Mr Iain gave, but she heard both men laugh before the closed door cut them off, and the sound made her feel distinctly uncomfortable. She scurried back across the black and white marble hall and through the baize door to find Mrs Kilby.

'It was Mr Iain,' she told the housekeeper. 'He has a guest with him and he wants brandy and a plate of Mrs Bellman's savouries.'

'William's just back, so he can take them up,' said Mrs Kilby. 'Tell him what Mr Iain asked for, and then get back to Mrs Bellman. There's a dinner party for twelve tonight, and she needs everything prepared.'

'How can there be so much work just to keep a family of four in comfort?' Mabel wondered aloud to her cousin one evening when there had been a dinner party for ten, followed by the inevitable clearing up. William, who was still sitting at the table, his work in serving the six-course dinner upstairs now done, overheard her and laughed.

'Because they don't lift a finger to look after themselves. From the moment they open their eyes in the morning till the moment they close them at night, everything is done for them. If we wasn't here to wait on their every little wish, they couldn't exist.'

'Enough of such talk!' Mr Felstead had walked silently into the room. Mabel had noticed that his voice tended to be rather high-pitched, particularly when he was pulling rank. Hearing him now, rebuking William, she had to repress a smile because it reminded her of the squeak of her recalcitrant window.

William, entirely unremorseful, replied, 'Well, it's true, ain't it? Which of them does a hand's turn in the running of the house?'

'That is your job, William,' Mr Felstead said loftily, 'and you're paid for it. You should not make outlandish statements like that, it is most disrespectful.' The butler turned on his heel and disappeared from the servants' hall, going, the others were certain, to join Mrs Kilby in her little sitting room.

'With a bottle of the master's brandy under his coat, I shouldn't wonder!' muttered William to the closed door.

Mabel thought he probably had, too, because one of her

morning jobs was cleaning Mrs Kilby's lair, and she had, more than once, found and removed two small glasses, empty but smelling of alcohol. Finding her holding these one morning, Mrs Kilby said, 'Be careful with my special glasses, Mabel. I use them for my evening cordial. Don't give them to Ada, or she'll break them. Wash them yourself.'

One sunny afternoon, Mabel saw her cousin going through the kitchen to the back door dressed in her own clothes rather than the uniform she'd been wearing during the morning.

'Where are you going?' She put out a hand to stop her. 'Lizzie, where are you going?'

'Home to see Mum,' Lizzie replied. 'It's my half day.'

Mabel had been looking forward to her first half day off, but though she had almost completed her month's trial, there had been no mention of such a thing.

'What about me?' she demanded. 'When's my half day?'

Mrs Kilby, coming into the kitchen at that moment, heard her question and snapped, 'Your half day? You haven't earned one yet. You'll get a half day when I say so and not before.'

'That's not fair,' cried Mabel. 'You told my mother I'd have half a day every two weeks and a weekend every month.'

'None of your cheek, my girl, you're still on trial,' retorted Mrs Kilby. 'I said if you could be spared, and at present you can't.'

'Why? Why can't I? What've I got to do that's so important?'

'Nothing you do is important,' replied the housekeeper sharply. 'What *is* important is that you learn your place and do as you're told. So, let me hear no more from you.' And with that she swept out of the kitchen to the privacy of her own parlour.

'Now you've done it,' muttered Lizzie. 'She won't give you a half day for ages now.'

'But that's not fair,' repeated Mabel angrily. 'It's not what was agreed!'

'Well,' said Lizzie, anxious to leave before Mrs Kilby changed her mind about her, too, 'the more fuss you make about it, the longer it'll be before she gives you time off. Keep your head down, that's my advice to you. I'm off now, I'll be back to help with the evening meal.'

'When you get home, will you go and see my mam and tell her why I haven't been back to see her?'

'Yes, all right,' agreed Lizzie, and hearing Mrs Kilby returning from her room, she ducked into the scullery, out across the yard and into the street, before anyone could stop her.

Mabel stared after her, and that was how Mrs Kilby found her moments later.

'Ah, Mabel,' she said, 'go into the house and collect all the chamber pots from the bedrooms and bring them down here for scrubbing out.'

It was not a job Mabel had been given before. Every morning, when she was making the beds and cleaning the bedrooms, Lizzie had to pull the 'chambers' from beneath the bed, empty them and then bring them downstairs to the scullery for Ada to scrub. Ada, as the lowest of the low in the servants' hall, was given all the most distasteful jobs. Mabel had seen her scrubbing the pots inside and out and had been intensely relieved that it was not one of her jobs.

Now, here was Mrs Kilby, telling her to do again what had already been done by Lizzie and Ada, first thing. She opened her mouth to protest, but before the words could escape, Mrs Kilby said, 'Straight away, Mabel, or you'll find it's your job every day.'

Mabel managed to bite her tongue and say nothing, for fear of making everything worse. She knew it was a punishment for what she'd said earlier and her face was mutinous as she turned towards the backstairs.

On reaching the family's bedroom floor, she went first to Miss Lucinda's room. There was no answer to her knock, so she opened the door and, finding the room empty, she went inside, pulling the door to behind her. She had not been into this room before and she paused to look about her and admire. How she would love such a room, spacious and stylish. It was furnished simply, but with elegance. The bed opposite the fireplace was flanked by two small bedside tables, and an elegant dressing table stood by the window. There was a bowl and ewer atop a chest of drawers and a tall wardrobe completed the suite. Afternoon sunlight flooded the room, its slanting light shining on the peignoir thrown carelessly across the bed, shimmering on an evening gown of peacock blue silk hanging on the wardrobe door and sparkling on the cut-glass bottles and jars laid out on the dressing table.

Mabel had never seen such make-up. Mam didn't wear any, nor Auntie Jane; only Auntie Susan always appeared with rouged cheeks and powdered nose. Mabel thought it made her look like a clown, though of course she had never dared to express this thought, not even to her brothers. Slowly she walked across to the dressing table and picked up one of the cut-glass bottles and, removing its glass stopper, closed her eyes, inhaling the scent that wafted from within.

'And just what do you think you're doing?'

The voice was so unexpected that Mabel very nearly dropped the bottle, spilling some of the scent as she juggled it in her fingers. She turned to find herself face to face with Miss Lucinda.

Lucinda was framed in the doorway, hands on hips, glowering at her. Her brown eyes gleamed with anger as she saw the scent bottle in Mabel's hand.

'N-n-nothing, miss!' Mabel stammered. 'I was just—'

'Just helping yourself to some of my scent.'

'No, really. I mean I was admiring the bottle and—'

'And were about to help yourself!'

If Mabel were completely honest, she might have admitted to thinking of taking a dab, but as she had not actually done so, she felt able to say, 'I just wondered what it smelled like.' She had replaced the stopper and set the bottle down carefully on the dressing table. Miss Lucinda gave her a knowing look.

'Very likely, I'm sure,' she drawled. 'You're new, aren't you? I've seen you about. So, what's your name? Did the lady of the house at your last place allow you to wear her perfume?'

'This is my first job, miss,' said Mabel, remembering at last to bob a curtsy.

'You should address me as Miss Lucinda.'

'This is my first job, Miss Lucinda.'

'And it could well be your last. You should be turned off without a character for what you were doing.'

Mabel said nothing, considering that silence was her best defence in the face of Miss Lucinda's anger.

'What were you supposed to be doing in my room, anyway?'

'Mrs Kilby told me to come and fetch...' Mabel faltered. How could she speak of chamber pots to a gently brought up young lady like Miss Lucinda?

'To fetch what?' snapped Lucinda. 'My scent?'

'No, Miss Lucinda... to fetch,' she dropped her voice to almost a whisper, 'the gazunder.'

Lucinda looked at the maid for a long moment and then burst out laughing. 'You mean the chamber, don't you?'

Red-cheeked with embarrassment, Mabel nodded, murmuring, 'Yes, Miss Lucinda.'

'Well, you'd better get on and take it to... wherever you're supposed to be taking it.'

She stood and watched as Mabel bent down and felt under the bed for the handle of the large ceramic pot, white and decorated with pink roses. As she dragged it forth and saw its design, for one moment Mabel wondered if the roses were supposed to make the contents smell sweeter, and she almost laughed aloud at the idea, but managed to school her expression before turning to face Miss Lucinda. Thank goodness, she thought, there are no contents just now.

She got to her feet and, holding the pot a little away from her, said, 'May I go now, Miss Lucinda?'

Lucinda sniffed. 'I think you'd better.' But as Mabel turned to the door, Lucinda said, 'Wait! You never did tell me what your name was.'

'It's Mabel Oakley, Miss Lucinda.'

'Well, Mabel Oakley, if I ever catch you touching any of

my things again, you'll be out of this house in a flash.' She glowered at Mabel. 'Understand?'

'Yes, Miss Lucinda. Thank you, Miss Lucinda.' And as Lucinda waved her hand in dismissal, Mabel bobbed one last time, made for the door and headed down the backstairs to the scullery.

She had to visit the other three bedrooms before her task was finished, but she encountered no one from the family as she did so. Although the scrubbing was unpleasant, it was not as bad as it would have been if Lizzie and Ada had not already completed it earlier in the day.

As she lay in bed that night Mabel considered her encounter with Miss Lucinda, the daughter of the house. She didn't know how old she was, but decided that she was probably not much more than two years older than she was herself. What a different life each of them had. Mabel within a loving family, all of whom worked hard for their bread, her parents strict but encouraging and supportive. Lucinda, brought up to expect her every wish to be granted, taught by a governess until she was thirteen and then attending an exclusive school for young ladies to prepare her for her place in polite society. Throughout her life it was most unlikely Miss Lucinda would have to support herself; she would move smoothly from the comfort and luxury of her parents' home to the comfort and luxury of a suitable husband. She would never be told that she could not visit her parents as she, Mabel, had been today.

When Lizzie had returned from her afternoon off, she told Mabel that her father was about to come out of hospital and her mother hoped she would soon be given her free afternoon, so she could come home and see them. They had not discussed this idea until they were safely in their own bedroom, under the eaves.

'You'll have to keep your nose clean if you want to have time off as soon as next week,' Lizzie advised. 'Make sure you don't cheek Mrs Kilby again, like you did today!'

'I've been punished for that already,' said Mabel, and told her of the fetching and scrubbing of the chamber pots, but she did not tell her about Miss Lucinda and the scent bottle. She had no wish to admit such stupidity to anyone, even to her cousin. She could only hope that Miss Lucinda wouldn't mention it to anyone, either.

17

Stephen Oakley slipped out of the house, along the lane and onto the main road. He was on a secret errand for his mother. Dad was asleep in his room and Eddie wasn't home yet. Only Mam and he knew where he was going and why.

His mother's fears about caring for her husband were realised almost as soon as he was established in his new, downstairs bedroom. Though Andrew had lost almost two stone in weight since the accident and looked little more than skin and bone, he was still a deadweight when it came to moving him between chair and bed or commode. He was still often in pain and was quickly overtired, which made him frustrated and irritable.

Mrs Doreen Finch, a retired nurse introduced to Alice by Andrew's sister Susan, came in each morning to help get him ready for the day. She was a motherly body, almost as round as she was tall. Her grey hair was pulled back into a ragged bun and her face was creased with wrinkles, with spots of high colour on her cheeks so that she looked rather like an overripe apple; but to Alice she was worth her considerable weight in gold. Unfailingly cheerful, she would wash and dress Andrew, so that when he was wheeled into the kitchen and seated at the table, one could almost forget he couldn't stand up at will… almost, but not quite.

Surprisingly, he found he didn't mind being subjected to Mrs Finch's ministrations; it was like being back in hospital. They both knew what had to be done and got on with it. She was experienced and strong, manoeuvring him with apparent ease, always speaking to him briskly, never treating him as an invalid. She was quite different from poor Alice, who was afraid of hurting him and worried he was in pain. She fussed him so much that it was all he could do not to snap at her, 'For goodness' sake! Leave me alone!'

When Nurse Finch found Alice in tears in the kitchen one morning, she made a pot of tea and, having poured for both of them, sat down at the table and said, 'Try not to fuss him, dearie. Let him do as much for himself as he can, even if it takes for ever. He needs as much independence as possible.'

'But there are some things he's never going to be able to do,' cried Alice.

'Of course there are,' agreed Nurse Finch, 'and that is something he's got to come to terms with… same as you. But he will eventually, and in the meantime, you must concentrate on what he *can* do, not what he can't. Take him a bowl of water in the morning and let him wash and shave himself. He can do it, even if he doesn't make a very good job of it.'

'But supposing he spills it? He'll be so upset!'

'He probably will,' said Mrs Finch with a smile, 'but don't make a fuss about it, simply mop it up again. It's not the end of the world.' She reached forward and took one of

Alice's hands in her own. 'Things *are* going to upset him,' she said gently. 'But you mustn't let them upset you.'

Mrs Finch was only supposed to come for Andrew's first week home, to help him get settled in, but she could see Alice was going to struggle with all that had to be done and with only Eddie to help her. The two of them managed to get Andrew into bed at night, but neither of them slept well as they lay in their own beds upstairs, one ear cocked for the sound of the bell on Andrew's bedside table.

'How would it be,' suggested Mrs Finch as she looked across the kitchen table at an exhausted Alice, pale-faced with dark smudges beneath her eyes, 'if I kept on coming for a little while longer? You know, just to get Mr Oakley up in the mornings? Once he's dressed, he and I can have a cup of tea here in the kitchen, while you sort out his room for him.'

Alice knew that she couldn't afford Mrs Finch for longer than arranged – even that was a stretch – but neither could she face the thought of losing her and having to cope on her own.

'Perhaps just for another week or so,' she said uncertainly. 'Until I've really got things under control.'

It was agreed, and Andrew, who hadn't been party to the original arrangement, shouldn't realise it had been changed. He was simply grateful Mrs Finch still came every day.

I know poor Alice is doing her best, he thought, as the nurse eased him from the bed to his indoor wheelchair, but she's not like Mrs Finch.

That afternoon, when Stephen came home from school, Alice called him upstairs to her bedroom. Andrew was supposed to be having a nap, but she wasn't going to risk him overhearing any part of what she was going to say to Stephen.

She beckoned him closer. 'I want you to do something for me, Stephen, but it has to be our secret, all right?'

Stephen nodded, intrigued. 'All right,' he said, 'what is it?'

From the drawer beside her, Alice took out a small velvet bag. 'You know Solomon's the jeweller just off Cuck Lane? Well, I want you to take this to Mr Solomon and ask him what he'll let you have against it.' She pulled out a small oval locket on a thin gold chain and held it up to the light to show him. 'It used to belong to your grandmother.' Alice clicked it open. 'See,' she held it out to him, 'those are my parents.'

Stephen took it and peered in at the two tiny faces captured inside.

'When they died, it came to me.'

'But what about their pictures?' asked Stephen. 'Don't you want to take them out?'

'I don't think I can, not without damaging them,' replied Alice. 'And it isn't as if I want to sell it, mind. Just borrow against it. We'll be claiming it back again next week. You know where to go?'

Stephen certainly did know Solomon's. He passed the shop on his way to and from school every day, and every day he paused at the window to peer inside. He was not the least interested in the items of jewellery displayed on velvet pads to tempt passing customers inside, but what did fascinate Stephen were the clocks and watches he could just see set out on shelves around the shop. He had never plucked up courage to go into the place to look properly; it would be clear to Mr Solomon who sat behind the counter, usually tinkering with the inner workings of some timepiece, that he had no money to buy anything and the old man wouldn't want him hanging about watching him mending things.

'But if it was your mother's, why are you trying to pawn it?' Stephen asked Alice.

'Because we need the money. At present I need more help with your dad, and this is the only way we can afford it. Don't worry, Stephen, we'll get it back very soon. We shan't need Mrs Finch for much longer, then we can claim it back with the money we'll save on her wages. The thing is,' she went on, 'it has to be our secret, yours and mine. I don't want your dad worrying about money, and Eddie is working so hard, he can't do any more.'

'But what about me?' demanded Stephen.

'Dearest boy,' Alice answered, a wave of love flooding through her as she looked at his earnest young face, 'you already give me everything you earn running errands in the market at the weekend. When you leave school next year, you'll find a regular job; you'll be able to give me a bit more and it will make all the difference.'

'I could leave school now,' suggested Stephen. 'I'm just thirteen.'

'So you are, but you're not allowed to leave school at thirteen unless you already have an offer of regular employment. Don't worry, I promise you we can manage, but a little extra cash against this locket will make things that bit easier.' Alice reached out, took his hand and gripped it tightly. 'Now, Stephen, promise me you won't mention our dealings with Mr Solomon to Eddie or your dad.' She fixed him with a steady stare and Stephen said, 'I promise, Mam. I won't tell them.'

'Our secret,' repeated his mother. 'Good lad!'

So now, here he was, approaching Mr Solomon's shop, the little velvet bag containing its treasure safely in his pocket. As always, Stephen paused at the window, shading his eyes against the reflection of the sun, and peered in. There was Mr Solomon, sitting as usual behind the counter with tiny pieces of something spread on a black cloth in front of him.

Well, thought Stephen, at least I have a reason to be here, and when I come back for the locket, I'll be able to come in again.

A small bell jangled above his head as he pushed the door open, and the old man looked up.

'Well, youngster,' he said, removing his eyeglass from his eye and putting a tiny wheel he had been studying into a small glass dish. 'What can I do for you?'

Joseph Solomon was a small man. His head, somehow too large for his body, was sparsely covered with thin grey hair; his beaky nose dominated his face and his mouth stretched, an unsmiling line, above a fleshy chin. These features melded into a face like many another until you noticed his eyes. Stephen noticed them now, a piercing blue, that seemed to drill into his head.

For a moment Stephen held their gaze, but then he dropped his eyes and, reaching into his pocket, said, 'My mother asked what you might lend against this.' He handed the jeweller the velvet pouch.

Mr Solomon lifted out the locket and held it up to the light. He clicked it open to look inside and then screwed the eyeglass back into his eye and peered at it more closely.

'And who are these people inside?' he asked.

'They're my mother's parents.'

'They should be removed,' said the old man, 'before the locket is left for pawn.'

'Mam's afraid they would be damaged if she tried to take them out. She says you'll only have it for a week or so before she can get it back.'

'Held for a month,' replied the old man. 'Two pounds.'

'That doesn't sound very much,' said Stephen, disappointed.

'Well, it isn't very much of a locket, is it? Take it or leave it.'

Stephen took it.

Mr Solomon pulled an order book towards him and, setting a pair of gold-rimmed pince-nez on his nose, placed a piece of carbon paper under a clean page and said, 'Name?'

Stephen gave his mother's name and address and watched as Mr Solomon wrote it all down in a crabbed hand, along with a description of the locket and the amount loaned. At the bottom of the page he wrote the date and term of loan, one month.

'Here you are, boy,' he said, passing the paper over to Stephen. He placed the copy and the locket into an envelope, with the name Oakley written on it.

'I'll put it in the safe,' he told Stephen. 'It'll be with me for a month. Then, if you haven't redeemed it, I shall offer it for sale. Please remind your mother of that.'

Stephen promised he would. He was just turning for the door, with the two pounds safely in his pocket, when the jeweller said, 'What's *your* name, boy?'

'Stephen, Stephen Oakley.'

'You look familiar. Have you been in here before?'

'No, but I do stop and look in through your window most days, on my way home from school.'

'So you do. I've seen you. Why's that? Shouldn't have thought you were in the market for anything I sell.'

'No.' Stephen spoke abruptly, and then added in a more conciliatory tone, 'You're always mending things.' He pointed to the pieces on the black cloth on the counter. 'What's those?'

'I'm repairing a watch for a customer. It's been overwound and the mainspring has broken. I'm replacing it.' Using a pair of tweezers he picked up a tiny coil of wire. 'See this?'

Fascinated, Stephen leaned forward to have a closer look. 'How do you know what to do?'

'I started learning when I was no older than you,' replied the old man. 'Many moons ago, that was!'

'But the works are so tiny!'

'They are,' agreed Mr Solomon, 'and I have to admit there are occasions these days when I struggle, even with my loupe.'

'Your... loupe?'

Mr Solomon picked up his eyeglass and held it out. 'That's what this is,' he said. 'It magnifies what I'm looking at. It's particularly helpful with gemstones. So if someone brings me a ring, I can inspect the stone with this and decide on its worth. Too many stones are actually coloured glass these days. You have to know what you're looking for. It's a trade like any other. You have to learn it from the beginning. There's no shortcuts.'

The bell over the door jingled just then and a woman came in. She looked at Stephen and turned away.

'Good afternoon, Mrs Shaw,' said Mr Solomon. 'How can I help you today?'

She didn't answer straight away, and Mr Solomon said, 'Off you go, boy. Your mother will be waiting for you.'

Stephen opened the shop door, the bell jingling again as he went out into the street.

18

Mabel made sure she was promptly obedient the following week. She longed for her afternoon off so she could go home and see her father. By the end of the week she waited to be told by Mrs Kilby when she might go, but nothing was said.

'It's not fair,' she complained to Lizzie again. 'I'm entitled to my afternoon off once every two weeks!'

'There's nothing you can do about it,' replied Lizzie philosophically. 'You just have to wait. I had to wait nearly six weeks for my first half day. She'll make you do the same. You have to put up with it.'

'I could go and ask Lady McFarlane,' she snapped. 'She's the person I work for, not Mrs Kilby.'

Lizzie looked at her in horror. 'Oh, Mabel,' she cried, 'for goodness' sake, don't do that!'

'Why not?' Mabel demanded mulishly.

'Even if she gave you permission to go, you'd never hear the end of it from Mrs Kilby, going over her head. She'd make your life a misery!'

'It's a misery already,' snapped Mabel. 'I hate it here!'

'It's a job, Mabel,' said Lizzie. 'And you need one. Don't throw it all away!'

Mabel wasn't convinced, but finally decided Lizzie was probably right; going to her ladyship wouldn't help.

Later that afternoon Mrs Flick, the washerwoman who came in twice a week to collect the dirty laundry and return it clean, pressed and folded, arrived with a basket of freshly ironed sheets and pillow cases. Mrs Kilby called Mabel from the scullery where she was washing up with Ada.

'Take this up to the linen cupboard,' she said, 'and look sharp about it. Remember to sort it onto the right shelves, and bring the basket back down for Mrs Flick.'

Mabel picked up the basket and took the backstairs up to the bedroom floor. As she edged her way through the door onto the landing, she caught her foot on the doorsill and tripped, dropping the basket and spilling the pile of ironed sheets all over the floor. She was just scrambling to her feet when Mr Iain came out of his room and almost trod on some of the scattered linen.

'Goodness!' he exclaimed. 'What are you doing, girl?'

'I tripped,' said Mabel crossly. Wasn't it clear what she was doing?

'So I see,' replied Iain with a grin. 'Come on, I'll help you gather these up.' He bent down and picked up one of the sheets. It was only partially unfolded and he dumped it into the basket.

'I can *do* it,' Mabel said fiercely. 'I'll have to fold them all again, properly.'

'Now, now, don't be awkward,' said Iain with a laugh. 'Here, catch hold of this!' He picked up another sheet and shook it out. With a shrug, Mabel did as she was told and together they refolded the sheet. With two to stretch and fold, it didn't take very long to do them all and Mabel was grateful for the help.

'Thank you, Mr Iain,' she said, and smiled up at him.

With everything safely back in the basket, Iain said, 'Here, I'll carry it to the linen cupboard for you. It's quite heavy.' And without waiting for an answer he picked up the basket and walked along the landing. The linen cupboard was set into an alcove between his bedroom and his sister's. When they reached it, he said, 'Open the door for me and I'll put this inside.'

'They have to go on the right shelves,' Mabel said, standing aside to let him unload the sheets from the basket.

'Well, Mabel... it is Mabel, isn't it? You can do the sorting out when you've given me my reward.' He was smiling as he dumped the sheets onto the nearest shelf and turned back to her.

Mabel looked at him, confused. Reward? Then he reached out to her and pulled her close, holding her firmly, so they were crushed together inside the linen cupboard.

'My reward for helping you,' he murmured. 'Just a little kiss to say thank you? You wouldn't refuse me that now, would you?' And before she could answer, he lowered his face to hers. He kissed her, first on her cheek and then full on the lips.

She could feel his tongue pressing against her mouth and she tried to turn her head away, but he held her firmly against him for another kiss, before he let her go and laughed.

'There, now,' he said teasingly, 'that wasn't so bad, was it? I bet you haven't been kissed before, have you? You're a pretty little thing and next time you'll get to like it. Now then, it's time you sorted out that linen. Mrs Kilby will be after you if it's all on the wrong shelf!' And with that, he disappeared along the landing and down the stairs.

For a long moment Mabel stood there, her cheeks burning, fighting tears, the lump in her throat making her feel sick. Angrily she grabbed a pillow case and scrubbed at her mouth, trying to wipe away the feel of his lips on hers, the dampness of his probing tongue.

Next time! He'd said it so casually. Next time!

Well, there wasn't going to be a next time if she could possibly help it, and she wasn't going to hang about here as if waiting for him to come back. She stuffed the crumpled pillow case to the back of the cupboard and, leaving the pile of linen exactly where he had put it, she closed the cupboard door, picked up the empty basket and scurried back to the stairs.

'You took your time,' snapped Mrs Kilby when she got back down to the kitchen. 'Doesn't take that long to sort the linen.'

Mabel almost told her what had happened, but she realised just in time that it would be a mistake. She could make no complaint about Mr Iain. He would either deny it or suggest she had offered herself to him. So all she said was, 'Sorry, Mrs Kilby.' And returned to the scullery where Ada was finishing the washing up.

Unfortunately for Mabel, the next time Mrs Kilby went up to the bedroom floor, she checked the linen cupboard and saw none of the clean laundry had been sorted; it was all in a heap on one shelf. She went straight back downstairs and, grabbing Mabel by the arm, pulled her into her parlour.

'I thought you said you'd sorted the linen onto the right shelves,' she said angrily. 'How dare you lie to me!'

Mabel couldn't think of an answer. There could be no truthful explanation, so she simply said, 'I'm sorry, Mrs Kilby.'

'So I should think,' expostulated the housekeeper, completely unmollified. 'You're a wicked, stupid girl. I was going to send you on your afternoon off tomorrow, but now your punishment for lying will be no afternoon off this week and probably not next, either. I will not tolerate disobedience and dishonesty. Now, go at once, sort out that cupboard and be quick about it.'

Reluctantly, Mabel returned up the backstairs. When she reached the landing she eased the door open a fraction and peered out. Mr Iain's bedroom door was open, but there was no sign of him. Her heart was thudding. Suppose he came back while she was dealing with the linen? He might think she was there because she wanted to be.

She hurried along the landing, giving a quick glance in through his open bedroom door, but thankfully the room was empty. She opened the linen cupboard and set to work sorting the sheets and pillowcases onto the appropriate shelves. She worked quickly and it was a relief when she was able to close the door again and hurry back down to the kitchen.

That night she told Lizzie what had happened. 'I don't know what to do,' she said, tears coming to her eyes again, as she recounted how he'd kissed her.

'You shouldn't have let him,' Lizzie said. 'You should have pushed him away. Now he'll think he can do it again, because you let him!'

'I didn't let him,' Mabel replied furiously. 'He had me trapped in the linen cupboard. He was too strong, I couldn't break away from him!'

'Well, you shouldn't have let him pick up the laundry in the first place,' said Lizzie. 'That was asking for trouble.'

'Why?' demanded Mabel. 'Why was it?'

'How old are you?' Lizzie asked with a sigh.

'Fifteen, why?'

'Well, you're old enough to know now what to expect from men, especially men like Mr Iain. Men who like to flirt.'

'Did he try it with you?'

'No, certainly not,' snapped Lizzie. 'But he... well, just steer clear of him, that's all. There's always consequences if you don't.'

That might be easier said than done, Mabel thought as she lay in the darkness. And because of him she'd lost her half day. She hated him for that, almost more than for kissing her and trying to lick her mouth.

The next morning she went about her usual duties and was surprised to see no sign of Mrs Kilby.

'Mrs Kilby is in bed with a temperature,' Mrs Bellman told them at breakfast. 'She won't be down today.'

Thank goodness for that, Mabel thought, and then as she drank the last of her tea she had an idea. Before she continued with her usual chores, she managed to speak to Mrs Bellman without being overheard.

'Please, Mrs Bellman, I was to have my afternoon off today, would it be all right if I took it as planned?'

'I should think so,' replied the cook. 'As long as you're back to help clear away after dinner.' Mrs Bellman had noticed Mrs Kilby had allowed Mabel no half days since her arrival and she had thought it unnecessarily harsh. The girl worked well, doing what she was asked. True, she was too ready with her tongue, too quick at answering back, but she would soon learn that didn't pay. 'You can go off when you finish this morning.'

While they were serving the family luncheon in the dining room, Mabel went up to their room and changed out of her uniform. For the first time since she had arrived, she put on her own clothes. It was wonderful the difference it made to how she felt. She felt free, as if she'd been released from a cage, and she couldn't wait to get out of the house. She had not yet received any wages, due on the last day of the month, but she still had the few shillings her mother had given her when she'd left home for Chanynge Place.

'Just in case of emergency,' Mam had said. 'Don't just spend it.'

Spend it! she thought now. What chance have I had to spend anything? I haven't left the house since I got here.

It more than covered her bus fare home and the afternoon stretched before her as she walked from the bus stop and turned into Cockspur Lane. They wouldn't know she was coming, she thought, and longed to see the delighted surprise when they saw who was at the door.

It was her mother who let her in, gathering her into her arms with cries of delight.

'My dearest girl, why didn't you let us know you were coming? We've been surprised and a little worried that you haven't been home before. Indeed that we heard nothing from you until Lizzie came home last time and explained you had to earn your first half day. Not what we expected…

but never mind, you're here now! Your father will be thrilled to see you. Come on in. He's in the kitchen. Have you eaten? Oh, my dear, it's so good to see you.'

Mabel followed her mother into the kitchen, and there, sitting in a chair at the table, was Dada. For a moment she paused by the door and then she was across the room and kneeling beside his chair, her arms around his waist, her head against his chest.

'Dada.' Her voice broke on a sob as she saw his wasted frame and the pallor of his face. 'Oh, Dada, how I've missed you.'

'Me too, Mabel. How grown up you've become. Not my little girl any more.' His arms had come round her and she could feel his hand on her head, stroking her hair. He eased her away from him and looked down into her face.

'You look tired,' he said.

'It's a tiring job,' she admitted. 'I'm always being told to do something... often two things at once.' She glanced up at her mother who was standing in the doorway watching them. 'I am a bit hungry, Mam,' she said, belatedly answering her mother's question, 'and dying for a cup of tea.'

Ten minutes later she was sitting down to a plate of scrambled egg on toast and drinking a cup of strong tea.

'So, tell us all about it,' said Mam. 'How are you getting on? I thought that Mrs Kilby was nice enough, but what about the rest of the servants?'

'Mrs Kilby is a tyrant,' stated Mabel. 'Nothing's ever good enough for her. I don't like her and I know she doesn't like me.'

'Oh, Mabel, don't talk like that,' chided her mother. 'What makes you think she doesn't like you?'

'She's always picking on me for things she says I've done wrong.'

'And have you?'

'Sometimes. She says I answer back.'

'And do you? You really should watch that tongue of yours.'

'Never mind about her now,' said Dada. 'You're home here with us. Stephen'll be back soon and he'll be pleased as punch to see you.'

'Tell me about you, Dada,' Mabel said. She hadn't meant to complain about the McFarlane household. The family needed her to stay there and she didn't want her dad to know quite how much she hated it. She certainly made no reference to Mr Iain and his advances. They would be horrified, but there would be nothing they could do. If they complained about his behaviour, she would be out on her ear, and as Lizzie had said, at least she had a job. 'How are you doing?'

'Oh, I'm doing all right, you know. Your mother looks after me wonderfully well, and we take life one day at a time. You can see I'm happily sitting at the table. I still get tired, but I have a snooze in the afternoons and that keeps me going for the rest of the day.'

'But you're stuck in the house.'

'Much of the time, but young Eddie and his friend have taken me to the Cockerel a couple of times. They wheeled me there in the chair your friend Mr Clarke gave us. It's a bit bumpy on the way, but they get me there safely and we have a pint.'

Alice continued to smile at him as he said this; she was truly glad that Eddie was able to take Andrew out sometimes.

She couldn't manage the wheelchair along the cobbled lane, and she couldn't regret the beer money. Andrew needed some enjoyment, but it stretched their depleted finances even further. Nurse Finch still came in the mornings, but Alice was working with her closely now; she had learned how to move Andrew on her own, and Andrew had learned how to help her do so. It wouldn't be long before she would feel confident enough to manage by herself, but both she and Andrew looked forward to Nurse-Finch-free days with trepidation.

At first, their conversation seemed stiff and stilted, but as the afternoon wore on, all three of them relaxed a little and their talk became more natural.

'Lizzie told me you were coming home, Dada,' she said, 'and I couldn't wait to see you. I feel so shut away at Chanynge Place.' She sighed. 'I have to be back to help clear the dinner table.'

'What, even on your half day?' cried her father in surprise.

'Afraid so,' Mabel said ruefully. Even as she said it, she thought of Mrs Kilby and wondered if she'd get away without her knowing she'd been home. Unlikely, she thought, but it was worth the risk just to be here.

'Sounds most unfair to me,' said Andrew.

At that moment Stephen got home from school and greeted his sister with delighted surprise. 'They let you out at last, then,' he said as he gave her a hug.

'Not for long,' grinned Mabel, 'but it's lovely to be home, even if it's only for an afternoon.'

When it was time to leave again, Andrew asked, 'Do you pass where this Mr Clarke works?'

'Yes,' she replied, even though it was only a half truth.

She had already decided she must stop in to see him, if only for five minutes or so, and she had allowed the extra time in her mind.

'Will you go and see him, just for a moment or two? Ask him if he'll come and see me. I want to thank him for his kindness in giving us the wheelchair and... and things.'

'Course I will,' replied Mabel. 'And I'm sure he'll come.'

She had tears in her eyes as she said goodbye to them all. She reached down to give her father a hug and saw his eyes were bright with tears, too.

'Look after yourself, Dada,' she murmured, and turned quickly to kiss her mother.

She was leaving before Eddie got home, but she sent him her love and gave her mother an extra hug, saying, 'Give that to Eddie for me, Mam.'

'We'll see you in two weeks,' Alice said as she hugged her close. 'Not long really.'

As she walked out into the street, Mabel supposed it wasn't long really, but just now it felt like an eternity.

19

As Mabel reached the bridge she heard the reassuring sound of the printing press. She had been afraid that Mr Clarke might have gone home already and she wouldn't have had time to go to his house to see him. As usual, the door stood open and as soon as he saw her, Mr Clarke's face split in a welcoming smile.

'Hello, stranger,' he said, his hands and feet continuing to work the press without a break in their rhythm. 'Come on in and put the kettle on.'

Mabel went in, but she said, 'I haven't time for any tea. I'm on my half day and I have to be back in time to work in the evening.'

On hearing this, Mr Clarke took his foot off the pedal and the press sighed into silence.

'So, Mabel my dear, it's lovely to see you, just for a minute or two.'

'First, I have a message for you, from my father. He's home again now and he asks if you would go and visit him. I think he wants to thank you for all your kindnesses himself.'

'Of course I will,' replied Mr Clarke. 'I'm sure life must

be very difficult for him at the present. Is he able to go out in the chair?'

'Eddie takes him to the Cockerel for a pint sometimes, but otherwise he's at home. I'm sure Mam would be delighted to see you, as well.'

'Then I'll go soon. I just have this commission to finish and then I'll be able to close up early one evening.'

'Thank you.'

Mabel's thanks were so heartfelt that it made Mr Clarke look at her more narrowly.

'And you,' he said, 'how about you? Are you getting on well in the house where you work?'

'Not too bad,' replied Mabel, but it was clear to him that there was more to say, so he waited, and it all came tumbling out. All the things she hadn't been able to say to her parents.

'I *hate* it,' she cried. 'I hate every minute of it. *Do this, do that, do the other, do them all at the same time*. It's a nightmare. Nobody simply talks to you, they just tell you what to do!'

'I suppose that's to be expected. Houses with several servants are expected to run like clockwork, and when something goes amiss, the blame is on the nearest person. What are the other servants like? Isn't your cousin there too? It must be nice to have one of the family living there as well.'

'Lizzie?' Mabel scoffed. 'Lizzie just does as she's told. She always has. She never has her half day taken away.'

'But you do?'

Mabel explained what Mrs Kilby had said.

'And had you lied to her?'

'Yes, it was a stupid lie. I should have known she would find out.'

'So what was the truth, that you didn't tell her? And why didn't you?'

'She wouldn't have believed me, or would have said it was my fault.' She raised anguished eyes to him. 'Even Lizzie said it was my fault, but it wasn't, really it wasn't.'

'I believe you if you say so,' said Mr Clarke quietly. 'But why don't you tell me the truth? What happened?'

'It was Mr Iain.' Her voice broke on a sob. 'Oh, Mr Clarke, will I be pregnant now? He kissed me more than once! Suppose I'm going to have a baby now? How can I tell my parents I let it happen?'

Thomas Clarke listened in silence, but the expression in his eyes darkened with every word. When she finally fell silent he reached over and took her hand. He had seen at once that Mabel had no idea how babies were conceived, and so he set about dealing with her main worry.

'Listen, Mabel,' he said gently, 'I can promise you that you aren't going to have a baby from this encounter.'

Mabel looked up at him with a glimmer of hope in her eyes. 'Are you sure? Lizzie says there's always consequences.'

'I'm certain,' he said firmly, 'and I have to tell you none of this was your fault.'

'But Lizzie said I let it happen. She said I should have stopped him!'

'I doubt if you could have in the circumstances,' said Mr Clarke wryly. 'Have you told anyone else but Lizzie? The housekeeper perhaps. Your parents?'

'Oh no, I couldn't do that!' Mabel cried in alarm.

'But you told me.'

'You're different.'

'Would it be so difficult to tell one of them?'

'They wouldn't believe me,' she said flatly. 'Or else they would say it was my fault. I don't know what to do. He said next time it would be better, but,' she sobbed, 'I don't want there to be a next time!'

'Of course you don't,' he agreed. 'You could give notice and leave the house?'

'But I need the job. My family haven't enough money for me to leave and come home.'

'Listen,' Mr Clarke said again, 'you must make every effort to avoid the man, especially try not to be alone with him, even if it means simply walking out of the room if he comes in when you're working alone. And if the worst comes to the worst, you will have to tell someone there… or leave. This man has no rights over you. You work for his family and they pay you to do so. It is a business arrangement, that is all.'

He handed Mabel a hankie and she blew her nose. 'Come on,' he said. 'You don't want to be late back. I'll come with you.'

Leaving the printing press all set up for him to continue his work in the morning, he locked up and they went to the bus stop together. He paid the fare and when they finally reached Chanynge Place he put a hand on her arm.

'Now then,' he said, 'have you got any money?'

'Oh yes, I've still got half a crown that Mam gave me for emergency money.'

'That's not enough,' he said and, pulling a wallet from his pocket, he took out a sovereign. 'Here, take this and keep it safely somewhere. I want you to be able to walk out of that house if you need to. All right?'

Mabel nodded. 'Thank you,' she said. 'I promise I'll keep it safe.'

'Good,' he replied with a smile. 'In you go then, and come and see me again on your next half day.'

'I don't know when that will be,' Mabel said in a small voice.

'Never mind when it is, I'll look forward to seeing you. And I promise I'll go and visit your father.'

'You won't tell him...' Mabel faltered.

'I won't tell him,' he promised.

Mabel pushed open the back gate and crossed the courtyard to the servants' entrance. As she opened the door, she found herself face to face with an irate Mrs Kilby.

'And just where do you think you've been?'

20

As Mr Clarke and Mabel were walking away from the bridge, there was a knock on the Oakleys' front door. Now that Mabel and Stephen had left, the house seemed quiet and empty, and Alice and Andrew would have been happy for it to remain so, but when Alice peeped out of Andrew's window to see who was there, she sighed.

'It's your sister.'

'Jane?' he asked, and his expression brightened. He always enjoyed Jane's visits.

'No, Andrew. Susan... and James.'

Andrew pulled a face. 'Let's pretend we're out,' he suggested with a grin.

'Pointless,' replied Alice. 'Where else would we be?'

'Down the pub?' he responded hopefully.

'I don't think she's going to go away, you know,' Alice said with a weary smile. And sure enough at that moment there came another, louder knock on the door and then Susan's voice floated in through the letter box.

'Hello? Alice? Can you hear me?'

'Can't miss you,' breathed Andrew.

'I'd better go and let them in.' Alice went to the door and opened it, feigning surprise at seeing who her visitors were.

'Susan! James! How lovely! Come on in. Andrew and I were just going to have a cup of tea.' She led the way into the kitchen and offered them chairs at the table.

'Andrew's in his room just now,' she explained. 'He won't be very long.'

Susan nodded and said, 'And how is the poor man?'

'You can ask him yourself in a minute or two,' Alice said with an edge to her tone. 'He's not deaf and he's not dumb and he's not stupid. He's quite able to hold a conversation, you know.'

'Of course,' Susan said hurriedly. 'But one doesn't like to ask, you know.'

'Why not?' demanded Alice. 'He's still Andrew. Talk to him as you always used to!'

This conversation was cut short as Eddie appeared, pushing his father in the indoor wheelchair.

'Susan,' Andrew said. 'What a lovely surprise.'

'Well, we thought we ought to come and see you,' said his sister. 'Didn't we, James?'

James looked a little embarrassed at his wife's words, but he said, 'Just wanted to see how you were getting along, Andrew.'

'As well as can be expected, I suppose,' interposed Susan with a sigh.

'We've had Mabel here for the afternoon,' Andrew told her. 'She seems to be doing well at the McFarlanes'.'

'Just what I said,' cried Susan. 'Didn't I say the silly girl was lucky to get a job with such a prestigious family? Didn't I say those very words, James?'

'You certainly did, my dear,' replied James, who had no recollection of any such conversation. 'You must be glad the girl's doing well, Alice.'

Alice had made the tea and as they sat round the table, Susan suddenly said, 'But where's Stephen?'

'Stephen goes down to the market at the weekend to earn a few pennies,' replied Alice. 'He works very hard to help us out.'

'Does he now?' replied Susan. 'Well, and so he should with his father unable to earn a penny piece!'

There was a moment's silence at this remark, broken as Stephen appeared through the door.

'Hello, Auntie,' he said, staying the other side of the table in case she expected him to kiss her.

'I was just hearing what a good boy you are, helping your parents,' remarked his aunt.

'Just running errands down the market,' Stephen said, bristling at being called a good boy.

'Well, it won't be long before you can leave school and get a proper job, will it?'

Before Stephen could answer, Andrew said, 'Sorry, Susan, I'm very tired. I'm afraid I'm going to turn you and James out. I need to go to bed. It's been a long day.'

James immediately got to his feet, looking relieved. 'Of course, old man, quite understand.'

His wife pursed her lips at this dismissal, but, pushing her chair back from the table, said to the room at large, 'Well, we'll see you all another day. Come along, James, we mustn't keep the invalid up late.'

'Someday, I might actually slap that woman's face,' exploded Alice as soon as she came back from the front door. 'You know there are times when I can hardly believe she can be your and Jane's sister! Are you sure she isn't a changeling?'

Andrew laughed. 'Oh, Alice love, just take no notice. It's just Susan being Susan!' He reached for her hand. 'Now, if you can wheel me back into my room, Eddie, I really do need to go to bed.'

Family, he thought as he lay in the dark. So precious, even the damned awkward ones! What would I do without mine?

21

Mabel looked at the housekeeper in dismay. She had assumed she would still be in bed, nursing her cold, and from the look of her, she certainly should have been. Her hair, though caught up in its familiar bun, looked lacklustre and straggly; her eyes, usually so sharp and penetrating, were dull and watery, and her face was blotchy and red, but whether from anger or as a symptom of her cold, Mabel couldn't tell. She simply looked tired and sagging, and yet here she was, waiting at the servants' door for her.

'Surprised to see me, eh? Well, no more surprised than I was, seeing you out and about instead of where you should be, helping Mrs Bellman in the kitchen.'

Mustering her defiance, Mabel said, 'But it was Mrs Bellman who said I could go. You were ill in bed, so of course I didn't disturb you…' Mabel had hoped that news of her absence would never reach the housekeeper, and though it had, she could see a hint of uncertainty in Mrs Kilby's eyes, so she went on, 'When Mrs Bellman heard it ought to be my free afternoon, she said she didn't need me until this evening, and here I am, back for the evening!' Mabel knew she had to brazen it out and hope Mrs Bellman remembered the conversation.

'You'd better come in,' grumbled Mrs Kilby, her voice scratchy. 'There's plenty of work—' She broke off in a paroxysm of coughing and buried her face in a handkerchief.

Mabel grabbed her chance of escape and slipped past her, through the scullery and into the kitchen. Mrs Bellman looked up as she appeared through the door.

'Good girl, Mabel,' she said. 'You're nice and early. We could do with another pair of hands. There are two extra guests coming tonight. Run up and get changed.'

Mabel needed no second bidding; she hurried out of the room and took the stairs to their attic two at a time. As she reached the top she almost collided with William coming out of the staff bathroom.

'Hey!' he cried, catching her arm. 'Steady on!'

'Let go!' she cried, pulling away. 'I'm in enough trouble as it is.'

'But where've you been?' William released her.

'Home,' Mabel replied shortly. 'My dad's come out of hospital. I went to see him.'

'Better get a move on then,' said William, giving her a gentle push, 'if the Killer-bee's after you?'

'Killer-bee?' For a moment Mabel was confused.

'Mrs Kill-bee... and she's in a foul mood.'

'I know,' said Mabel. 'I've just seen her.'

'Then get a move on. If you rush about like mad, making yourself useful, you might get away with it, I suppose.'

'Thanks.' Mabel dived into her bedroom, only to find Lizzie getting changed to wait at the dinner table.

'Oh, Mabel, thank goodness you're back. Mrs Kilby's

been looking everywhere for you. There'll be a frightful row.'

Surprisingly, Lizzie was wrong. As Mabel arrived at the kitchen door, she heard Mrs Bellman saying, '... So, I said she could go. The poor child has been here over a month and has had not a single half day.'

'She has to earn it first,' came the sharp retort.

'Well,' said Mrs Bellman staunchly, 'I thought she had, and as you were lying in your sickbed, you weren't there to ask, so I told her she could go if she was back in time to help with the dinner. She was even early, good girl that she is. Now if you'll excuse me, I've a sauce to make.' There was a clatter of pans on the stove and a short silence before Mabel heard the sound of the door to Mrs Kilby's parlour closing behind her. She waited another moment or two so that Mrs Bellman wouldn't realise that her conversation with Mrs Kilby had been overheard, and then stepped into the kitchen and said, 'Here I am, Mrs Bellman. What would you like me to do?'

She had got away with it, there was no frightful row, but Mabel knew that she must be extremely careful in the coming weeks, not to forfeit her next free day.

In fact, the next two weeks were quite different from the previous ones. Mrs Kilby returned to her bed for three days, and she wasn't the only one to go down with the heavy cold. It was a virulent strain that laid its victims low with headaches, coughs and streaming noses; it ran through the whole household, except for Mrs Bellman and Mabel. Everyone else, including Sir Keir and Lady McFarlane, succumbed, and took to their beds for at least two or more days. It meant far more work for those left: Mrs Bellman cooking light, nourishing dishes to tempt those who had lost their appetites; Mabel being sent to do work that was not usually among her duties. Lizzie and Ada were both ill, but luckily not at exactly the same time, so not everything fell on Mabel's shoulders. She missed her next free afternoon because she could not be spared, but was promised a weekend at home when everyone was better. Only Chalmers remained aloof. She steered resolutely clear of everyone in the servants' hall, coming into the kitchen and carrying a tray upstairs to eat alone in her room. She still took care of Lady McFarlane's personal needs and stayed close while her ladyship was laid low, but she mixed with no one else, and managed to avoid infection.

It was Miss Lucinda who was the worst affected, running such a high temperature that the doctor had to be sent for. He diagnosed influenza and recommended she stay in her bed for at least a week, and then, provided her temperature came down and remained down for two days, including in the evening, she would be allowed to sit by the fire in the morning room in the afternoons until she was fully restored to health. While Lizzie was confined to bed for a couple of days, it fell to Mabel to carry Miss Lucinda's trays up to her. It was up to her to remake the bed, morning and evening, to draw the curtains back and forth – though never to open the window for fear Miss Lucinda should become chilly – to bring hot water for washing, and to deal with the chamber pot. It was obvious to anyone seeking Mabel that she could often be found on the family's bedroom landing; and that is where Iain McFarlane decided to lie in wait for her again. He thought back to his encounter with her beside the linen cupboard and found himself anxious to repeat it.

She was very young, of course, but she intrigued him. She seemed far more self-contained than other housemaids who had come and gone. When she had been summoned to the library the day he was entertaining his friend Everette, both he and Everette had looked at her with frank approval.

'Wouldn't mind an armful of her,' remarked Everette when she left the room.

'Nor me,' agreed Iain with a grin. 'Taking little thing.'

One afternoon, Mrs Kilby, now back on her feet, sent Mabel with a tray of tea up to Lucinda's room. Mabel tapped on Lucinda's door and went straight in. Lucinda was propped up in bed, her face pale against her white pillows. A book lay face down on the covers, Lucinda having given up the wearying task of reading.

'I've brought you some tea, Miss Lucinda,' Mabel said, putting the tray on the dressing table while she moved the little bedside table nearer to the bed. 'Shall I pour you a cup? There are some of Mrs Bellman's biscuits too. She thought you might fancy something to nibble on.'

'I'm bored,' complained Lucinda, as she watched Mabel pour the tea. 'Is Iain in his room?'

'I don't know, miss. You know he hasn't been well either, but I think he's downstairs again today.'

'Well, go and see,' said Lucinda petulantly. 'Knock on his door and tell him to come and have tea with me. I want someone to talk to.'

Reluctantly, Mabel left the room and went along the landing to Iain's room. She had followed Mr Clarke's advice about keeping away from Iain McFarlane, but there had been a couple of occasions when it had been impossible. Now, when she knocked, she was called to come in.

Iain was sitting in an armchair by the window, looking out over the gardens. He smiled when he saw who it was and said, 'Well, Mabel. How are you today? Have you caught this dreadful cold?'

'No, sir,' she replied.

'Come in and speak to me properly,' he said. 'You look like a frightened rabbit, standing there.

Mabel took a half step into the room. 'Please, sir, your sister asks you to come into her room and have tea with her.'

He sighed. 'Oh dear, does she?'

Mabel took a step backwards and said, 'What shall I tell her, sir?'

'Oh, you'd better tell her I'll be in in a minute. Is there enough tea for me?'

'Plenty, sir, I just need to fetch another cup.' And with that, Mabel beat a hasty retreat.

Iain watched her go with amusement before getting to his feet and preparing to join his sister. He would wait in his room until he heard Mabel coming back and then step out on the landing. The idea amused him.

When he heard footsteps on the stairs, he walked out onto the landing and found himself not facing the pretty housemaid as he'd expected, but William the footman, carrying a tray with a single cup and saucer on it, along with a plate of scones and some cream.

William said, 'Good afternoon, sir,' as he stopped outside Lucinda's door and knocked. 'Mrs Bellman thought you might like some scones as well as the biscuits she sent up earlier.'

At a call from inside the bedroom, William opened the

door and went in. 'A cup for Mr Iain, Miss Lucinda,' he said.

'Where's Mabel?' demanded Lucinda.

'Mrs Kilby had a job for her below stairs,' he replied smoothly. 'So she sent me.'

Mabel was relieved. William had come to her rescue this time, but would she be able to avoid Mr Iain so easily another day?

The next afternoon, when Mabel went up to remove Lucinda's tea tray, to her dismay she found him waiting for her on the landing, smiling.

'Well,' he said, 'if it isn't our pretty little Mabel.' He reached out and took her by the wrist. 'No laundry today? What a shame! It was cosy in the linen cupboard, wasn't it?'

At first Mabel made no reply and he said, 'What's the matter? The cat got your tongue?'

'I've been sent up for Miss Lucinda's tea tray,' she muttered.

'Have you?' He glanced along the empty landing. 'Well, there's no hurry, is there? She won't mind if you're a few minutes late.' His grip on her wrist was tight, and she couldn't break away.

'Please, sir,' she cried. 'Let go. You're hurting me.'

At that moment another door along the landing opened and Miss Chalmers emerged from Lady McFarlane's room. Iain just had time to release Mabel and say loudly and cheerfully, 'Never mind, Mabel, I'm sure it'll all be all right in the end.' And so saying, he disappeared down the main staircase.

Released from his grasp, Mabel forgot about the tea tray and scurried back down to the kitchen. She had only been there a couple of minutes when Miss Chalmers followed her in.

'You, girl,' she said. 'I wish to speak to you. Come here.' Obediently, Mabel followed her out into the passage.

'Now then, I saw you upstairs. What were you up to with Mr Iain?'

'Nothing,' answered Mabel defensively. 'I was fetching Miss Lucinda's tray.'

'Were you indeed? It didn't look like that to me! You're a stupid little girl, a nobody. If I see you trying to flirt with Mr Iain again, Lady McFarlane will hear of it and you'll find yourself out in the street without a character.'

'I didn't!' Mabel almost shouted. 'I don't, I don't go near him. He's horrible.'

'And that is no way to speak of your employer's son!' snapped Miss Chalmers. 'I shall be watching you, my girl, and woe betide you if you make eyes at those above your station.' With this warning, Miss Chalmers turned away and disappeared up the stairs.

Red-faced at the injustice of these accusations, Mabel went back into the kitchen to find Mrs Kilby demanding to know why she had been so long, and then seeing her empty-handed, where the tray was.

'Go straight back upstairs and fetch it. I can't think what you've been doing.'

'Miss Chalmers wanted to speak to me,' murmured Mabel.

'Did she now? Well, she's no business to keep you from your work. Off you go!'

On the second occasion, she had returned some towels to the linen cupboard when she heard Iain's voice in the hall below and then footsteps running up the stairs. To reach the backstairs she would have to pass the top of the main staircase; she could not get past in time. On the instant, she made a decision, opened the door to Lucinda's room and slipped inside, closing it behind her. She had known the room was empty because she knew that Miss Lucinda was now downstairs taking tea with her mother, but had she been quick enough? Had Iain seen her on the landing and guessed where she'd gone? If so, she was trapped; if he came into the room after her, there would be no escape. She pressed herself against the wall behind the door, so if he opened it he wouldn't immediately see her. Holding her breath, she kept her ear against the door, listening, straining to hear anything, his voice, or his footsteps. Had he paused outside the door, or were his steps too soft to be heard? The seconds passed, turned into minutes, and she could hear nothing from the landing.

Surely, she thought, he couldn't be waiting this long, simply to catch her out. She couldn't stay here indefinitely, Miss Lucinda would be coming upstairs herself very soon. What excuse could Mabel give for being alone in her bedroom this time? She had been sent to the linen cupboard with a pile of clean towels. She had no excuse to be in here. She stared across the room, racking her brains.

The dressing table under the window was in its usual state, its surface untidy with bottles and jars. A small silver tray at the back, beneath the tilting mirror, held an assortment of hairpins, hat pins, some earrings, a watch, a ring, a string of beads and, to one side, a silver-backed hairbrush with a tortoiseshell comb tucked into its bristles. Nothing helpful there!

It was when she looked at the bed, neatly made as she had left it that morning, that the idea came to her. The chamber pot! Quickly she hurried to the far side of the bed, reached underneath and pulled it out. It was, to her relief, empty, but beside it, neatly folded, lay the cloth with which it was covered when on its way to the bathroom. If she met anyone they would see, though pretend not to, the chamber in her hands and assume it was on its way to be emptied. Surely no one would ask to see the contents!

Arranging the cloth as she had in the morning, Mabel opened the bedroom door and stepped onto the landing. There was no one there, and she was about to turn back and close the door, when the door to Lady McFarlane's room opened and Miss Chalmers appeared.

She stopped short at the sight of Mabel coming out of Lucinda's room.

'Mabel! What are you doing? Why were you in Miss Lucinda's room at this time of day?' she demanded.

Mabel extended the chamber pot. 'Seeing to this, Miss Chalmers.'

Miss Chalmers glanced at the covered pot with obvious distaste. 'At *this* time of day? Surely that should have been done this morning!'

'Lizzie was called away before she had time, miss,' Mabel improvised. 'I said I'd come back and do it for her.' She was shaking inside and wanted to get away. Suppose Mr Iain was in his room and came out? Chalmers would think she'd had an assignation with him! With a quick bob in Miss Chalmers' direction, Mabel went into the bathroom further along the landing, and for the moment out of sight, pulled the chain, flushing the lavatory. Then she went to the basin, as she did in the mornings, and rinsed the pot before covering it again with the cloth and returning to Lucinda's room. Miss Chalmers was still standing outside, and she waited there, as Mabel went in to replace the chamber pot under the bed. As she came out again and closed the door, she ignored the woman now standing at the head of the main staircase, and scurried along the landing, down the backstairs.

Gradually, as everyone recovered, the house returned to a type of normality. Mabel was allowed her half days regularly and, to her delight, she was given an occasional Saturday night at home. At twelve noon, she would put on her hat and let herself out of the servants' door into the little street. If she had been given enough warning, she was able to send her mother a postcard to say that she was coming.

22

July 1912

Alice received the postcard from her daughter with delight. Mabel was going to be home again from Saturday lunchtime until Sunday evening. In the past weeks, she had been allowed her half days regularly, but it had been a long time since she had been spared for a proper weekend.

Alice showed the card to Andrew. 'Look,' she said, 'Mabel's staying the night on Saturday, so I thought we'd have a special family meal.'

As soon as Stephen got home from school, she took him aside and slipped off her wedding ring.

'Take this to your friend Mr Solomon and see if he'll advance me a little on it, just until next Friday.'

'But Mum,' Stephen looked at her wide-eyed, 'it's your wedding ring! You can't sell that!'

Alice patted him on the shoulder, smiling. 'I'm not going to sell it, silly boy, any more than I'm selling the locket. I'll redeem them both very soon, but I just need a little extra cash this weekend, what with Mabel coming home and that.'

So Stephen went back to Mr Solomon's shop where, over the weeks, he had become a regular. Since he had first taken his mother's locket and borrowed two pounds against it, he had been back several times, either to redeem the locket or to pawn it again. Today the locket was already resting in Mr Solomon's safe, and when the old man saw it was Stephen, he got up from his place behind the counter, ready to open the safe and return it. Joseph Solomon liked Stephen and had begun to allow him to come into the shop on his way home from school, letting him stand by the counter and watch while he worked, repairing clocks, watches and small pieces of jewellery. He was intrigued by the concentration with which the boy watched what he was doing, asking intelligent questions and remembering the answers. He wished his son had shown half that amount of interest as a young lad; but no, Adam had shown none. When he left school he'd worked at odd jobs until he had saved enough to buy a passage to America and disappeared to seek his fortune.

'I haven't come for my mother's locket,' Stephen said.

Mr Solomon looked surprised. 'Then what have you come for? I was about to shut up shop.'

Stephen put his hand in his pocket and produced his mother's ring, wrapped in a scrap of cloth. 'This.' He extended his hand, uncurling his fingers so that the ring lay in his palm. Solomon took the ring between his thumb and forefinger.

'A wedding ring,' he said carefully. 'Your mother's?'

'Yes.'

Joseph Solomon's loan dealings were strictly business; he never asked his customers why they needed the cash.

If they did not return to redeem their valuables at the appointed time, he placed the item for sale in the shop window and sold it to recoup his loan. But the boy had been into the shop so often to leave his mother's locket and then to redeem it that Solomon was intrigued. He had been offered wedding rings before, but for some reason he knew he couldn't accept this one.

'I cannot take it,' he said, and seeing the look of dismay on the boy's face, he went on, 'Suppose she were not able to redeem it? If she's offering it against a loan, she must be in great need. I know where you live, boy, and people from Cockspur Lane seldom need my services to meet their bills.' He cocked his head enquiringly. 'So, tell me why, and then I will decide.'

For a long moment Stephen didn't answer. His mother had said it was to be their secret and he was not sure if he ought to tell Mr Solomon, but if he didn't, the old man might refuse to lend the cash and then where would they be? Mr Solomon waited, and eventually Stephen said, 'My sister is coming home for the weekend, and my mother wants to have a special family meal.'

'For a special meal?' Mr Solomon stared at him. 'There must be something more.' He pointed to the door and said, 'Put up the closed sign, boy, and pull down the blind. We will have a talk.'

Stephen went to the door, wondering what Mr Solomon was going to say. The wedding ring lay on the counter between them.

'Sit down, sit down,' instructed the jeweller, waving a hand to the upright chair set for customers, 'and tell me.'

Stephen sat and for a moment he said nothing. Again

Mr Solomon waited and at last Stephen told him; told him everything from the day when his father had stepped into the path of the brewer's dray. Slowly at first, he searched awkwardly for words, but as he began to tell everything that had been bottled up inside him since his mother had begun to pawn her locket, the whole story came flooding out, like the bursting of a dam. Mr Solomon listened without interruption as Stephen told of the accident and its dreadful results, of his mother struggling to look after her injured husband, the breadwinner who would never be able to work again. The lack of money which haunted them. Mam trying to make an income from sewing piecework, Eddie giving up the chance of an apprenticeship for immediate work in Smithfield market, Mabel going into service and Stephen's own frustration at still having to go to school.

'I'm useless stuck at school,' he said wretchedly. 'I can only give Mam a few pence I earn running errands in the market at the weekend.'

When he finally fell silent he suddenly felt light. It was as if someone had lifted an enormous weight from his shoulders. He could feel tears pricking his eyes and he sagged against the chair.

'Thank you, Stephen, for telling me all this.' Mr Solomon nodded his head as if confirming something in his mind. 'Your mother is a brave woman. I had heard about the accident, of course, but had not realised it was your father who was so badly injured.'

'So will you lend Mam the money for her wedding ring? I know I'll come back for it when Mr Moses has paid her next week.'

'No,' replied the old man. And before Stephen could

protest he went on, 'I have a better idea.' Again he cocked his head like an inquisitive bird. 'Would you like to hear it?'

Stephen nodded, wondering what on earth was coming next.

'I'm getting old and can't do everything I used to do. You are an intelligent boy, and I could use you in the shop. If you wanted to learn, I will teach you my trade, like an apprentice. I will lend the money your mother needs against your work for me... I will not take her wedding ring.' He waited for a moment as Stephen, stunned, stared at him. 'What do you think, young man?'

'Will you teach me to mend watches and clocks?' Stephen's face was suddenly alight with hope.

The old man smiled at his enthusiasm. 'I have no son to teach,' he replied, 'so why not you, eh? Don't think it will be easy, I will work you hard, day and night. We'll feed you upstairs, but we have no extra room for you in the flat, you'll have to sleep down here in the shop.'

'In the shop?'

'As I did in my father's shop.'

'But I still have to go to school!' said Stephen flatly.

'How old are you?'

'Just thirteen.'

'Then I think not. I am offering you full-time work. You can leave school at thirteen if you have a proper job, and that's what I'm offering you.'

Stephen looked at him, wide-eyed. Could he really come and work here with Mr Solomon? Learn how to mend delicate things, clocks, watches, brooches and necklaces? Have a real trade and money to give to Mam?

'But what about Mam's things?'

'Ask your mother to come and see me. If she agrees to the arrangement, I'll give her the locket then,' said Mr Solomon, 'against your first month's wages.'

'She doesn't want my dad to know that she's been pawning things,' Stephen said anxiously.

'And he won't. You simply tell him that you're working for me and living in.' He picked up the wedding ring from the counter and handed it to Stephen. 'Take this home with you and return it to your mother. It is worth more to her than any amount I could lend her!' The old man got to his feet and glanced at the curtain at the back of the shop that shrouded the stairs to his flat above.

'I will tell Mrs Solomon about you. She will enjoy having a boy about the place.' He walked across to the shop door and unlocked it. 'Off you go now and talk to your mother. Our arrangement will be between the three of us? Yes?'

'Yes!' Stephen's reply was heartfelt.

'Good! I'll wait for her to call on me.'

As the door closed behind him, Stephen broke into a run. He couldn't wait to get home and tell Mam what Mr Solomon had offered him. A chance to earn some money! To learn how to mend watches and clocks. To learn it properly!

When he reached Cockspur Lane, he found Eddie had come home and was helping his mother move Andrew from the bedroom to the kitchen for the evening meal. He was bursting to tell her the great news, but he'd promised secrecy to Mr Solomon and had to say nothing. His mother raised an eyebrow and waited hopefully for the money he should have brought with him. He shook his head and mouthed the word 'Later'. He needed to get her on her own to explain.

It wasn't until nearly ten o'clock, when Eddie had lifted his father into his bed and he'd been settled for the night, that Stephen had a chance to say anything to his mother. Each evening Eddie would scoop his dad up in his arms and lay him on his bed. Dad had lost weight and Eddie could lift him as easily as a child. No heavier, Eddie often thought to himself as he picked him up, than when he carried the half carcass of a pig across the market each and every day; indeed, lighter if anything. Certainly not something he could ever express aloud, but he thought it every night.

At last Alice kissed Andrew and turned out the light. Andrew liked his bedroom curtains open at night so he could see the eerie green light of a street lamp outside. Because of the summer heat, his window was left open a crack and he could hear the street noises beyond the glass, recognise the sounds that he'd heard unconsciously ever since they had moved into the house all those years ago; recognise them and long, with a physical ache, to feel part of the street where he lived.

Eddie went immediately to bed because he had to be on the market floor at four o'clock the next morning, and at last Stephen and his mother could sit down in the kitchen together and talk.

'Did you get the money?' Alice asked at once. 'How much did he lend against my ring?'

'Nothing,' Stephen replied, and handed her back her wedding ring.

'Nothing?' echoed his mother in dismay. 'Why not? It must be worth something.'

'It is,' answered Stephen. 'Mr Solomon said it was worth more to you than anything he could lend on it.'

'But didn't you explain it was only for a week?'

'Of course I did. I told him I'd be redeeming it in a week's time, but listen, Mam, he had a better idea.'

'What do you mean, a better idea? How does he know what I need and when?' She looked at Stephen narrowly and demanded, 'What have you been telling him?'

'He refused to lend against your ring until I told him why. I thought we needed the cash, so I told him. He said he wouldn't take your ring, but that he had a better idea.'

'Did he now?' Alice said bitterly. 'Well, come on then. What's this better idea?'

'He's offered me a job and if you agree, I shall be working for him full time!'

'Working for him? Doing what? What about school? You still have to go to school.'

'No I don't, not when I'm thirteen and working.'

'But what can you do? Working in a jeweller's shop? What use would you be?'

'He's going to teach me to mend watches.'

'Mend watches! What on earth good will that be to you? Who's going to employ you to mend watches? Really, Stephen, this is a mad idea. You must stay at school and finish your education.'

'You wouldn't let Mabel do that,' snapped Stephen. 'Why should I have to?'

'Because, my dear boy, you'll have to earn your living for the rest of your life. One day Mabel will marry and her husband will earn their bread.'

'I might marry too!' pointed out Stephen.

'So you might. You almost certainly will, and what will you feed a family on? Mending the odd watch?'

'Mam, you don't understand. Mr Solomon said he would teach me to be useful to a jeweller...'

'Cheap labour for a Jew,' interjected his mother. 'That's what he'll be after!'

'Mam, I've told him I want to do this. I'm so excited that I nearly burst, not saying anything earlier when Dad and Eddie could hear.' He looked at her stern face with an appeal in his eyes. 'Just go and see him, Mam. Please? Just go and hear what he's suggesting. I'll be living with him and his wife, so you won't have to feed me, and he'll return your locket as part of my wages.'

'No!' Alice's answer was firm. 'I won't have you taken advantage of like this, and that's the end of it.'

'If you don't at least go and talk to Mr Solomon, and really understand what a chance it is, I shall ask Dad,' threatened Stephen. 'Then he'll find out about pawning your locket and trying to pawn your wedding ring. He'll be horrified, and so worried about us not having enough money to live on. This way, we simply say that I've got a job and am learning a trade.'

'Mending watches isn't a trade,' retorted Alice, but she was surprised at Stephen's determination. 'And don't you dare tell your father! It would upset him to no purpose.'

'Mam, please,' Stephen tried coaxing, 'just go and see Mr Solomon. I told him you would!'

'Certainly I will,' returned Alice. 'I'll tell him I refuse to let you give up the last year of your education for some hare-brained idea that will come to nothing.' She got to her feet and sighed. 'You'd better go to bed, Stephen, and we'll talk about this in the morning. I'm too tired to discuss it now.'

They both went upstairs to their rooms. Once he was in bed, Stephen found he couldn't sleep, his mind full of Mr Solomon's offer. How could he persuade Mam to let him take it up? And if she didn't? Could he simply go anyway? Did he have the courage simply to move out of Cockspur Lane and in with the Solomons? When at last he drifted off to sleep he was no nearer an answer.

The following morning, Stephen was sent reluctantly off to school.

'I'm not going unless you *promise* me you'll go and see Mr Solomon,' he said. 'If you don't promise, I'll play hooky and go to see him myself.'

'And if you don't promise to go into school as usual,' returned his mother, 'I won't go and see Mr Solomon!'

For a moment they stared each other out, Stephen defiant, Alice half smiling at his belligerence. 'All right,' she said at last. 'I promise I'll go.'

She went early, while Mrs Finch was preparing Andrew for his day.

'I won't be very long,' Alice said, 'just an errand I need to run.'

'You take your time, dearie,' said Mrs Finch. 'I can stay here for a while.'

Knowing that Andrew was in safe hands, Alice closed the front door behind her and stepped out into the lane. She paused on the pavement for a moment and drew in a deep breath of fresh air and knew a moment's freedom. The sun was bright and the sky a clear cerulean blue; it was going to be hot. It was not that far to walk to Cuck Lane and ten minutes later she was pushing open the door of Joseph Solomon, Jeweller and Clockmaker.

At the sound of the bell on the door, Mr Solomon emerged from behind the curtain at the back of the shop and approached the counter, rubbing his hands together as if they were cold.

'Good morning, madam,' he said with a smile. 'How may I help you?'

'Mr Solomon,' Alice said, 'I'm Alice Oakley. I've come to see you about Stephen.' It was clear from her tone that she was not going to beat about the bush.

'Ah, yes,' replied the old man mildly. 'Your boy Stephen. You are lucky, Mrs Oakley, to have such a loyal and trustworthy son.'

'Oh!' The wind was rather taken out of Alice's sails.

'An intelligent boy.'

'Yes, well, I know that,' said Alice, regaining her composure, 'that's why I am determined he shall finish his education before he sets about getting a job.'

'I understand that, Mrs Oakley,' said Mr Solomon. 'Education is important. One must develop one's talents and your boy has several. However,' he went on, raising a hand to stop her interrupting, 'have you considered how much it means to your son to be contributing to your family's income? He wants to help relieve the financial stress you are under—'

'I don't know what he's been telling you,' Alice said sharply, 'but we aren't so strapped for cash that I would put his education at risk.'

'He hasn't had to tell me that you're strapped for cash,' pointed out Mr Solomon. 'The fact you are having to pawn your locket regularly tells me that. Your husband's accident has changed your lives, and adjustments must be made.

I have offered Stephen a job in my shop, but I have also offered to teach him the trade that goes with it. In a few years' time, when I have taught him all I know, he'll be able to work for any jeweller in London.' He smiled across at her and went on, 'And in the meantime, he will be contributing to your family's income. Not much, I have to agree, but it's important. Anything he can contribute will make him feel he is pulling his weight with your other children.' When Alice said nothing, he waited in silence for few moments before adding, 'I am asking him to live in, so he's no drain on your pocket. I will return your locket as a sign of my good faith and I will pay him ten shillings a week. If I have read the boy correctly, I assume almost all of that will come to you.'

Alice sank onto the chair beside the counter and put her head in her hands.

'Stephen is very keen not to let his father know quite how difficult things are financially, as I believe you are too, so accepting my offer of a job would help keep that secret. Your boy has been coming into my shop after school for some time now to watch me at work. I think he will soon be able to help me make simple repairs. He is a good boy with a good heart and I would like to see him do well.'

So Alice agreed. It was still against her better judgement, but she could see how important it would be to Stephen. He might still only be a boy, but in his own eyes he would be a wage-earning man.

'I'll have to clear it with the school,' she said uncertainly. She could only hope Miss Chapman would understand. 'When do you want him to start?'

'He can start as soon as he likes.'

Alice realised that this was the second time since Andrew's accident that she had received and accepted help from complete strangers. She knew she needed help to survive, but to have it offered so freely and without reciprocation made her feel humble. Once again she had misjudged a man. Joseph Solomon was not exploiting a young boy, he was setting him on the road to independence and self-esteem. Before she left his shop, he went to the safe and took out her locket. The deal was sealed.

23

Mabel left Chanynge Place at lunchtime that Saturday. She changed out of her uniform and hurried to the top of the backstairs. If she was quick, she might catch the next bus from the square. William was just coming up and for a moment he blocked her way, looking at her appreciatively in her blue cotton frock scattered with daisies.

'You scrub up well,' he said with a grin.

'Oh, William, what are you doing up here? Aren't they having lunch?'

'Yeah, about to.'

'Well, I'm off, so get out of my way or I'll miss my bus!'

William grinned again and stepped aside, saying, 'Have a good weekend with your family.'

Mabel flashed him a smile and with a joyful, 'I will!' ran on down the stairs.

Halfway down she nearly cannoned into Mr Blundell. He put out a hand as if to ward her off, but apart from a sniff of distaste as she stood aside, he ignored her and went on up the stairs to the servants' landing.

It was as she was crossing the kitchen to the servants' door that she was halted by the sharp voice of Mrs Kilby.

Mabel froze. Surely the Killer-bee wasn't going to refuse, at this last minute, to let her have her Saturday night at home.

'Mabel, her ladyship wishes to see you.'

Mabel paused and turned slowly towards the housekeeper. 'Her ladyship? What does she want?'

'How would I know?' snapped Mrs Kilby, who was indeed annoyed that she had not been told why Lady McFarlane wanted to speak to the tweeny. 'But I do know she won't want to be kept waiting. She's in the morning room.'

Reluctantly, Mabel took the stairs to the baize door and, drawing a deep breath, pushed it open. The hall was empty, there was no one on the staircase or the landing above, and with a sigh of relief she hurried across to the morning room and tapped on the door.

Lady McFarlane was sitting at her writing desk as usual, and standing beside her was Miss Chalmers. Mabel bobbed her curtsy and waited just inside the door.

'That'll be all, Chalmers,' Lady McFarlane was saying. 'I'll speak to her myself about it.'

'Yes, my lady.' Chalmers didn't look very pleased to see Mabel standing by the door, and the girl moved hurriedly aside.

Lady McFarlane waited until the door closed and then said, 'Come here, Mabel.'

Mabel took a step forward and waited. Lady McFarlane surveyed her for a moment. The girl had been a find, she decided. She wasn't afraid of hard work. She had rallied round, doing everybody's job while the household was laid low with colds, with no complaint and using common sense, seeing what needed to be done and doing it. It would be worth training her up as something better than a between-maid.

She had plans for Mabel which, though she wasn't prepared to divulge just at present, would give the girl a future to look forward to. However, time enough for all that when they got back from Haverford Court, in the autumn.

'Now, Mabel,' she said. 'I hope you've settled in well here?'

Mabel bobbed and murmured, 'Yes, thank you, my lady.' What else could she say? She could hardly speak the truth if she wanted to remain in the house, and remain she must.

'Good.' Lady McFarlane gave her a brief smile, before continuing, 'It is our custom to move to our house in Suffolk during the summer,' she said, 'and we shall be leaving in ten days' time. Mrs Kilby does not come with us to Haverford Court, because Mrs Scott is our permanent housekeeper there. Felstead and William usually accompany us and last year we took Ellen. I have decided that you should come with us this year, Mabel. You show promise and I think it will be useful to have you there when we are all in the house.' Lady McFarlane paused, as if waiting for some reply or comment from Mabel, and in the end Mabel said, 'Thank you, my lady.'

'We shall just be a small party most of the time. Mr Iain and his friend Mr Everette will only be staying a few days, before they set off on a bicycling holiday in France, but there may be other visitors from time to time.'

'Yes, my lady.'

'Good, well, enjoy your weekend and tell your parents not to expect you home again for at least six weeks. It's always a busy time packing up and preparing to leave for Haverford, so there will be plenty to do and I'm afraid there'll be no more half days for you before we leave. Now, run along and ask Mrs Kilby to come and see me please.'

Mabel bobbed another curtsy, but Lady McFarlane had already returned her attention to the papers on her desk.

Mabel scurried back to the kitchen, gave the message to Mrs Kilby, and then slipped out of the door, before the housekeeper could ask what her ladyship had wanted.

As she sat on the bus heading for home, Mabel considered the news. She was going with the family to the country. It didn't sound as if Lizzie and Ada were coming too. What would they be doing, stuck with the Killer-bee in London? William was coming and Mabel smiled at that thought. She liked William. He teased her like Eddie did at home and she felt comfortable with him. The only cloud on the horizon was the fact that Mr Iain and his friend were going to be there. She could only hope their stay, before they left for France, would be a short one.

What would Mam and Dada think? she wondered. Had Lizzie ever been to Haverford Court? What would it be like, living in the country? She had never lived anywhere but London, never even travelled to any other town. She knew what 'the country' was supposed to be like, quiet and peaceful, but would quiet and peaceful suit her, she who had lived all her life in tune with the sounds and rhythm of the city?

When at last she reached Cockspur Lane she found the front door of 31 open, awaiting her arrival.

'Hello!' she called as she pushed it wider. 'I'm home!'

Her mother emerged from the kitchen, and gathering her into a hug, held her close for a moment before leading her back to where her father was sitting at the table, drinking a cup of tea. Mabel went to him and put her arms round him from behind, leaning her cheek against his.

'Dada,' she said softly, and then releasing him, moved to the other side of the table so she could look at him.

At that moment Eddie, having heard her arrival, came rushing downstairs and, giving her a punch on the arm, greeted her with a careless, 'Hey, sis!' before asking, 'Any tea left in that pot?' He grinned across at her and said, 'Sorry I missed you last time, but some of us have to work!'

Alice made a fresh pot of tea and cut them each a slice of cake.

'Now, no more than a piece each,' she admonished. 'Family supper coming up later.'

'Where's Stephen?' asked Mabel as she sipped her tea.

'Working his last day at the market,' replied Eddie. 'He starts a proper job on Monday.'

'What sort of proper job?' demanded Mabel.

'Now then, Eddie,' said his father, 'let the lad tell her himself when he comes in.'

'I've got some news, too,' Mabel said, and over the tea and cake she told them of her unexpected interview with Lady McFarlane.

'Is Lizzie going too?' asked her mother.

Mabel shook her head. 'No, I don't think so. I think she's staying here, in London.'

'Her ladyship must think very well of you,' remarked Alice, 'taking you with her into the country, when you're so new in her service.'

Mabel shrugged. 'Dunno,' she said. 'She didn't say, just said she hoped I'd settled in all right.'

Her father's eyes searched her face. 'And have you?' he asked.

'Yes, Dada. It's not as bad as I'd expected.' She gave him her brightest smile and went on explaining. 'Not everyone goes to the country,' she said. 'As I said, Lizzie isn't and nor is the Killer-bee.'

'The Killer-bee!' exclaimed Alice.

'It's what William calls Mrs Kilby.'

'Who's William?' asked Eddie.

'Oh, Eddie, I've told you about him before. He's the footman. He always goes to Haverford with them, and so does Mrs Bellman, the cook, but they have another housekeeper there, so they don't need the Killer-bee.'

'So you won't be coming home for a while again, now,' sighed her father. 'Not if you're going to be at this Haverford House.'

'Haverford Court, Dada,' Mabel corrected him with a smile, and for the first time Alice thought her daughter had at last come to terms with being in service and heaved a mental sigh of relief. Indeed she was partially right. Mabel was looking forward to seeing the McFarlanes' country seat.

Just then Stephen burst into the house, calling, 'Is she home yet?' Wreathed in smiles when he saw Mabel at the kitchen table, he gave her a hug and moments later he was explaining with great excitement about his new job with Mr Solomon.

'He's going to teach me to mend clocks and watches,' he enthused, 'and I'm going to live at the shop. I'm to go there tomorrow afternoon, ready to start on Monday morning.'

Alice still wasn't sure, but Andrew had understood

Stephen's need to leave school and start out on the rest of his life; his need to contribute.

'Let the boy go,' he'd said when she had expressed her doubts. 'He's thirteen, almost an adult, and you can be sure Mr Solomon wouldn't have suggested taking him on if he didn't think he was worth it.'

'That's what I'm afraid of,' replied Alice. 'That he's using him as cheap labour.'

'He'll be learning a trade at the same time.'

'Strange trade to learn,' Alice said with a shake of her head.

'But a useful one. There are watches and clocks in almost every home these days, and they break or go wrong. I think he'll have steady work as he gets older.'

Now, as Stephen was telling Mabel all about it, Alice remained silent, her doubts still with her, but not expressed to spoil Stephen's delight.

Later, when she had her mother alone, Mabel took the two pounds wages she'd been paid by Mrs Kilby, and put them into her hand.

'I shan't need these, Mam,' she said. 'Not if I'm going into the country. And I've still got the emergency money you gave me when I first went.'

Alice gave her a hug. 'You're a good girl, Mabel,' she said. 'I know you hate it there.'

'I'm getting used to it,' Mabel sighed, 'and you need the money for Dada.' She felt a pang of guilt that she didn't hand over the pound that Mr Clarke had given her, that she didn't even mention it, but it had been given to her for a specific purpose and she would use it for nothing else.

The house fell silent as the clock struck ten, but it was

some time before most of its occupants went to sleep. In the darkness of his downstairs bedroom, Andrew lay still, fixed in the position in which he would finally fall sleep. They had all enjoyed a family meal together, the first for nearly three months, but as they were sitting round the table he looked at his wife and each of his children, all determinedly cheerful, and it nearly broke his heart. He blamed himself entirely for the way the lives of his family had been changed by that moment's inattention on his part. His mind had been in turmoil. He'd given no thought to the street or to the people around him and he had stepped out into the road without looking.

He could accept blame for the accidental misaddressing of the envelope, containing Peter Everette's private documents. He should have checked and not relied on Bevis, but to be dismissed on the spot, with less than a week's wages in his pocket for an error that wasn't actually his, still filled him with bitter frustration. Tears squeezed from under his lashes and soaked into his pillow, as he stared into the darkness and recognised that the dreams of his children had been swept away. No apprenticeship for Eddie, just the exhausting job of a Smithfield porter; no secondary school and typing course for Mabel, just a job in service which she had always sworn to avoid. Leaving school underage for Stephen, to work as a 'hey you' for an elderly Jew; and Alice, his beloved Alice, taking in sewing from a sweatshop round the corner. And all his fault. Andrew had never felt closer to complete despair. The only thing that kept him from trying to end his life was the possibility Peter Everette might pay for his silence.

Upstairs, in the bedroom which had once belonged to

Mabel, Stephen lay awake. He no longer had to share a room with Eddie. He had Mabel's room to himself. His last night in his own bed until...? Until when? Stephen didn't know if he would ever come back to live at 31 Cockspur Lane. How long would it take to learn to mend watches? He didn't know, but now his immediate future had been decided, he was anxious to get started. He was going to be out in the world while his school mates were still struggling with lessons. The thought made him grin with pleasure. He could hear Eddie in the next room, tossing and turning and grunting in his sleep. His work as a porter was gruelling, and he fell into exhausted sleep every night the moment his head hit the pillow.

Sleep eluded Mabel, too. She lay, not in her old familiar room, in her own bed. That had been moved downstairs for Dada. Now, she slept in the double bed next to her mother. They lay side by side, each of them thinking back over the evening, but neither of them voicing her thoughts about Andrew. It was only when she heard her mother's quiet, steady breathing from the other half of the bed that Mabel found herself able to think of anything else. She was used to Lizzie sleeping in the same room, snuffling and muttering in the other narrow single bed, and she had soon learned to fall asleep despite it. Now, in the privacy of the dark bedroom, she thought about going to Haverford Court. It meant not only that she wouldn't be home again for several weeks, but also that she wouldn't be able to call in on Mr Clarke as she had promised. She must write to him and explain her absence. She would do it in the morning and put the letter in the post so he would get it the very next day. With this decision finally made, Mabel drifted off to sleep.

The next day passed too quickly for all of them. Stephen left after dinner, his few belongings in a carrier bag. Eddie offered to go with him, but Stephen shook his head.

'No thanks,' he said. 'I'd rather go by myself.' He gave his mother a quick hug. 'I'm not far away, now, am I? I'll come back and tell you and Dad how I'm doing.' And with that, he was gone.

The house seemed empty without him and Mabel found she wasn't sorry when it was time for her to leave as well. She had written her note to Mr Clarke and had it with her to drop into the pillar box at the end of the lane.

They kept their farewells brief. She hugged her parents, and walked with Eddie to the bus stop.

'It's going to be weird without either you or Stephen living at home,' Eddie said as they waited for the bus. 'The house will seem even more peculiar than it is already. Mum can't manage without Mrs Finch, you know, but it's a real stretch, paying for her to come every day.'

'I gave her my wages this time,' Mabel said. 'That should help. I'll have more next time, when we come back from the country.'

24

For the first time, Mabel was anticipating returning to Chanynge Place with something other than resentment. Despite her dislike of being in service, she found she was looking forward to going to the country with the family. It would be completely different from working in the London house... and no Killer-bee. She wondered what Mrs Scott would be like. Maybe she'd be worse!

It was still early evening when she reached the servants' entrance and she was surprised to find the door locked, so she had to knock to gain admittance. She heard the bolts being drawn from the inside and expected to see Lizzie's welcoming smile as the door opened. Instead she found herself face to face with Felstead.

'Oh, Mr Felstead,' she said, flustered at finding the butler opening the servants' door. 'I'm sorry I had to knock, but someone had bolted the door and I couldn't get in.'

'That, Mabel Oakley, was because we wanted to know when you came back... if you did.'

Mabel looked confused. 'What do you mean, "if" I did? Mrs Kilby knew I would be back this evening... and I'm not late,' she added, a note of defiance in her voice. If anything she was earlier than they might have expected.

'Come inside, girl,' snapped the butler, and stood aside to let her pass. 'And go immediately to Mrs Kilby. She's in her sitting room.'

'Shouldn't I change into my uniform first?' Mabel asked in surprise.

'I said immediately,' returned Felstead. 'And speak to no one on the way.'

Mabel was about to protest when her sense of caution kicked in. She had no idea what Mrs Kilby wanted her for, but she could tell that it was serious. Without another word she passed through the kitchen and the servants' hall, where William and Ada were sitting at the table. Neither of them looked at her, or spoke to her as she passed through, just kept their eyes fixed on the table. She was about to ask them what the matter was, when Felstead came in behind her, and so she said nothing, but knocked on the housekeeper's door and went in.

Mrs Kilby was sitting at her desk. She didn't speak, just looked Mabel up and down as if she were something the cat had brought in.

Eventually Mabel said, 'You wanted to see me, Mrs Kilby?'

'I can assure you, Mabel Oakley, that I'd be happy never to see you again.'

Amazed, Mabel simply stared at her and said nothing.

The silence lengthened before Mrs Kilby broke it and said, 'You had a good place here, Oakley, and you've just thrown it away.'

'But why... how... what have I done? I've just been home

for the weekend, that's all. You knew I was going. Her ladyship knew I was going. I was told I might go.'

'Very convenient for you,' said Mrs Kilby. 'Gave you a chance to sell the watch, I suppose.'

Mabel looked confused. 'Watch? What watch?'

'The watch you took from Miss Lucinda's dressing table before you left. The gold and emerald watch on a diamond brooch, left to her by her grandmother.'

'But I didn't... I haven't, I've never touched Miss Lucinda's dressing table.'

'Liar,' snapped the housekeeper. 'Miss Lucinda herself caught you touching things on her dressing table.'

Mabel's brain raced back over the times she had been in Miss Lucinda's room and the blood suffused her face. Miss Lucinda had caught her at the dressing table some weeks ago, holding one of the cut-glass scent bottles.

Seeing her blush, Mrs Kilby said, 'Ah, so you do admit it. Taking things from Miss Lucinda's dressing table.'

'No, I don't,' Mabel said fiercely. 'I've taken nothing from Miss Lucinda's room or anywhere else.'

'Then how did a valuable moonstone ring find its way into your bedside locker?' demanded the housekeeper. 'You're a thief, Mabel Oakley. You deserve to be turned over to the police.'

Mabel stared at her. A ring found in her bedside locker? How could one of Miss Lucinda's rings be in her bedside locker? When she'd been looking after Lucinda while she was ill, Mabel had seen rings on the ring stand, but she'd never touched them, or any of the other jewellery so carelessly left on the dressing table.

Mabel drew a deep breath and said, 'I have never taken

anything from Miss Lucinda's room, and if I had, I wouldn't be stupid enough to leave it in my bedside locker.' It was said with defiance and, as she said it, Mabel realised that it was a mistake. It meant that she was calling Mrs Kilby and whoever else had 'found' the watch a liar.

'Your cousin was in the room when it was searched,' snapped Mrs Kilby. 'She was there when the ring was found. Is she a liar?'

'No,' Mabel said, 'I'm sure she's not, but I didn't take the ring and I didn't hide anything in my bedside locker.'

'Are you saying someone else put it there?' Mrs Kilby fixed her with a gimlet eye. 'That is quite ridiculous. It is clear to us all that you took the ring and almost certainly the watch as well. When you left the house yesterday, the watch went with you.'

'I never touched Miss Lucinda's watch. I don't think I've ever seen it. You can look in my pocket and my bag, but you won't find it.'

'No,' agreed Mrs Kilby, 'I'm sure I won't, you'll have sold it by now.'

Silence fell between them and Mabel knew she must hold her tongue. Anything she said now would make the whole situation worse. In the end it was Mrs Kilby who spoke.

'You're to come with me to see her ladyship,' she said. 'She will deal with you.'

'Should I go and put my uniform on first?' asked Mabel. She didn't know what else to say.

'No, certainly not,' snapped the housekeeper. 'You are a disgrace to that uniform.'

With a bleak heart, Mabel followed Mrs Kilby through

the baize door and across the hall to the morning room. Mrs Kilby stepped into the room, pushing Mabel before her.

'Mabel Oakley, my lady.'

'Thank you, Mrs Kilby. That will be all.'

It was clear to Mabel that the housekeeper was disappointed at being dismissed.

She wanted to stay and see me get the sack, thought Mabel, and in a tiny corner of her mind she was pleased the Killer-bee had been thwarted.

Lady McFarlane waited until the door had closed and then, sitting back in her chair, looked at Mabel for the first time.

'Well,' she said. 'What have you to say for yourself, girl?'

'I didn't take a watch or a ring from Miss Lucinda's room,' exclaimed Mabel. 'I didn't take anything.'

'Did you not?' Lady McFarlane cocked her head as she studied Mabel's face. 'Then how do you account for the ring being in your bedside locker?'

Mabel felt the colour flood her cheeks. 'I can't,' she muttered. 'I don't know how it got there, but I didn't take it, and I didn't hide it in my locker.'

'And yet it was found there when we searched,' stated Lady McFarlane.

'Why were you searching?' Mabel asked bravely. 'What made you look there?'

Lady McFarlane looked at her for a long moment and Mabel thought she had gone too far, but in the end her ladyship answered, 'The ring and the watch were missing. Lucinda had seen them on her dressing table the evening before you left. When she went to put them away after luncheon the next day, she couldn't find them.'

So you decided that *I* must have taken them, thought Mabel, but she had enough sense not to give voice to that thought. Lady McFarlane waited for her reply, but when none came she went on, 'So we conducted a search in all the servants' quarters, and found the ring in yours. Your cousin Lizzie was in the room at the time and she witnessed its discovery among your belongings.' Lady McFarlane raised an interrogatory eyebrow. 'How do you explain that?'

'I can't, my lady. I can only say again that I didn't take the ring or the watch, or anything else.'

'Your father has been injured in an accident, hasn't he?'

Her employer's change of tack took Mabel by surprise. 'Yes, my lady. He's in a wheelchair.'

'And never likely to walk again?'

Mabel shook her head and whispered, 'No.'

'I imagine it's very difficult for your poor mother, with the breadwinner unable to work and feed the family.'

'It is hard for her,' agreed Mabel, wondering where this was going. 'But she manages.'

'With your wages helping out?'

'Yes, I gave her what I was paid last month.'

'It would be very tempting, I imagine, to add to the family coffers by taking a few small items from here, little things which might not be missed. I could understand that, but why something as valuable as Lucinda's ring, or her watch? They would be missed at once, and I doubt if you could find a jeweller who would give you very much for them. He'd realise that they were stolen, wouldn't he? And now you've risked losing your place here, all for nothing. You can't even help your mother with your wages.'

'I didn't take anything from Miss Lucinda's room,' asserted Mabel. 'I wouldn't, I'm not a thief.'

'And yet Lucinda says, not so long ago, she caught you with one of her scent bottles in your hand when she walked into her room unexpectedly. What do you say to that?'

'I was admiring the bottle. It was beautiful, but I didn't use any of the scent, and Miss Lucinda knows that.'

'Be careful what you say, Mabel,' warned Lady McFarlane. 'Are you saying that Lucinda is lying?'

'No, my lady. I am saying she saw me with the bottle in my hand and believed me when I said I was simply admiring it; when I told her I had not taken any of the scent.'

'The thing is, Mabel, Miss Chalmers has seen you several times up on that landing, and she was suspicious of what you were doing. Can you explain?'

Mabel sighed. She knew it would be hopeless to mention Mr Iain, so she simply said, 'One time when Miss Chalmers saw me, I'd been sent by Mrs Kilby to sort things out in the linen cupboard, and another time I was checking that the chambers under the beds had been emptied. Miss Chalmers saw me coming out of Miss Lucinda's room with a covered chamber. I was taking it to the bathroom to empty and clean. I returned it to the room immediately and then went back downstairs. She saw me do both.'

'I see. And you still maintain you took nothing from my daughter's bedroom?'

Mabel took her courage in her hands and, holding Lady McFarlane's gaze, said firmly, 'I have taken nothing from anywhere.'

Lady McFarlane sighed. 'And yet the ring was found in your possession.' For a moment she was at a loss. She had expected, in the face of the evidence, that Mabel would break down and admit the theft, and then she might have been magnanimous and given her a second chance, but there was something about the girl's stance which made that impossible.

'You'd better go to your room and stay there for the time being. Sir Keir is away from home until tomorrow. It will be up to him how we proceed from here, whether we hand you over to the police or simply dismiss you without a character. You will stay in your room until I summon you. You will be fed, but you will speak to no one about what you have done; and when Sir Keir decides what to do with you, you will be informed. Now, go to your room.'

Mabel stood her ground for a moment before saying, 'I can't not speak to Lizzie when we're sharing.'

'Lizzie will sleep with Ada until further notice. She will have removed her things by the time you get up there. Now go, before I lose patience with you.'

Mabel gave the briefest of bobs and left the room. As she closed the door behind her, she met Iain in the hallway. He gave her a grin and took her arm to delay her.

'You look pretty glum,' he said. 'What's up?'

'If you don't know, your mother will tell you,' snapped Mabel, and pulling free, pushed him aside and went through the baize door to her own part of the world.

For a long moment Iain stared after her, then he crossed to the morning room door and pushed it open. Lady McFarlane glanced up in annoyance until she saw who it was.

'Hello, darling,' she said. 'When did you get back?'

'Just now,' replied Iain.

'Good weekend?'

'Not specially,' grumbled Iain. 'Everette's being awkward about our bicycling holiday. But never mind him, what's up here? I've just seen Oakley in the hall with a face like a wet weekend.'

'So she might have,' retorted his mother, and she told him the whole sorry story.

'And they were both found in Mabel's locker?'

'No, we think she took the watch with her when she went home for her Saturday night. It was the more valuable. The thing is, Iain, her family are in great financial difficulty as her father has been injured in a traffic accident and won't be able to walk again, let alone work. I think she took the watch to sell to give her mother the money.'

'But what does the girl herself say?' asked Iain.

'Well, she denies it, of course. Says she's never taken anything from Lucinda's room.'

'But you don't believe her?'

'All the evidence is against her. Chalmers saw her up on that landing a couple of times with no reason to be there, coming out of Lucinda's room, and pretending to sort the linen cupboard.'

'Well,' said Iain, 'I certainly saw her up there and she was indeed sorting out the linen cupboard.'

'Did you? But that still doesn't account for the ring being found in her locker, does it?'

'No,' agreed Iain, 'but if I had stolen stuff from my employer, I certainly wouldn't keep it in my bedside table. You say she went home for her Saturday night? If I'd been her, I'd have taken everything I had stolen with me, wouldn't you?'

Lady McFarlane shrugged. 'I don't know. I just know what we found. Anyway, I've sent her to her room. Your father is attending a gentleman's dinner at his club tonight and won't be home until the morning. I shall leave him to sort it out. If she still has the watch we want to get it back, it's an heirloom after all. Perhaps if she agreed to return it we'd simply dismiss her rather than involve the police.'

'Good idea,' agreed Iain. 'Let's leave it to the gov'nor,' adding with a grin, 'After all, he's a judge!'

'Well, until your father gets home, we shan't discuss the matter any further.'

'It's no good telling the servants that,' said Iain. 'They'll be discussing it below stairs, without doubt... and taking sides. Isn't Lizzie some relation of Mabel's?'

'You seem to know a lot about them.'

'Only what I've heard, you know, at table and things.'

'Well, you steer well clear of Mabel Oakley,' his mother said coldly. 'We want no more trouble of *that* sort.'

'Don't worry, Mama, Mabel is quite different.' With that he gave her a smile and left the room. As he went upstairs to his own room he thought about the situation and knew a twinge of guilt. Perhaps he shouldn't have teased the poor girl, for she was certainly different from that flirt Ellen. At least Chalmers hadn't seen him with Mabel at the linen cupboard, that would have been as bad if not worse than the accusation of theft. The poor girl would have been out of the house in two minutes flat.

25

When Mabel reached her room she saw that all Lizzie's things had been removed, making it clear she was to have no contact with her cousin, or anyone else. She wished she could have spoken to her as she would have liked Lizzie to explain exactly what had happened while she was away. For example, had they really searched all the servants' rooms, or had they simply homed in on theirs, on her bedside locker? Feeling more alone than she could ever remember, Mabel lay on her bed and fought back the tears. It wasn't fair. She had *not* taken anything from Miss Lucinda's room. Clearly someone had, but who and when? She remembered that she'd bumped into William on the backstairs as she was leaving on Saturday. What was he doing going up to that landing in the middle of the day? Surely he hadn't taken the ring and put it in her locker? Not William, she couldn't bear it if it was William, whom she'd grown to like over the past weeks. No, of course not William. Why on earth should he do such a thing? What had he to gain, except her dismissal, if and when it was discovered? And Lizzie? She wouldn't have done it. She knew how much Mabel needed her job, she wouldn't have wanted to get her sacked. She'd have nothing to gain, either. But then Mabel thought of the trip to the country; she had been chosen to go with the family and Lizzie had been left behind. Had Lizzie been jealous because it was she who was going? She might have been disappointed, but surely she'd never have schemed to get Mabel sacked?

Beyond the tiny window, the sun sank in a blaze of colour. As it dipped below the skyline, the evening sky deepened, first to twilight, slashed with streaks of fire, orange, cerise and plum, before drifting through the deep purple of summer darkness into full night.

Mabel didn't see the brilliance of the sunset, or watch it fade to a warm afterglow; nor did she switch the light on, to keep the darkness at bay.

Though she'd heard footsteps on the landing as the rest of the staff came up to bed, no one had come near her since she'd been sent up to her room.

Just like a naughty child, she thought. And the turmoil of her thoughts turned from confusion to anger. No one would believe her, of course. They'd all think she'd taken the watch and the ring, and deserved whatever was coming.

She thought of Mam and Dada at home. What would they think? Would they believe her?

Surely they'll believe me, Mabel thought bitterly. They'll believe I didn't steal.

Finally, exhausted and hungry, she was just drifting off into a muddled slumber when the door opened softly and a shadow slipped in.

'Mabel?' Lizzie's voice was a whisper as she closed the door gently behind her.

Mabel sat up at once. 'Lizzie?' she whispered back. 'Is that you?'

'Yes, I've brought you a sandwich. I thought you might be hungry.'

As her eyes grew accustomed to the darkness, Lizzie came over to the bed and sat down beside her cousin. 'Here,' she said. 'It's only cheese, I'm afraid.'

Mabel took the sandwich. 'Thanks, Lizzie, you're a pal.'

'I'm not supposed to see you,' Lizzie said. 'But I think they're all in bed now.'

'Just be careful you're not caught,' Mabel warned. 'They'd sack both of us, then.'

'Have you been sacked?' Lizzie asked.

'Not yet,' replied Mabel. 'But it's only a matter of time. Her ladyship is waiting to discuss it with Sir Keir when he gets back tomorrow, but they think I stole those things and I'll be lucky if they don't call the police.'

'You could simply slip out of the house tonight,' suggested Lizzie. 'Run away before Sir Keir gets home.'

'Run away?' Mabel shook her head. 'They would say that proved I was guilty.' She heaved a sigh. 'I didn't take anything from Miss Lucinda's room, but I can't prove it, can I? They told me you were there when they found the ring. Please tell me exactly what happened.'

'Yes, I was there. It was yesterday evening, long after you'd gone. Mr Felstead and Mrs Kilby came up here and insisted on searching all our rooms, William's, Ada's, ours. They didn't say what they were looking for, just that some valuables were missing and they were searching everyone's things.

'Mr Felstead opened your locker drawer, and tipped

everything onto your bed. Mrs Kilby did the same with mine and then they began to go through it all. He unfolded each of your handkerchiefs and that's when he found it. One of the handkerchiefs had the ring knotted into a corner.'

'You *saw* him find it?'

'Yes, he put the pile of hankies onto your bed and unfolded them, one at a time.'

'You're sure he couldn't have slipped the ring in there himself?'

'No, he saw that there was something there and he told Mrs Kilby to come and look. He couldn't untie the knot, it was too tight, so she did it. But the ring was definitely tied into the hankie before they came into the room.'

'Did they go into everyone else's room after that? Mrs Bellman's, Miss Chalmers', each other's? Mr Blundell's?'

'No need,' answered Lizzie. 'They'd found the thief, hadn't they?'

'No!' snapped Mabel. 'They had not! *You* don't think I've stolen anything, do you?'

'Nooo,' said Lizzie slowly. 'But I can't explain how that ring got there.'

'Nor can I,' said Mabel. 'Someone must have hidden it there, but I don't know who and I don't know why.' She looked across at her cousin. 'All I can think is that someone wants me to be dismissed.'

A silence fell between them as they sat side by side on the bed. In the end, it was Mabel who spoke first. 'You'd better go, Lizzie,' she said. 'No point in risking you being caught in here with me.' She reached out and took her cousin's hand. 'Thanks for the sandwich. That was kind of you.'

Lizzie gave Mabel's hand a squeeze, then left the room

as silently as she'd come, leaving Mabel alone with her thoughts.

It's no good sitting here in the dark, she thought, and switching on the light she got ready for bed. She found she wasn't hungry any more, but she ate the sandwich anyway. If it was found there in the morning, they would know that someone had been in to see her. When she'd finished it, crumbs and all, Mabel opened the drawer of her locker and peered inside. Her things were all there, her books, her notepad, her pencil case, her hankies, not tidily laid out as she had left them, but all dumped back in a jumble. She picked up the pencil case and emptied it out onto the bed, looking at the contents. Two pens, several pencils, a rubber, some paper clips, a small penknife for sharpening the pencils, some spare nibs for the pens, a tiny bottle of blue ink, a couple of safety pins. If I'd been hiding anything small like a ring, she thought, I'd have put it in here with all these bits. I certainly wouldn't have tied it into the corner of a hankie where it would have been obvious.

Sudden fury shafted through her. How dare they search her things? How dare they accuse her of stealing? She scooped up the contents of the pencil case and tossed them back into the drawer, then flung herself onto the bed. Angry tears scalded her cheeks, and burying her face in her pillow she finally cried herself to sleep.

When she awoke the next morning, there was one glorious moment of calm before the events of the previous evening crowded her mind and everything came flooding back. Sitting up and scrubbing the sleep from her eyes, she knew this would be the last day she would wake in this tiny attic bedroom. Tonight she'd have been sent home in disgrace.

Well, she thought, let them! She wasn't going to apologise for something she had not done. If they turned her off without a character, well, so be it. She would find another job, not a place in service, so the lack of a character wouldn't matter. She would go home and get on with the rest of her life and never think of any of the McFarlanes again.

Mabel slid off the bed and went to look out of the window. It was another beautiful summer morning, the sun, already warm, beamed down from a clear blue sky, striking brilliance on the gardens far below. It must be later than she thought, well past the time she should be down in the kitchen.

Suddenly conscious she needed the bathroom, she went to the door and cautiously peered out onto the landing. No one about. Nothing to see or hear. Quickly, she hurried to the tiny staff bathroom and made her ablutions, using the lavatory, washing her hands and face, before returning to her room to get dressed, brush her hair and make herself presentable. She looked at the clothes she had been wearing the day before, her own clothes now neatly folded, but leaving them where they were, she put on her uniform. It had been washed and neatly pressed by the laundress, the cap and apron spotless and starched as they were at the beginning of every week. She did not like it any better now than on her first day, but she had not been dismissed, not yet, and she was determined to appear dressed and ready for work.

Once she was ready, she sat on the bed, and opening a

copy of *Pride and Prejudice* that she had bought for a penny in the market, she began to read.

Sometime later, Mabel could not have said how long, she heard footsteps on the stairs and, opening her door a crack so that she could see who was there, found herself face to face with Mrs Kilby. Behind her was Ada, carrying a tray with some toast and a cup of tea.

'Set it down there, girl,' snapped Mrs Kilby, indicating Mabel's bedside locker. Ada did as she was told before scurrying off downstairs again.

Mrs Kilby stood by the door and looked Mabel up and down. 'Who told you to dress in that uniform?' she demanded.

'Why shouldn't I?' answered Mabel. 'I'm still a maid here.'

'Not for long,' sneered the housekeeper. 'A common thief is what you are!'

'No.' Sticking to her decision not to admit anything, Mabel replied firmly, 'I have stolen nothing.'

'Sir Keir will want to see you,' Mrs Kilby told her. 'You're to wait here and you'll be sent for.'

Mabel wasn't hungry – indeed – she felt rather sick, but she wasn't going to give them the satisfaction of knowing that, and she ate the toast and drank the tea. When she had finished she pulled her canvas bag from under the bed and packed it with her few possessions, tucking *Pride and Prejudice* back into the top. Only her own clothes were left, folded, on the bed. She would change out of her uniform when she had been sacked and not before. Whatever happened in her interview with Sir Keir, she had no intention of remaining in the house once it was over. She would shake the dust of Chanynge Place off her feet and go home to Cockspur Lane, where she belonged.

When Sir Keir had returned from his club that morning, it was to find Felstead, rather than William, waiting in the hall. As soon as he had removed his coat and hat and handed his cane to the butler, Felstead murmured, 'Her ladyship is in the morning room, sir. She asks that you'll join her there as soon as is convenient.'

'Thank you, Felstead,' replied Sir Keir. 'Perhaps you would tell her ladyship that I'll be with her within the quarter hour.'

What can be so important, he wondered irritably, as he changed into the suit Blundell had laid out for him, that Isabella needs to see me so immediately? I'm due in court later and I really don't have time for any domestic dramas.

'Well, my dear,' he said, when he joined her exactly fifteen minutes later. 'What's the matter? I have to leave for the Old Bailey in less than an hour.'

As they sat together in the morning room, his wife explained the case of the stolen ring and the still-missing watch.

'The thing is,' Lady McFarlane said, 'I wouldn't have expected it of her. She's an intelligent girl with decent manners. I had hopes of bringing her on, you know. I thought she could be trained up as a lady's maid for Lucinda. She'll need someone very soon, and definitely when she marries and sets up her own household. I told Chalmers this was my plan and had enlisted her help. She was going to teach the girl the necessary skills. Dressing hair, use of make-up, cleaning delicate fabrics, looking after jewellery…' She waved a hand in the air. 'You know the sort of thing. Chalmers knows her job inside out and though Lucinda will need someone with experience, it should be someone nearer her own age. It seemed to me Mabel was suitable, a cut above the other maids, and she could gain the necessary experience in the coming months, working with Chalmers as she attends me. I was already searching for another between-maid to replace her in the general household. And now this!' Lady McFarlane looked at her husband wearily. 'And now this.'

'Bella, are you absolutely sure she did take the ring?' asked her husband.

'It was found in her belongings,' replied Lady McFarlane. 'And the watch, which is far more valuable, is still missing. She must have taken that with her when she went home on Saturday.'

'But why leave the ring?' wondered Sir Keir. 'Why not take both items?'

'Because she couldn't sell both at once without arousing suspicion?' suggested his lady with a shrug. 'I don't know, do I?'

'What does the girl herself say?'

'Oh well, she denies it all, of course.'

'I see,' replied her husband. 'Well, let's have her in and see what she has to say for herself, after a night to sleep on things.'

Before he could ring the bell, the door opened and Iain came in. 'What's going on, Gov'nor? Has Mama been telling you about Lucy losing her valuables? She shouldn't leave them lying about, too much temptation.'

'I agree,' said his father, 'but that's beside the point. We can't employ anyone untrustworthy.'

'Miss Chalmers saw her coming out of Lucinda's room on two occasions,' put in Lady McFarlane. 'She had no reason to be there if she was sorting things in the linen cupboard as she maintains.' Delicacy forbade her to mention the emptying of chamber pots in front of her menfolk, but she added, 'So you see, she had ample opportunity to take the ring and the watch from Lucinda's dressing table.'

'But when is she supposed to have taken the things?' Iain asked.

'Lucinda's not sure, she can't remember exactly when she last saw them. But some time ago she herself caught the girl with one of her scent bottles in her hand, and Chalmers definitely saw her coming out of Lucinda's room when she had no reason to be there. What else can we think?'

Iain felt the blood warm his cheeks. He was tempted to say nothing in Mabel's defence, but in the end he said, 'I'm afraid that might have been my fault... I think she was probably hiding from me.'

'Hiding from you!' exclaimed his mother. 'What on earth were you doing, playing hide and seek with one of the maids?'

'I had been teasing her... a bit,' admitted Iain. 'Nothing serious, of course, just a bit of fun, you know...' His voice tailed off.

'Yes, Iain, I'm afraid I do,' interposed Sir Keir. 'And I shall deal with you later. Just now we have to decide what to do with this maid. Whatever the rights and wrongs of where she was and why, we can't get away from the fact that one of the stolen items was found in her possession.'

'Among her possessions, Gov'nor,' pointed out Iain. 'That's not quite the same thing.'

'Possibly not,' retorted his father, 'but in this case it amounts to the same thing.' He glowered at his son and added, 'And if what you think is true, you are very much to blame for the difficult situation the girl finds herself in now.'

For a moment they were encased in silence and then Sir Keir walked across the room and pulled the bell. Moments later William appeared, and Sir Keir despatched him to fetch Mabel.

'You're to go and see Sir Keir in the morning room,' William said when he reached Mabel's room. 'And it don't look good.'

'I can't help what it looks like,' snapped Mabel. 'I'm not a thief.'

'Of course you ain't,' agreed William. 'Problem is, them finding that stupid ring.'

'You really don't believe I stole anything?'

'Course I don't,' said William stoutly.

'I think Lizzie's not so sure.'

'That's cos she's a silly girl,' William replied, as he led the way downstairs. As they reached the hall, the morning room door opened and Iain came out. They stood aside to let him pass, but as he climbed the stairs he heard William say, 'Good luck, Mabel. I know you ain't a thief.'

And, Iain thought, he's probably right.

26

Mabel drew a deep breath, knocked on the morning room door and, without waiting for a reply, turned the handle and went in. Lady McFarlane was sitting in her usual chair and Sir Keir was standing by the window, looking out onto the street. Both turned to face her as she paused just inside the door. She bobbed her curtsy but said nothing.

'Mabel Oakley,' Lady McFarlane spoke first, 'I'm very disappointed in you. I have told Sir Keir the sorry tale of your thieving, and we want to hear what you've got to say for yourself.'

'I've stolen nothing,' Mabel replied firmly, clasping her hands behind her so that they shouldn't see them shaking. 'I am not a thief.'

When she said nothing more, simply stood there looking at her employers, Sir Keir said, 'Then how do you account for the ring being found in your drawer?'

'I can't, but I did not put it there.'

'And you expect us to believe that?' drawled Lady McFarlane, raising an eyebrow.

Mabel shook her head. 'No, I don't,' she said, 'but it is the truth.'

'You can't think that someone else put it there?' Her ladyship's tone was sharp.

Mabel dug her fingernails into her palms. 'I have to,' she replied, 'because I didn't.'

'You're a very silly girl,' Lady McFarlane said stiffly. 'If you'd admitted your guilt and returned the missing watch to us, we might have found it in our hearts to give you a second chance. You're only young and we know your family are in difficulties with your father so badly injured. Though that doesn't excuse what you've done, it does explain why you did it.'

'No,' replied Mabel. 'I'm not a thief and I am not a liar.'

'Oh, for goodness sake, girl,' said Sir Keir in exasperation, 'the money you get for that watch won't be anything compared with its value. Far better to keep your job here—'

'I won't get anything for it,' Mabel interrupted him, 'because I haven't got it.'

There was a moment's stunned silence at her interruption, before Lady Oakley said, 'Then, Mabel Oakley, I'm afraid we have no option but to dismiss you from our service with immediate effect for dishonesty. Collect your belongings and be out of the house in half an hour.'

'Half an hour?' Mabel gave a bitter laugh. 'I can assure your ladyship, it won't take me that long.'

'How dare you speak to me like that!' exploded Lady McFarlane. But Mabel ignored her and without another word, turned on her heel and closed the door behind her.

'How dare she?' repeated Lady McFarlane, quite astounded by the girl's audacity.

Sir Keir ignored her question and put one of his own. 'Did she do it, do you think?' he asked.

'I neither know nor care,' replied Lady McFarlane, still bursting with righteous indignation. 'But Iain has clearly been showing interest in her, and we can't afford another scandal. She has to go, whether she was telling the truth about the theft, or not.'

Sir Keir nodded; he felt bound to agree, but he also felt a little uncomfortable with the decision.

Moments later the door opened again and Iain reappeared. 'Have you sacked her?' he demanded.

'She is leaving our employ,' replied his mother stiffly. 'She's not suitable for our household. I believe she has a disruptive influence below stairs.'

'Gov'nor?'

'Your mother's right,' said Sir Keir. 'Whether she's a thief or not there will always be a question mark over her honesty here. She'll be better off working somewhere else where her integrity is not in question.'

'You're giving her a reference, then.'

'Certainly not,' snapped Lady McFarlane. 'How can I testify to her honesty when I have dismissed her because it was in doubt?'

'Now perhaps you can see where your "bit of fun" has led to,' said his father. 'I can tell you now, you won't be going to France with your friend Everette, I shall not allow it, and that girl will have to try and find a new job without a good character.'

'And we can only hope you manage to stay out of trouble until you go up to Cambridge again in the autumn,' remarked his mother.

Iain almost laughed. 'But at Cambridge I'm allowed to

get into trouble again?' he nearly asked, but did not. His mother wouldn't see the joke.

As for his father forbidding his and Everette's bicycling holiday, that was not so dreadful. Though Iain had been looking forward to it, Everette had already gone off the idea.

'Sounds like damned hard work to me,' he'd said. 'All that pedalling! How does Brighton appeal to you? Plenty of talent down there, I imagine.'

It hadn't appealed to Iain, not until now, but if France was off, Brighton might be fun. His parents had made no mention of cutting his allowance or anything drastic like that. In fact, Iain thought as he left the room, suitably scolded and dutifully remorseful, he'd got off pretty lightly.

Certainly more lightly than Mabel. When she left the morning room, she went back upstairs and changed out of her uniform into her own clothes. The uniform she left hanging on its hanger, the starched cap tied with it. She wondered who would wear it next. They'd have to replace her and fairly quickly because the family were due to depart for Haverford in a few days' time. They'd probably take Lizzie after all, leaving the new maid, whoever she was, in London to settle in.

With one final look round the cramped bedroom, she picked up her bag and went down the backstairs to the servants' hall.

Preparations for luncheon were under way, and Ada was in the scullery at the sink, peeling potatoes and carrots. She glanced up at Mabel as she walked into the kitchen, head held high, carrying her bag, dressed in her own clothes.

How Ada wished she was brave like Mabel, ready to stand up for herself. William had listened for a few moments at the morning room door and had heard the answers Mabel had given. When Mrs Kilby and Felstead were in the room he said nothing, but when they'd gone, he regaled the other servants with what he'd heard. Mrs Bellman had been listening. She'd made no comment, but neither had she added condemnation. Miss Chalmers sat on a chair in the corner with closed eyes, a silent ghost, saying nothing.

'Goodbye, everyone!' Mabel's voice rang out loud and clear, and though nobody actually returned her farewell, there was an air of sympathy in the kitchen as she passed through.

Mabel was just leaving through the back gate when William called her name and hurried across the yard.

'Tell me where you live, Mabel,' he said as he followed her out of the gate into the mews beyond.

Mabel paused and looked back at him. 'Why?' she said.

William looked a little nonplussed. 'Well,' he said awkwardly, 'I thought I might come and see how you're going on,' he said, 'on me evening off.'

Mabel gave him a quick smile. 'Better not,' she said, going on with sudden insight, 'I'm a different person out here.'

'So you won't tell me?'

'No, I won't tell you, William,' she said. 'You've been kind to me while I've been here, and I think it's better that we say goodbye now. You have a good place as footman and they think well of you. You don't want to risk that.' She gave him a little push. 'Go on, go in now, before they notice you followed me out.' She held out her hand, an awkward gesture, but after a moment's hesitation William shook it and, as he released it, said, 'I shan't forget you, Mabel. I'll come and find you.'

He stood at the gate and watched her round the corner and disappear into the streets beyond, before he turned back to go indoors.

Mabel walked quickly along the road and then waited for a bus at the stop. She wondered what Mam and Dada were going to say when she arrived home so unexpectedly. Would they be angry? Disappointed? Sympathetic? Her thoughts were interrupted by a man's voice, one she recognised.

'I'm sorry they turned you off, Mabel.'

She spun round and found herself face to face with Mr Iain. 'Oh,' she said, disconcerted. 'It's you!'

'You left before Mama was able to give you the wages that were owing,' he said.

'I was sacked without wages or character, as you well know,' snapped Mabel. 'Your ma probably thought I could live on the proceeds of the theft.'

'Difficult if you didn't do it,' remarked Iain casually.

'You don't know I didn't!' challenged Mabel.

'Yes, Mabel, I think I do.'

'If not me, then who?'

Iain shrugged. 'I don't know,' he replied, 'but I believe you when you say you didn't. Here.' He reached into his pocket and pulled out two sovereigns.

Mabel stared at the coins in his hand for a long moment before saying firmly, 'We don't need your charity.'

Iain continued to hold out the coins and said, 'Not charity, Mabel, wages. They're what you're owed.'

It was so tempting, seeing the money there in his hand, knowing how much it would help Mam, but somehow, irrationally, Mabel felt if she accepted them, it would be admitting guilt to the theft.

'Your mother didn't send you with that money,' was all she could think of to say.

'No,' admitted Iain, 'but she should have done. I am simply making good her omission.'

The bus came round the corner and Mabel put out her hand to hail it.

'Please take it, Mabel,' Iain said. 'I'm sorry you're leaving...' The bus slowed and as it did he reached for her hand and put the two coins into it, closing her fingers over them.

'You gettin' on, or what?' the conductor's voice came from inside the bus.

'Get on,' Iain urged, 'or it'll go without you.' He gave her a little push. From the platform she looked back, but Iain McFarlane was already walking away, without a backward glance.

Once Mabel was settled in a seat, she slipped her hand, still holding the precious sovereigns, into her bag and pushed them down to the bottom for safety. At least now when she arrived home, jobless and with no reference, she would not arrive empty-handed.

27

Miss Enid Chalmers stood at the window of her bedroom on the servants' floor and looked down into the road. She had not been present when her employers dealt with the between-maid and, she assumed, gave her her marching orders. She knew the girl had been sent for, and surely would be faced with an accusation of theft. Despite Mabel's protestations of innocence, the evidence of the ring was incontrovertible, and the watch was still missing.

It had been a few days earlier that Lady McFarlane had called Chalmers in and explained the plans she had for the new between-maid.

'She is a girl of intelligence, far more so than her cousin,' said her ladyship. 'Oh, Lizzie is a competent housemaid, but it's unlikely she'll ever be anything more, whereas Mabel has something about her. Look at the way she coped with such common sense when we were all taken ill. I am sure you can see it yourself.'

Chalmers had agreed that she could and indeed it was true, but she didn't like it at all. Nor did she relish the task her ladyship had in mind, training Mabel up as a lady's maid for Lucinda, teaching her the duties and the skills she would need to succeed. Lady McFarlane had suggested that, once trained by an experienced maid like Chalmers, Mabel would make an admirable lady's maid for Lucinda. Chalmers, at almost fifty, immediately suspected that whatever her ladyship said, what she was really being asked to do was train her own successor.

'I've decided to take her to Haverford Court with us,' Lady McFarlane went on. 'It will do her good seeing how a country house runs. You can keep an eye on her in a general way. If all goes well, when we get back to London in the autumn, I shall find a new tweeny for Mrs Kilby and you can start teaching Mabel.'

Though she assured Lady McFarlane she readily agreed with this plan, from that moment on Chalmers had looked on Mabel as a rival and began to consider how she might get rid of her. In this, she hoped to use Iain's weakness for a pretty face. Twice she had heard him coming up the stairs when Mabel was working on the family's landing, and she had hoped to surprise them together, but to no avail. It was when she found Mabel emerging from Miss Lucinda's room when Lucinda was downstairs with her mother that the idea came to her. Just before Mabel left for her home, Chalmers slipped into Lucinda's room and, casting an eye over the jewellery left lying on the dressing table, she removed the moonstone ring and the gold watch on a diamond brooch.

How ironic, Chalmers thought, as she slipped the ring and the watch into her pocket, that if Mabel had already been Miss Lucinda's personal maid, *she* would have been looking after her jewellery, putting each piece away in its case at the end of the day. No valuable jewellery would have been left out on the dressing table for anyone to find.

Now, as she watched Mabel emerge from the mews behind the house carrying her bag and trudging along the road towards the bus stop, Chalmers allowed herself a smile of satisfaction. Her rival, if she had indeed been one, had gone and would be no threat to her ever again.

She was about to turn away when another figure appeared and, although she was three storeys up, Chalmers stepped back behind the curtains, afraid he might look up and see her.

In amazement she watched as Iain McFarlane caught up with the disgraced maid who stood waiting for her bus. She saw him speak to Mabel and after a brief exchange she saw Mabel turn away from him. But Mr Iain did not move away. He reached for Mabel's hand and thrust something into it. Mabel looked down and he said something else to her before giving her a push so that she stepped forward at last, to board the bus.

As the bus began to move, Iain was already returning to the house, disappearing from Chalmers' sight as he neared the front door.

What on earth had been going on there? she wondered. Why had Iain hurried out after Mabel Oakley? And what had he pressed into her hand? Money? Perhaps Lady McFarlane had relented and paid her what she was owed. As she continued to stare down into the street, Chalmers knew a flooding relief; thank goodness she had not actually accused Iain of flirting with the girl, or it might have been she who was catching a bus, suitcase in hand.

For a moment or two she sat down on her bed. She needed to think. Obviously, when she went back downstairs and heard officially of Mabel's dismissal, she must be shocked and horrified at what the disloyal, thieving girl had done.

Now she had to decide how she was going to dispose of the watch. The ring, of course, had been returned to its rightful owner, but she had expected that. It had served its purpose and was far less valuable than the watch. Sir Keir might well have asked the police to alert jewellers in case that was offered for sale. She realised now that she should have chosen something less distinctive, and knew she must wait before trying to dispose of it. It would be worth the wait to make sure of her retirement nest egg. In the meantime, she needed to find somewhere safer than the small pocket she had made in the ticking of her mattress. Although it was unlikely there would be any more searches of the servants' quarters, she decided she must, henceforth, keep it about her person at all times. She retrieved the watch from its hiding place and for a moment held it up to the light. The summer sunshine sparked fire from the diamonds that encrusted the brooch and from the tiny nibs of emerald that marked the hours on its golden face. She set it down on the bed and took down her hair. Carefully winding the brooch into its thickness, she pinned the bun back into place at the nape of her neck. It was slightly enlarged and she could feel its unaccustomed weight against her skin, but to the casual observer, it would pass unnoticed. Putting on her white lace cap, she glanced in the mirror that hung near her bed, assuring herself that her treasure was well hidden.

She went down to Lady McFarlane's bedroom where she sorted through the clothes for the laundress, and the delicate underwear that she would launder herself. She was still busy with this chore when the bell rang to summon her to her ladyship.

'Chalmers, you'll be distressed to hear that I was quite mistaken in the girl, Mabel Oakley. She refuses to admit her guilt, even though the ring was found in her possession. Sir Keir and I felt we had no option but to dismiss her.'

'I see, my lady,' replied Chalmers. 'That must have been very distressing for you.'

'Indeed,' agreed her ladyship. 'And we still have no trace of the watch. I'm afraid that has disappeared for good. I imagine that the wretched girl took it with her on Saturday and has already disposed of it.

'However, for the moment we must consider the arrangements for our move to Haverford Court. As you know, I had planned to take Mabel with us, but now she has gone, I shall have to take Lizzie.'

'Lizzie is a good girl,' remarked Chalmers. 'She always does what she's told. You'll have no trouble with her.'

'I certainly hope not,' said Lady McFarlane. But she thought, even as she spoke, that this was true in more than one way. Iain had never shown any interest in Lizzie. 'So,' she went on, 'I shall speak to the rest of the staff later today and apprise them of the situation. We certainly don't want any speculation as to why Mabel has left us.'

'I think they already know, my lady,' ventured Chalmers. 'They have discussed little else since the ring was found.'

Lady McFarlane sighed. 'I suppose that was unavoidable,' she said, 'but let's hope something else will engage them before long.'

'Certain to,' replied Chalmers. 'The kitchen is always

a hothouse of rumour, and if you announce who is accompanying the family to Haverford Court this year, it will give them something else to gossip about. And presumably you'll need to find a new between-maid…?'

'I suppose we must,' said her mistress. 'And I had such high hopes of Mabel Oakley. It makes her dishonesty even more disappointing, don't you think?'

'I certainly do,' replied her maid, reaching up to touch her hair. 'Most distressing!'

28

When Mabel got off the bus she stood on the pavement for a moment and watched it disappear. It was a short walk back to Cockspur Lane, but suddenly she wasn't ready to face her parents yet, to tell them how she had been accused and dismissed. She knew she would have to do so in the end, but wanting to put off the evil hour, she decided to go and see Mr Clarke first. Still clutching her canvas bag, she turned in the opposite direction. Somehow she knew it would be easier to explain to him what had happened. Mr Clarke wouldn't be affected in the way her family would. He would listen to her story unemotionally, as he had when she'd told him about Mr Iain's advances. He had listened then with a sympathetic ear, and given her good advice; perhaps he would do so again.

As she approached the end of the alley, she saw Albert Flood, sitting outside his newspaper kiosk on the corner. Albert was a small, rotund man with a bald pate fringed with iron grey hair and topped by a disreputable-looking flat cap. He spent all day selling papers to the crowds that used the bridge to the station platforms below. He knew all his regulars by name, knew their choice of newspaper, greeting them all with a ready smile and a cheery word come rain or shine.

When Albert saw her he waved and called out, 'Tom ain't there yet this morning, me duck.'

'Oh.' Mabel's disappointment was clear in her voice.

'Don't s'pose he'll be long though. You want him special like?'

'No,' said Mabel. 'Just thought I'd look in to say hello.'

She didn't have long to wait. Though Thomas Clarke was late coming to work, he was in good spirits. As he walked to his workshop, he thought about the meeting he'd had this morning and was pleased with how it had gone. He'd had a plan in his mind for some time and today he'd put it into action.

As he came round the corner he heard Albert call out, 'Hey, Tom, you got a visitor!'

'Mabel!' he exclaimed. 'What a lovely surprise! Didn't expect to see you this morning.'

For a moment she hung back. She didn't want to explain in front of Mr Flood why she was here and not at Chanynge Place. Always a fount of information, Albert chatted to everyone, and she certainly didn't want it noised abroad that she had been sacked from the McFarlanes' house for stealing.

Seeing Mabel's reluctance, Mr Clarke gave her a smile and said, 'Fancy a brew before I start work?'

'Oh, yes please,' answered Mabel, and together they walked to the workshop.

He made no further comment about her being there on a Monday morning when she ought to be in Chanynge Place, but simply filled the kettle and set it on the gas ring.

Mabel perched on her usual stool and watched him. He was so unhurried; it was one of the things she'd grown to like about him, he was never rushed, never pressed her about anything. Once the tea was made, he sat down as well and smiled at her across the rim of his mug. Clearly there was something wrong, or Mabel wouldn't be there, but he wouldn't ask. He simply sipped his tea.

'I've been given the sack,' Mabel said suddenly. Her tone was belligerent. 'But I didn't do it.'

He had his opening and said gently, 'Do what?'

'Steal Miss Lucinda's ring and her watch.'

'Of course you didn't,' returned Mr Clarke. 'What makes them think you did?'

So Mabel told him the whole story. Mr Clarke listened without interruption until at last she fell silent.

'It sounds to me as if someone wanted to get rid of you,' he said. 'But who? Someone who didn't want you to go to Haverford Court with the family?'

'I don't know,' answered Mabel miserably. 'I don't think anyone else knew I was going. Lady McFarlane only told me as I was leaving on Saturday. No one else was in the room at the time. Mrs Kilby knew I'd been sent for, but she didn't know why. At least she said she didn't. I certainly didn't tell any of them before I left.'

'What about William?' suggested Mr Clarke. 'Or Sir Keir's manservant? You said they were going upstairs as you were coming down?'

'Oh no, not William,' asserted Mabel. 'I'm sure it's not him. And Mr Blundell? Why would he do such a thing? Let's face it, anyone could have gone up to the servants' landing, unnoticed, after I'd gone.'

'Hmm,' said Mr Clarke thoughtfully.

'They tried to make me admit it was me, Sir Keir and Lady McFarlane,' Mabel said with a tremor in her voice, 'but I wouldn't, so I'm sacked without a character.' She swallowed hard, determined not to cry. 'The thing is, they need my wages at home, and without them, things are going to be even more difficult.'

Mr Clarke nodded. 'Yes,' he said, 'I can see they will be.'

'I'll have to try and find another job,' Mabel said, 'but it won't be easy without a reference.'

'At least you have something to take home with you,' Mr Clarke pointed out. 'You said Iain McFarlane gave you what you were owed.'

Mabel nodded. 'But I don't think he was meant to.'

'Probably not, but it was because of him you had taken refuge in Lucinda's room, and he must have realised that. Not something he was going to admit to his parents maybe, but perhaps he felt guilty enough to give you the money.'

'I didn't want to take it,' Mabel assured him. 'It felt as if I was being, I don't know, paid off somehow.'

'I understand that, but in the circumstances I'm glad you did. You'll be able to give it to your mother when you get home. Now,' he said, leaning over with the teapot to top up Mabel's mug, 'we must give thought to what you are going to do now you are back at home.'

'I might be able to sew things for Mr Moses, like Mam does,' Mabel suggested. 'Only plain sewing, not the setting of sleeves and stuff like that.'

'Well, that's certainly something you could look into,' agreed Mr Clarke, 'and there must be other jobs that you could do perfectly well.'

'Not without a character,' Mabel sighed, 'you know, from a previous employer?'

'What about your headmistress, from the school?'

'What, Miss Chapman?'

'Why not? She'd surely give you a good reference based on what she knew of you at school.'

'But they don't want to know about how I behaved at school. They want to know what I can do.'

'And that's the sort of thing she can tell them. She can say you are a hard worker, because it is true. She can say that you're trustworthy. She knows you are. I really do think you should go and see her and ask her to put something in writing that you can show a prospective employer.'

Tom Clarke could see that Mabel was beginning to respond; these were practical ideas to make her feel she was taking control of her life.

'Now,' he said, setting down his mug, 'you'd better be getting home. It's no good putting it off. Just tell them as you told me.'

'Supposing they think I'm a thief...' began Mabel.

'Mabel, dearest, they won't,' replied Mr Clarke. 'You're their daughter. They know you better than anyone else and they know you aren't a thief. Come on.' He stood up and reached for Mabel's hand. 'Time you were off. I'll walk with you as far as the Cockerel.'

Reluctantly, Mabel set down her mug and got to her feet. She knew he was right. She had to get it over with.

Mr Clarke locked the workshop door and they set off. All too soon, they were standing outside the pub on the corner of Cockspur Lane.

'Come and see me again soon,' he said as she paused on

the corner. 'Let me know how you're getting on. And don't forget to go and see that Miss Chapman, all right?'

'I won't,' she promised, and with a brave smile, she turned into the lane.

Mr Clarke waited for a moment or two and then headed back to his workshop. He'd done all he could to help at the moment, but he would go and see Mabel's father in the next day or two and suggest an idea that had occurred to him as they sat beside his printing press, drinking tea.

29

When Mabel reached number 31, the front door was on the latch as usual. She paused on the step and then pushed it open.

'Mabel? Is that you?' There was surprise in her dad's voice. She looked in and saw him sitting at his bedroom window in his indoor chair, looking out into the lane. He must have seen her coming.

'Hello, Dada,' she said, pausing in the doorway.

'What's happened?' asked Andrew. 'Why've you come home? Is everything all right?'

Mabel set down her bag and went across to kneel beside him. 'No,' she said. And at that her resolve gave way and she began to cry. Andrew immediately reached out to her, awkwardly drawing her closer. 'Don't cry, pet,' he said as he stroked her hair. 'Tell me. It can't be that bad!' But once she had started, Mabel found that she couldn't stop. The tears streamed down her cheeks as she sobbed, unable to speak, unable to explain.

Realising she couldn't help herself, Andrew just held her until the flood of her tears faded to dry, gulping sobs, and having scrubbed her eyes with her handkerchief and blown her nose, she managed to ask, 'Where's Mam?'

'Gone to the market,' he replied. 'She won't be long. Why don't we go into the kitchen and make a cuppa? You can push me along there, can't you?'

'Yes, of course.' Mabel got to her feet and manoeuvred her father along the passage to the kitchen where she installed him at the table, before setting the kettle to boil.

Once the tea was made and poured, they sat opposite each other. For a moment neither of them spoke and then Mabel said, 'I got the sack, Dada. I was sent away this morning.'

'The sack?' echoed her father. 'Why? What did you do?'

'Nothing,' replied Mabel. 'I haven't done anything, but they accused me of stealing. They say I'm a thief.'

'Stealing?' Andrew sounded incredulous. 'They say you stole something? What? What did they say you stole?'

'A ring, belonging to Miss Lucinda, and a watch. They were both missing.'

'A ring and a watch? But why do they think it was you who took them?'

'They found the ring in my bedside locker, on Saturday night, while I was here at home.'

'They found the ring in your locker?' he echoed. 'What made them look for it there? And what about the watch? Where's that?'

'Lizzie says that when Miss Lucinda noticed that the ring and the watch had gone from her dressing table, they began to search all the servants' rooms, going through their belongings. Lizzie's things were searched as well, but once they found the ring in my drawer, they didn't bother to look any further. They haven't found the watch, but they think I brought it home with me on Saturday, to sell. It's more valuable than the ring.'

'But how did it get in your drawer? The ring?'

'I don't know,' Mabel replied miserably. 'Someone must have put it there, but it certainly wasn't me.'

'And they simply dismissed you?'

'They tried to make me admit that I'd done it. They wanted me to give back the watch. Lady McFarlane said she understood that our family was in great need of money because of your accident...' Mabel trailed off, horrified at what she'd just said.

'I see,' he said. 'And she suggested this was what might have made you do it?'

'Yes,' whispered Mabel.

'And what did you say?'

'I kept on saying it wasn't me, and in the end they just said I was sacked... without a character.'

'But what made them think it was you in the first place?'

'I'd been seen on the family's bedroom landing a couple of times, and once I had been coming out of Miss Lucinda's room when I shouldn't have been there.'

'So why were you?'

'It's complicated, Dada.'

'Then uncomplicate it for me. Why were you in Miss Lucinda's room when you shouldn't have been?' He waited and the silence stretched out between them.

Eventually she said, 'To hide from Mr Iain.'

'To hide?'

So, at last, Mabel explained about Mr Iain, finishing

with, 'I couldn't tell them that. They would say I'd been encouraging him, like the last girl.'

'I see.' Andrew's face was a mask of anger. 'So this Mr Iain has allowed you to be dismissed without telling his parents that he'd been making a nuisance of himself, accosting you.'

'I couldn't tell anyone, Dada. They'd say I encouraged him, Lizzie said so. And Mr Clarke had said to make sure I wasn't alone with him. I heard him coming up the stairs one day and I knew Miss Lucinda was downstairs with her mother, so I just slipped into her room, out of the way.'

'Mr Clarke said…?'

'I didn't know what to do, and that's what he said.'

'You told Mr Clarke about this Mr Iain being a nuisance?' remarked her father. 'You didn't think to tell us? Your mother and father?'

'I couldn't, Dada. I needed the job.'

Her father looked at her hard and long, before he said, his voice tight with anger, 'You may have needed a job, but you are not required to put up with unwelcome advances from the son of the house.' His voice softened. 'Dearest Mabel, if you'd told me when it happened, I'd have written to Sir Keir, removing you from his employ and saying why. We don't live in the middle ages now, and girls like you do not have to put up with such behaviour.'

At that moment they heard the front door open and Alice calling Andrew's name.

'In the kitchen,' he called back, and she pushed open the door, saying, 'How did you manage—' before seeing Mabel sitting there with her father.

'Mabel? What are you doing here?'

'I've been sacked,' Mabel replied.

'Sacked!' exclaimed her mother. 'Why? You silly girl! What on earth have you done?'

Before Mabel could reply, her father said, 'Mabel's done nothing, Alice. Come and sit down and we'll tell you why she's safely back with us.'

'Safely back…?' said Alice faintly. 'What's happened?'

It was Andrew who told the story, while Mabel simply sat and listened. Dear Dada, she thought, as his anger grew with the telling, he believes me.

'But stealing,' said her mother at last. 'You didn't, did you?'

Before Mabel could answer, Andrew snapped, 'I don't think you need to ask that question, Alice.'

'No. No of course I don't,' Alice said, shamefaced. 'I know you would never steal anything, Mabel. I'm sorry.'

'I think I shall write to Sir Keir anyway,' Andrew said. 'I will not have my daughter branded a thief and then turned off without a farthing.'

'Please don't, Dada. It would make things even worse.'

'How could they be worse?' muttered her mother.

'They will say that the evidence was found in my locker,' sighed Mabel. 'It's what they've said all along. And it was. The ring was there and Lizzie was in the room when they found it. It was tied into the corner of one of my handkerchiefs. The knot was so tight, Mr Felstead couldn't undo it at first. Lizzie said there was no way they could have put the ring there then.'

'But what about this watch?' asked her mother. 'That wasn't there, was it?'

'No, but they think I brought that home with me on Saturday, to sell.'

'Well, I think our Mabel is well out of that house,' said Andrew firmly. 'She can soon find another job.'

'But not in service,' pointed out Alice. 'Anyone looking for a housemaid will want a reference.'

'I don't want to go into service again,' cried Mabel, just as her father said, 'There are other jobs.'

Later, when Andrew was having his afternoon rest, Mabel took the two sovereigns that Iain McFarlane had given her and handed them to her mother.

Alice stared at them. 'Where did they come from?'

Mabel told her. 'At least we have something to keep us going until I find some work,' she said. 'I didn't mention them to Dada, in case he thought I shouldn't have taken them.'

Alice sighed. 'Yes,' she said. 'Better not.' She reached over and gave Mabel a hug. 'I'm sorry I said what I did, Mabel,' she said. 'I know you'd never steal anything.'

When Eddie got home, he was told the whole sorrowful story and his anger rivalled his father's.

'How dare they suggest such a thing?' he exploded. 'You'd better not let me meet up with that Iain bloke, I'll knock his block off, trying it on with my sister.'

As the four of them sat round the supper table that evening, they discussed what Mabel might do. Remembering how annoyed her father had been that she had told Mr Clarke about Iain McFarlane first, she didn't mention she had been to see the printer on her way home this morning. However, she did mention his idea about approaching Miss Chapman for a school leaver's reference, passing it off as her own.

Alice looked doubtful, but Andrew thought it was a good idea. 'As I remember, Miss Chapman thought well of our

Mabel. There's no reason why she shouldn't put that on paper for her, is there?'

'I'd have to tell her what's happened,' Mabel said, 'and she might not believe me.'

'I agree you'd have to explain why you need a reference, but I bet she won't think you're a thief,' Eddie maintained.

'Perhaps you could work at the school,' suggested her mother. 'You know, helping with the little ones. Surely you could teach them to read, or their times tables?'

When Mabel finally fell asleep that night, sleeping in the room Stephen had so recently vacated for under the counter in Mr Solomon's shop, she had decided to go and see Miss Chapman the following day. If the headmistress was willing to help, the sooner she asked her, the better. If she was not, well, the sooner Mabel knew that, the better. She would go at midday, when most of the children would have gone home for their dinners, and hope that Miss Chapman could spare her a few minutes. The decision made, she fell into an exhausted sleep, the first real sleep she'd had for nearly forty-eight hours.

30

John Sheridan arrived at his office that Monday morning knowing that his first appointment was with Peter Everette. More and more he wished that he'd never taken Everette Enterprises on as clients. When he got to the top of the stairs he found Miss Harper waiting for him. He nodded a quick 'Good morning,' but she remained resolutely in his way.

'Mr Everette's secretary telephoned,' she told him, 'to say that Mr Everette will be late for his appointment.' Knowing a moment's relief, Sheridan thanked her.

'I shall be busy until he arrives,' he said. 'No calls or interruptions please.'

It was almost noon when Miss Harper finally announced that Mr Everette had arrived. Sheridan had hardly stood up to receive him when the man flung into the office and, with a dismissive hand, waved at the papers that lay ready upon the solicitor's desk.

'You can put those away, Sheridan,' he said. 'We shan't be signing them today.'

John Sheridan's expression of enquiry masked his profound relief. It sounded as if the deals within those papers were to be deferred or even, he hoped, scrapped altogether.

'Is there a problem with them, sir?' he asked, his voice neutral, the fiasco with Andrew Oakley still invading his mind.

Peter Everette did not immediately answer the question. He was facing a definite setback, but that was none of the solicitor's business and he did not intend to enlarge upon it; he would deal with things in his own way.

'No,' he said. 'Not if they are as I requested. If they are all drawn up ready, they can be actioned another day,' he said. 'I'll take them with me for my man Clegg to check.'

'You realise they have to be properly witnessed?' asked Sheridan as he gathered the documents back into their folder.

'Of course.' Everette was already on his feet and when Sheridan passed him the folder he almost snatched it from him and pushed it into his briefcase, snapping the locks closed. 'You have copies, I take it?'

'Of course,' answered Sheridan.

'Then I'll take those as well. And indeed any other paperwork you still hold relating to my company.'

Sheridan stifled his surprise at this, and, ringing for Miss Harper, he despatched her to find the required files. While she was out of the room, Peter Everette paced the office like a caged bear, and when Miss Harper returned he pounced on the files, cramming them into his already full briefcase.

'Is there anything else?' Sheridan asked mildly.

'Not at present,' snapped Everette. 'I'll be in touch if there is.'

As soon as he had gone, Sheridan summoned Miss Harper and dictated a letter regretting that as Mr Everette had removed all the documents Sheridan, Sheridan and Morrell had been holding for him, the firm would no longer be able to represent Everette Enterprises. With this letter, they would also present Everette Enterprises with a final invoice for the consultation and the work completed to date.

'Please make sure that this catches the afternoon post,' he said to Miss Harper, 'or better still,' he said, remembering the previous error, 'tell Bevis to hand deliver it... to the address in Myddelton Square.'

When she had left the room to type the letter, Sheridan sat back in his chair and considered Peter Everette's actions. He didn't know what had panicked the man, but whatever it was, he was pleased that all paperwork relating to Everette Enterprises had been removed from his office and he could terminate their association.

Once he had signed the letter, he decided, he would go straight home. It seemed prudent to be unavailable for a while.

When Mabel arrived at school in the dinner hour, she went to the office to ask the secretary, Miss French, if she could see the headmistress.

'It's not convenient,' said Miss French. 'Miss Chapman's having her lunch.'

'I won't keep her long,' said Mabel. 'I'm Mabel Oakley, I used to come to this school.'

'I know fine well who you are, Mabel Oakley, my memory's not that short, but Miss Chapman's on her lunch break and she won't want to be disturbed by you, or anybody else.'

Mabel was about to protest when the door from the head's office opened and Miss Chapman herself appeared. She greeted Mabel with a surprised smile.

'Mabel Oakley!' she said. 'What brings you here?'

Now she was here, facing her old headmistress, Mabel was suddenly tongue-tied. What she wanted to ask seemed such an enormous favour that she didn't know where to start.

Seeing her erstwhile pupil looking so nervous, Miss Chapman said, 'Come on into my office, Mabel, and tell me how you've been getting on since you left us.' She glanced at her secretary and said, 'Thank you, Miss French, for protecting me, but I have got a few minutes to talk to Mabel.'

Once in her office with the door closed behind them, Miss Chapman waved Mabel to a chair and said, 'How nice to see you. And how are you getting on in your job? Everything going all right?'

Mabel sat down, perching awkwardly on the edge of the chair. 'I haven't got a job, just at present, Miss Chapman,' she admitted, and as she saw Miss Chapman's raised eyebrow, went on hurriedly, 'Please can I ask you something?'

'Yes,' Miss Chapman replied a little cautiously. 'What can I do for you?'

'Well, first I have to explain why I haven't got a job...'

Miss Chapman put aside the sandwich she'd been eating for her lunch and said, 'I see. Well, go ahead.'

'I was accused of stealing a ring and a valuable brooch-watch from my employers, so they sacked me.'

'But you didn't, I assume?' The question was gently put.

'No!' exclaimed Mabel hotly. 'I did not!'

'So why do they think you did?'

For the third time in two days Mabel told what had happened while she was working for the McFarlanes. Miss Chapman heard her out without interruption, but when at last Mabel fell silent she said, 'I see. How difficult for you.'

'Do you believe me?' asked Mabel in a small voice.

'Of course. Why shouldn't I?' replied Miss Chapman. 'You've always been truthful before, but what I believe and what the McFarlanes believe, are two different things.' She looked across at Mabel. The child, for as far as Miss Chapman was concerned Mabel was still a child, was in a difficult situation. Like Mr Clarke, she could only assume that someone had planted the ring to get Mabel sacked, but she couldn't fathom the reason for that. Had she fallen out with one of the other servants? Whatever the matter, Mabel had been dismissed and must have come to her for help.

'What is it you want me to do, Mabel?' she asked. 'You do realise you can't go back into school again, don't you? The exam date is long past and there is no point in you coming back to this school in the autumn.'

Such a possibility had never crossed Mabel's mind and she said, 'Oh no, I know that. I wasn't thinking of that.'

Miss Chapman knew a moment of disappointment because, despite her words, she'd been wondering if she could still manage to get Mabel into the secondary school.

'I have to earn my own living,' Mabel explained, 'or at least contribute to the family income. My father will never work again, and so we all need to support him. But that's my problem, you see. I was dismissed without a character or reference, which makes getting another job very hard.' She paused and, drawing a deep breath, said, 'I wondered, please could you give me a reference, Miss Chapman? Just something to say that I'm hardworking and honest? Something I could show to a prospective employer?'

Miss Chapman didn't answer immediately and Mabel sat, her hands in her lap, her fingers tightly crossed as she waited for the reply. As the silence lengthened she said softly, 'Mam thought I might be able to get work here at the school, you know, teaching the little ones their letters and numbers. I could do that, I know I could.'

'I'm sure you could,' agreed Miss Chapman. 'I always said you'd be a good teacher, but you'd have to be trained. You could come and do that today, but you wouldn't be paid.' Seeing the disappointment on Mabel's face, she said, 'Look, I am happy to give you a reference of the kind you mention. From my own experience I know you are all those things and more, but whether it would help you find work, well, that would depend on other things too: the sort of employer, the type of job.' A bell sounded in the playground, summoning the children in for afternoon school. Miss Chapman stood to look out of the window for a moment and Mabel could hear the children lining up outside.

'If you can wait until the end of school,' said the headmistress, 'I'll dictate something to Miss French. In the meantime, if you'd like to pass the time hearing the infants saying their tables, you can go into Miss Hatchard's class and say I sent you.'

Miss Hatchard, faced with a large class of six-year-olds, was delighted to let some of them chant their two and three times tables with Mabel Oakley. It was only a few years since Mabel had sat at a desk in this very room, chanting tables herself, and Miss Hatchard remembered her well.

At the end of afternoon school, Mabel presented herself to the secretary's office and was handed a sealed envelope. Hearing her voice, Miss Chapman appeared from her office.

'That's the best I can do,' she said. 'With luck, it will help you find some sort of employment. You're a determined young woman, Mabel, and whatever you decide to do, put your heart into it and I'm sure you'll succeed.'

Filled with gratitude, Mabel thanked Miss Chapman for everything and put the envelope safely into her pocket. As she walked out into the yard, Miss Chapman watched her from the window and thought, That's a girl with a future. I hope she grasps it with both hands.

When Mabel reached the park, she turned in through the gate and found an empty bench. She sat down and took the envelope out of her pocket. She wanted to read what Miss Chapman had written before she showed it to her parents. The envelope held a single sheet of notepaper, with the typed heading *Walton Street Elementary School* and dated 16th July 1912, under which was the testimonial.

To whom it may concern.

This is to say that Mabel Oakley has been a pupil at Walton Street Elementary School for the last seven years. I can recommend her as intelligent and hardworking and she leaves us as a well-mannered and respectful young woman, whose honesty and loyalty have never been in doubt.

This was followed by her signature in royal blue ink, beneath which was typewritten

```
Signed:- Grace Chapman, Headmistress
```

Mabel read it through twice. Brief though it was, it might be enough for an employer to look at her with favour.

Well, thought Mabel as she tucked it back into its envelope and got to her feet, at least I've got something to show now.

She considered dropping in on Mr Clarke, but was reluctant to bother him again. He had given her good advice yesterday, but her father had clearly been hurt that she had confided in him first and she didn't want to make that mistake again. However, she was about to pass Mr Solomon's shop and, on impulse, she stopped outside and peered through the window. She could see both Stephen and Mr Solomon, heads together, looking closely at something on the counter. She was about to walk on, leaving them to whatever they were doing, when Stephen looked up and saw her outside. He left the counter and came to open the door.

'Mabel?' he said anxiously. 'What are you doing here? Is everything all right? Nothing's happened to Dad or Mam?'

'No,' said Mabel, 'nothing like that.'

'Mr Solomon says to come in for a minute,' said Stephen.

'No,' answered Mabel quickly, 'I can see you're both busy.'

'Just for a minute, Mabe. He says he wants to meet you.'

Still she hesitated, and Stephen said, 'Come on. He won't bite!'

'All right,' she agreed, 'just for a minute.'

Mr Solomon set aside the tweezers he'd been holding and said, 'Good afternoon, Miss Oakley. How do you do?' He did not offer a hand, but he gave her a warm smile. 'Have you come with a message for your brother? Is all well at home?'

'Yes, thank you,' Mabel replied, and then added, 'I did want to speak with Stephen though, just for a moment, if you don't mind.'

The old man shrugged. 'Of course,' he said. 'We can finish this later, Stephen. I have to go upstairs just now, anyway.'

The two Oakleys watched him shuffle away towards the stairs. Stephen said, 'What's up, sis? What are you doing here? Has Mam sent you?'

'No,' answered Mabel. 'There was just something I wanted to tell you.' Briefly she outlined what had happened and as Stephen listened his expression became serious.

'But surely they don't really think you've stolen those things?'

'I don't know what they really think, but the result is the same. I've been sacked, and I've got to find another job quickly. Mam needs my wages.' She went on to tell him about Miss Chapman's reference. 'I'm hoping Mr Moses might have work for me, like Mam. Sewing and stuff. I'll go to see him tomorrow. I wouldn't have to bring the sewing home like Mam does, I could work with the other girls in his sewing room.'

'In that sweatshop!' Stephen sounded horrified. 'You couldn't work there, Mabel!'

'I could if I had to,' replied Mabel, 'if he had a job for me!'

'There must be something else.'

'I'll have to take what I can get,' said Mabel flatly. 'Anyway,' she said, edging towards the door, 'I'd better be going. I don't want to upset your Mr Solomon.' She punched Stephen gently on the arm and said, 'See you soon, Stephen.'

Moments later, the curtains concealing the stairs flicked open and Mr Solomon came back into the shop.

'Your sister has gone?'

'Yes, thank you, sir,' Stephen answered. 'She had to get home to help my mother.'

'Ah,' said the old man with a smile. 'That's as it should be. Now then, come and look at this.'

The two of them turned their attention back to the movement of the clock that they'd been working on, and for the moment, all thoughts of Mabel and her dilemma faded from Stephen's mind. He watched, fascinated, as Mr Solomon carefully replaced the clock's innards into its case, delicately adjusting the balance and turning the tiny screws that held it in position.

'Your sister has leave before she goes into the country?' asked Mr Solomon when he had finished and placed the clock back onto the repairs shelf. The previous evening Stephen had told the Solomons how Mabel had been chosen to travel with the family she worked for.

Stephen felt the colour flood his face as he said, 'No, not exactly.' And then, to change the subject, he asked, 'When will we be looking at Mr Talbot's grandfather clock, sir?'

Mr Solomon glanced across at the tall longcase clock standing silent in a corner of the shop. 'Ah,' he said. 'That will require some time. It is old and needs a good clean, both the movement and the case itself. We'll leave that until tomorrow or the next day. It's not a job to be hurried, so we'll see what else comes in, eh.'

31

When Mabel did not visit him the next day, Thomas Clarke decided he would go to Cockspur Lane and see her father. He had already dropped in a couple of times to see Andrew Oakley. Looking after Emma as he had during the last months of her life, Tom Clarke knew only too well the difference it had made to her, having visitors to keep her in touch with the world outside; the importance of occasional fresh air and the relief of a change of scene. He knew how frustrating it was, being tied to the house like Andrew, only able to escape when Eddie was at home to take him out, to manoeuvre the chair over the cobbles. Clarke had met Eddie once, and he thought very well of him. Not easy, Thomas thought, for a lad of his age to have to take over the role of breadwinner.

He knew, too, that Alice, with the best will in the world, hadn't the strength to push Andrew's wheelchair over the cobbles of Cockspur Lane. She could manage to move him around the house in the indoor chair, but it meant that Andrew had very little change of scene.

Lying awake last night, Thomas Clarke had given a lot of thought to the idea he'd had after Mabel went home.

He would have to convince her family – and, Thomas thought, her mother in particular – that his plan was not only a viable one, but was one that would appeal to Mabel herself. He was aware of the guarded way Alice Oakley viewed him, even now, and he didn't want to make things worse. It was only proper that he approach her parents before speaking to Mabel, but if he could convince her father of his plan, perhaps Andrew would be able to bring his wife round to the idea, too. If not, well, that would be that. He'd certainly not mention it to Mabel unless her parents agreed. If her father thought it had merit, then he could leave it up to him to persuade Alice. He wondered if Mabel had told her parents that she'd been to see him on her way home that Monday morning. He guessed not, and if he were right he'd need to tread very carefully; the last thing he wanted to do was to upset her family. He decided to wait until he closed up the print shop that evening, and then call in on his way home.

When he knocked at the door of number 31, it was opened by Mabel herself, her face lighting up with pleasure when she saw who was on the step.

'Hello, Mabel,' he said. 'I've come to see your father. Is it a good time?'

'Mr Clarke,' she cried. 'Of course, come in.' Calling over her shoulder, 'Dada, Mr Clarke's come to see you,' she turned back to their visitor and said, 'I'm afraid we're all in the kitchen, do you mind coming in there?'

'Not in the least,' he replied, though, as he followed Mabel through to the back of the house, he wondered how Alice would feel about him invading her kitchen.

Alice was standing at the stove and Andrew was seated at

the table. When she saw they had a visitor and who it was, Alice gave a cry of dismay. 'Oh, Mabel, you shouldn't bring Mr Clarke into the kitchen.'

'There's nowhere else to take him,' pointed out Mabel. 'He's come to see Dada.'

On his previous visits Mr Clarke had sat with Andrew in his front room bedroom. Taking in the awkwardness of the situation now, he said, 'I was on my way home, and I fancied a beer. I came to see if you felt like joining me for a pint at the Cockerel, Mr Oakley? But it looks as if you are about to have supper, so perhaps we should leave it till another day?'

'No, indeed,' Andrew answered at once. 'A pint at the pub would be most welcome. I'm sure supper can wait for half an hour, can't it, Alice?'

The hope in his eyes turned Alice's refusal to agreement. 'Of course,' she said. 'Go for your pint. Will you be able to manage the wheelchair over the cobbles, Mr Clarke?'

Clarke assured her that he would. Ten minutes later, they had transferred Andrew from his indoor chair to the outdoor one and the two men started the bumpy journey to the corner of the street and in through the door of the pub.

Once seated at a corner table with two pints of bitter in front of them, Andrew took a taste of his beer and then said, 'Well, Mr Clarke, this is a surprise visit. What's it all about then?'

'Over a pint perhaps we could be Tom and Andrew?' suggested Mr Clarke.

Andrew nodded and said with a smile, 'Tom it is. Now then, what can I do for you?'

'It's about Mabel.'

'Yes, well, I thought it might be. What about her?'

'I see she's at home again…'

'Indeed she is.'

'And I wondered if there is anything I can do for her.'

'You know she's been sacked from that house up west?'

'Yes,' admitted Tom. 'She did tell me.'

Andrew gave him a lopsided grin and said, 'Yes, well, I thought she might have. She thinks the world of you.'

'And I think the world of her,' replied Tom. 'She's very strong, you know. I don't mean physically, though she's strong in that way too, but as a person. She has a strong character and doesn't give up.'

'That's what that Miss Chapman, her headmistress, says. Mabel went to see her yesterday afternoon and she's written her a testimonial. Nothing fancy, but a commendation she can show to a prospective employer.'

'Did she indeed?' Tom took a swallow of his beer. 'Good for her.'

'Mabel told you why she's been sacked?'

'Yes, some nonsense about stealing a piece of jewellery.'

'Yes, but that's just rubbish! She would *never*…'

'I know that; I know Mabel.'

'But the trouble is,' said her father, 'if that ridiculous idea became common knowledge, she might never get another job. Not if her honesty was in question.'

'Well,' said Tom – it was now or never – 'well, that's what I wanted to talk to you about.'

'Oh yes?'

'I've had an idea that you might like to consider, as a possibility, you know?'

'Yes?'

'I would be very happy to give Mabel a job, if she would like to work for me.'

'Work for you? What, as a housemaid? I don't think so.'

'Nor do I,' Tom said quickly. 'I don't want to employ her in a domestic way; no, not at all. She would hate it and I don't need a housemaid.'

'I see. So what are you suggesting? I won't have any funny business, or anything to suggest there might be something improper between you.'

'Nor will there be,' Tom assured him. 'It's just that I'm getting on a bit now and for some time I've been considering employing a young lad as an assistant; someone to run errands, deliver completed work and the like.'

'Mabel? An errand boy?' said Andrew in disbelief.

'An errand girl, if you like,' Tom answered with a smile. 'To start with, but I would hope to train her to set type, and...' And eventually use the press? But this last idea he did not voice, finishing his sentence with 'And generally help me in the workshop.' He'd said enough already; he could see the doubt in Andrew's eyes. 'And what difference a lass or a lad? I'd pay her the same as a lad; ten shillings for a six-day week.'

Tom Clarke sat back in his chair, took another mouthful of beer and waited. He watched Andrew's expression change as he considered what was actually being suggested. Would he go for it? Would he be able to accept they were talking about his daughter, not one of his sons?

Surely, thought Tom, if I'd made such an offer to Stephen, they would have grasped it with both hands. But an errand *girl*?

'But how would she get about, making these deliveries?' wondered Andrew.

'I've a bicycle she can use. Used to ride it myself not so long ago.'

'A bicycle?' echoed Andrew. 'She don't know how to ride a bicycle.'

'She'll soon learn,' replied Tom. 'It's not difficult once you've got your balance.'

Andrew shook his head in disbelief. Who'd ever heard of such a thing? What would Alice say? Her daughter working for a single man? Being sent out on the streets by herself? Riding a bicycle!

Mr Clarke knew enough to say no more now. If Andrew thought he was being pushed into something he'd probably reject the idea out of hand, but if he were left cogitating, well, he might gradually accustom himself to the thought and see its many advantages.

'Well,' said Andrew, downing the last of his pint, 'better be getting back, Alice'll have my tea on the table. My round next time, eh?'

'You're on,' said Tom cheerfully.

When Andrew was safely back in the house, Tom Clarke said goodnight and walked home. He hoped the idea he had planted in Andrew Oakley's mind would take root and Mabel's parents would see the advantages it offered.

Back in Cockspur Lane, Andrew said nothing of his conversation with Thomas Clarke until Eddie and Mabel had gone to their beds and he and Alice were alone. He wanted Mabel kept in the dark about Tom's suggestion, unless he and Alice decided in favour of it. And that was the thing – were they going to? They knew that for some reason

Mr Clarke, a man in his sixties, and their daughter Mabel, rising sixteen, had established a firm friendship, and neither of them was quite comfortable with the idea.

'You don't think, well, that he has something more sinister in mind, do you?' asked Alice.

'I didn't think so,' he replied. 'When he was explaining what he was offering, it all sounded very reasonable. He would pay her ten shillings a week and she would work as a general assistant, running errands, helping in the workshop, things like that.'

'There must be more to it than that,' pointed out Alice. 'Ten shillings a week for doing almost nothing? He must want more of her, and that's what I don't like.'

'She'd be living at home,' Andrew reminded her. 'She wouldn't be living with him. Not like Stephen with the Solomons.'

'I should think not!' exclaimed Alice, conveniently forgetting she had not approved of that arrangement at first, either. 'That is something entirely different. Stephen's living with a man and his wife, a live-in servant, if you like. Perfectly proper and above board.'

'Well,' Andrew said slowly, 'Mabel would be here with us. You'd hear how her day had been every evening.'

'She might not tell us everything,' answered Alice doubtfully. 'I can't agree to the idea. It's not right for her to work for a man fifty years older than her. I don't know what Susan would say!'

'Susan?' Andrew sounded surprised. 'What has Susan to say to anything?'

'Your sister always has something to say about everything,' replied Alice tartly, 'whether it's her business or not. I dread to think what she'll be saying when she hears why Mabel is in need of a job.'

'Then we won't tell her!'

'Oh, Andrew,' Alice said with a rueful laugh. 'This is Susan we're talking about! She'll get to know in the end, she always does. She's always so critical, so different from Jane.'

'But you don't have to take any notice of her!' cried Andrew. 'I never have!'

'She doesn't think I should be working for Saul Moses. She was horrified when I told her. She said wives in our family don't go out to work and you wouldn't like it.'

'So what did you say to her?' asked Andrew, really wanting to know.

'I said, then you'd have to lump it, and she called James to heel and they got up and went home.'

'Well, I should prefer you didn't have to take in sewing,' Andrew conceded, 'but at present it helps keep us fed.' He reached over and took her hand. 'I'm proud of you, Alice, proud of you for keeping us afloat. Both the boys doing their bit and Mabel too, until this stupid accusation.'

'She'll have to get a job of some sort,' sighed Alice. 'She's another mouth to feed.'

'She'll want to contribute,' Andrew said. 'She feels guilty that she's been sacked, and we have to admit it will be almost impossible for her to get another job in service, without a proper reference from Lady McFarlane.'

'But as an errand girl?' Alice sounded despairing.

'An errand girl working for a man she knows and likes and who doesn't for a minute believe she's a thief. Should we put the idea to her and see what she thinks?'

'Oh, she'll want to take it,' replied Alice, 'you know that,

I know that, and once you've asked her and she says yes, we'll have to let her.'

'There's no need to decide now,' Andrew said soothingly. 'Why don't we sleep on it and discuss it again in the morning?'

Because I shan't sleep, thought Alice, as she went upstairs to bed. I shall be churning and churning all night and I still won't know what to do in the morning.

32

Alice Oakley was not the only one who slept badly that night. John Sheridan was exhausted, but as he lay in the darkness beside his sleeping wife, listening to her regular breathing, his mind was wide awake as he tried to decide what to do. Should he sit tight and hope that Everette Enterprises weathered the storm, whatever that was, or might there be some sort of investigation which could involve him? When at last he did manage to doze off, he slept only fitfully and awoke in the morning, unrefreshed. He was still as undecided as to his course of action as he had been the night before.

'You look tired, John,' remarked his wife across the breakfast table. 'Didn't you sleep well?'

'Oh, not too bad,' he said casually. 'I've a lot on my plate at the office just now.'

'You work too hard, darling,' said Anne. 'Why don't you take today off? It looks a beautiful day. We could go out somewhere.'

'Can't, I'm afraid,' her husband replied ruefully. 'I've got a couple of important meetings I really can't cancel. Things'll probably get easier in a few days.'

'I was thinking we might go and spend the weekend in Hove,' Anne said a little tentatively. 'I haven't seen my parents for ages, and I'm sure Lavinia would love a few days by the sea.'

'Sounds a lovely idea,' agreed John, though the thought of a dreary weekend with his in-laws was the last thing he wanted right now. 'Why don't you arrange to go?' he suggested. 'See if Lavinia would like to go and I'll come down and join you all if I can.' Better than having them here, he thought. At least if they went to Hove they could come home again after the weekend. The last time Anne's parents had come to visit them, they stayed nearly ten days.

Anne gave him a knowing smile. She was well aware of how difficult John found her parents, but she knew they ought to make the effort as her father, in particular, seemed to have aged suddenly.

'I'll phone them and see if they'd like us to come,' she said.

'Good,' said John getting up from the table. 'You do that.' He reached over and kissed her forehead. 'I must go or I'll miss my train. Don't wait dinner for me this evening. I've a late meeting so I'll probably eat at my club before I come home.'

'Well, don't overdo it,' warned Anne. 'I'll expect you when I see you.'

Sheridan bought a paper at the station and read the headline:

Everette Enterprises Cease Trading

He read the article and sighed. Everything would

probably come out now, but with luck Sheridan, Sheridan and Morrell would not be implicated in any of the illegal dealings.

When he reached the office he found there was a letter from Everette Enterprises in reply to his own. It was short and to the point, refusing to pay the invoice he had sent and using the error with the delivery of earlier papers as the reason.

> This error has already cost my firm a great deal of money, and we feel no obligation to pay the invoice that has been submitted.

It's a bit late to use that as an excuse, thought John wryly, but knew he had to accept it. It was the price they would have to pay for severing all connection with Everette Enterprises. Despite the bill being dishonoured, which was a hefty blow, Sheridan could only feel relief. His firm could survive the deficit and he felt well rid of Peter Everette.

Perhaps, he thought, it wouldn't be a bad idea to be out of town for the next few days.

'You were right, as always,' he said to Anne when he got home. 'I do need a break, so I'm going to take a couple of days off. Which means I can come with you to Hove after all!'

'Oh, darling,' Anne cried in delight. 'That's wonderful, you really are so good to make the effort to come with us. I know you don't find my parents easy.'

'But they are your parents,' John said with a smile, 'and it's important to you. That's what matters. Let's hope the weather doesn't break and we can all enjoy some fresh sea air.'

'If we're to go in the morning as planned,' beamed Anne, 'I must do some packing for you.' And getting up from her chair, she hurried out of the room to tell Lavinia the good news. 'Daddy's coming with us! Isn't he a dear man?'

33

The following morning Mabel woke early and couldn't get back to sleep, her brain in turmoil, all her problems without resolution. With what seemed like the weight of the world on her shoulders, the days ahead of her seemed to stretch endlessly into the future. She had no job and no prospect of one, and she felt she was a burden on her parents when they were already in tight financial circumstances. Like her mother, she was prepared to take almost any job to make her contribution, and she decided, as she lay watching the grey light of the pre-dawn gradually turn to a golden glow as the sun rose, that today she would go out and secure something, even if it paid a pittance and meant exhaustingly long hours. She gave a shuddering thought to Mr Moses' sweatshop.

'Even that!' she said defiantly as she got out of bed.

Washed and dressed, wearing a flower-patterned cotton frock and a white cardigan, she went quietly downstairs to the kitchen. She would start the day with a cup of tea and a piece of toast and then make tea for her parents before she set off in her search for a job.

But, when she entered the kitchen, Mabel was surprised

to find Mam there already, pouring boiling water from the kettle into the teapot.

'Mabel,' cried her mother, 'you *are* looking smart.'

'Because I'm going job hunting,' Mabel told her. 'You're up early, Mam. I was going to make you and Dada a cup of tea before I went out.'

'Where are you thinking of going?'

'I'm going to buy a newspaper and look in the personal columns and the situations vacant, and see if I can find anything.' She paused for a moment and then added, 'I thought maybe at Mr Moses' in his workshop?'

Her mother, maintaining her expression with difficulty at this suggestion, said, 'Well, before you do that, will you take this cup of tea to your dad and have a little chat with him; cheer him up a bit? His spirits are often low first thing in the morning when he wakes up and sees another day like all the other days stretching out ahead of him.'

'Of course, Mam.' Mabel picked up the two cups of tea and headed for her father's room. As she left the kitchen her mother called after her, 'Tell him I'll be in in a minute.'

Alice had also woken early and as she'd emerged from slumber, Mr Clarke's offer had come flooding back to her, crowding her mind with worry and doubt. Lying in bed, she thought over the discussion she'd had with Andrew the previous night. Her brain must have been working on the problem as she slept, for as she considered the idea again, she realised what Andrew had been saying was right. Mabel felt she had let her family down and made their financial situation worse. None of them considered her dismissal to be her fault, but it was important that Mabel should know she could still contribute to the family's finances. What Mr

Clarke had suggested was one way in which she could. Perhaps, Alice thought now, I should set aside my doubts and agree to Mabel working as his assistant.

An early sunbeam had forced itself between her curtains, promising another warm summer's day, and for some reason, Alice felt a ray of hope. They must all move forward as best they could.

I'll go down and talk to Andrew again, she thought, and if he still feels the same as he did last night, then I'll agree too; I won't stand in her way.

Knowing he was probably awake already, Alice got out of bed and, crossing to the window, threw back the curtains. Below her, in the early morning sunshine, Cockspur Lane was beginning to wake up. A young lad riding a bicycle rattled his way over the cobbles, laughing out loud as he bounced and jounced in the saddle without slowing and, skidding round the corner, disappeared.

A young lad so full of life and hope, thought Alice. And our Mabel should be the same, laughing as she looks forward to the day ahead.

She realised now that, while Mabel had been in service, it was unlikely she had ever woken up and looked forward to what the new day would bring. That was something Mr Clarke's offer might put right.

Alice put on her dressing gown and padded down the stairs to Andrew's room. As she had guessed, she didn't have to wake him, he was wide awake already and greeted her with a smile.

'Good morning, dearest,' he said. 'Did you sleep?'

Alice crossed over and perched on the end of his bed. 'Yes,' she replied. 'Did you?'

'After a while,' he admitted. 'I did a lot of thinking before I fell asleep.'

'I seem to have done my thinking while I *was* asleep,' Alice told him. 'And I woke up with my mind made up.'

'And your decision?'

'It's an unusual job for a girl like Mabel,' Alice said, 'but I think we should put it to Mabel herself, and if she wants to accept Mr Clarke's offer, we should let her.' She reached over and took Andrew's hand. 'But you're her father, so only if you agree with me.'

Andrew returned the squeeze of her hand and said, 'I completely agree.'

'Should we suggest a trial period, do you think?' wondered Alice. 'So that if it doesn't work out as we hope, she can give it up?'

'Only between ourselves. We mustn't let her think we doubt her... or him.' Andrew gave her a brave smile, the one he managed when he felt particularly helpless. 'Is Mrs Finch coming this morning?'

'Yes, she'll be here once you've had your breakfast,' replied Alice.

'Then why don't you give Mabel a call and we can put the idea to her now, before Mrs Finch arrives?'

'I'll put the kettle on,' said Alice getting to her feet. 'And when the tea's made, I'll give her a call.' But surprisingly, Mabel had beaten her to it and appeared in the kitchen ready to go out. Alice gave her a few minutes to settle with her father and then, picking up her own cup, went in to join them.

'You're up early,' she heard Andrew saying as she pushed open the door.

'Of course,' Mabel replied. 'I've got to go and look for work and the sooner I start the better.'

'Well, sit and drink your tea first,' said Andrew. 'Your mother and I have something to say to you.'

Mabel turned and saw her mother coming into the room.

'I'm not going back into service,' Mabel said, determined to get in first. 'You can't make me.'

'My dearest girl,' her father answered evenly, 'we have no intention of making you do anything. Will you just listen for a moment or two?'

Mabel gave a reluctant nod, but it was clear she didn't want to hear what they had to say.

'I had a drink with Mr Clarke last night,' began Andrew.

'I know. I was here when he came, remember?'

'Mabel!' her mother reproved. 'Please don't speak to your father like that.'

Mabel looked chastened. 'Sorry, Dada,' she murmured. 'Go on.'

'Well, Mr Clarke has come up with an idea we think might appeal to you. Do you want to hear it?'

Now her father had caught Mabel's attention. 'Yes, please, Dada, I really do.'

'He wondered if you'd like to work for him… with him, in his print workshop.'

For a moment Mabel couldn't believe what she was hearing. Work with Mr Clarke!

She stared at her parents incredulously.

'You really mean it?' she whispered. 'You mean I can go to the print workshop every day and learn to be a printer, like Mr Clarke?'

'You'll start as an assistant, running errands, taking messages, clearing the workshop at the end of the day,' said her mother.

'You mustn't expect too much to begin with,' put in her father. 'Once we see how things go, we can look further into the future. What do you say, Mabel?'

A stupid question, he thought, even as he uttered the words, for he already knew the answer.

'Oh, Dada, Mam, can I? Can I really go and work for Mr Clarke?' A sudden thought struck her. 'Will he pay me? I need to be earning money.'

'He says he will,' replied her father. 'When you've had your breakfast, why don't you ask him here, so we can sort out the details?'

'Oh, Dada, I don't need breakfast,' cried Mabel. 'I'll go now!'

'Steady on now, Mabel,' warned Alice. 'It's very early and the poor man probably hasn't had his breakfast yet.'

'Give Mrs Finch a chance to help me get ready for the day,' said her father, 'and then you can take a message to him. All right?'

'Oh yes!' cried Mabel, her eyes bright with happiness. 'Oh yes!'

Once Mrs Finch had been, Mabel ran all the way to Mr Clarke's workshop, only pausing to catch her breath when she reached the newsagent's kiosk on the pavement. For a moment she stood looking along the alley and wondering. She could see Mr Clarke's door was standing open, so he was already there at work. Dada had said Mr Clarke had made his suggestion last night in the pub, but Dada hadn't said yes straight away. Suppose Mr Clarke had changed his mind overnight! It was too awful to contemplate. Slowly she walked to his door and peeped in.

'Aha,' came a voice from inside, 'here's my assistant at last!' And as Mabel stood poised on the threshold, her new employer had the pleasure of seeing delight suffuse her face at his words.

34

It was on a beautiful morning several days later that Sir Keir McFarlane, seated at the breakfast table in Haverford Court, picked up the ironed and folded copy of *The Times* which lay beside his breakfast plate. Ignoring the personal columns on the front page, he shook the paper open and turned his attention to the news on the inside pages. What he read there brought him up short. He glanced across the breakfast table to where his son was calmly buttering a piece of toast. Iain's friend, Alfred Everette, had not yet put in an appearance, and nor had Lucinda, and Sir Keir knew he must speak to Iain privately before they did.

He got up from the table and said, 'I'd like to see you in the library, Iain, as soon as you've finished your breakfast. There's a matter I must discuss with you.' And with that he left the room, his scrambled eggs untouched, his coffee left to grow cold.

Surprised at this summons, Iain hurriedly finished his toast, and forgoing another cup of coffee, followed his father out of the room, almost bumping into Alfred Everette as he pushed through the dining room door.

'Have you finished your breakfast already?' Alfred asked.

'Yes, just got to have a word with the gov'nor. I'll be back for another cup of coffee in a while.'

Alfred nodded and went to the sideboard to help himself to a generous helping of scrambled eggs and bacon from the chafing dishes. It suited him very well. Lady McFarlane often took her breakfast on a tray in her room, and with Iain and Sir Keir already absent from the table, it meant that when Lucinda came down for her breakfast, he would have her to himself. The thought delighted him.

Leaving Alfred to his daydreams, Iain crossed to the library and went in to his father. Sir Keir was seated behind his desk with the newspaper spread out in front of him.

'You wanted me, sir?'

'Yes, Iain. Come and read this,' replied Sir Keir and pointed to a short article with the headline *Everette Enterprises Investigation*.

Iain skimmed through it and then reread it again more thoroughly, before looking up enquiringly.

'The Peter Everette mentioned in connection with this apparent fraud, is that Mr Alfred Everette's father?'

'Yes, Gov'nor, I believe it is.'

'Then that young man must leave this house at once. We must have no connection with him.'

'That sounds a little harsh, sir,' protested Iain. 'I mean, it's nothing to do with him.'

'We have no idea if it's to do with him or not,' returned his father, 'but should the case come to court, it might come up before me and there must be absolutely no question of bias. You must see that.'

'Yes, I suppose,' Iain said slowly. 'Do you want me to tell him he has to leave?'

'No, my boy, I'll do that. However, I need to speak to your mother first, so carry on as normal until we decide exactly what we are going to do and say, and then leave it to me.'

As promised, Iain returned to the dining room for his second cup of coffee and was greeted with a look of resentment from Alfred and an expression of welcome release from Lucinda.

'What are our plans for today?' Alfred demanded as Iain poured himself his coffee. 'I was just asking your beautiful sister if she would care to join me for a drive and a picnic... you too, of course,' he added as a hasty afterthought.

'Unfortunately,' Lucinda cut in before her brother could reply, 'I have a fittings appointment with my dressmaker today. I need so many new things before the winter, and as she's coming down from London especially to discuss everything with Mama, I can't possibly cancel.'

'Well,' Iain said, turning to Alfred, 'I did think as it's such a beautiful morning that we might go for a cycle ride. It won't be long before we're back in London where cycling in the traffic is awful.'

'It sounds very energetic to me,' grumbled Alfred.

'Well, you two must decide between you,' said Lucinda, setting aside her napkin and getting up from the table. 'I promised Mama I'd go and see her as soon as I'd had my breakfast.'

She found both her parents in her mother's bedroom, her mother still sitting up in bed with a bed-table across her knees holding the remains of her breakfast, and her father standing by the window staring out into the garden.

As Lucinda opened the door there was a sudden silence, as if she had interrupted a private conversation.

She paused in the doorway and then stepped into the room and said, 'Good morning, Papa, Mama.'

'Good morning, Lucy,' answered her mother. Turning back to her husband, she said, 'Well, I'll leave it up to you, but you must come up with something to allow him to leave with some dignity.'

'Of course, my dear,' agreed Sir Keir, and with that he left the room.

'Who's leaving?' asked Lucinda, sitting down on the end of her mother's bed.

'Alfred,' replied Lady McFarlane. 'Family problems. He must return to London straight away.' A look of profound relief crossed Lucinda's face, and her mother knew it was reflected in her own expression. She had been well aware that Alfred's attentions to Lucinda had become too marked to be ignored for much longer, and considered him an entirely unsuitable match for her daughter.

Pushing such thoughts aside for the moment, she said, 'Now, I must get up. Ring for Chalmers, will you, Lucy? Croxton will be meeting Madame Chantal off the half past ten train, and we must be ready when she gets here.'

Downstairs in the library, Sir Keir decided exactly what he was going to say and then asked Felstead to find Mr Everette and invite him to join Sir Keir in the library.

Alfred was happy enough to comply, thinking it might even be the chance to ask the judge for permission to address his daughter, but by the time he left the library fifteen minutes later, he was filled with mortification and rage. How dare Sir Keir speak to him as he had? Instructing him to leave the house almost as if he were dismissing a servant! He was to depart that very afternoon, with some story of there being a phone call from his family summoning him back to London.

'It's hardly my fault,' he protested angrily to Iain. '*I* haven't been buying inside information.'

'No,' agreed Iain, 'but it could be awkward for my father if yours happened to come up before him and you were residing in his house. You must see it from his point of view.'

Alfred, who never considered any point of view other than his own, scowled and said, 'What *I* see is the sins of the father being visited on the son.'

That had made Iain give a shout of laughter. 'Never thought I'd hear you quoting the Bible, old chap,' he said, before adding, 'And think, you'll be able to get back to the bright lights of town, while I'm still in exile here for casting my eyes on one of the maids.'

Alfred left the same afternoon. So that there was no chance of him missing his train, the dog cart was brought to take him to the station. For a moment, Alfred stared at it in mortification... only the dog cart, not even the car!

As, red-faced, he stepped up into it, he said, 'Well, Mac, old chap, I'll see you when you're back in town. I imagine this scandal about the pater will all have blown over by then. Drop me a line when you get back and we'll have a night on the town.'

'Yes, of course,' Iain agreed, knowing even as he spoke that they would not. He watched the trap disappear round the corner and heaved a sigh of relief. Unadulterated Alfred Everette, behaving as if he owned the house rather than living as an invited guest, had proved to be extremely tiring.

'I can't see what you ever saw in him,' Lucinda remarked as they sat companionably in the peace of the rose garden that evening, admiring the sunset and enjoying a glass of wine. 'He's a toad and I'm glad he's gone. I don't have to make sure I'm not left alone with him any more.'

For a moment Iain looked at her in horror and said, 'He didn't lay a hand on you, did he, Luce?'

'No, of course not,' scoffed Lucinda. 'I'd have walloped him one if he had.'

Looking at his sister's indignant face Iain could well believe it and said with a grin, 'I bet you would have, too.'

'I think poor Lizzie will be pleased he's gone as well.'

'Lizzie?'

'I sometimes wonder about you, brother dear,' said Lucinda. 'Do you walk about with your eyes and ears closed? All the staff loathe him. They call him Carrot-top, you know.'

That made Iain laugh. 'Really? Well, I suppose it suits him.'

'And as for the parents,' Lucinda continued, 'I think Daddy was very pleased to find a reason to ask him to go, and Mama certainly was. Everyone's delighted that he's gone.'

What she said was true; with the departure of Alfred Everette the house settled to its normal, peaceful, summer routine, and Iain began to see his erstwhile friend for what he really was: a loud-mouthed braggart, happy to dominate any conversation and to think that his father's money gave him immediate entry to any society in which he found himself. John Sheridan, had he met him, would have recognised him at once as the true son of his father.

As the Alfred Everette-free days followed, Iain became more and more relieved that the gov'nor had decreed that his friend must leave and not return.

35

The McFarlane household moved back to Chanynge Place during the second week in September. For the first time, William was pleased to be back in London. Normally he was happier in the country, where the daily routine was more relaxed and the workload less pressured. Mrs Scott was far easier to work with than the Killer-bee and even Mr Felstead seemed to unbend a little in the fresh air of the Suffolk countryside. However, now they were back, William was looking forward to his next half day. He had decided that he would go and see Mabel, a surprise visit. He had grown fond of her while she was at Chanynge Place, gently teasing her and enjoying making her smile, but it wasn't until she had left that he realised quite how much he would miss her.

Now he was back in the normal London routine he noticed her absence even more than he had in the country. She had refused to tell him where she lived, but William hoped her cousin Lizzie might be persuaded to do so. One evening, as they lingered over a cup of tea before they turned in for the night, William brought Mabel's name into the conversation, wondering how she was doing now she wasn't in service any more.

'Mabel? Oh, she'll be all right. Falls on her feet, that one does,' responded Lizzie. 'I'm off on Saturday and I'll probably see her while I'm home. Find out what she's up to an' that.'

'Live near you, does she?' suggested William lightly.

'Yes, not far. My mum and her dad are brother and sister, an' we all live quite close.'

William decided to take the plunge. 'Where's that then?' he asked with studied indifference. 'Will you tell me exactly where she lives? Her address?'

Lizzie gurgled a laugh. 'Mabel's address? Why d'you want that?' She gave him an arch look. 'Are you going calling, William?'

'I might,' William replied with a shrug. 'Just to see how she is.'

'Well, if I do see her, I'll tell her you was asking, shall I?' Lizzie said with a quizzical smile.

'No, don't,' William said quickly. 'I want to surprise her.'

'Hmm.' Lizzie nodded. 'Like that, is it?'

'It isn't like anything,' replied William hotly. 'I just thought it would be kind to go and see how she is!'

'Oh, kind,' laughed Lizzie. 'Of course! Well, if that's all it is, kindness, I can tell you how she is when I get back.' Seeing his face redden, she relented and said, 'They live at 31 Cockspur Lane. It's a little street not that far from Liverpool Street station. The Cockerel pub is on the corner. And,' she added in a half-whisper, 'I'll keep your secret for you.'

'I haven't got a secret,' snapped William, annoyed that her teasing had made him reveal more than he had intended, but at least he'd got what he wanted – Mabel's address.

When the day came, he left Chanynge Place as soon as luncheon had been served in the dining room. Lizzie came back down to the servants' hall and saw him leaving. He was dressed in dark blue trousers and a jacket, a white shirt with a tie, and though he was clearly wearing his Sunday best, Lizzie couldn't help thinking he seemed somehow diminished without his usual footman's uniform, smart and close-fitting.

'Enjoy your day,' Lizzie said to his departing back, but if he heard her, he showed no sign, simply walked out through the scullery door and disappeared.

William had in fact heard Lizzie, but he wasn't prepared to stop to answer. After her Saturday at home, Lizzie had told him Mabel was still living at home with her parents, helping her mother with the care of her injured father.

'I didn't see her myself,' Lizzie told him, 'but my mum says she has got a sort of job somewhere, though we aren't sure what it is. Said Mabel's parents were being a bit cagey about it.'

Well, thought William, as he took his place on a tram, clanging its way through the crowded streets towards the city, I shall soon find out.

He took two more buses and several wrong turns before he found the Cockerel, but at last he saw it, built astride a corner, its painted sign swinging in the breeze, and there, opposite, was the end of Cockspur Lane. He paused, looking at the brick houses, not dissimilar to the one in which he had been brought up by his widowed grandmother, while his parents worked in service to provide for them. It was the sort of street where he had played football with his school friends – that was, until he was ten, when he got a Saturday job as the boots boy in the house of Dr Dean, a Harley Street physician. He had been well taught by Dr Dean's butler, and had learned what service was required of a manservant in a smart household. At twenty-one, he had been offered the job of footman in the McFarlane establishment, and grabbing it with both hands, had moved into the Mayfair house. Yet now, as he walked along Cockspur Lane, the narrow cobbled street seemed as familiar and welcoming as the street where his gran still lived.

It's a place I could easily belong, he thought, if I wasn't employed by the quality in Chanynge Place.

He paused outside the gate of number 31, summoning up his courage to open it and knock on the front door. He almost turned away, but as he was about to go back the way he'd come, the front door opened and Mabel herself appeared in the front yard.

'William!' she cried. 'I *thought* it was you. I saw you from the window. What on earth are you doing here, standing about in the lane?'

William could feel the colour rising in his cheeks, but he managed to say, 'I was coming to see you, Mabel. But I weren't sure this was the right house.'

'Well, it is,' she replied cheerfully. 'You'd better come in, hadn't you?'

Obediently, William opened the little gate, stepping into the yard and then following Mabel indoors. As she went inside she called, 'Mam, we've got a visitor.'

'Who is it?'

'It's William, you know, the footman from McFarlanes'. I told you about him.'

Alice appeared from the kitchen, wiping her hands on her apron.

'Well, you'd better bring him in. I'm about to put the kettle on.' And then turning to look at William properly and liking what she saw, she added, 'I hope you won't mind the kitchen, Mr William.'

'Certainly not,' asserted William. 'It's where I spend much of my working life.'

'Then come you in, young man, and take a seat by the fire.'

And thus William was introduced to the Oakley family. He knew Mabel's father had lost the use of his legs, but William, seeing him sitting at the table, appeared unaware of the fact, and Mabel felt a surge of gratitude; all too many of their friends either became embarrassed and tongue-tied or loudly loquacious to cover their embarrassment. William did neither, he simply leaned forward, offered his hand, and said, 'Good afternoon, sir.'

As they sat and drank tea and ate Alice Oakley's scones, warm from the oven, William heard how Mabel was now working as an assistant to a printer.

'That's a funny job for a girl,' he said, unwary.

'What do you mean?' Mabel was immediately defensive.

Startled by her reaction, William said, 'Only that not many girls would be happy working for a printer. I mean, where does it lead you?'

'It brings me a wage,' answered Mabel tightly. 'And so far, I've been learning to set type.'

'And sweep the workshop,' added her father with a grin. 'That's women's work.'

For a moment William thought Mabel was going to explode, but suddenly she broke into laughter, and to William it was as if the sun had burst from behind a cloud.

During the afternoon, both Eddie and Stephen had looked in.

Hearing that Stephen was working in a jeweller's shop, William said, 'Is there any way we can hear if someone is trying to sell the watch?'

Stephen shook his head. 'Snowflake's hope in hell.'

'Stephen!' cried his mother in dismay. 'Mind your language! What will Mr William think of you?'

Entirely unabashed, Stephen laughed and said, 'Only repeating what Mr Solomon said when I told him about it. But,' he went on, 'he did say he'd put the word about, cos if the thief had any brains at all, he wouldn't be trying to sell it in the West End.'

'Let's face it,' added Eddie, 'that watch is long gone. We have to forget the whole thing and get on with our lives. The only thing all of us know for sure is that Mabel didn't steal it.'

'That's all right,' ventured William, 'unless she's trying to get another job.'

'Well, I'm not,' said Mabel sharply. 'I've got a perfectly good job, and even if I hadn't, nothing would make me go into service again!'

'So you've said before,' interposed her father quietly. 'No need to jump down our throats!'

By the time William had to depart, he was sorry to have to leave the comfort of the Oakleys' home. He'd had no chance to speak to Mabel alone, but he'd been made welcome by the entire family. As he was saying goodbye, Mrs Oakley had said, 'Don't be a stranger, Mr William. Come and visit us again, if you've a mind to.'

Mr Oakley had shaken his hand and Eddie, who had disappeared upstairs, came down to say goodbye. Stephen said, 'I'm going your way, I'll walk with you.' And then waited out on the pavement as Mabel showed William to the door.

'It was lovely to see you, William,' she said. 'But please don't tell anyone else at Chanynge Place that you have, will you?'

'No, I won't,' agreed William readily enough. He didn't want the two parts of his life to cross over. Cockspur Lane must be kept secret. 'Of course Lizzie knows, that's how I found you,' he added.

'Guessed it was,' Mabel said. 'Well, you tell Lizzie from me, she's to keep quiet!'

'I will,' promised William. Awkwardly, he held out his hand, and as Mabel gave it a brief shake, she said, 'But come again... if you want to.'

'Yes,' said William, 'I will.'

As he and Stephen walked back to the bus stop, Stephen said, 'Mr Solomon has already passed the word about the missing watch. Didn't want to say much, in case it builds up their hopes, but the word has gone out that it's stolen. Probably come to nothing, cos there's hundreds of jewellers in London, but you never know.'

They parted outside Solomon's shop, where Stephen let himself in with a key and William walked on briskly to catch his bus. He'd never had a family as such, being the only child of middle-aged parents and the only grandchild of a doting old lady. The warmth of the family kitchen had enclosed him and as he walked away down the road, though it was a temperate September evening, he felt the chill of exclusion. He had been made welcome, but as a guest; hardly surprising, but as he left the house, William found he wanted more.

36

For Enid Chalmers, the return to Chanynge Place was a great relief. She always found the sojourn at Haverford Court particularly boring. She considered the family's social life at Haverford extremely countrified; dinner with the rector, Reverend Paul Medway, and his wife, Elfrida; or lunch at The Manor, a far less imposing residence than Haverford Court, with squire Jonas Hale, a rotund bachelor in his mid-fifties, a man of neither class nor distinction.

The time it took Chalmers to oversee the care of Lady McFarlane's clothes was minimal. Apart from her ladyship's fine underwear, which Chalmers laundered herself, all she had to do was ensure that each garment hung mended, clean, pressed and ready to wear whatever the occasion demanded. Despite the extent of her country wardrobe, Chalmers considered her mistress's choice of clothes embarrassingly plebeian. She couldn't wait to return to London where her ladyship wouldn't feel the need to 'dress down for the country'.

'Only two more weeks of relaxing here in Suffolk,' Lady McFarlane said one morning while Chalmers dressed her hair. 'You must make the most of your leisure time here at Haverford, life is going to be busy when we return to town. I shall be hiring a maid for Miss Lucinda, of course, ready for her come-out in April, but until I find someone suitable, you'll be looking after both of us.' Lady McFarlane sighed and added, 'How I wish that stupid Oakley girl had not given in to temptation. I'm not usually so mistaken in a person's character, and I'm certain she would have made an admirable lady's maid, once you'd taken her in hand.'

'Certainly, madam,' Chalmers had replied, touching the bun at the nape of her neck to ensure it was still securely in place. 'But I am sure you'll be able to find another suitable woman; someone older perhaps? With more experience? And of course, in the meantime I shall be perfectly able to take care of both you and Miss Lucinda as we prepare for her first season.'

They were all back in London now, and the missing watch was a thing of the past. As October slid into November, Chalmers decided that it might be safe to attempt its sale. She was well aware that she would get nothing like its actual value, but even so, she was certain some unscrupulous jeweller would be happy to pay a reasonable amount without asking too many awkward questions about its provenance, knowing he could sell it on for a sizeable profit. There was no point in visiting any of the prominent jewellers in the West End. Everyone in the house knew Sir Keir had made sure they were alerted at the time of the theft. He had offered a reward for information leading to the discovery of the watch and they might still be on the lookout.

Still, she thought, there'll be jewellers in the East End

who know nothing about it. I could go there on my next afternoon off and see what they might give me.

Carefully she considered her options: should she pawn it, or try to sell it outright? She might get more with a sale, but if she borrowed a sufficient amount against it, she could simply disappear with the cash. A false name and address, and there would be no way it could be traced back to her. Eventually it would be unclaimed and the jeweller would be entitled to sell it, almost certainly for more than he had lent her. Unlikely, she thought, that the jeweller himself would inform the police of the watch's unexpected appearance; surely he'd be far more likely to remain silent and take his profit. Chalmers decided the risk to her would be minimal.

She just had to come up with a plausible story for having the watch in the first place. She turned over various stories in her mind: a legacy from an aged aunt? No, she knew she did not look like someone with a wealthy aunt. A gift from a grateful employer on her retirement? A possibility, but unlikely with a piece of such obvious value. And then she came up with an idea that she thought might work. She went to sleep thinking about it and by the time she woke the next morning, her brain had refined it so that it seemed a decidedly workable plan.

As soon as she had been released for her free afternoon, Chalmers went up to her bedroom and took down her hair. There was the watch, sparkling on its brooch in the shaft of sunlight that pierced the small window; her future nest egg. She smiled at the sight of it, before wrapping it in a handkerchief and stowing it in an inner pocket in her bag. Quickly she changed out of her black dress, into a grey skirt, with a white blouse and dark blue jacket. She piled her hair onto the top of her head, securing it firmly with several pins before tucking it up into her hat, and then surveyed herself in the mirror. She looked ordinary, unexceptional, like any other lady's maid on her free afternoon. Satisfied, she strolled down to the servants' hall where nobody gave her a second glance, and out through the yard into the street.

Her relief at reaching the anonymity of the busy West End made her realise how tense she had been as she'd made her way through the house with the watch in her bag. Suppose someone had stopped her? Suppose they'd had reason to search her before she left?

'Don't be so stupid,' she muttered as she hurried along to the bus stop. 'What possible reason could they have to suspect me of anything?'

She was right, there was no reason to suspect her, but as she rounded the corner, she saw a man standing talking to a young boy and realised with a stab of panic that it was Iain McFarlane. Swiftly, she turned in through the nearest gateway and approached the front door, as if she were about to ring the doorbell. Had she been quick enough? she wondered. Had Mr Iain seen her? She fought the urge to look back into the street for what seemed an age, but realising she couldn't stand at an unknown front door any longer, she risked a quick glance along Chanynge Place. Neither Iain McFarlane nor the boy were anywhere to be seen. They must be long gone. With a huge sigh of relief, Chalmers stepped out onto the pavement and after a moment's pause, continued towards the bus stop. As she boarded the bus she looked along the street again, but there was still no sign of Iain McFarlane and her pounding heart began to slow.

Stupid! She admonished herself as the bus continued to carry her away from Chanynge Place towards the city. Why had she felt the need to hide? What if Mr Iain had seen her? It was her afternoon off and she was perfectly entitled to be out. Why would it have mattered if Mr Iain had seen her?

It was exactly the question Iain McFarlane was asking himself as, concealed in a doorway himself, he waited for her to re-emerge on to the street. When she did, she paused for a moment to look around, before stepping out onto the pavement.

Furtive! The word came unbidden into Iain's mind. Chalmers looked extremely furtive. Why would she take cover the way she had? Where was she going? To meet a man? Iain almost laughed out loud at the thought of the stiff, supercilious Miss Chalmers off for an assignation with an unknown admirer. Good grief, Iain thought, as he watched her scurry away to catch the oncoming bus, she's fifty if she's a day! The bloke she's meeting must be desperate to want someone like her. And yet, Iain had to admit, there had been an occasion, when he was about fourteen, when he had seen the kitchen-maid carrying water up to Chalmers' bedroom to fill the hipbath. His adolescent mind tried to imagine her getting into the bath, wondering how she could fold her angular body into such a small space. Her knees would have to stick up out of the water and her bosoms float on the top. At the time Iain had never seen anyone's bosoms, but conjuring up what they *might* look like, he had found that his own body was somehow aroused in a peculiar way. Now, nearly seven years on, when he knew far more than he ought about such things, the whole idea of Chalmers' bosoms made him hoot with laughter; the bloke, whoever he was, was welcome to them.

But why was she trying to hide from him? Would his mother dismiss her if she realised that her maid was carrying on a clandestine affair on her afternoon off? He doubted it, but it was a useful snippet of information to have; information, he had found, was a form of power and could be used in more than one way.

Chalmers had no particular direction in mind when she got off the bus near Liverpool Street. The crowded streets were a jumble of houses, offices and shops. She walked slowly along one of the narrow streets, looking out for the three golden balls, the sign of a pawnbroker. At the end of one twisted lane she spotted what she had been looking for and approached the shop. Three golden balls suspended from a wrought-iron spike jutted out from the wall. Above the door was the name, Jacob Levy, Jeweller and Pawnbroker.

Perfect! A Jewish jeweller! Everyone knew the Jews were grasping people, always trying to make their money on the backs of the poor. Surely, Chalmers thought, as she peered in through the dusty window at the goods on display, the Jew who ran this shop would see the value of the watch brooch and want to buy it. She would say it was not for sale and come up with her prepared story, insisting she just needed a short term loan and she would be back to claim it within the month.

He'll offer a pittance, compared with its real worth, she reasoned, but it will be enough for me, and what he does with the watch after that is no concern of mine.

Pulling her hat down to shade her face, she opened the shop door and went in. Jacob Levy was just as she had imagined he would be, a small man with a straggly beard, wearing a black skullcap and sitting behind his counter, rather like a spider in its web.

He peered at her through rimless spectacles and said, 'Good afternoon, madam. How may I help you?'

Chalmers drew a deep breath and began her prepared story.

'I've brought something to pawn,' she said. 'Not for myself, but for my mistress, Lady Rafferty. Just a short term loan to pay off her gambling debts.' She reached into her bag, unwrapped the watch and laid it on the counter.

Jacob Levy did not pick it up, but looking down at it, said neutrally, 'I see. This is a very valuable piece.'

'I know, but her ladyship is desperate for some ready money as she does not want her husband to know the extent of her debts.'

'Who did you say this lady was?'

For a split second Chalmers faltered before saying, 'Lady Rafferty. She and her husband are visiting London from Ireland. They are staying at Brown's Hotel, but they return to Dublin at the end of the month, so she needs the money now.'

Chalmers had done her homework by reading the court and social columns in *The Times* over the last few days, and had learned all she could about Lord and Lady Rafferty and their movements.

When Jacob Levy made no comment and the silence lengthened, Chalmers felt obliged to explain further.

'Her ladyship just needs some cash to pay off her debts,

until she is in the funds again. It is a precious piece and without doubt I will be back to redeem it for her within the week.'

'I see.' Jacob Levy still did not pick up the watch. 'And how much did her ladyship have in mind?'

Chalmers had been ready for that question and she said, 'She needs at least five hundred pounds.'

'Does she indeed? Well, I can assure you I don't keep that sort of money in the shop. If I was to lend you that much, you'd have to wait until tomorrow.'

This was a problem Chalmers had not anticipated. 'But she needs the money today,' she said, her mind racing. She might not be free to come back tomorrow. Perhaps she should try somewhere else.

At that moment the door opened and a lad came in.

'Ah, Leon,' said Jacob, slipping a cloth over the watch still lying on the counter, 'go through to the back and wait there, I've got another errand for you.'

The boy nodded and disappeared behind a curtain.

Jacob removed the cloth and took up the watch. For the first time he screwed in his eyeglass and began a detailed inspection of the stones and their setting. For several minutes there was no sound to break the silence except for the steady tick of an ornate bracket clock on a shelf behind the counter. Staring at it, Chalmers wondered if it was pawned, or if it was for sale and if so, how much it was worth.

Her attention jerked back to Jacob Levy when he said, 'Now, madam, I'm prepared to lend your mistress £450 against this piece.' He cocked his head and looked at her quizzically. 'If that suits you,' he paused, 'and her... then come back first thing tomorrow morning and I'll have the money you need.'

'Only £450?' cried Chalmers. 'That's too little and probably too late.'

'Then she'll have to raise the rest of the money from someone else,' replied the jeweller firmly. 'Take it or leave it.'

For a moment Chalmers hesitated. Was the old man going to check up on her story? Well, even if he did, he might discover that Lord and Lady Rafferty were indeed staying at Brown's, but nothing more. The discreet hotel staff would not divulge anything about one of their guests. It was extremely unlikely that Mr Levy would actually ask to speak to either of them, particularly as there was the question of Lady Rafferty's gambling debts.

'I'll take it,' Chalmers said. It wasn't as much as she had hoped for, but even so, it was a lump sum worth having.

The jeweller pushed the watch back across the counter and Chalmers picked it up, stowing it in her jacket pocket.

He said, 'I'll see you tomorrow morning, unless of course you, or her ladyship, have changed your minds.' He turned to the curtained door behind him and, as Chalmers paused to take note of his address, to ensure she could find her way back through the myriad of streets next day, he was already calling for the boy, Leon.

The narrow street outside was busy with people in and out of the small shops that lined its pavement, and as Chalmers stepped out into the busyness of Brock Street, she paid no attention to the man and boy who were standing, half hidden, in the doorway of the White Horse Inn, opposite. Entirely unaware of their interest, Chalmers set off down

the street, her bag slung over her shoulder. At a nod from
the man, the boy turned and vanished down a nearby alley.

Chalmers had never been to this part of the city before
and as she made her way along the narrow streets, looking
at the strange variety of shops and market stalls, she noticed
several other jewellers displaying the three golden balls of
their trade. She wondered with a pang if she might have
got a better deal from one of these. Perhaps she should try
another before she returned home. Pausing outside one
of them she saw, reflected in the glass, two young men on
the opposite side of the road, eyeing the bag she carried.
Clutching it more tightly, she turned away. She was, she
realised, out of place and conspicuous in this rundown area
of the city and knew it was time she went back to the West
End. As she turned towards the station where she could
catch a bus, she was nearly knocked flying by a boy hurtling
round the corner. She staggered and might have fallen if
another pedestrian had not caught hold of her.

'My dear madam,' he cried, as he held her for a moment
to steady her. 'Are you all right? That scoundrel didn't get
your bag, did he? No, no, I see you have it safe.'

Embarrassed by the whole incident, Chalmers jerked her
arm free of his hand and said, 'Thank you, sir, but as you
see I am quite all right. Good afternoon.' If this stranger
thought she was going to give him something for coming to
her aid, he was quite wrong.

'So I see,' the man replied with a twisted smile. 'Well,
good afternoon.' And he walked away, disappearing down a
side street, leaving her standing there, feeling a little foolish.
Of the boy who had cannoned into her, there was no sign.

Well, she thought, as she set off towards the station once

more, her rescuer was quite right, at least the wretched boy hadn't succeeded in snatching her bag, but the incident had shaken her and suddenly she couldn't wait to leave this insalubrious area and get home.

It was with some relief that an hour later she got off the bus and walked back along the familiar safety of Chanynge Place to number eleven.

All she had to do now, Chalmers thought as she entered through the door in the yard, was find a reason to be out again in the morning, and she could collect her £450, the cushion for her old age.

Her shadow, who had followed her all the way back, noted which house she entered and returned, unobserved, to report to his master.

37

As soon as Chalmers disappeared from view, Jacob Levy had told Leon what he wanted him to do and the lad had set off immediately. Once he was alone in the shop, Jacob took a piece of paper and wrote down exactly what he had observed when studying the piece of jewellery the woman had brought in. He'd recognised it at once. The watch had been stolen several months ago, and news of the theft had travelled its way round the smart jewellers' shops in the West End and, to a lesser extent, among several of the smaller ones across the city. The word in the East End jewellery trade was more specific; if anyone was offered a gold fob watch, with or without its diamond brooch, for sale, they were asked to contact Joseph Solomon of Dundas Alley, off Cuck Lane, at once.

For the first time in years Jacob shut his shop early and set off to walk the mile or so to Cuck Lane. As he walked through the late afternoon streets, he wondered why he was actually going. What did it matter to him if the woman was hawking stolen property about? He was not a fence, well, not often anyway. He'd been offered stolen jewellery before and occasionally he bought it and sold it on, but this was different. It would be very difficult to sell such a distinctive item without breaking it up, but that wasn't the only reason he was on his way to see Joseph Solomon. Joseph was family, his mother's cousin. And if it was a family matter, then they would stand together.

When he reached Cuck Lane and turned into Dundas Alley, it was getting on for five o'clock. When Joseph saw who had come in, he greeted his cousin with surprise and pleasure, saying, 'Jacob! To what do I owe this honour? Will you come upstairs and take a cup of tea with Miriam… or something stronger?'

'A cup of tea,' agreed Jacob. 'But before we go up to see your dear wife, I have some news for you.'

'Then let me close the shop and you can tell me.' Joseph locked the front door and turned the sign to closed. 'Come through to the back and we can talk there in peace.' He led the way into the tiny office beyond an inner door and waved his cousin to a chair.

'What news then, Jacob?'

'I think I've been offered that fob watch on the diamond brooch you've been looking for.'

'You have!' exclaimed Joseph. 'When? Who by?'

'Woman who came in off the street this afternoon. Scrawny-looking piece. Sharp-faced. In her fifties. Says she's a lady's maid.'

'And she offered you a gold fob watch? Are you sure it's the one that was stolen?'

'Not absolutely as I've never seen it, but it sounds like the one you were asking about a couple of months ago. Gold case; face set with emerald snips to mark the hours, and depending from a bar brooch, set with some very fine diamonds.' He passed Joseph the piece of paper on which he had written the description.

'Certainly sounds like it,' agreed Joseph as he scanned the paper. 'Did you buy it? Have you got it?'

'Wasn't for sale,' Jacob replied. 'She said it belonged to her mistress, a Lady Rafferty, who simply wanted to pawn it for a month. Gambling debts. Wanted £500.'

'Did she indeed? Sounds unlikely. What did you say?'

'Told her I didn't keep that sort of money in the shop, and the most I could lend against it was £450.'

'And what did she say then?'

'She said that wasn't enough, so I said then she'd have to go somewhere else for the rest, because, take it or leave it, £450 was my last and only offer.'

'Don't tell me she decided against and went somewhere else,' groaned Joseph.

'No, no. She wanted the money, well, some money anyway. I told her she'd have to come back again tomorrow morning and I'd have the money ready for her then.'

'So she'll be coming back again tomorrow, bringing the watch with her?'

'She was disappointed by the amount,' replied Jacob, 'but I think she'll come. I don't think Lady Rafferty, if there even is such a person, knows anything about the watch and the loan she's trying to make.'

'So,' began Joseph thoughtfully, 'we need to organise a welcome party... but supposing she doesn't show up?'

'I thought she might try her luck with someone else,' said Jacob, 'so I've set my lad, Leon, to follow her. Discover where she lives, so we always know where to find her.'

'And hope she doesn't sell it elsewhere in the meantime,' sighed Joseph.

'I don't think she's going to sell it at all,' Jacob said. 'I think she'll leave it, pawned, just never come back to claim it. That way she gets a lump sum, but she can never be traced.'

'Far less than if she sold it.'

'Yes,' agreed Jacob, 'but a large sum to her, even so.'

At that moment the back door opened and Stephen Oakley came from the alley. He stopped abruptly when he saw that Joseph had company and began to apologise, but Joseph cut him short.

'Ah! Stephen!' he cried. 'Jacob, this is Stephen, my apprentice. Stephen, this is my cousin, Jacob Levy. He's in the same business, and he thinks he's found the watch.'

Stephen swung round. 'Where? Where did you find it?'

'It was brought into my shop this afternoon to be pawned.'

'Who brought it?' demanded Stephen. 'Who had it?'

Surprised by the boy's vehemence, Jacob said, 'Tell me first why it's so important to you, this watch?'

'Because my sister Mabel has been accused of stealing it,' Stephen replied fiercely. 'And she didn't.'

So Jacob explained again what had happened, and when he'd finished Stephen's eyes were gleaming with anger. He turned to Joseph. 'So what are we going to do? How do we catch her? D'you think she'll come back tomorrow?'

'We don't know for sure, but let's assume that she will.'

'And you don't believe she's pawning it for her mistress? Perhaps she is and it isn't the right watch at all.'

'I don't think she is acting for her mistress, if indeed

she has one,' replied Jacob. 'She kept on insisting who it was for and why she needed it. I think if she had really been carrying out such an errand, she would have been more circumspect. She would have told me as little as possible, to protect her mistress's reputation. She would not have given me all that information about Lord and Lady Rafferty.'

'So what do we do now?' Stephen asked.

'That's just what we're about to decide, my boy,' replied Joseph.

'When she comes into Mr Levy's shop, we should lock the door,' Stephen said, 'and not let her out.'

'That's all very well,' protested Jacob, 'but we've no actual evidence she stole the watch, have we?'

'Except she's trying to pawn it,' Stephen almost shouted at him. 'What more d'you need?'

'Enough, Stephen!' snapped Joseph. 'That is no way to speak to your elders. Kindly be quiet, and let us consider the possibilities.'

'I bet it's someone from the McFarlanes' house,' muttered Stephen under his breath, before he retreated into sullen silence.

'This girl who was accused of taking the watch,' said Jacob thoughtfully. 'Would she be able to recognise the woman? I mean, if the boy is right and she is part of the McFarlane household?'

'She might,' agreed Joseph, 'but even if she did, she could be accused of having a vested interest. We need someone there who is an entirely unbiased witness.'

Stephen seemed about to interrupt again, but another frown kept him silent.

'If she's faced with the watch and the fact that she is not Lady Rafferty's maid, but works for the McFarlanes, she really has no defence to the charge of theft,' Joseph pointed out.

'But if she continues to maintain that she is acting on this Lady Rafferty's behalf, unless we confront Lady Rafferty and ask her, which means touching on her gambling debts…'

'I don't think Lady Rafferty will know anything about her,' said Joseph.

'No, nor do I,' conceded Jacob.

There was a moment's silence and Joseph, glancing across at Stephen, saw he was almost bursting with the need to speak. 'Well, Stephen, if you can speak politely, you may say what you have to say.'

Stephen took a gulp of air and then said in his mildest voice, 'If Mabel was hidden in the shop she could say if it was someone from the McFarlanes' and nothing to do with this Lady Rafferty, and we could lock the door and keep the woman there until we fetched a policeman?'

Joseph Solomon looked at his apprentice and said with a wry smile, 'You make it sound very easy, boy.'

'I can go home and get Mabel now, if you like,' suggested Stephen, edging towards the door.

'Just a minute, Stephen,' Joseph said. 'Do we want your sister to think that the watch has been found when we aren't even sure that it's the right one?'

'We have to do something or the woman will get away with it,' said Stephen, his voice full of frustration.

'Not necessarily,' said Jacob. 'I could refuse to accept the watch against the money.'

'And I'd be there, as witness to the fact that she'd brought the watch in,' said Joseph.

'But she'd just go somewhere else,' cried Stephen.

'He has a point, Joseph,' Jacob said. 'And all we do is lose track of the watch.'

'Let me go and get Mabel,' begged Stephen. 'If she knows the woman who comes, and recognises the watch, she can confront her and then surely we can lock the door and call the police.'

'Is there somewhere she can hide until the watch is laid on the counter again?' Joseph asked Jacob.

'In the back workshop,' replied Jacob.

In the end, they sent Stephen off to Cockspur Lane to fetch Mabel, and the cousins went upstairs for the promised tea with Joseph's wife Miriam.

When Stephen returned with Mabel, the girl was full of excitement.

'Tell me what this woman looked like,' she said, when she had been introduced to Jacob.

Jacob repeated the description he had given to Joseph earlier and Mabel said, 'Well I can tell you who that is. It's Miss Chalmers. She's Lady McFarlane's personal maid. She was the one who said she'd seen me coming out of Miss Lucinda's room.'

And so they laid their plans to trap Chalmers.

'But what if she doesn't come?' sighed Mabel.

'She will, if she wants the money,' Joseph said reassuringly. 'And we'll be waiting.'

Thus, their plan was made and Mabel went back home bursting with excitement. She and Stephen had agreed that she should say nothing to their parents until the thief had been identified once and for all.

When Jacob got back to his own shop he found Leon waiting for him.

'Well?' he said. 'Did you follow her home?'

'Yes, sir. I followed her and she went to a house in Chanynge Place in Mayfair. Number eleven. Posh house and she went in round the back, like she were a servant.'

'Well done, Leon,' said his master, decidedly relieved that she had indeed been followed to Sir Keir McFarlane's house. 'That's very good news.'

'Not all of it, sir. You ain't heard the half of it yet.'

'Go on then, what haven't I heard?'

'Well,' said Leon, 'when I followed her down the street she were lookin' in the shops like, and she stopped outside Mr Isaac's shop and looked in the window and I thought she was goin' in. But suddenly she turned and walked away.'

'So she didn't go inside Isaac's?'

'No, she hurried off towards the station and then it happened.'

'*What* happened?' demanded Jacob with irritation. 'Speak up, boy!'

'She was about to cross the road when a lad come running round the corner and knocked into her, tried to grab her bag. She hung on to it, but he nearly knocked her over.'

'And?'

'And Lenny the Dip was right there beside her, caught hold of her so's she didn't fall. He weren't interested in her bag, but he took something outta her pocket.'

'You're sure?'

'Yeah. He's a smooth operator is Lenny. And I think the boy what bundled her was his lad, Spike.'

Jacob sighed. So much for all their carefully laid plans, he thought in frustration. The woman, Chalmers, if that's who it was, almost certainly no longer had the watch. She would not be coming back in the morning. He must warn Joseph that the whole plan was off.

'I need you to take a note to Mr Solomon in Dundas Alley,' he said to Leon. And disappearing into his back workshop, he scrawled a note to Joseph.

They must have been watching her when she left my shop. When she took the watch back I was surprised to see her put it into her jacket pocket, not her bag. The apparent attempt on her bag must have been a ploy to distract her so that Lenny could simply remove the watch from her pocket. Almost certainly Lenny now has the watch and even if we can get it back, we can't prove who brought it to me. So all bets are off and we can't prove your girl didn't take the watch in the first place. Unless of course you can come up with another idea!

Jacob sealed the note and sent Leon round to Dundas Alley.

'You're to wait for an answer,' instructed Jacob.

The answer came more slowly than Jacob was expecting and he was beginning to wonder if Leon had got into trouble, as the sun slipped below the horizon and darkness invaded the sky, but at last the boy reappeared at the shop door and Jacob unlocked it to let him in.

'Leon!' Jacob exclaimed. 'Where on earth have you been?'

'Wiv Mr Solomon. You said wait for an answer.' He delved into the pocket of his trousers and pulled out a rather dog-eared envelope. 'An' here it is.'

When Jacob had read the message, he smiled and said, 'One more errand this evening, Leon, and then you can go home.' He scribbled another note. 'Take this to Mr Solomon and say I'll expect him tomorrow morning.'

With a sigh, Leon crammed the new message into his pocket and was about to leave again when Jacob held out a sixpence. 'Here you are,' he said, as Leon stared at the coin. 'Get yourself a pie on the way home, and I'll see you in the morning.'

Leon almost snatched the sixpence. A sixpence would buy three tuppenny pies – one for him, one for Ma and one for his sister Rochelle. What a feast!

He turned and hurried to the door before Mr Levy could change his mind and take the coin back.

Jacob smiled as he watched him run out into the darkness and thought, He's a good lad really, always looking after his family in place of his vanished father.

Picking up the note from Joseph, he read it through again. It was a plan. It might work for them, it might not, but it was definitely a plan.

38

Chalmers finished her tea and was just walking out of the kitchen door when her ladyship rang the bell. Chalmers was not officially on duty that evening, but that had never stopped her mistress sending for her, if she knew that she were actually in the house. As she walked along the family's landing, Mr Iain came out of his room. He greeted her with a knowing smile and said, 'Hello, Miss Chalmers, did you enjoy your afternoon off?'

She felt the colour flood her cheeks. He had seen her after all! What had he thought she was doing?

'Yes, thank you, Mr Iain,' she replied tightly.

'It must be nice to have a few hours entirely to yourself,' he said conversationally, still barring her way.

'It is indeed, sir,' she said. 'Now if you'll excuse me, your mother is ringing for me.'

Iain stood aside and said with a wink, 'So glad you enjoyed yourself!'

How dare he speak to me like that? Chalmers fumed. As if we shared a secret! She was a senior member of the staff and he had no right to patronise her. With a face like thunder she pushed past him and knocked on his mother's door. As she opened it, she heard him laugh behind her and thought viciously, you'd be laughing on the other side of your face if you knew where I've really been this afternoon.

'Ah, Chalmers,' said her ladyship. 'I'm glad you're back early. Sir Keir has just telephoned from his office to say that he has tickets for the theatre tonight, so I have to get changed at once.'

Chalmers went through the familiar motions of preparing Lady McFarlane to go out for the evening but, all the time, she was thinking about her afternoon. She would, she decided, go back to the Jew in the morning and take his money. With that amount she could retire when she wanted to. If it weren't for Miss Lucinda's coming out in the spring, she would give in her notice at once, but there must be no suspicion that she had come into money. She would continue to work for the McFarlanes until the end of the summer and then she could give notice because she was retiring, and no one would think anything of it. As she laid out silk lace undergarments for her mistress, she thought of the incident with the street boy who tried to rob her and her heart contracted with fear. What if that boy *had* managed to snatch her bag? She would have lost her purse, certainly, but far, far worse, she would have lost the watch as well! But then another fear, even worse, came hard on the heels of the first as she realised that the watch had not been in her bag. In her hurry to leave the jeweller's, she had put it in her pocket; and now she didn't know if it was still there.

'Chalmers,' snapped her ladyship, 'that's the second time I've asked you to fetch my pearls. I'll wear the necklace and the matching earrings. Get them out and look sharp, or I'll be late meeting Sir Keir. Really, Chalmers, what *is* the matter with you this evening?'

Chalmers murmured an apology and tried to keep her mind on the job in hand, but by the time she had finished helping Lady McFarlane to dress and had arranged her hair twice before her mistress was satisfied with how she looked, it was more than an hour before Chalmers was free to return to her own room. Her bag and jacket were lying where she had left them, on her bed. She immediately picked up her jacket and put her hand into her pocket to take out the watch, only to find that her worst fears had been realised; the pocket was empty. She knew a moment of blind panic and rammed her hand back into the pocket again and again, as if she might have overlooked the watch, but there was nothing, nothing at all. She turned the jacket over and felt in the opposite pocket, but that yielded nothing, either. Shaking, she grabbed her bag and turned it upside down on the bed. The contents came cascading out, but there was no glittering fob watch on a diamond brooch. She put her hand into the empty bag, running her fingers round its base, feeling the lining, in case there was a hole through which the piece might have slipped. Nothing. No hole in the lining; nothing caught up in the inner pocket where she had put the watch on her way out, earlier in the afternoon. She returned to her jacket and felt it through and through, hoping that somewhere she'd feel the shape of the watch, the weight of it, but there was nothing there. Once again she turned her attention to the heap of things she had tipped out of the bag, in the forlorn hope that she might have missed it, but all she found was the jumble of items she always carried: her purse, another hankie, a comb, her notebook and pencil, several hairpins and, daringly, a red lipstick and an enamelled powder compact, both of which she had rescued from the make-up lying on Lady McFarlane's dressing table the day they'd packed up to leave Haverford Court, but neither of which she'd used today. Her bag was empty, her jacket pockets were empty... the watch which was going to fund her old age had vanished.

For a split second she wondered if she had left it on the counter in the shop, but no, no, she remembered, definitely remembered, hastily putting it in the pocket of her jacket.

She thought of the boy who had nearly knocked her flying as he made a grab for her bag. She had clung on to the bag, and she had not fallen, because a stranger had grabbed her and held her steady... and, she realised now, must have picked her pocket at the same time.

She gave a howl of misery as she saw how she had been tricked.

That Jew must have tipped them off, the boy and the man, she thought in fury. They were a gang of thieves; the Jew had seen her put the watch in her pocket, so although it looked as if the boy had tried to grab her bag, it had been the watch they'd been after all the time.

Chalmers couldn't remember the last time she had shed a tear, if ever, but now tears of rage, misery and frustration poured down her cheeks. She flung herself on the bed among the debris from her bag and sobbed into her pillow.

A little later there was a tap on the door and when Chalmers didn't answer, Lizzie called timidly, 'Miss Chalmers, Mrs Bellman asks if you're joining us for supper.'

'No!' Her answer was a shout. 'No, I have a headache, I've gone to bed.'

'She didn't sound very headachey,' Lizzie confided to William after she had passed on the message to Mrs Bellman. 'She just sounded angry.'

'Better she doesn't come down then,' murmured William.

'Will you send Ada up with a tray after?' suggested Mrs Kilby to Mrs Bellman.

'No,' replied the cook firmly. 'She was perfectly all right when she got back earlier. If she wants her supper, she can come down for it, like the rest of us.'

Miss Chalmers did not come down, and the supper table was a noticeably friendlier place without her.

39

Sir Keir McFarlane was about to enter the morning room for a quiet breakfast with his wife, when Felstead stopped him in the hall.

'Good morning, sir,' the butler said, proffering a silver salver on which lay a long white envelope inscribed with Sir Keir's name.

'Just been delivered, sir, by hand.'

Sir Keir picked it up and looked at it. He didn't recognise the writing, though it was clearly an educated hand.

'Who delivered it?' he asked.

'A young lad. Well turned out. Not a street urchin earning a penny.'

'Is he still here?'

'No, sir. He handed me the envelope and having wished me good morning, he went back into the street.'

'I see.' Still holding the letter, Sir Keir continued into the morning room, where his wife was already sitting at the table with a steaming cup of coffee at her elbow, buttering a piece of toast.

'Good morning, dearest,' he said, and taking his place

opposite her, he laid the envelope down beside him. 'I trust you slept well after our evening out.'

'Indeed I did,' responded her ladyship. 'We were quite late home, you know, and I was soon asleep. I'd told Chalmers not to wait up, so she's having to sort my evening clothes out this morning. She's not in the best of moods, so I decided to breakfast downstairs today and left her to it.'

'I don't know how you put up with her sometimes,' said Sir Keir. 'Her moods and her arrogance.'

Lady McFarlane sighed, 'Because she's good at her job, I suppose. But she certainly wasn't herself when she got back yesterday from her afternoon off and she's not much better this morning!'

She leaned forward to pour her husband a cup of coffee, while he picked up the envelope and slid his letter opener under the seal.

'What's that?' she asked. 'Who's it from?'

'I don't know,' replied Sir Keir. 'It was delivered by hand this morning. Felstead's just given it to me.'

The letter it contained was written in the same handwriting as his name on the envelope. He started to read and as he took in what the letter said, his eyes widened and he glanced across at his wife.

'Bella, did Chalmers have the day off yesterday?'

Lady McFarlane looked up. 'Afternoon, yes, though I was very grateful she came home early, as I needed her to help me dress for the evening. Why?'

Sir Keir shrugged, saying, 'Just wondered, that's all.'

Surely, he thought, this whole thing must be some sort of tasteless, inappropriate joke. And yet, as he read the message through again, he couldn't help feeling there might actually be some truth in what it suggested. It wasn't anonymous rubbish, sent by some crank, it was dated and signed with a return address. Of course he mustn't accept it as gospel, but surely it was worth investigating further. As he considered the matter he realised that Bella was speaking to him again.

'I don't think she can have enjoyed her free time yesterday. She's been like a bear with a sore head since she got back. Why the sudden interest?'

Sir Keir passed her the letter, saying, 'Because of this note that came this morning. It's a strange one.'

His wife took the letter and scanned it quickly before starting to read it again, more thoroughly. When she'd finished, she tossed it aside and said, 'That's just preposterous! We already know who took the watch.'

'Do we?' asked Sir Keir. 'We had to assume someone from the house was the thief, and on evidence given by Miss Chalmers herself, we accepted it was the housemaid... what was her name?'

'Mabel Oakley,' supplied his wife. 'And we know she took it, because the ring, taken at the same time, was found among her belongings.'

'She always denied she had taken it,' Sir Keir reminded her.

'Well, she would, wouldn't she?'

'Certainly she would... if it were true.'

'Even if it wasn't,' retorted his wife, 'all it achieved was getting the girl the sack. What reason would Chalmers have to do that?'

'I don't know,' he answered. 'You tell me!'

'I can't think of a reason. But do you know? I wasn't that sad to see Mabel go in the end. I was disappointed in her, yes, but I was also aware Iain had been taking too much interest in her, and I certainly wanted that nipped in the bud.'

'I thought you said you had been planning to get Chalmers to train her as a lady's maid for Lucinda,' remarked Sir Keir.

'Well, yes I had been, but that was before I realised she was a thief.'

'How much credence should we give to this letter, do you think?' Sir Keir asked.

'None at all,' snapped his lady. 'We should burn it and forget all about it.'

'And yet it gives chapter and verse of her movements yesterday afternoon. I'm inclined to think we ought to speak to Chalmers herself. Enquire where she went when she was out yesterday.'

'On her free afternoon, Keir, that is surely none of our business.'

'But according to this letter, perhaps it should be.'

At that moment the door opened and Iain appeared. He seemed surprised to find his parents still sitting at the breakfast table.

With a casual, 'Morning, Mama, Gov'nor,' he strolled over to the sideboard and began to load a plate with eggs and bacon from the chafing dish.

'Good morning, Iain,' replied his mother.

'Let's see what Iain thinks,' suggested his father.

'I doubt if he has anything to add,' returned Lady McFarlane. 'It has nothing to do with him, and I think the whole letter is mischievous and should be ignored. The idea is outrageous.'

Intrigued by this exchange, Iain asked, 'What letter, Gov'nor?'

'Some anonymous letter that arrived this morning,' his mother answered.

'But that's the point, my dear,' said Sir Keir. 'It is neither anonymous, nor without a return address.'

'Some down-at-heel address in the East End,' his wife reminded him. 'And signed Jacob Levy. Who is Jacob Levy? It could be anyone. I think you should treat it with the contempt it deserves.' She finally got to her feet and crossed to the door, turning back to say, 'I shall do so, anyway.'

When the door closed behind her, Sir Keir handed the letter to his son and said, 'What do you think, Iain?'

Iain read the letter and then looked up at his father. 'I think it's worth investigating. I mean, whoever this Jacob Levy is, he's approached us, knowing that a fob watch such as he describes was stolen from us back in the summer. If this is it, well, we might even have the chance to get it back.'

'But Chalmers? She's been with your mother for over seven years.'

'She has,' agreed Iain. 'But she's never really fitted in, has she?'

Recalling how he had described her earlier, Sir Keir had to agree that she had not. 'But just because she's arrogant and moody doesn't mean she's a thief.'

'Well, we can confirm she was certainly out and about yesterday afternoon. I saw her myself, and I have to say she was acting rather strangely. She turned the corner and saw me standing in the street, and immediately turned in through the gate to one of our neighbours. I watched her because I wondered what she was up to. She clearly hoped I hadn't seen her.'

'But it was her free afternoon, so why would it matter?'

'That's what I wondered at the time. She was pretending to ring the doorbell of number fifteen, but as soon as she thought I'd gone, she came back out and caught a bus into town.' Remembering the word that had occurred to him the previous afternoon, he added, 'Furtive. She was furtive. I thought so at the time. It made me wonder if she had an assignation with a man, but perhaps it was something else.'

He picked up the letter again and said, 'Let's consider the situation again. This letter is from a jeweller who says he has been offered the watch by a woman wanting to pawn it. He says he agreed to give her £450 against it if she brought it back again today, but now he admits he no longer expects her. Says he needs to speak with us. What's all that about?'

'Perhaps he's heard she pawned it somewhere else?' suggested Sir Keir. 'Jacob Levy, a Jewish jeweller. Why didn't he simply give her the money and keep the watch?'

'Perhaps he didn't have it. Or perhaps he's just an honest man,' suggested Iain. 'And knew the watch must be stolen.'

'But from us? Our watch?'

'The Jews tend to stick together,' Iain said. 'Especially those in a similar business. They have a sort of bush telegraph. They know things.'

'Your mother doesn't believe a word of it.'

'No,' agreed Iain. 'But she could be wrong, you know.'

For a moment there was an awkward silence and then Iain said, 'Well, perhaps I should go and see him. At least if this is a nonsense, we can write it off as such, and you will never have been involved with it. If we dismiss it out of hand, we'll never know if it was genuine. I'm happy to go and find this man, Gov'nor, and talk to him. If I believe his story when I've met him, then I think we can decide what to do next. Perhaps face Chalmers with the accusation. Give her a chance to defend herself. That's only fair, isn't it?'

'But if she's already pawned it elsewhere?'

'Well, if she hasn't got the watch, she'll probably have a great deal of unexplained money in her possession, don't you think?'

'You're already assuming that she is guilty,' remarked his father.

'We did the same for the maid,' pointed out Iain. 'Assumed she was guilty.'

'She did have the ring.'

'It was among her things,' Iain agreed, 'but she always maintained that she had not taken it, or the watch. And once the ring was found, I don't think they searched anyone else's belongings. It was assumed she was the thief and that she'd already disposed of the watch, or at least removed it from here.' Iain found he was thinking of Mabel Oakley. He'd liked the girl, she had spunk! Thinking of Mabel and looking across at his father, he went on, 'You know, Gov'nor, I think we should at least investigate further.'

Sir Keir could see the sense of what he was saying and so, a little reluctantly, he agreed Iain should go and find Jacob Levy, Jeweller, and see what he had to say.

When Iain walked into Jacob's shop, one look told Jacob that he was not a customer. His clothes, his manner, even his hairstyle proclaimed him a toff from the other side of London. As the jingle of the doorbell died away, Iain turned

the sign on the door from open to closed before approaching
the man behind the counter.

'Good morning, sir,' Jacob said, making no comment
about the closed sign.

'Mr Jacob Levy, I presume,' said Iain.

'Indeed.' Clearly the old man had guessed who he must
be, but remained unmoved.

'My name is Iain McFarlane,' said Iain. 'I believe you
wrote to my father this morning about a watch you have
been offered for sale.'

'As collateral for a loan,' corrected Jacob.

'And you took the watch?'

'No, sir. I don't keep that sort of money in my shop.
The woman concerned intended to come back again this
morning. She said she was acting for her mistress, a certain
Lady Rafferty staying with her husband at Brown's Hotel.
An Irish lady, I believe.'

'So why did you write a letter to my father, Sir Keir
McFarlane, and not to the husband of this Lady Rafferty?'

'I was suspicious, right from the start,' replied the jeweller.
'So when she left the shop, I sent my lad out to follow her.
I wanted to know if she went back to Brown's Hotel... or
somewhere else. It was somewhere else. He followed her to
number 11 Chanynge Place, which I believe is your family
home.'

When Iain nodded assent, Jacob went on, 'She was seen
to go in through the servants' door at the back, letting
herself in without knocking or ringing a bell.'

'And you'd recognise this woman again?'

'Oh yes, most certainly.'

'And you're saying that she has in her possession the fob watch on the diamond brooch stolen from my sister?'

'No, sir, I'm afraid not.'

Iain looked startled. 'So where is it? You say you haven't got it, and now that she hasn't either? What is this cock and bull story?'

'Unfortunately that is true...' began Jacob. This was the difficult bit.

Iain rounded on him. 'You mean you've dragged me round here on a wild goose chase? How dare you! How dare you cast aspersions on a member of our household without a shred of evidence? I should have the police on you, wasting my time like this!'

Jacob Levy remained calm and said, 'Before you do, perhaps you'd like to hear the evidence from someone else who's involved.' He turned to the curtain behind him. 'Leon!'

The boy edged unwillingly out from behind the curtain and waited, pale and frightened, behind the counter.

Iain looked him up and down, and said in a voice of ice, 'Well?'

At a nod from Jacob, Leon related his journeys to and fro the previous evening. As he spoke, his nerves seemed to come under control, for when Iain asked him what buses he had taken and the colour of the house when he finally reached his destination, the boy answered with confidence.

'And all those answers are right, Mr Iain, aren't they?'

Another voice spoke from behind the curtain, before, to Iain's amazement, Mabel Oakley stepped out into the shop.

'Mabel? Mabel Oakley? What are you doing here?'

'Trying to help you catch the real thief,' she replied.

'So, who has the watch now? Where is it?'

'We know who has it,' she answered, 'and we can almost certainly get it back provided the reward offered at the time of the theft is honoured.'

'I don't think you're in any position to make conditions,' stated Iain firmly.

'That's up to you,' answered Mabel, not backing down. 'We'll let the man who has the watch now, keep it. The original thief will get away with the theft, of course, even though she no longer has it.'

'You are telling me Miss Chalmers came here to pawn the watch and she was robbed in turn on her way home? A bit ironic, don't you think?'

'To be honest I'm delighted she was robbed. I'd rather *anyone* other than Chalmers had it. She lost me my job and my reputation. Thanks to her, I was dismissed without a character. Whether you believe what we've been telling you this morning or not, *we* are now certain of the truth. The watch was stolen by Miss Chalmers. Take her to task for it. Get her to explain where she was and what she was doing yesterday afternoon. You are harbouring a thief in Chanynge Place, Iain McFarlane, but I no longer care.' Then, turning to Jacob, Mabel said, 'Thank you for letting us know about the watch, Mr Levy. I'm very grateful, it means that among my friends at least, my name has been cleared. I need to go back to work now. We've an order to complete before the end of the day.'

'Mabel—' Iain started to speak, but Mabel cut him off.

'I have nothing further to say to you,' she snapped, 'now or ever.' And before Iain could say anything else, she walked past him, her head held high, and out into the street, the door closing behind her with a jingle of its bell.

Iain found he had nothing more to say, either. Seeing Mabel again, suddenly much more grown up than he remembered, gave him a jolt, as if he'd touched a live wire.

When he turned back to the counter he saw that the little jeweller was watching him. There was a long moment of silence between them and then Iain said, 'I'll go home and tell my father what you have all told me. I can't promise he will act, but I will certainly encourage him to do so.'

'That's all we can ask of you, sir. I only wish the woman had not been robbed on her way home, but if the reward is forthcoming I think we can retrieve the watch for the price you were prepared to pay at the time it was stolen.'

'The reward being for you.' It was a statement, not a question, and as soon as he spoke, Iain knew he'd made a mistake.

The jeweller fixed him with an icy stare and said, 'No, sir. For the man who has it safely in his possession now.' After another pause, he went on, 'I'll bid you good morning, sir.'

Iain knew this was his dismissal and replied quietly, 'Thank you. Good morning to you, sir,' and left the shop.

Once the bell had sounded his departure, the curtain opened again and Joseph Solomon came into the shop.

'Well, Jacob, do you think he'll do any more?'

'I think he will,' replied his cousin. 'I saw the way he looked at young Mabel.'

'And can we get the watch back from Lenny?'

'Why not? He can't sell it as it is, can he? If he's given the reward money with no further questions asked, I think he'll happily part with it.' Adding with a wry smile, 'It'll be more than he'd have got from either of us.'

40

When Mabel left the shop, she headed back to the printery by the bridge. She felt almost light-headed. She had been vindicated. She had spoken up to Iain McFarlane, not allowing him to reply, before she swept out. He had been a contributor to her sacking, she knew that. Not because he thought her a thief, but because he had not actually admitted why she had been hiding in Miss Lucinda's room. Well, she had told him what she thought and could now dismiss him from her mind and get on with her life.

As she reached Mr Clarke's workshop, she heard the rhythmical sound of the printer hard at work and found herself smiling. This was her life now and she loved it.

Tom Clarke had opened the door to his workshop that morning, knowing Mabel was going to be late. The previous evening, she had returned from Joseph Solomon's shop and explained the situation to him.

'Someone has tried to pawn the gold and diamond fob watch I was accused of stealing,' she told him. 'And Mr Solomon, where Stephen works, and his friend Mr Levy are going to catch her in the morning.'

Tom looked concerned. 'How are they going to do that?' he'd asked.

'I'm not quite sure,' admitted Mabel. 'But they want me there to identify her.'

'So you know who it is?'

'Almost certainly,' Mabel said.

Tom had not been happy with her news. Since Mabel had been working with him, she had changed. The schoolgirl she had been was maturing into a confident young woman. She seemed to have put the accusations of theft behind her and moved on, out into the world. None of her friends believed her to be a thief, and surely, Tom thought, as he set up the press, surely that was all that mattered? He didn't want the old wound to be reopened. Mabel had blossomed as she had begun to work with him and learn his trade, her confidence re-established by his trust in her.

Well, he thought, I suppose we shall have to see what happens and deal with the consequences if it all goes wrong.

Now, when Mabel pushed open the door, Tom Clarke could see at once that things had not gone wrong; she was beaming as she greeted him.

'Well,' he said without missing a beat, as he operated the press, 'how did it go? Did she turn up?'

'No,' answered Mabel. 'But Mr Iain came.'

'Iain McFarlane? I thought you were expecting this Chalmers woman.'

'We were,' replied Mabel, 'but by this morning everything had changed.' And she began to tell him what had happened to Chalmers.

'It got a bit difficult when Mr Levy had to admit that Chalmers had been robbed on the way home. Mr Iain was furious at first, but in the end I think he began to believe what we said, but goodness only knows if he'll do anything about it.'

'Well, you've all done the best you can,' said Mr Clarke. 'If they want the watch back it's up to them.' He doubted that anything further would be done and wanted to change the subject back to their own business. As long as Mabel was happy with the result of the morning's meeting, that was all he cared about.

The press fell silent as the print run was finished, and he said, 'Put the kettle on, Mabel. I could do with a cup of tea.' Even as he spoke, he sat down suddenly and heavily on his chair, causing Mabel to look at him anxiously.

'Are you all right, Mr Clarke?' she asked.

'I'm fine,' he replied. 'Just ready for a brew, that's all, and while we wait for the kettle, you can pack up this order for Miss Chapman.'

Mabel picked up the printed pages, admiring the smart headed paper:

Walton Street Elementary School, Walton Street,
London E.

She wrapped them carefully in brown paper, ready for delivery. As soon as she'd finished her tea, she put the parcel into her bicycle basket.

'I'll be back as soon as I can,' she said. 'Is there anything else we can offer to Miss Chapman?'

'I doubt it,' replied Mr Clarke. 'I doubt if she has the funds for anything else,' adding as she reached the door, 'Take it steady now, on that bike.'

'I will,' promised Mabel, and with a wave she left him finishing his tea and set off for her old school. Learning to ride a bicycle was one of her new accomplishments, and she loved the freedom it gave. It also meant Mr Clarke was now able to offer a delivery service. She worried continually, though unnecessarily, that they needed to get more work to cover her employment. She couldn't bear the thought Mr Clarke might not be able to afford her wages. She still had some more business ideas to suggest, but she hadn't mentioned them to him yet.

Since she had been employed by Mr Clarke Mabel had never been happier. She was out in the world and earning money to help support her family. It wasn't a great amount, but her wages, and those of her brothers, added to the modest amount her mother still made, sewing garments for Mr Moses, put bread on the table and they could afford Mrs Finch to continue with her father's care.

She often wondered how she had ever endured her life in service; the remembered monotony of endless, identical days now seemed unbearable. Working for Mr Clarke every day was different. She was learning to set type and, despite the letters being fiddly and back to front, her speed and accuracy were improving. She also knew, in principle, how to work the press, though Mr Clarke had not allowed her to do that yet. He had promised she should learn, but just at present they had enough work to keep them going; mostly small jobs, printing leaflets, advertisements, invoice forms, wedding invitations, business cards – the bread and butter of his trade.

He promised that when they had a slow day, she could, under his close supervision, have a try at working the treadle and feeding the paper onto the platten. Mr Clarke made it look so easy, his movements smooth and rhythmical, but she knew that came with years of practice.

Looking at the headed paper she was going to deliver, Mabel thought it looked very smart. If Miss Chapman approved it, Mabel had decided, despite Mr Clarke's doubts, she was going to suggest other work they might do for her: printed record cards, achievement and progress sheets.

Mabel's parents were pleased she was happy in her work, but they were also concerned that Mabel, following her determination to become a secretary, was taking evening classes in short-hand, typing and book-keeping, and it was Mr Clarke who was paying her night school fees.

'It's not right,' Andrew had said to Alice. 'We should be paying those.'

'We should,' Alice agreed, 'but we can't and he's promised they will only be a loan, which she can pay back when she's earning more.'

'And when will she be earning enough to pay him back?' Andrew enquired, a bitter note in his voice. 'If she's working for him, he'll be repaying his own loan! It's all wrong!'

Alice had to agree, but she also had to accept that without Mr Clarke's help Mabel would have no job at all, and with only Miss Chapman's short testimonial to offer a prospective employer, and a question mark still hanging over her honesty, she was hardly in a position to return to service in some other household, even if she could be persuaded to.

Now, when Mabel arrived at the school it was the dinner hour and the playground was filled with children letting off steam in the winter sunshine. Several of the older ones, once her class mates, waved to her as she parked her bicycle against the wall and, as an adult, entered the front door of the building.

When she knocked on the school secretary's door, Miss French greeted her with a scowl, eyeing the parcel.

'Miss Chapman is busy,' she said. 'You can leave your package here with me and I'll see she gets it.'

'Thank you, Miss French,' Mabel said, 'but I have a message for her as well, so if you don't mind, I'll wait to speak to her.'

When she had come to Miss Chapman for a reference Mabel had admitted she'd been accused of theft. Miss Chapman had believed her when she'd said she was innocent and provided the reference. Unfortunately, the rumour about Mabel Oakley being sacked from her job up west for stealing had circulated over the following weeks and Miss French had no intention of leaving a thief alone in a room on the school premises. Who knew what she might slip into her pocket and take with her when she went?

Keeping her eye firmly on Mabel, she tapped on the headmistress's door. 'Mabel Oakley has come with a package to deliver, but she says she has a message for you as well.' She didn't ask what she should do with a thief in the office, but the question hung in the air for a moment between them.

'Thank you, Miss French,' Miss Chapman said. 'Please ask her to come in.'

It was not the answer Miss French had hoped for and, with disapproval on her face, she waved Mabel forward.

'Miss Chapman will see you now,' she said, and walked

back to her desk, making a point of checking that all was exactly as she'd left it.

Mabel went into Miss Chapman's room and closed the door behind her. 'Good morning, Miss Chapman,' she said as she laid the parcel on the desk. 'I've brought the printing from Mr Clarke.'

Miss Chapman glanced at the package. 'Our headed paper?'

'Yes, Miss Chapman, and it looks really good. Shall I show you?'

The headmistress nodded and Mabel unwrapped the parcel and passed a sheet of paper across to her.

'It looks splendid,' agreed Miss Chapman with a smile.

'It does, doesn't it? And I wondered,' Mabel said, going on quickly, 'if there is any more printing work we could do for you. I was thinking about printed record cards which you could fill in with all the children's details. They would all be the same and they could be filed year by year. Parents' names, date of birth, home address, that sort of thing.'

Miss Chapman smiled at her enthusiasm. 'That sounds a lovely idea, Mabel, but we already have such forms, you know. I'm not sure paying for a different sort would be worth the money it would cost me.'

'Oh, we would give you a special price,' Mabel assured her.

'I'm sure you would,' agreed Miss Chapman, 'but in the current financial climate, they are not something the school can afford. At present Miss French draws up the cards and then fills them in as a new pupil joins us.' Seeing Mabel's disappointment, she went on, 'Don't look so downcast, Mabel. If we need any other printing done, Mr Clarke is the first person we'll come to for a price. In the meantime, why don't you go round to some of the other local schools? You could show them a piece of our headed paper. The heads there might be very pleased with some of your ideas, if not now, maybe in the future?' She smiled as she saw the look of purpose light Mabel's eyes.

'Yes,' Mabel said. 'Yes, of course! Why didn't I think of that!'

'You're clearly enjoying your new job, Mabel,' remarked Miss Chapman.

'I love it,' Mabel replied. And Miss Chapman could see that it was the simple truth.

'I'm so pleased for you,' she said, getting to her feet. 'Good luck with the other schools.'

Mabel left the school to return to Mr Clarke, pedalling fast, fizzing with sudden energy. Despite everything, Miss Chapman still had confidence in her, and today her life was good.

She thought back to her encounter with Iain McFarlane earlier and longed to know if anything had been done about Chalmers. Would she ever know? Then she remembered.

William had a night off tonight and would probably be coming round to Cockspur Lane where he was always sure of a warm welcome. Since his first visit, and encouraged by Alice, William had started to visit the family on his evenings off. Alice had taken to him immediately, and though it was too early to make plans for Mabel's future, Alice considered he would, in time, make an excellent husband for her. He always arrived at the house in the early evening, often with some meat, vegetables or eggs given to him by Mrs Bellman. The cook knew where he was going and also knew that a few slices of cold beef, or some onions or carrots, would not go amiss. The whole family soon accepted him and treated him as one of their own. He never revealed in Chanynge Place where he went, but Lizzie had heard of his friendship with her cousin from her mother, and it was she who'd mentioned it to the cook.

Dear William, Mabel thought as she pedalled her way through the busy city streets, he's never doubted me.

That was true, and though there had been nothing he could do to prove that Mabel was not the thief, he remained staunch in his belief of her innocence. But would he have news from Chanynge Place this evening? Surely, Mabel thought, he'll know if anything untoward happened in there today. Surely he will. Servants know everything.

41

Iain walked to the taxi rank at Liverpool Street station and took a cab home. All through the journey he wondered what his father would think of what he had discovered. The story the jeweller was asking him to accept seemed, on the face of it, quite ludicrous, but as he considered it again, he began to come round to the idea. Surely no one could have made up such a story. That the thief, whoever she was, had been robbed herself in the open street was, if true, ironic in the extreme. The trouble was, even if they did face Chalmers with the accusation, if she denied it, which he assumed she would, there was no evidence to prove she had ever had the watch in her possession.

He thought of his mother's reaction that morning to the letter. She certainly wouldn't believe such a story. She would simply dismiss it as a clumsy attempt by a Jew to extort money from them. He, himself, had been quite ready to dismiss the idea when he first heard it, but the boy, Leon, had known all the answers to his questions and had clearly followed Chalmers as she returned to Chanynge Place. He might have been coached in what he was to say, but on balance, Iain didn't think so. And then there was Mabel Oakley. She had appeared from the back of the shop and faced him down, not accepting any doubts about what had happened the previous day. Mabel still had the same streak of honesty which had impressed him before and he found himself wanting to believe her, wanting to believe it was not Mabel but Chalmers who'd stolen the watch and taken it to Jacob Levy's shop yesterday.

When he got home, Iain found his father still in his library.

'How did you get on?' asked Sir Keir. 'Was it our piece?'

'I don't know,' admitted Iain, 'because they haven't got it and nor has the thief any more.'

Sir Keir looked incredulous. 'Then what was that letter all about? It's a good thing we didn't face Chalmers with an accusation!'

'I'm not so sure,' replied Iain. 'Let me tell you the whole thing.'

Sir Keir listened without interruption to Iain's account before he said, 'So we could force them to tell us, threaten them with the law!'

That was the last thing Iain wanted. Now Mabel was involved personally again, he wanted to follow up on what he knew without involving the forces of law and order. He realised it would be difficult, with his father a judge at the Old Bailey, but he was going to try to convince him.

'We could,' agreed Iain cautiously, 'but I'd rather not. Why don't we show Chalmers the letter and see what she says?'

'She'll simply deny it and then what do we do? We have no proof she has ever been near Jacob Levy's shop.'

'No,' sighed Iain, 'but it would be extremely interesting to see her reaction.'

'Maybe it would, but it still wouldn't prove anything.'

'If we don't face her with it, we shall continue to suspect she might be the thief. Surely she's entitled to know the accusation has been made and to have the chance to defend herself. She may well be able to prove she was somewhere else entirely.'

Sir Keir considered this argument and said, 'Perhaps. But I tell you one thing, your mother's not going to like it.'

Sir Keir was right. Lady McFarlane, having listened to Iain's story, said, 'If you show Chalmers this letter, and she denies everything, what happens then? Will you really take the word of some East End Jew over hers?'

'I think it might be worth a telephone call to Brown's Hotel,' suggested Sir Keir.

'If you say so,' sighed his wife. 'Though what Lady Rafferty will have to say when you suggest she has gambling debts, I can't imagine!'

The telephone conversation was, understandably, short; Lady Rafferty angrily disclaimed any such debts, and said that her personal maid, Panton, had been with her in the hotel all the previous afternoon.

Sir Keir apologised for the intrusion and rang off.

'So, don't you think we should speak to Chalmers now?' asked Iain. 'If we don't tell her what's being said about her and allow her to give her side of the story—'

'We don't even know if she has a side of the story,' interrupted his mother.

'Exactly,' said Iain, 'and we shan't know unless we ask her.'

'Well,' said his mother, 'if you are determined, so be it. But I think you're wrong and I insist that it is your father who talks to her about it. You,' she said, pointing her finger at Iain, 'are being influenced by the Oakley girl.'

Sensibly, Iain did not make a comment on this last observation, but accepted that his father should conduct the interview.

Sir Keir rang the bell, and when William came in answer, he said, 'Ask Miss Chalmers to step into the library, please, William.'

When Chalmers found herself facing the three McFarlanes, the colour fled her face, but she held her head up high and addressed herself to her mistress.

'You wanted me, my lady?'

'Yes, Chalmers. Sir Keir would like to ask you a couple of questions. It won't take long.'

Sir Keir was standing with his back to the window, so his face was in shadow.

Chalmers turned to face him and said, 'Yes, sir?'

'Was it your afternoon off yesterday, Chalmers?' he asked.

'Yes, sir. I went out after luncheon had been served.'

'I see.' Sir Keir spoke quietly. 'And how did you spend your afternoon?'

Remembering that Iain had seen her in the street, she said, 'I was going to go out with a friend, but when I called round, she wasn't able to come.'

'A friend? Working for one of our neighbours?'

So Iain had seen her go into number 15.

'I called, but she was needed by her mistress, so I came away.'

'And where did you go after that? When your friend couldn't come?'

'I caught a bus and went into town. Regent Street.'

'So if I told you we have information that you went to a jeweller's in Brock Street yesterday afternoon, it would be wrong?'

'Certainly it would,' she replied firmly. 'Where is Brock Street? I've never heard of it.'

'So you went to Regent Street. Anywhere else while you were out?'

'Yes, I walked down the Haymarket to Trafalgar Square and went to the National Gallery.' Even as she spoke, she realised that it was a mistake. If he asked about the current exhibition, she wouldn't know what to answer.

He did not, and Chalmers gave a mental sigh of relief. Say as little as possible, she warned herself. Answer his questions simply and don't embroider what you say.

'Did you meet anyone, another friend, who was with you for any part of the afternoon? Someone who could vouch for your whereabouts at any particular time?'

'No, I spent the afternoon alone. Why are you asking?'

'So you weren't anywhere near Liverpool Street station?'

'No, sir, I was not. Please, Sir Keir. Why all these questions?'

'I will explain,' her employer replied. 'I have received a letter from a jeweller in Brock Street, not far from Liverpool Street, stating that you went into his shop and tried to pawn a piece of jewellery. Did you?'

'No, sir. I did not,' Chalmers answered angrily, but inside, she was shaking. 'I've never been to that area of London. Why would I go to a rundown area like that?'

'You might have been meeting someone at the station,' suggested Sir Keir.

'Well, I wasn't. I was nowhere near there.'

'The thing is, Chalmers, the piece of jewellery that was offered sounds remarkably like the fob watch that was stolen from Miss Lucinda's room in the summer.'

'Well, if it was, surely you should be questioning that Mabel Oakley, not me. We all know she stole it, and the ring too. It must have been her trying to sell it... or her mother.'

'Whoever it was, wasn't trying to sell the watch,' remarked Sir Keir. 'Just to raise money against it. I understand the woman concerned claimed to be a lady's maid to a certain Lady Rafferty who is at present staying at Brown's Hotel. She told the jeweller that she was raising money to pay off that lady's debts.'

'Then, with respect, sir, shouldn't you be questioning this Lady Rafferty and her maid?'

'I have been in touch,' replied Sir Keir, 'and Lady Rafferty knew nothing about any watch, or indeed the need for money. I have to say she was quite offended at the idea.'

'Well, I know nothing of a Lady Rafferty, or her debts,' maintained Chalmers. 'So whoever it was, it certainly wasn't me.'

'Fair enough,' said Sir Keir. 'But it does seem strange that the woman who brought in the watch was followed here after she left the shop, don't you think? To this house. And she was seen to enter through the servants' door at the back. You say that wasn't you?'

Chalmers felt sick. How could they know so much? But she still held a winning hand; she no longer had the watch in her possession. She raised her chin and looked Sir Keir straight in the eye. 'If you really feel it is necessary, sir, you can search my things, but I can assure you, you will find nothing.'

'Thank you,' replied Sir Keir, 'I think that is a very sensible idea. It will decide the question without doubt. Lady McFarlane and I will come with you to your room now.'

When Iain got to his feet, his father said, 'No need for you to come, Iain. Your mother and I will see to this.'

Determined to show she had nothing to hide, Chalmers marched up the staircase in front of them.

Thank goodness I haven't still got the watch, she thought. Who would have imagined that sneaky Jew would have me followed and then write and tell them what I'd been trying to do? He's probably after the reward. Well, he certainly won't get that. They can search all they like, but they won't find anything here.

When they reached her bedroom, she opened the door and said, 'After you, my lady.'

Lady McFarlane went in, but then stood to one side to let her husband pass ahead of her. It was clear to Chalmers that her mistress didn't like what they were doing.

I shall give notice after this insult, she thought, as she watched Sir Keir pull out her carpet bag from under the bed. He upended it and shook it, but it was empty, only used when they all travelled to Haverford Court. Leaving it aside, he turned his attention to the two drawers in the bedside locker. Nothing in there, she thought triumphantly, as he moved on to the small chest of drawers containing her clothes. However, he left that to be searched by his wife, and as she watched Lady McFarlane search through her underclothes with distaste, she suddenly realised Sir Keir had picked up her handbag. He turned to her and held it out. 'Perhaps you'd empty this out onto your bed,' he said. 'Then I think we'll be finished.'

With an exaggerated sigh, Chalmers upended her bag, spreading the contents for all to see. Sir Keir picked up several items and put them down again as of no interest, but when he picked up a small notebook and flicked through it something caught his eye. He smoothed the page out and glanced at it again, before closing the book and tossing it back onto the bed. He continued his search, running his hands around the inside of the bag, making sure there were no concealed compartments.

Glancing across the room, Lady McFarlane saw her enamelled compact among the things the bag had contained, and the red lipstick she thought she had left in the country by mistake. She looked sharply at her maid, but said nothing; Chalmers was watching Sir Keir peering inside the bag.

'Have you seen enough?' Chalmers demanded, brave now she was sure he had found nothing to link her to Jacob Levy and his shop.

'Almost,' replied Sir Keir. He picked up the notebook again and, holding it out for her to see, asked, 'Why have you written this in your book?'

It was Lady McFarlane who took the notebook from her husband and with widened eyes read out, '"Jacob Levy, Opposite White Horse, Brock Street."'

She looked up at her maid, who was now deathly pale.

'So, Chalmers,' she said. 'You lied to us. You do know

where Jacob Levy's shop is, don't you? I begin to believe it *was* you who went there yesterday with Lucinda's watch.'

'That proves nothing,' stated Chalmers.

'It proves a connection with Mr Levy's shop,' said Iain, who had been listening to the exchange from the landing and now stepped into the room. 'And why would he make up a story like this?'

'I haven't got Miss Lucinda's watch, as you can see' – Chalmers waved her hand at the drawers that had been searched – 'and I never have had. You should be going round to see that Oakley girl. She'll be the one.'

'Oh, we know you haven't got the watch now,' said Iain. 'A pickpocket stole that from you on your way home, didn't he? The lad who was following you saw the whole thing. It was very neatly done, and I doubt if you realised just what they *had* done, the boy who bumped into you and the man who steadied you.' He paused and, when she made no comment, he went on, 'When did you realise what had happened, I wonder? Perhaps you didn't discover until you got back here?' Iain saw the flash of fury in Chalmers' eyes. 'I see from your expression that you didn't.' He laughed and said, 'Funny, don't you think? The thief being set upon by thieves? Rough justice, wouldn't you say?'

His laughter finally made Chalmers lose her temper. 'They were all in on it,' she snarled. 'The jeweller must have told the other two what I was carrying in my pocket; they were lying in wait for me.' She gave a twisted smile. 'So now none of us have that watch, and it's all been for nothing.' She crossed the room and began stuffing her bits and pieces back into her handbag. 'I'm leaving now,' she announced, 'and you can't stop me. You have no evidence that I ever touched that watch.' She reached for the discarded carpet bag and began to fill it with her clothes.

Lady McFarlane stepped forward and, reaching down to the bed, retrieved her compact and lipstick. 'I think I'll have these back,' she said softly. 'They prove you're a thief, if nothing else does.'

42

When Mabel got home that evening, she found William had already arrived.

'You got here early,' she said as she greeted him with a smile.

'They didn't need me, so I slipped away,' William said. 'I've got some wonderful news and I couldn't wait to tell you.'

'Chalmers?' asked Mabel.

For a moment William looked crestfallen. 'You already know? Who told you? Did the McFarlanes send you a message?'

Mabel took his hand. 'No,' she said, 'but I do know some of it and I'll explain in a minute, but first you tell me what's happened in Chanynge Place. I'm dying to hear it all.'

'Well,' William said, brightening, 'it was this morning, Sir Keir rang for me and asked me to send Chalmers to the library… no, actually,' he broke off, 'no, it started earlier than that. A letter come early, addressed to sir. Mr Felstead received it and gave it him as he was going in to breakfast.'

'A letter?' prompted Mabel. 'Was it delivered by hand?'

William looked surprised at the question. 'Yes, it was. How did you know?'

Mabel didn't answer his question but asked one of her own. 'What did it say?'

'We don't know, not for sure, but we think it was from someone who knew something about that brooch watch thing what was stolen, you know?'

'I certainly do,' agreed Mabel wryly.

'Well, they was arguing in the dining room and Lizzie, who just happened to be polishing the banisters in the hall, heard your name mentioned, and so she listened in a bit. It seems that Chalmers went into some jeweller's shop down the East End to try and pawn it. The watch.'

'So who wrote the letter?'

William shrugged. 'Don't know, but her ladyship was right cross. Said they should destroy the letter and forget all about it. Sir Keir was considering that when Mr Iain came down. Lizzie had to do some hurried polishing so that he wouldn't realise she'd been earwigging.'

'What did he say?'

'To Lizzie? Nothing, just gave her his usual grin and went into the dining room. An' then, few minutes later, Lady M come out looking angry and Lizzie melted away before she caught the edge of Lady M's tongue.'

'So you don't know what happened next?'

'No,' conceded William, 'not exactly, but as soon as he'd finished breakfast, Mr Iain went out and was away for a good hour and a half. Don't know where he went, but I saw him come back in when I was taking sir his tiffin.'

'Iain went to the jeweller's shop to see what he could find out—'

'Did he? But Mabel, how d'you know all this?'

'Cos I was there...'

'Was you? Why was you?'

'Because we were trying to catch the real thief. I'll explain it all when you've finished telling me what happened back at the McFarlanes'.' She looked at William expectantly. 'Go on,' she urged. 'What happened then?'

'He went into the library and I was expecting a call to bring him something to eat as well.'

'And?' Mabel tried to curb her impatience.

'And sir rang for me and asked me to send Chalmers in to see him. Lady M was there with them by that time.'

'And did she go?'

'Course she did,' said William. 'She had to, didn't she?'

'I suppose.'

'Well, when she went in we couldn't hear nothing from the outside, not at first anyway. But after a bit their voices got louder and the next thing we knew was that the door burst open and Chalmers was going upstairs, up the front staircase too, followed by Sir Keir and Lady M. She didn't look too happy about it, but she followed them up. Chalmers was spouting off about search all they liked, but they wouldn't find nothing.'

'What about Iain? What did he do?'

For a moment Mabel's question brought William up short. 'Mr Iain?' he said, as if he didn't know who she meant.

'Yes, Mr Iain.'

'What d'you want to know about him for?'

'I told you, it was Iain who went to the jeweller's to check up on what had been written in the letter.'

'Oh,' said William, less than enthusiastically, 'is that

where he'd been?' For a moment he looked confused. 'But how d'you know that, then?'

'Cos I was there,' repeated Mabel. 'I know what happened in the shop. Promise I'll explain in a minute. Go on, what happened next.'

'I see,' sighed William, who didn't. He didn't see at all, but at Mabel's insistence he went on with his story.

'Well, to begin with Mr Iain stayed downstairs, but Lizzie an' me, we was watching from the drawing room, and it weren't long before he was creeping up the stairs behind them. Anyhow, Felstead come through the baize then and sent us downstairs, sharpish.'

'So, you don't know what happened next?'

'Well, I do and I don't,' admitted William. 'We didn't see it, but the Killer-bee said at dinner that Chalmers had packed her bags and walked out. Just like that! She said it was because they'd caught her thieving. Said she'd heard Chalmers saying that she wouldn't stay in the house for another minute, not if they begged her to, and then she swept out, through the front an' all, an' slammed the door behind her.'

'Where was she going?' wondered Mabel.

William shrugged. 'How should I know? As long as she's gone, we're all better off.'

'Except for Lady M who's been left without a lady's maid for herself, and Miss Lucinda, getting ready for her come-out,' pointed out Mabel. 'But it serves Chalmers right, and I'm glad they got rid of her.'

'Well, Mr Blundell, who was in Sir Keir's room at the time, said that when Lady M told Chalmers she was to be dismissed, Chalmers snapped, "Too late! I've already given notice." And then she said, "And heaven help poor Miss Lucinda if you get someone like that Oakley girl to dress her. Train her up to replace me, was that the idea? Well, madam, no chit of a girl is going to take my place."'

'And Mr Blundell heard all this?'

William shrugged again. 'Says so.'

'So that was it,' mused Mabel. 'That's why she wanted to get rid of me.'

'Sounds like she wanted that watch as well,' pointed out William. 'We know she was a thief, cos she'd taken some things of Lady M's from Haverford Court. They was hidden in her bag, which proves she's a thief, but she didn't have no watch, which they thought she had.'

'No, William, she didn't,' agreed Mabel. 'Thanks for telling me all that. I can tell you a bit more, but you must promise me you won't let any of it slip in the servants' hall. You won't, will you?' She looked at him anxiously.

'I can't see why not,' began William, who had relished being in the know.

'Because it may spoil the end of the story.'

'Isn't *this* the end of the story?'

'No, not quite. I can't tell you all of it just now, but one day I will.'

'You don't trust me.' William sounded resentful.

'Course I do, silly,' replied Mabel, 'but at present it's a secret, and it isn't my secret to share.'

'Bet it's something to do with Mr Iain,' mumbled William.

'For goodness' sake, Will, forget Mr Iain. I don't give a fig about Iain McFarlane and I told him as much this morning; I told him I never wanted to speak to him again, and I meant it.' She reached for his hand and went on, 'Come on, Will, let's go and tell Mam and Dada that they know now who the real thief was, even if she'll never be caught.'

William liked it when Mabel called him Will. She was the only person who did, or ever had, for that matter. Now he held her back for a moment and, squeezing her hand, said, 'Mabel, you do know I'm fond of you, don't you?'

Surprised, Mabel left her hand in his and replied with a smile, 'And I'm fond of you, William.'

'Yes, I know that,' he said awkwardly, 'but is it the same sort of fond?'

'Same sort of fond?'

'Real fond, like the way I feel about you.'

Mabel turned to face him. 'I don't know, William. It's too soon to tell, don't you think?'

'But you aren't, like, well, fond of Mr Iain?'

'No, William.' She spoke slowly and, enunciating each word clearly, as if speaking to a backward child, said, 'I am not fond of Iain McFarlane and never will be.'

'Only you refer to him as Iain, not Mr Iain as you used to,' persisted William.

'That's because I can,' she said. 'I no longer have to call him "Mr" as a sign of respect, cos I don't work for him and I don't respect him.'

There was a moment's silence as William held her gaze and then he sighed. 'That's all right then,' he said, but he still wasn't quite sure.

Mabel tugged at his hand. 'Come on,' she said, 'let's go and tell them the good news.' And together they went into the kitchen, to deliver the cake William had brought from Mrs Bellman and to tell Alice and Andrew the whole story.

43

It was two days later, on Saturday morning, that Andrew, sitting at his window as he so often did, saw the car turn into the street, a large and gleaming car which had no business to be driving into a street like Cockspur Lane.

'Hey, Alice,' he called. 'Come and look at this. Did you ever see such a car?'

Alice came in, closely followed by Mabel, and all three watched in amazement as the car drove slowly up the road and drew to a halt outside their house.

Mabel had no trouble recognising the beautiful blue car she had first seen in the mews behind 11 Chanynge Place, the car that was Mr Croxton's pride and joy. And now here it was outside their house with Croxton at the wheel, and sitting behind him, Iain McFarlane.

For a moment Mabel closed her eyes, half expecting that when she opened them again the car had been a figment of her imagination. However, when she did re-open her eyes, there was the car, with Iain McFarlane stepping out of it.

Her parents were still staring in amazement at the magnificent vehicle. Several of their neighbours came out onto the street to see the wondrous sight, but Mabel drew back from the window so that she couldn't be seen.

'It's Iain McFarlane, Mam,' she breathed. 'Don't let him in. Tell him I'm not here.'

'But what on earth can he want?' wondered her mother.

'I don't know and I don't care,' retorted Mabel. 'I'm going upstairs. I'll come down again when he's gone.'

Leaving her parents below, she hurried up the narrow staircase and into her room. As she was about to close the door, she heard the doorbell, followed a few moments later by a hefty banging on the front door with the knocker. She heard her father say, 'You'll have to answer that, Alice, or we'll be providing entertainment for the whole street!'

'Mabel doesn't want to see him,' replied her mother.

'She doesn't have to,' said Andrew, 'but we do have to open the door.'

Mabel watched through the banisters as her mother went to the front door and opened it. At once she heard Iain McFarlane's annoyingly familiar voice saying, 'Good morning, Mrs Oakley. It is Mrs Oakley, isn't it? You look so like Mabel, that I'm sure you must be. I'm sorry to intrude unannounced like this, but I was hoping to have a few words with Mabel herself.'

Even as she listened to him from upstairs, Mabel knew that he was treating her mother to his most charming smile.

That's just like him, she thought angrily. He switches on the charm like a lamp and everyone does exactly what he wants them to! Well, I won't! Mam can say I'm not at home, just like they would if I knocked unexpectedly on their front door in Chanynge Place.

Iain was still speaking. 'Is she at home? I have an important message for her from my parents.'

'I think she may have gone out,' responded Alice a little uncertainly. Mabel had asked her to say she wasn't at home, but Alice hated lying and wasn't very good at it.

'Then perhaps I may wait, until she comes back,' suggested Iain.

All charm and smarm, thought Mabel. Say no, Mam, she willed her mother. Say no!

'I'm afraid I don't know how long she'll be,' answered Alice.

'That's no problem, Mrs Oakley,' Iain assured her. 'I wouldn't dream of inconveniencing you, I can wait in the car until she's back. My parents are very keen for me to deliver their message.'

'I see,' said Alice. 'Well, of course, that's up to you, Mr Iain.'

'Don't call him that!' hissed Mabel. 'Send him away.' But she knew now that he wouldn't go away. He would sit outside their house in his posh car with all the neighbours gawping at him until she agreed to speak to him. Speaking to him would be the only way to get rid of him. If it had been a normal Saturday she wouldn't have been at home, she'd have been at work and he wouldn't have known where to find her, but Mr Clarke said he wasn't going to the workshop this weekend, and had told her not to come in.

She heard her father call from his room. 'Bring the chap in here, Alice. He can't simply sit out there in the car as entertainment for the neighbours.'

So her mother invited Iain into the house and Mabel was

trapped upstairs. She heard Iain's cheerful greeting to her father, and that seemed to be the last straw. How dare he patronise her parents?

After a while, she heard her mother bring them tea and then, at last, her footsteps on the stairs.

'Now, Mabel, you'll have to come down,' she said. 'He's come with a message from his parents and you can't ask the man to wait all day for you.'

'I didn't ask him to wait at all,' retorted Mabel. 'I don't want to talk to him, but if he decides to wait, that's his business.'

'Don't be childish,' snapped her mother. 'If you want to be treated as a grown-up, you'll have to behave like one. He seems very charming, so come down and talk to him.'

'He's always "very charming" when he wants to be, Mam,' said Mabel bitterly.

'Well, he's in with your father and they're getting on very well.'

'All right,' Mabel sighed. 'You can tell him I'm upstairs and I'll be down shortly.'

A quarter of an hour later, Mabel came down to find Iain sitting with her father, chatting cheerfully as if they were old friends. Mabel had been determined to take her time and not run downstairs as if she were still a housemaid. She spent some time putting her hair up in a manner that wouldn't have been allowed in Chanynge Place. She scrubbed her face, pinching her cheeks and biting her lips to give them colour, and wished she had some face powder to take the shine off her nose. At last she couldn't put it off any longer and, drawing a deep breath, she went down. When she walked into her father's room Iain came to his feet immediately as he would have done for a lady of his own class.

'Miss Oakley,' he said with an appreciative smile, as if he knew the trouble she had taken with her appearance. 'How do you do?'

'Very well, thank you,' she replied coolly. 'I was about to go out, so do tell me why you have come.'

'I bring an invitation from my parents,' he answered. 'They would very much like you to come to Chanynge Place to see them. I believe there is much they would like to discuss with you.'

'That sounds more like a summons than an invitation,' remarked Mabel calmly. She saw the colour touch Iain's cheeks and knew she had made her point.

'If you will feel able to accept, I'll take you in the car and of course bring you home again, later on.'

Mabel couldn't help glancing out of the window at the car waiting in the street, Croxton patiently polishing the windscreen. A thought crossed her mind and she wondered how much of his life was spent polishing the car and how much actually driving it.

Iain was waiting for her answer. He did not press her, which made it all the more difficult to refuse. Both her parents waited expectantly for her reply. How could she refuse?

Reluctantly, she turned back to Iain. 'All right,' she said. 'I'll fetch my hat and gloves.' It wasn't the most gracious of acceptances, thought Alice, but at least she had said she would go, without making a scene.

Her parents watched her from the window as Iain led her to the car and Croxton hurried to open the door for them. He and Mabel had always got on well enough in the servants' hall but he disapproved of Iain treating her as an equal as he was now, and retreated into silence. Iain handed Mabel into the back of the car and then got in beside her. Watched by most of the neighbours, they were driven out of Cockspur Lane, heading towards the West End and Chanynge Place.

At first they travelled in silence, Mabel leaning back against the leather seats, enjoying being seen travelling in such a grand car. She had never been in a motor car before, let alone anything as splendid as this one, and Iain left her to her thoughts.

At last Mabel broke the silence: 'I suppose Lizzie told you where to find me.'

'Yes,' Iain replied. 'She was most helpful.'

'What do your parents want?' she asked after another lengthy silence.

'I don't know, exactly,' Iain said. 'They just asked me to come and fetch you.'

'Did they, now!' Mabel's hackles were up. 'What if I had absolutely refused?'

'I would have encouraged you to change your mind.'

'And do you think you could've?'

'Well,' he replied with his usual grin, 'you're here, aren't you?'

'Yeah,' she managed a rueful smile. 'I s'pose I am.'

'You know something, Mabel? That's the first time you've ever smiled at me.'

'Probably because it's the first time I've had reason to.'

'You're very beautiful when you smile,' he said, and then immediately realised that he had made a mistake. Her expression changed, her eyes hard and cold, before she turned away and looked out of the window. Neither of them spoke again until Croxton drew up at the front of 11 Chanynge Place.

'Wait here, Croxton,' Iain said. 'We'll be driving Miss Oakley home again later.'

Croxton touched his cap. 'Yes, Mr Iain.'

Iain led Mabel up to the front door and rang the bell. It was opened by Felstead. Seeing Mabel first, he was about to reprimand her for coming to the front door, but just in time he saw Iain behind her and stepped aside.

'Where are my parents?' Iain asked.

'I believe they are in the drawing room, sir.' He took Iain's hat, and then, somewhat reluctantly, accepted Mabel's hat and gloves when she handed them to him.

'Thank you, Felstead,' she said. And in that moment Iain knew whatever his parents offered Mabel, it would not be enough to bring her back into service.

He led the way up to the drawing room, where they found Sir Keir and Lady McFarlane waiting for them.

'Iain,' said his mother, 'you've been so long, I was beginning to think you must have got lost.'

'Miss Oakley was not at home when I first arrived. So I had to wait for her return.'

Mabel glanced at Iain in surprise, wondering why he had lied. Oh well, she thought, that's up to him.

'Thank you for coming, Miss Oakley.' Sir Keir stepped into the silence that followed Iain's explanation. 'Please, do sit down. Ring the bell for William, Iain, I'm sure Miss Oakley would like some refreshment.'

Ian rang as he'd been asked and then sat down in the chair next to Mabel's.

'I'm sorry you had to wait, but Iain was lucky to find me at all,' Mabel said. 'I'm normally at work on a Saturday morning.'

'Oh.' Lady McFarlane looked surprised by Mabel's use of her son's Christian name. That must certainly stop. But all she said was, 'You have a job already, do you?'

'Yes.' Mabel gave no further explanation.

'Before we go any further,' Sir Keir said, 'we owe you an apology. All of us. We have now discovered the identity of the thief who took Lucinda's jewellery. We know now that you had nothing to do with it, and we should have investigated further at the time, not just accepted the evidence against you without scrutiny.'

'Yes,' agreed Mabel. 'You should.'

Surprised at her forthright speech, Lady McFarlane said, 'Well, we want to put all that behind us now and we're happy to give you your job back. I shall have to employ a trained lady's maid for myself, but she can train you so that you can look after Lucinda, and—'

'Excuse me, my lady,' interrupted Mabel, 'but I already told you, I have a job.'

'Yes,' Lady McFarlane sounded surprised, 'but in whose household?'

'No one's.'

'But you say you have a job...'

'I'm an assistant to a printer. I'm learning his trade.'

'A printer?' echoed her ladyship. 'That's no job for a girl. I should think I'm offering you something far better than that! A chance to be trained, so when Lucinda is married and sets up her own household, you'll be able to move with her as her personal maid. A great step up for you, as you'll realise when you think about it.'

At that moment William appeared and, without even looking at Mabel sitting next to Iain, took the orders Sir Keir gave for refreshment. He'd already heard that Mabel had been fetched in the car by Mr Iain; and when Felstead had opened the front door to her, she'd addressed him as plain Felstead, without the courtesy of 'Mr'. Now that he'd seen her for himself, sitting next to Mr Iain as an equal, William turned and left the room, stony-faced.

'Thank you, Lady McFarlane,' Mabel answered. 'But I am perfectly happy in what I am doing now.'

'But your prospects—'

'I am very happy with my prospects,' interrupted Mabel, 'and I have no wish to go back into service, either here or anywhere else.'

'But for goodness' sake, child, you can't become a printer!'

'With respect, my lady, I am not a child. I am an adult earning my own living and paying my own way. I can do that in any way I choose. I thank you for your offer, but I do not choose to accept it.'

'I hope you know what you're giving up,' said Lady McFarlane tartly.

'What I'm giving up,' repeated Mabel. 'Yes, I assure you I do. I don't wish to be in service.' She could have said more, listed all the reasons she hated being in service, but her father's words echoed in her mind. *Remember, people who can afford to employ servants provide jobs and livings for hundreds of folk who wouldn't otherwise have any work.*

'I know many people feel happy and safe working in a household like yours, but it's not for me. I need to be out and about in the world.'

'In that case we have nothing further to say to each other,' replied Lady McFarlane, getting to her feet and ringing the bell. 'I've rung for William, Iain. Miss Oakley is leaving.'

Mabel stood up, about to leave, when Iain surprised her by saying, 'I promised to take Miss Oakley home, Mama. I believe Croxton is waiting to drive us.'

'That surely is unnecessary, Iain,' answered his mother. 'I'm sure Miss Oakley would be far happier travelling home by bus, particularly if you give her the fare.'

'I really think, Mama...' began Iain, who had seen the flash of anger in Mabel's eyes, but he was interrupted by his father.

'Make sure you're back before luncheon, Iain. I need the car this afternoon.'

'Certainly, sir.' Iain could see his mother's furious expression at being overruled by her husband and he said quickly, 'If you're ready, Mabel?'

As they were passing through the hall, William emerged through the baize door carrying the tray of refreshments Sir Keir had ordered. He stopped short as he saw Iain hand Mabel her hat and gloves.

'Not sure my mother will want those now, William,' Iain said, 'but you'd better go in and ask. I'm just taking Miss Oakley home.' And opening the front door himself, he stood aside to let Mabel precede him.

'I take my hat off to you Mabel,' he said, once they were settled in the car and Croxton had started the engine. 'You know how to stand up for yourself. Not many girls would take on my mother like that.'

'Well, I didn't want the job she was offering me,' replied Mabel. 'I know she doesn't understand and thinks I'm mad to refuse, but I never want to earn my living that way again.'

'Well, I admire your spunk,' Iain said. 'I'm down from Cambridge for the next week, so I shall be keeping an eye on you to see you don't get into any more trouble.'

'You can keep your eyes to yourself,' retorted Mabel. 'I am happy in what I am doing and I don't want any further contact with you or your family.'

'Well, that's certainly telling me,' said Iain with a laugh. 'You don't pull your punches, do you?'

'Then I wish you'd listen to what I'm saying,' Mabel snapped, 'and believe I mean it.'

The arrival of the car in Cockspur Lane caused less excitement the second time, though one or two curtains were twitching as Iain walked Mabel to her front door. She pushed it open, but Iain caught her hand, holding her on the threshold, and said, 'I shall come and visit you next time I'm home. To see how you're getting on with your printer.'

'I hope you won't.' Despite the anger boiling inside, Mabel managed to keep her voice cool. 'I've no wish to see you ever again.' And with that she pulled her hand free and closed the front door in his face.

Unseen, another pair of eyes watched as Iain returned to the car and was driven away.

44

As Iain and Mabel had been driven up to the McFarlanes' house, Alfred Everette was just approaching it from the opposite direction. He stared in amazement at the girl who was sitting beside Iain in the back of the Rolls. Surely that was the chit they'd both lusted after earlier in the year. The pretty one with the blue eyes who had served them in the library. What was she doing, riding in the back of Sir Keir McFarlane's car? She'd been caught stealing and sacked, hadn't she? Had she been reinstated? Even so, how could she be allowed to ride as an equal with Iain McFarlane, in the back of the judge's car?

Alfred hadn't seen Iain McFarlane since that mortifying day he had been told he was no longer welcome at Haverford Court. That was several months ago now and as the hubbub around his father had long been overtaken by other, more interesting news, Alfred had decided it was time to try and reinstate his friendship with Iain McFarlane. He had once hoped that the McFarlane family would be his ticket out of 'trade' and into social respectability, a move he was sure would give him the life he craved, so when he heard Iain was down from Cambridge for a few days, he took the opportunity to call. However, when Felstead opened the door, Alfred had been informed that Mr Iain was not at home. Alfred did not believe the man, but he simply left his card and walked away; he would call another day.

Seeing Iain and the girl together now emboldened him to try again. Once the door closed behind them, he waited for a few minutes before approaching himself.

When Felstead answered the bell, Alfred took a step forward and said, 'Good morning, Felstead. Mr Everette, to see Mr Iain McFarlane.'

Felstead did not stand aside or give the usual response that he would see if Mr Iain was in, he simply stood in the doorway and replied. 'I'm sorry, sir, but Mr Iain is not at home.'

Angry at this abrupt refusal, Alfred snapped, 'I know he is, Felstead. I saw him walk in through the front door just now.'

The butler straightened his back and, remaining firmly on the threshold as if he expected Alfred might try and push him out of the way, said, 'Mr Iain is not at home to you… sir.' The door closed and Alfred was left, humiliated, on the doorstep.

He glanced along the street to see if anyone had seen the refusal, but few people were about.

Furious at this treatment, Alfred walked down the steps to the street where Croxton was waiting, polishing the windscreen of the car.

Pulling his hat down to shade his eyes and effectively covering his distinctive red hair, Alfred paused beside the car. 'Nice motor,' he said conversationally. Croxton looked up to see a thin-faced young man looking admiringly at the car.

Showing no recognition, he replied, 'It is, sir,' and returned to his polishing.

Alfred crossed the road and went into the Chanynge Place communal gardens. He sat on one of the occasional wrought-iron benches set between the flower beds and settled down to wait. From his seat he had an uninterrupted view of the front door of the McFarlane residence, while being sheltered himself by a small growth of evergreen shrubs.

It was half an hour later when Iain and Mabel emerged from the house. Alfred watched them from his vantage point, safe in the knowledge that they would be entirely unaware of him. As Croxton came to attention and opened the rear door of the car, it was obvious that Iain was only interested in looking after his companion, handing her into the back seat, while Mabel seated herself as far away from him as the car allowed, and stared out of the window.

For a moment it seemed to Alfred she was looking straight at him, but if she saw him, she gave no sign.

As the Rolls pulled slowly away to join the morning traffic, Alfred cut across the garden and out through a further gate, so that he was ahead of the car as it proceeded towards him down the main street, almost at walking pace.

Stopping and starting in the morning traffic, they drew to a halt yet again to allow a waggon drawn by two shire horses to edge past them from the opposite direction. The horses, loath to pass the shining motor car, had to be coaxed by their driver to pull the waggon through.

Alfred walked past the car and waited at the next corner to see which way it went. Probably, Croxton was simply driving the girl home, and if so, where was that?

But, Alfred thought, if he isn't, it'll be interesting to

see where Iain *is* taking her. A love nest somewhere? The idea made Alfred grimace. Surely not in his father's Rolls! Anyway, Alfred could see that though Iain was attentive, he was getting little response from the girl.

As the car finally turned into a narrow lane, Alfred held back, afraid that he might be seen now and recognised. He had managed to keep up with the car's ponderous journey through the area's twisted back streets; it was clear Croxton was taking no risks with his master's car.

Well, now I know where she lives, thought Alfred, as from the shelter of the Cockerel's yard he watched Iain leave a house with a blue door and get back into the car.

Still unaware that he was being watched, Iain's mind was full of Mabel. What a wonderfully strange girl she was. He could hardly believe his ears when he heard her stand up to his mother as she had. And a printer? What on earth had made her become a printer's assistant? He wondered where her printer had his workshop. He would be fascinated to go there and see the press in action, to see Mabel at work. He wondered what she would say if he just turned up?

'Give me a tongue-lashing,' he answered himself. 'And serve me right!'

As the car headed back to the West End, Alfred walked slowly up Cockspur Lane, giving number 31, the house with the blue door, a cursory glance as he passed. He too was thinking of Mabel.

Inside the house, Mabel joined her parents in the kitchen and related the events of the morning.

'Lady McFarlane really couldn't believe I wasn't going to take the job she was offering,' Mabel told them.

'I'm not surprised,' said her mother. 'It was a good offer.'

'But not what I want to do, Mam,' Mabel said firmly.

'Well, let's hope you made the right decision,' Alice answered.

Alice had accepted Mabel was now working for Mr Clarke, but she still wished her daughter had a more suitable job to go to. She worried about her, out and about by herself, running errands, riding a bicycle, making deliveries all over the place.

'Oh, Mam,' sighed Mabel. 'Don't worry about me.'

All right to say that, Alice thought ruefully. But it's hard not to.

That night, Mabel lay awake and thought about her day. It had certainly been an eventful one, and though she really didn't like him, Mr Iain had been entertaining company. But she couldn't even begin to think like that. She had told him in no uncertain terms that she didn't want to see him again, and she hoped he knew she meant it.

She had enjoyed the journeys in the car, but it certainly hadn't been a speedy form of transport. As they'd eased their way through the traffic, there had been one young man, muffled in hat and scarf against the cold, who seemed to be keeping pace with the car and sometimes even overtaking it. He had disappeared as they had turned in by the Cockerel, but until then he'd been beside them much of the way.

I'm not surprised, Mabel thought. I'd certainly have been quicker on my bike.

Tomorrow was Sunday but Mabel was already looking forward to Monday so that she could tell Mr Clarke about her visit to the McFarlanes', Lady McFarlane's offer of her job back, and best of all, being chauffeured about in Sir Keir's beautiful car.

45

In the weeks that ran up to Christmas, Mabel was completely happy. She heard from Joseph Solomon that Lenny the Dip had parted with the watch and gratefully accepted the finder's reward, before fading back into the alleys of Whitechapel. To keep his father from being compromised by such a deal, Iain McFarlane made the exchange at Jacob Levy's shop.

Though Sir Keir and his wife resented having to pay a thief for the return of their property, Iain reminded them they'd have paid the reward if it had been found at the time it disappeared. This they had to accept as the only way they could prevent the heirloom from being broken up and sold for the value of the gold and its stones.

Mabel's name was cleared and her honesty had been re-established, but even so she was surprised and pleased to receive a formal letter from Sir Keir McFarlane, to the effect that Miss Mabel Oakley was entirely exonerated from the theft of the fob watch belonging to Miss Lucinda McFarlane and that there was no taint of dishonesty attached to her name. The envelope also enclosed a character reference signed by Lady McFarlane, stating she had found Mabel

Oakley to be of good character, honest and hardworking. It was not a glowing reference, but that didn't surprise Mabel after the way she had spoken to her ladyship. It was, however, something she could offer if she were ever asked for a reference again. At last she could put the whole affair behind her, and continue working with Mr Clarke.

The only change after Mabel's visit to Chanynge Place that day, was that William ceased to visit Cockspur Lane on his evenings off. Alice received a letter from him, explaining that he was now walking out with a young lady working in one of the other houses in Chanynge Place and he would no longer be able to spend his free time visiting the Oakleys.

'And there was I thinking he was getting fond of you,' Alice said, when she showed Mabel the letter. 'But why did he write to me rather than you, I wonder?'

Mabel could guess, but she shrugged and said, 'Don't know, Mam, but I think he came here because he was rather lonely. He always enjoyed his chats and games of draughts with Dada.'

'Yes, I know your dad will be disappointed he won't be coming again,' Alice sighed. 'He looked forward to William's visits. He'll miss them.'

'Yes,' agreed Mabel. 'So shall I.' And she found as the days and weeks went by that she did. She thought of William often but, in every other way, her life was just as she would have chosen.

'We should print some leaflets of our own,' she suggested to Mr Clarke one day when she was parcelling up some pamphlets for the local church advertising its upcoming Christmas bazaar. 'The vicar is arranging for some of his parishioners to deliver these around the local streets. We could do the same, something that people could tuck behind the clock on the mantelpiece and keep until they need it, rather than relying on small posters or cards in the local newsagents.'

'I suppose we could,' replied Mr Clarke thoughtfully, 'but the distribution would take a good deal of work.'

'Oh, don't worry about that,' cried Mabel. 'I can deliver those on my bike. It would mean we could advertise further afield.'

She had already procured two small orders for invoices and some headed notepaper from a local building firm; even small jobs like these helped to keep them afloat, but work was coming in more slowly than she would have liked. On the plus side, Mr Clarke had kept his word and allowed her to try her hand working the press.

She had watched him over the months and she knew in theory the various procedures necessary to run the press, but when it came to putting those into practice it took her longer than she had thought. With Mr Clarke standing beside her, she worked her way through the set-up, preparing for the first pull of some type she had set. The huge flywheel on the side of the press ran smoothly, and her first effort, working the press by hand rather than with the treadle, came out reasonably well. Over the next few weeks she gradually improved her technique and produced prints that though not good enough to offer for sale, were as good, clear and centred as they should be. Learning to work the treadle to power the press was more difficult as she had to learn the joint rhythm of hand and feet; a rhythm that appeared so easy when she was watching Mr Clarke, and so difficult to maintain in practice.

Mabel continued to find ways of increasing their output. 'I can set type now,' she said. 'So I can set the type for the next job, while you're printing off the job before.'

Tom Clarke was a perfectionist and corrected Mabel in the smallest mistake, but privately, he was proud of her progress. He had learned from his father, and knew all the little things that could go wrong when there was a novice at the press or if there was the slightest mistake in the set-up.

As she had suggested, they devised a leaflet advertising their services, and in the winter afternoons Mabel kept warm pedalling round the area slipping the leaflets through the doors of local businesses and dwellings alike.

'Is it really worth delivering these to private homes?' Mr Clarke wondered as she bundled up another pile and got ready to set off on her bike.

'Of course it is,' Mabel assured him. 'Who knows, someone there might need headed paper, or some invitations. We're local, so it's easy to call in with an order and easy to deliver the work afterwards.'

She had been proved right and their workload gradually increased as people realised where they were and what they could do.

One morning in late January, Mabel arrived at the workshop to find the door still padlocked. She was surprised as it was rare for her to arrive before Mr Clarke himself. However, she had a key to the padlock and so she opened up and went inside. The press had been prepared the night before, because they had an order for invoices to be delivered today. She waited for over an hour before she took the plunge and, making the final preparations, she spread the ink on the disk, moving the rollers by hand for an even spread and then, using the flywheel, pulled off a test copy. She took it to the window and scrutinised it in the daylight. It looked good, but was it good enough? Should she wait for Mr Clarke or should she try printing the hundred copies required?

She knew she shouldn't activate the press in his absence, but on the other hand the work was to be delivered today to a builders' merchants, Topperly and Co, the firm she had talked into putting in this very order. If Thomas Clarke, Printer failed to deliver on time, there'd be no more work from them. She went to the door and looked out along the alley. Albert Flood had been in his kiosk when she passed by that morning, too cold to sit outside on this raw day. She ran up the alley now and looked out into the road. There was no sign of Mr Clarke.

She stuck her head into Albert's kiosk and asked, 'Have you seen Mr Clarke this morning?'

'No, luv,' Albert replied, 'but I ain't been sittin' out.'

Mabel went back to the workshop. It was only marginally warmer inside than out and Mabel switched on the one bar electric fire Mr Clarke had allowed himself in the winter.

'Can't set type with cold hands,' he'd said on one particularly chilly day. 'Always have it here in the winter.'

She decided she would make some tea and if Mr Clarke wasn't there by then, well, she would try the print run. If that proved a disaster, no one would know but herself and she would visit Mr Topperly and explain the situation, that the printer was indisposed, but would be back to fill the order as soon as possible.

Once she heard footsteps approaching and sighed with relief – it must be Mr Clarke. But though the footsteps paused for a moment outside the workshop, it wasn't Mr Clarke. A shadow and movement at the grubby window let her know that someone stopped to peer in. Mabel went to the door and looked out, but whoever it was had disappeared. This wasn't the first time Mabel had felt she was being followed. Of course, she knew she wasn't. Who would do that? But now she came back inside and dropped the snib on the catch, locking the door.

When the kettle boiled she made the tea, and setting the pot aside to brew, turned her attention to the job in hand.

An hour later there was a neat stack of invoices complete with the name and address of Topperly's. She looked at each one carefully and discarded several that didn't match up to the required standard, because she'd put uneven pressure on the treadle. Even so, she was proud of what she had achieved, and packed them up carefully in brown paper for delivery, adding two copies of an invoice of their own.

There was still no sign of Mr Clarke, so she put the parcel in her bicycle basket and closed the padlock on the door. She would go round to Mr Clarke's house and see where he was. He'd been a bit husky the last few days, so perhaps his cold had settled on his chest. On the way, she would deliver the promised invoices to Mr Topperly. As she emerged from the alley she saw Albert outside his kiosk with a woman who, rocking a pram with one hand, was chatting to him as she chose a magazine.

'I'm going out on a delivery, Mr Flood,' Mabel called. 'I won't be long. If Mr Clarke comes back can you tell him where I've gone and say I'll be back soon.'

Albert waved his hand in acknowledgement. He liked the girl Tom Clarke had taken on as an assistant; unusual job for a girl, of course, but she seemed to be useful to Tom who, like Albert himself, wasn't getting any younger.

Mr Topperly was in his office at the builders' yard. He unwrapped the parcel Mabel handed him and looked at the stack of printing.

'Good work,' he announced. 'Tell your boss we'll use him again; quick and efficient is what we like to see.'

'I'll tell him,' Mabel promised, adding as Mr Topperly was turning away, 'Our invoice is there too, sir. The terms you agreed were cash on delivery.'

Mr Topperly looked at her. 'More usual to fall due in a month,' he said.

'Of course, sir,' said Mabel, and picked up the pile of invoices.

Topperly looked at her through eyes deeply pocketed in the bags beneath them. 'If I pay you cash,' he said, 'how do I know it'll get back to your boss?'

Mabel gave him her sweetest smile. 'Because I will have signed the invoice as paid,' she replied. And as he still seemed to be hesitating, she said, 'It's what we agreed, sir.'

Mabel was determined to stand her ground, though what she was going to do if he actually refused to pay, she wasn't sure. Walk out, carrying the printed work? If necessary, she decided, that's exactly what she'd do. Topperly would never use them again, but they couldn't and wouldn't deal with a man who didn't keep his side of the bargain.

Topperly saw by the determined expression on her face she was not going to go until the bill was paid and gave a rueful grin. 'You're a one, I must say. I'll have to watch you!'

And I'll have to watch *you*, thought Mabel, but managed not to say it. 'Thank you, sir,' was all she said.

Mr Topperly went to a drawer in his office desk and, pulling out a cash box, counted the money into her hand. She put it safely into her pocket and scrawled 'Paid', her name and the date on the bottom of their invoice. She did the same with her own copy which she stowed in her other pocket.

'Thank you for using Thomas Clarke, Printer,' she said. 'We look forward to serving you again.' And with that, she mounted her bicycle and rode off, leaving a slightly incredulous Mr Topperly watching her go. And a thought crossed his mind as he went back into his office: Good thing she's a Judy. If she was a bloke, she'd be dangerous!

Having successfully delivered the morning's work, Mabel pedalled her way to Barnbury Street to find Mr Clarke. Number 27 was halfway along and when she reached it she parked her bicycle in the tiny front garden and went up the steps to the front door. There was no answer to her first gentle knock, nor to her second, louder one. She pushed open the letter box and peered in, calling his name. All she could really see was the bottom of the staircase and the hallway leading to the back of the house. There was no answer to her call; all was silent.

Mabel was about to leave and go back to the workshop, but she gave one last knock and tried the front door. It remained firmly locked.

As she walked back to her bike, she noticed that there was a side gate allowing access to the rear of the building. She had only ever been to the house once, so she left the bike where it was and tried the gate. It wasn't locked and she was able to lift the latch to let herself through. The path led sharply downwards into the back garden and here she found she was now level with another door, beneath the kitchen window, and she realised it was a basement. She tried that door but it was locked, too. Then she walked up the steps to what must be the back door. She peered through the window beside it and saw a heap of... something? Clothes? It was half concealed by the kitchen table; and then she saw it, a hand, outstretched as if reaching for something, and she gave a gasp of horror as she realised what she was looking at was Mr Clarke, lying on the kitchen lino. She rapped hard on the window, calling his name, but there was no response. She turned the handle of the back door and to her surprise it opened easily. For a moment she paused on the threshold and then she hurried to the man lying awkwardly on the floor. Mabel stared down at him, saying his name over and over again. His face was turned away from her, but there was something about the stillness of the body that told her he couldn't hear her, and would never hear her again. After a long and silent moment, she steeled herself and knelt down beside him, touching his outflung hand. His fingers were stiff and stone cold. With a moan of desolation, she sat back, tears springing to her eyes. Mr Clarke was dead and he'd died alone. She had been working on the printing press when she should have come here first. If she'd come as soon as she'd realised he was late for work, she would have found him earlier; might have been in time to get help; to have got him to hospital; to have saved his life. And there she'd been, trying to be clever and show him she was perfectly able to work the press without his supervision. She was too late, and with that knowledge she sat beside him on his kitchen floor and wept.

She had no idea how long she remained in the house

before she realised that she needed to get help. Mr Clarke wasn't going to come back to life and he had to be moved.

Not knowing quite what to do, she went up into his bedroom. Taking a blanket from his bed, she brought it downstairs and gently laid it over him, covering him from head to foot, as if to keep him warm on this chilly winter's day. She didn't want to leave him alone, but she knew she had to get help, and so she said softly, 'I love you, Mr Clarke. I can't bear that you're dead,' and went out through the front door, taking the key from its hook and pulling it closed behind her.

Mabel remembered very little of the rest of the day. She had wandered out into the street, looking for someone to help. The street seemed strangely empty, but then, on a corner further along, she saw the tall figure of a policeman on his beat. He was looking in the opposite direction and didn't hear Mabel until she was almost at his side. One look at her tear-stained face told him she was in need of help.

'Now then, Missy, what's the trouble? I can see you're upset. I'm Constable Tiney.' He looked down at her from his height of six foot five and gave a brief smile. 'You can see I'm aptly named! So how can I help you?'

'It's my friend, Mr Clarke. He's on the floor and he's dead.' Mabel's voice broke on a sob.

'I see. And what's your name?'

'Mabel Oakley.'

'Right, Mabel Oakley, now where is your friend, eh?'

Mabel pointed dumbly at number 27.

'In there, is he? Well, let's go and see, shall we? He might not be dead, you know, just because he's on the floor. He may have fallen and been knocked out.'

Mabel shook her head and murmured, 'He's cold; so cold. I've never seen anyone dead before.'

'And maybe you haven't now,' soothed the policeman. 'We'll go and have a look and see what we can do. All right?'

Once he had seen Tom Clarke's body, Constable Tiney locked the back door and took the front door key from Mabel, then he took her next door and left her sitting with the elderly Mrs Frost, who gave her hot sweet tea for shock. Constable Tiney went to the nearest police call box and rang in what he'd found. Help arrived in the person of a doctor, who pronounced Mr Clarke dead, before disappearing again. A message was sent to Alice and within half an hour she was sitting beside Mabel in Mrs Frost's front room, sharing the tea.

'I should have come straight here,' Mabel sobbed. 'I shouldn't have stayed at the printing shop. If I'd come here, I might have been able to get help in time and saved him.'

'I doubt it, darling,' soothed her mother. 'Constable Tiney told me that he must have been dead for several hours before you found him. It's not your fault he's dead.'

'But he was by himself,' cried Mabel. 'All by himself!' And her tears continued to flow.

'He had a dicky heart, lovey,' Mrs Frost said gently. 'He knew he had, and that he could go any time. He probably knew nothink about it, poor man.'

When she and her mother got home again, Alice made Mabel some cocoa and put her to bed. 'Try and sleep, dear,' she said. 'Mr Clarke wouldn't want you to cry for him.'

'You don't know that,' replied Mabel fiercely.

'I think I do,' answered Alice. 'He was very fond of you,

you know, and he wouldn't want you to be sad. He's in heaven now, with his wife.'

'I don't believe that,' said Mabel. 'I don't believe in God. If God was real, he wouldn't let things happen, like Dada's accident and Mr Clarke dying by himself.'

'Bad things do happen in life,' Alice said, sitting on the edge of the bed and taking Mabel's hand. 'But good things do as well, you know.'

'Like what?'

'Like you meeting Mr Clarke in the first place. You met him and loved him, and I know he loved you too. Those are the things we have to hang onto, Mabel. If you remember those things, no one can take them away from you.'

46

Tom Clarke's funeral was a small, quiet affair. There was a short service in St Saviour's church, after which he was laid to rest in the cemetery beside his wife, Emma. Alice and Mabel attended, and Joseph Solomon gave Stephen the time to push his father to the church in his wheelchair. Once the final prayers had been said at the graveside, the Oakley family turned away, ready to go home. Mabel had been determined not to cry. Remembering what her mother had said about Mr Clarke not wanting her to be sad, she clenched her teeth, not allowing the lump in her throat to dissolve and break her resolve. She could hear the gravediggers filling in the grave, the thud of clods of cold, damp earth falling onto the coffin, and it hit her once more that she would never see Mr Clarke again. She had nothing to remember him by, no keepsake except the wheelchair he had given to her father. Walking beside her mother, her sight blurred by unshed tears, she didn't see the man waiting by the gate. Andrew, being pushed by Stephen in his chair, saw him and could hardly believe his eyes.

'Good morning, Oakley,' said John Sheridan. 'Mrs

Oakley.' He tipped his hat to Alice and then continued, 'A sad day.'

'Indeed,' replied Andrew stiffly, wondering why Mr Sheridan should be there. He hadn't seen him in the church.

'Mr Clarke was a client of ours,' Sheridan went on. 'Well, of Mr Morrell's actually, but unfortunately he is indisposed today and so I have attended the funeral on his behalf.'

Andrew still didn't know what Sheridan was doing there, so he said nothing, waiting for an explanation. After all, he knew very well that the partners at Sheridan, Sheridan and Morrell did not normally attend the funerals of their clients.

'Would it be possible for me to call at your house, perhaps later today?' Sheridan suggested.

'For what purpose, Mr Sheridan?' Andrew's voice was cold. 'To offer me my job back?'

The solicitor felt the colour rising in his cheeks. He knew he had treated Andrew Oakley shabbily, but Hugh Morrell was ailing, so now he had to have more dealings with him.

He ignored the question, but said, 'It's with regard to Mr Clarke's will.'

That did bring Andrew up short. 'Mr Clarke's will? What has that to do with me?'

'Well, if I might call upon you this afternoon, I can explain,' responded Sheridan. 'It's hardly a subject we should discuss publicly, here at the cemetery gate. Would three o'clock be convenient?'

'I suppose so, if you must,' Andrew said grudgingly, but interested, despite himself, in what the solicitor might have to say. 'Three o'clock,' he said. 'Right-ho, Stephen, let's go home.'

'What was all that about, I wonder,' said Alice as they walked away.

'Can't imagine,' replied Andrew. 'Maybe something about the various things he lent us, about what we should do with them now.'

Stephen needed to return to Solomon's as soon as he had delivered his father back to Cockspur Lane, but Alice heated up some soup and laid out bread and cheese for herself, Andrew and Mabel. The day was raw and cold and they were all three in need of hot food to warm them up after standing at the graveside.

'I'm not hungry, Mam,' Mabel said, as she watched Alice pour the soup into bowls.

'Just try and eat a little,' encouraged Alice. 'Come on, Mabel, it'll warm you up. It was bitter out there.'

Mabel tried a spoonful or two and found the warm savoury soup did make her feel better, but when she'd eaten she went upstairs to her room. She needed to be alone to consider her future. Her life, as she'd grown used to it, had suddenly come to an end. What was she going to do now? She still needed to earn her living.

'I s'pose I'll have to find another job,' sighed Mabel. The horror of going into service loomed, but for the moment, she wouldn't confront that. She lay down on her bed. All she wanted to do was sleep and sleep and sleep, and then wake up again to find it had all been a nightmare; that Mr Clarke was at work at the press and she was out and about on her bicycle making deliveries; that nothing had changed.

Downstairs, over another cup of tea, Andrew and Alice's conversation was running along very similar lines.

'What's she going to do with herself?' Alice wondered.

'I can tell you one thing,' Andrew said, 'she won't go back into service.'

'She may have to,' Alice said briskly. 'She can't live on thin air.'

'She won't like it.'

'Lots of people have to do work they don't like simply to earn their crust,' Alice pointed out.

'It's a pity she hasn't finished that night school course she was doing,' said Andrew. 'Then she'd have a qualification to offer.'

'That was pie in the sky.'

'I suppose we can't afford to continue—' began Andrew, but Alice cut him off.

'No, we can't,' she said sharply, 'and don't you go raising Mabel's hopes in that direction! We can't afford the fees and that's that.'

At that moment the doorbell rang. John Sheridan had arrived. He raised his hat to Alice when she opened the door, saying, 'Good afternoon, Mrs Oakley. Is your daughter at home?'

'Mabel? Yes, she's upstairs.'

'I think it would be helpful if she were down here with us.'

'What's it got to do with Mabel?' asked Alice.

'I'd rather not explain it all twice, Mrs Oakley,' replied Sheridan. 'If you wouldn't mind asking her to come down and join us.'

'Better give her a call,' Andrew said resignedly. 'Let's get this over.'

Mabel was surprised at being summoned to the meeting with Mr Sheridan. She got up from her bed where she was dozing, and came down to sit on the edge of her father's bed.

Sheridan opened his briefcase and took out a folder. 'I have here the last will and testament of Thomas David Clarke of 27 Barnbury Street London. It was duly signed and witnessed on the twelfth of July 1912.'

Just about when I was given the sack, thought Mabel.

'The will is a simple one,' continued Sheridan, 'of which my partner Mr Hugh Morrell is the executor.' He turned to the will and read: '"I bequeath everything I own, both in the funds and in property, to Mabel Oakley of number 31 Cockspur Lane. My wife and my son are both deceased and Mabel has become like a daughter to me. She is a girl whose determination and vision will take her far. My only regret is that I will not live to see her make her dreams come true."'

There was a gasp from Alice, and Andrew's eyes widened with surprise, but Sheridan ignored both of them and continued, now addressing his remarks to Mabel. 'Mr Clarke has left you everything he owns, Miss Oakley. It is in a trust and the trustees are your father and Mr Morrell. You may have the use of any income accruing during the term of the trust, but you may not touch the capital without the consent of both the trustees until you are twenty-one, or you are married, whichever is the sooner. In that case the trust will be wound up and you will have control over your affairs without reference to anyone else.'

He looked across at Andrew and added, 'Mr Morrell will be able to advise you on all things legal. It is unfortunate he is not able to come here today to explain the contents of the will in more detail. I have done my duty, making you aware of Miss Oakley's change of circumstances. There is a bank account in the name of the trustees, with a current balance of £743 10s 6d from which you, Miss Oakley, will be made an allowance of £50 per annum. You now own the freehold of 27 Barnbury Street with its contents and the lease of the printery workshop with its contents, all of which may be disposed of, with the agreement of both trustees.'

John Sheridan shuffled his papers together, ready to leave. He had carried out the job that ought to have been Hugh's. Damn the man for being ill. He had told a child, a mere child, that she had become an heiress. She had an inheritance well beyond her station in life, with only a crippled father and an elderly solicitor to guide her and prevent her from wasting every penny of it within the next five years.

'Just one more thing before I go.' Sheridan put his hand into his briefcase and took out an envelope, addressed to Mabel. 'This was kept with the original copy of the will,' he said. 'To be handed to you in person, when the terms of the will had been explained to you. I have now fulfilled that requirement and so am able to hand you this letter myself.'

Mabel took the letter and saw her name written in Mr Clarke's firm hand. She immediately put it into the pocket of her skirt. She had no intention of opening it until she was alone again.

John Sheridan closed his briefcase and got to his feet, but Andrew held up a hand as if to restrain him.

'One moment please, Mr Sheridan,' Andrew said. 'Before you go, I would like a certified copy of Mr Clarke's will.'

Sheridan looked annoyed. 'You must know I can't leave this will with you until it has been officially registered, Mr Oakley.'

'That's not what I asked for,' replied Andrew. 'But I am

sure Miss Harper, if she is still in your employ, can type up another copy, which you can attest is a true and faithful copy, and have it delivered to us here. There are many things that will have to be considered, and we need the exact wording, to be sure we know what Mr Clarke intended.'

'That is the sort of thing you must take up with Mr Morrell,' Sheridan replied stiffly.

'I am assuming Mr Morrell will be charging a fee for his work as joint trustee with me, and therefore my daughter and I have now become clients of your firm. In which case what I am asking can be easily achieved. As you know, I know exactly how your office runs.' The threat was veiled but implicit and John Sheridan knew it was there. Andrew Oakley knew too much and could still spread dangerous rumours about him and damage the firm.

'I will pass your request on to Mr Morrell, Mr Oakley, but I am sure there will be no problem arranging for you to have a certified copy.'

When John Sheridan had finally taken his leave, the three Oakleys stared at each other. Their financial worries were over.

'Explain to me exactly what Mr Clarke has left me, Dada,' Mabel said.

'As far as I can tell, you now own a house in Barnbury Street, the workshop and everything in both. You have money in the bank and a regular income. Not huge, but steady.'

'I'd rather have Mr Clarke,' murmured Mabel.

'Of course you would, love,' said her mother. 'But it's a generous bequest and you must be grateful for that.'

'But is the printing business mine?'

'Well, yes, in theory,' replied Andrew, 'but of course there is no way you can carry it on.'

'Why not?' Mabel spoke more sharply than she had intended and softened the question by saying again, 'Why shouldn't *Thomas Clarke, Printer* continue printing?'

'My dear child—' began her father, but she cut across him.

'I'm not a child, not any more,' she said, 'and I see no reason not to carry on the printing business. We've been building it up over the last six months, and surely Mr Clarke wouldn't want to waste all that progress we've made.'

'But, Mabel, don't you see,' began her mother gently, 'he isn't here to do it with you.'

'No.' Mabel swallowed hard to disperse the growing lump in her throat. 'I know that, Mam, of course I do. That's why I shall have to get on and do it myself.'

'We'll have to set up a meeting with Mr Morrell, once he's back in the office,' Andrew said.

'He's very old,' pointed out Mabel. 'Suppose he doesn't come back to the office, what then?'

'My dear... girl,' Andrew caught himself before he used the word 'child' again, 'let's cross that bridge when we come to it. In the meantime...'

'In the meantime,' Mabel said, getting to her feet, 'I'm going to the workshop to get on with the orders that came in last week. I shan't be anything like as quick as Mr Clarke, so I shall have to work late, but I will get them done, you'll see.'

47

Mabel arrived at the entrance to the alley and paused. She had not been back to the workshop since she had found Mr Clarke. She knew it was secure, because she had locked it herself before going in search of him. Since then, it hadn't seemed right to let herself in again. It was his place and without him there, it would feel as if she were intruding. But now, if that Mr Sheridan was to be believed, it was hers. Slowly she walked to the front door and, taking her key from her pocket, undid the padlock.

Once inside she shut the door behind her and stood in the middle of the room, looking about her. The press stood large and silent, dominating the room as it always had. The cabinet housing type, paper, ink and the other necessities of the business, stood against the wall. One of its drawers was slightly open, as Mabel, in her hurry to deliver Mr Topperly's order, had left it. The kettle was still sitting on the gas ring, her dirty mug was in the sink, everything as she had left it that fateful morning, only a week ago.

The workshop was cold and Mabel switched on the electric fire. As the room began to warm up, she sat down on her stool and took out the letter Mr Sheridan had given her. It seemed right that she should read Mr Clarke's last message to her here, where he had worked for all those years, where they had worked together for the last six months.

With trembling fingers, she slit open the envelope and pulled out the letter, a single sheet, closely written.

My Dearest Mabel, for that's who you are.

If you're reading this, then I have gone to my maker and may not have had a chance to say goodbye. You will have heard from Sheridan, Sheridan and Morrell, my solicitors, that I have left you everything I own. I've known Hugh Morrell for several years and he has handled my affairs honestly and efficiently. For this reason, I have made him my executor and your trustee. He insisted that I set up the trust you've now heard about, afraid you might not use your legacy wisely. I have more faith in you than that, but I thought your father would make an excellent trustee as well, so there'll be a check and balance between the two of them.

You may be surprised at the extent of the bequest, but my only relatives, my wife Emma, and our son George, both died before me, so no one will be left out because of you. Most of the money actually comes from Emma, left to her by her grandmother. It was always hers and I never touched a penny of it. It was she who decided to buy the house in Barnbury Street, so that George would have a home when he came back at the end of the South African war and got married. Sadly he never did and his fiancée is now happily married to somebody else, which is as it should be. Anyway, it is yours now, my dearest girl. You have dreams of building a better life for yourself and your family. The decision on how you spend the money will eventually be entirely yours, but if I may make a suggestion from beyond the grave, perhaps you could now buy Eddie that apprenticeship he had to give up after your father's accident. Both your brothers have stood by your parents, just as you have, so maybe you could think of some way to further Stephen's future, as well?

Dearest Mabel, I leave you my worldly goods, but most of all I leave you my love and my hopes that you will follow your dreams and make them come true.

Yours, Tom Clarke

As Mabel read the letter, and then read it again, tears began to course down her cheeks. She sat in the little workshop, surrounded by everything that was Mr Clarke's, and allowed herself one last burst of weeping before she wiped her eyes, blew her nose and carefully folded the letter back into its envelope.

'I will.' She spoke aloud in the empty room. 'I'll make you proud of me, Mr Clarke, I promise you.'

48

It was a week later that the doorbell rang just as the Oakleys were sitting down to their supper. Mabel got wearily to her feet and went to answer it, and there on the doorstep stood William. He was clearly embarrassed and for a moment seemed lost for words.

'William!' cried Mabel to fill in the silence. 'What a surprise! How lovely to see you! Come in.'

'Mabel, I… I don't know what to say.'

'Then don't say anything,' replied Mabel cheerfully. She really was pleased to see him and reached out her hand to pull him indoors. 'Come in, Will. We've missed you!'

'Have you? Have you really?'

'Course we have,' laughed Mabel. 'You were becoming one of the family.'

William allowed himself to be drawn along the hall and into the kitchen.

'Look who I found on the step, Mam,' cried Mabel.

'Mr William!' exclaimed Alice. 'This is a surprise. Pull up a chair and have some rabbit stew. There's plenty!'

Once the meal was cleared away, Eddie disappeared and Alice wheeled Andrew back to his room to set up the draughts board, leaving Mabel and William at the kitchen table.

'Lizzie was home last weekend,' he began.

'Yeah, I know, I saw her,' said Mabel. 'She and her mum came round for a cuppa on Saturday afternoon.'

'Well, she told me your sad news,' William said awkwardly. ''Bout your friend, Mr Clarke. That he'd died and it was you what found the body.'

'Yes,' replied Mabel quietly. 'That was the most dreadful day.'

'Wish I'd know'd at the time,' William said. 'I could have come then. But course, it was days later that I heard and this is my first free evening.'

Mabel smiled at him. 'Thank you, William, but you know, there was nothing you could have done.'

'I could've been there,' he said. 'As a friend.'

There was a moment's silence and then Mabel asked, 'How is the lucky girl you're walking out with, Will? Won't she miss seeing you on your free evening?'

'No,' answered William. 'No.' He drew a deep breath and then went on, 'There weren't no girl… I made her up.'

Mabel couldn't help laughing at that. 'Made her up! Oh, William, whatever for?'

'Because I'm stupid,' mumbled William.

'Stupid?' echoed Mabel. 'Course you're not stupid.'

'When I saw you with Mr Iain, sitting in the library, talking as equals; I seen the way he looks at you, well, anyone with half a brain can see…'

'Can see what?' prompted Mabel.

'That he… that he is interested in you.'

'Is he now? Well, I'm not interested in him!'

'You came in the car, both of you in the back. Not you in the front, like you was a servant.'

'Well, I'm not a servant, William. I'm a printer.'

'An' you called Mr Felstead just plain "Felstead",' William went on as if he hadn't heard her. 'As if you thought yourself better than him. An' I can tell you, Mabel, he was most put out.'

'If I still worked for the McFarlanes, I'd call him Mr Felstead, as we all did. But I don't and he looks at me down that nose of his as if I was nothing, so why should I respect him?'

'An' then you went home in the car with Mr Iain.'

'So? He said he'd drive me home and he did.'

'Lady M didn't like that either.'

'Will,' Mabel spoke more gently. 'That's her problem, not mine.'

'You ain't like any of the other girls I know,' said William, confused.

'How many others do you know?' asked Mabel with a grin.

'Well, not many, I 'spose,' admitted William, and rallying a little, went on, 'But I wanted to be sure you were all right, what with that Mr Clarke dying and you having no job an'—'

'What do you mean, having no job?' interrupted Mabel. 'I told you, I'm a printer.'

'But you haven't got a printing job no more, not now he's dead. What are you going to do? Not many printers'd give a girl a job. Must be heavy work just using that great press thing.'

'Not once you get the hang of it,' said Mabel. 'Mr Clarke

was a good teacher and I can work the press. I make mistakes and I'm nothing like as quick as he was, but I'm improving.'

'But who's paying you?'

'Don't worry about me, Will. I get paid.' And anxious to change the subject she continued, 'Now, I think Dada should be ready for his game of draughts. Shall we go through to his room?'

She followed William into the front room where they found the draughts board set up, ready. William took his accustomed seat and Mabel perched on the bed to watch the game, but her mind wasn't on it. She was determined that news of her legacy should remain within her immediate family at present.

She had followed Mr Clarke's suggestion and managed to convince Mr Carter that he might take Eddie on as an apprentice after all.

'And here's the money,' she said, and placed the necessary £25 on the table in front of an astonished Mr Carter to seal the agreement.

'But, sis,' argued Eddie, 'Mr Clarke left that money to you.'

'He did,' agreed Mabel, 'and there is plenty of it. It was his idea that I should use a little of it for your apprenticeship premium. So don't worry about it, just become a fantastic carpenter and make beautiful furniture for when we have a bigger house.'

She knew Eddie had no idea just how much her legacy was, but when she insisted he should take up the new offer from old Mr Carter, he flung his arms around her in an entirely uncharacteristic display of affection.

'I won't forget this, sis,' he said gruffly. 'Not ever.'

'It's what families are for,' she said. She said the same words again to her mother when she tried to insist they continue to employ Mrs Finch without Alice having to work for Mr Moses, but this time she did not have her way.

'No, Mabel. I must continue to contribute to the family income. I enjoy the sewing and it allows me to spend time with your father during the day while doing something constructive with my time. Don't worry, we'll still have Mrs Finch. You save your money for a rainy day.'

The wider family were not yet included in the news about Mabel's new-found wealth.

'If they all know, Mam, they'll be telling me what to do and never letting it rest,' she said, when her mother suggested she told her Aunt Jane. 'It's none of their business, is it?'

'They'll have to know eventually,' pointed out her mother. 'They'll find out!'

'I know,' sighed Mabel, 'and when they do, well, we'll deal with it then.'

Not knowing about Mabel's money did not, however, stop the family in general discussing her future.

'That girl should be out earning a proper living,' Aunt Susan said to her husband when she saw Mabel pushing leaflets through letter boxes in their street. 'Frank tells me they don't think she's a thief after all, so she could go back into service and save the drain on her poor parents' resources. Someone should speak to her.'

'Not our business, Susan,' James reminded her gently.

'Well, it should be! Andrew's my brother and I don't like to see a healthy girl of her age living off her parents. A delivery girl indeed! If she's paid at all, it must be a pittance.'

★ ★ ★

'How was poor Mabel?' Lizzie asked William when he returned to Chanynge Place that evening. 'She must be desperately sad that the old man died like that and her finding the body. What's she going to do now he's gone and she's left with no job to go to?'

'She seems to have decided to keep working as a printer,' replied William.

'But can she? I mean, does she know how? She was only a sort of assistant, wasn't she? You know, delivering stuff an' that?'

'She says she's doing all right,' answered William.

'Well, she would, wouldn't she?' said Lizzie. 'That's Mabel, isn't it?'

49

Iain McFarlane got off the train from Cambridge and headed out towards the taxi rank. As he walked through the station, he heard someone call his name. Turning, he found himself face to face with Alfred Everette and his heart sank. He had not seen Alfred since he had gone back up to Cambridge in the autumn.

'McFarlane,' Everette drawled. 'Haven't see you around much. Been avoiding me, have you?'

'Everette! No, of course not.'

'I did call round, but that stuffy butler of yours told me you weren't at home.'

'Well,' replied Iain, 'then I probably wasn't.'

'Oh, but you were. I'd just seen you get out of your gov'nor's car and walk in with that maid. The one that was sacked for stealing? What was her name? Mabel? How are you getting on with her these days?'

'I'm not "getting on with her", as you put it,' said Iain sharply.

'Really? You looked very chummy when I saw you. She prefers the lovesick footman, does she?'

Seeing a confused expression cross Iain's face, Everette

grinned at him. 'Your footman, William. Don't say you didn't know he was your rival for her affections?'

'William?'

Alfred gave a bark of laughter. 'You didn't know, did you? Fancy you, Iain McFarlane, being cast aside for a lowly footman.'

'You're talking complete rubbish, Everette,' snapped Iain. 'And, do you know? I think you always did!'

'She works hard, that girl, I give her that, but she shouldn't be alone in that workshop so often. Specially now the old man's dead. Makes her look fast, a woman trying to run a business on her own. Gives people the wrong idea.'

'You stay away from her,' growled Iain.

'Me? What would I want with her?' Alfred gave an unpleasant laugh. 'I don't want her, a cheap maid, run after by a footman and a fancy boy!'

Without conscious thought, Iain took a swing at his erstwhile friend, wanting to lay him out, but Alfred, ready for such a response, simply ducked away and walked off, laughing, leaving Iain rigid with fury.

His encounter with Everette made him face up to the reality of his feelings for Mabel. He did want Mabel himself, but not just for a secret liaison. The practical side of his brain told him there was absolutely no future with a girl from Mabel's background. Even trying to imagine his mother's reaction if he brought Mabel home as his fiancée was impossible. A maid and, worse still, *her* maid. His father might be less horrified, but his hopes of Iain following him into his Inn of Court would be completely dashed. Iain knew he had to accept the impossibility of any meaningful relationship between them. He knew he was attractive and had always enjoyed teasing the housemaids and making them blush; but Mabel had been different. At first he hadn't recognised the fact, not until she had been sacked for stealing. He remembered the day when Mabel had scuttled from the library to fetch the refreshments he'd asked for, and how disappointed he and Alfred had been when it was William who'd brought in the tray.

For the first time, he thought about William. He had already served the family for several years and was probably about twenty-five. Was he really a rival? He was a nice enough chap, Iain thought now, and probably a good catch for a girl like Mabel, a girl from straitened circumstances, but would he be enough to make her happy?

That evening, as the working day came to its end, Iain loitered on the street corner outside the Cockerel. When Mabel arrived on her bicycle, skidding round the corner into Cockspur Lane, he stepped off the pavement, nearly knocking her flying. She slammed her foot down on the pavement to avoid falling and turned on him in fury.

'Iain McFarlane, what on earth do you think you're doing, jumping out at me like that! You nearly knocked me off!'

'I'm sorry, Mabel,' he said, 'but I need to speak to you.'

'Well, I don't want to speak to you,' she retorted.

'I know,' he said with a wry smile. 'You did mention that before.'

'Then I wish you'd listen!'

'And I wish you'd listen,' Iain said. 'I've something important to say to you and I really need you to listen.'

'What?' demanded Mabel. 'What's so important?'

'Can we go indoors?' Iain asked quietly. 'I can't explain on the street corner.'

'Well, you're going to have to, because you're not coming into our house ever again.'

'All right,' Iain sighed. 'You probably won't remember a friend of mine who used to come to the house, a small bloke with orange hair.'

'Yeah, I remember. Had tufty ginger hair. Carrot-top, we used to call him below stairs.'

'That's him. Well, I think he's been watching you.'

'Watching me? Why on earth would he do that?'

'I don't know, not for sure, but you need to be careful.'

'You're talking nonsense,' Mabel told him. 'Just go away!' And hoisting herself back onto her bike, she pedalled off down the lane.

'Mabel! Please!'

But she was at the house, and getting off her bike she pushed it in through the front door.

'See,' said a familiar voice behind him. 'She won't listen to you!'

Iain spun round to find Alfred standing in the pub doorway. He had heard every word of their exchange.

50

After his encounter with Mabel and then Alfred, Iain realised Alfred was right. Mabel wouldn't listen to him. But who would she listen to? She needed protection, but he couldn't protect her, not all the time. He would have to take the initiative and deal with Alfred once and for all. But how? He couldn't do it on his own. He was pretty sure he could get the better of Alfred physically, but that might not be enough. If there were two of them, perhaps between them they could put the fear of God into the little creep, and coward that Alfred was, it would be enough to ensure that he never went near Mabel again. But who could he ask for help?

Of course the answer was obvious, it had to be William, but how could he enlist his help without disclosing his own feelings? And yet they were both fit young men, both physically bigger and stronger than Alfred. Surely, between them, they could teach him a lesson he wouldn't forget in a hurry. Much as Iain loathed the idea, if it were the only way he could get William to help him deal with Alfred, he realised that he was going to have to admit how he felt about Mabel to his footman... his rival, William.

Lying in bed that night he tossed and turned, but gradually came to the conclusion that he had to speak to William and see if, together, they could come up with a plan to fix Alfred Everette once and for all. It was only in the small hours that he finally fell into a fitful sleep, but he still awoke early, unrested and tense.

He joined the family for breakfast and then asked, as casually as he could, 'All right if I borrow William for the day, Gov'nor? I've got a few things to see to while I'm home and it would be helpful to have William on hand.'

'Provided your mother doesn't need him,' Sir Keir answered, 'he's all yours. I'm straight off to court.'

'Well,' said Lady McFarlane, 'I suppose I don't need him today.' She took a slice of toast and rang the bell. 'Fresh coffee please, William. This pot has gone cold.'

When Iain had finished his breakfast he too rang the bell, and when William answered its summons, Iain said, 'I need a word with you, William. My father is going straight out, so perhaps you'd join me in the library in about ten minutes.'

William's 'Yes sir,' was abrupt, his expression completely flat.

Ten minutes later there was a tap on the library door.

'Come in, William,' Iain said. 'Sit down, please, we need to talk.'

'I prefer standing,' responded William.

Iain could feel a tide of resentment flowing from him and decided not to push it. 'Fine,' he said. 'However you're more comfortable.'

For a long moment neither man spoke and then Iain, knowing it was up to him to start the conversation, said, 'I want to talk to you about Mabel Oakley.'

That got a reaction anyway, Iain thought, as he saw William stiffen.

'I believe you and she are walking out,' Iain said.

'If that's any business of yours,' replied William, adding a very belated, 'sir.'

'It isn't,' answered Iain smoothly. 'But her welfare is.'

'What has her welfare got to do with you?' demanded William, casting all deference to the winds. 'You sacked her for something she didn't do. You could've spoke up for her then, if you'd had a mind to, but no, you let her be dismissed. So her welfare ain't nothing to do with you no more.'

'You're entitled to that opinion,' replied Iain, 'but if you'll just hear me out, I think you'll see we both need to be concerned right now.'

'Oh yeah? An' why's that... sir?'

'Because I think she's in danger,' replied Iain, ignoring William's rudeness.

'She ain't in danger if *you* ain't nowhere near her,' snapped William.

'I promise you, William, she has nothing to fear from me, but even so, she could be in danger from someone else.'

'Who?' The question was less aggressive and for the first time Iain sensed he was actually getting through.

'You remember I had a friend called Everette?'

'Carrot-top,' said William with a sniff. 'Small, ferrety little bloke.'

'That's him. Well, he took a shine to Mabel while she was with us, and I have to admit at the time I didn't discourage him...' Iain's voice tailed off.

William said, 'And what's he got to do with Mabel now?'

Iain took a deep breath. 'He's been following her.'

'Following her?'

'Yes. He's found out where she lives and where she works.'

'And what's that to you?'

'The thing is, William... the thing is, I've come to love Mabel.' There, he'd said it.

William stared at him in astonishment. He'd always assumed that Iain's interest in Mabel was transitory: conquer and move on.

'Your mother's maid?' he said in disbelief.

'Not my mother's maid, no. Just Mabel. I've always admired her, not just because she's beautiful, which I'm sure you agree she is, but because she's different from any other girl I've ever met. She's strong and determined and believes in herself. But, though I wish it were different, you don't have to worry. She's made it very plain that she doesn't want me and I have to accept that we have no future together.'

There was another silence while William took in this last remark and then he asked, 'So what about this Everette bloke following her about?'

'I tried to warn her last night as soon as I realised what Everette's been doing. I went round to Cockspur Lane and stopped her on her way home, but she wouldn't listen. And he was already there.'

'What, Everette?'

'Yes. He was watching her from the pub yard and heard our exchange. He knows she doesn't believe me and so she won't be on her guard.'

'We need to warn her.' There was a note of panic in William's voice.

'We can try, or rather you can.' Iain gave a wry smile. 'She'll certainly take more notice of you.'

'She may not,' said William gloomily. 'She thinks she can look after herself!'

'You can at least try,' urged Iain. 'Who does she work for?'

'No one, not now,' replied William. 'He died, the printer she was working for.'

'So she hasn't got a job?'

'She's still doing the same one, but she works for herself now.'

Iain shook his head in disbelief. 'She really is some girl!' he said.

'The thing is, she'll be riding home on her own,' said William. 'S'pose he's lying in wait somewhere on the way!'

'She may think she's riding home alone, but with two of us we can watch out for her and if he comes anywhere near her, then we can deal with him.'

'Deal with him? How?' asked William.

'He's a bully, and like most bullies he's a coward too. We're going to scare the living daylights out of him. Are you up for that?'

William looked across at Iain. Who'd have believed it? he thought. Me an' fancy boy on the same side!

'And if there's any trouble after,' Iain promised, 'I'll take care of it. You were just following my orders!'

'Doubt if the rozzers would agree to that,' said William, and for the first time he grinned and said, 'You're on. Let's get the bastard!'

'Right,' said Iain. 'Better make a plan. Any ideas?'

51

Mabel was pleased with her morning's work. She had completed an order for some calling cards. It had been more time consuming than she had expected, but once she had the form set up and had drawn off several copies to ensure they were perfect, she got into her rhythm and the run went smoothly enough. She had brought a sandwich with her for her lunch and so she put the kettle on and sat down in Mr Clarke's chair to drink her tea. She always sat in his chair now, partly because she felt closer to him when she did and partly because she couldn't bear to sit and look at the empty chair. She finished her tea and decided she had time for another before she wrapped the cards and set out to deliver them. As she poured herself a second cup from the little brown pot, the door opened and a man came in.

'Miss Oakley, Mabel,' he said with a smile as he closed the door firmly behind him, 'how lovely to renew your acquaintance.'

For a split second, Mabel couldn't place him, but as he removed his hat with a gentlemanly flourish, she saw his ginger hair and knew at once who he was. Carrot-top! Iain had tried to warn her and she'd ignored him.

'Good afternoon, sir,' she said, her brain racing, wondering if she could get past him to the door. Pretend you don't know who he is! she thought. Pretend you think he's a client and try to get to the door. 'How can I help you?' She edged forward, but Alfred was squarely in the way. Seeing her intention, Alfred reached back and turned the snib on the catch so the door couldn't be opened from outside. They were locked in.

'Hey!' cried Mabel, really frightened now. 'What are you doing?'

'You very kindly asked if you could help me and you can, but I don't want us to be interrupted.' He took a step towards her, and though he wasn't a tall man, he was taller than she. She backed away, but Thomas Clarke's armchair was behind her and, catching the backs of her knees, tipped her onto its seat.

Immediately, she tried to get back to her feet, but Everette was on her at once, holding her easily enough with his weight and one hand firmly across her throat. With his other hand, he pulled at her blouse so it came free of her skirt.

Mabel was not going to give in easily and she fought back, kicking out with her legs, trying to escape, but she was squashed into the chair with her arms held down and her flailing was to no avail.

'Feisty little thing, aren't you?' Everette gloated. 'Always thought it would be fun to take you on. I like a bit of a struggle myself, makes things more interesting.' Still keeping Mabel pinned down, he pulled at the buttons on the waistband of her skirt and as they came free, he slid his hand downwards, tugging at the cotton of her chemise so that it rucked up and gave him access to her bloomers.

Mabel struggled and spat and for a moment he released her neck and slapped her backhanded across her cheek.

'Behave now, missy,' he scolded, and sitting astride her to keep her pinned down, he opened her blouse to expose her small breasts. Mabel continued to struggle, but even as she did, she realised that this was making him more excited and more violent. She managed to get one hand free and tried in vain to push him off, but without some sort of weapon she knew he was too strong for her. She tried to scream, but after one piercing shriek he stuffed his handkerchief into her mouth and laughed.

Below them, with a roar and a cloud of smoke, an express train thundered non-stop through the station, drowning any noise she might make.

'Waste of time, screaming,' he crowed as he squeezed her breast. 'No one can hear you from the outside.' He leant forward, rubbing himself against her. 'Be nice to me, Mabel,' he whispered, 'and you might even find you like what I'm going to do. You'll see what it's like with a *real* man, not a sap like your William or a fancy boy like McFarlane. I bet he couldn't have got it up with you if he tried. But he didn't even try, did he? Not really. And now it's my turn.' For a moment his weight came off her as he wrestled with his fly buttons and she took her chance. Reaching one arm behind her she snatched the kettle from the gas ring and swung it hard, catching him on his shoulder. The water, so recently boiled for her tea, exploded against his neck, causing him to scream with pain. He fell backwards, scrabbling at his face in an effort to sweep away the pain, but Mabel hadn't finished yet. She swung the kettle again, hitting the side of his head, and the last drops of scalding water flew through the air, spattering his hands and hair. He screamed again and collapsed on the floor.

At that moment there was a pounding on the door and shouts from outside. Alfred had been wrong – when there were no passing trains, screams could be heard from the outside. Someone had heard screams – hers or Alfred's she didn't know or care – but whoever it was outside had come to find out who was screaming and why.

Calling for help, Mabel pulled herself clear of the creature now moaning on the floor, but before she could get to the door, it exploded inwards as the combined weight of William and Iain broke the catch and burst it open. Albert Flood was waddling down the alley behind them, but by the time he got there, Mabel was in William's arms and Iain was removing his tie and binding the hapless Alfred's hands tightly together.

'Mabel! Oh Mabel!' William cried. 'Are you all right? He didn't hurt you, did he?'

'No!' she growled. 'I hurt him!' For a moment she clung to William and then, suddenly realising she was hardly decent, she pushed him away. 'Let me go, idiot.'

Reluctantly, William loosened his hold and Mabel made a grab for her new red coat that still hung on the back of the door. A small crowd was beginning to gather outside, wondering what the commotion was all about.

As soon as he realised what had happened, Albert hurried back to the street in search of a policeman. He'd always liked that little Mabel Oakley, but today he was in awe of her. How had she fought off the brute who'd cornered her in the printery? As he emerged onto the main road he saw the beat copper, PC Darke, approaching in his usual, leisurely fashion towards Albert's kiosk where he normally stopped for a brew of tea. Albert shouted at him and frantically waved his arms and at once the constable quickened his pace.

'Quick, Constable, there's a girl been assaulted down there.'

Darke wasted no time. With Albert trying to keep up, he set off down to Mr Clarke's workshop.

When he saw Mabel, her disordered clothes only partly covered by her overcoat, it was clear what had been going on.

As soon as Iain had restrained Everette, he'd fetched a bucket of cold water and tipped it over Alfred's head, hoping to cool his burns. Ten minutes later Alfred Everette was being led away in handcuffs, still whimpering with pain.

'Stop that caterwaulin',' Darke instructed. 'The police doctor'll see you once we've got you back to the station.'

Now she was safe, Mabel found she was shaking. She sat down in Tom's chair and dashed angry tears from her eyes. William knelt beside the chair, holding her hands.

'It's all right, Mabel,' he said soothingly. 'You're safe now and he'll never hurt you again, I promise.' He looked round to say to Iain, 'She didn't need us, you know...' But Iain had disappeared. Mabel was safe. She'd always said she could look after herself, and she had.

'Come on,' William said. 'Let's get you home. You've had an awful shock. You need to go to bed and rest.'

Mabel looked up into his dear, familiar face, a mask of concern as he helped her out of the chair.

'I'm all right, Will, really I am. I'm supposed to deliver

these cards this afternoon.' As she went to the bench to pick them up she gave a cry of dismay.

'Oh look, I spent hours on them this morning and now they're ruined and I'll have to do them again!'

William looked at the cards and saw that several of them were damp, spoiled by the water from the kettle.

'It ain't all of them, love,' he said. 'You can explain there was an accident an' you'll print some more very soon.'

They secured the workshop with the outside padlock and, as they walked home, with William wheeling Mabel's bike, she suddenly asked, 'What was Iain McFarlane doing here with you?'

'He came to warn me Everette was following you. We thought the two of us together might scare him off.' William gave a choking laugh. 'But I reckon you've done a first rate job of that for yourself!'

'He tried to warn me last night,' Mabel said in a small voice, 'Iain did, but I didn't listen to him.'

'No,' William said ruefully, 'but then, I think you don't listen to a lot of people. That's the trouble with you, Mabel. You're too independent for your own good.' An opinion repeated almost word for word by her mother when they got back to Cockspur Lane.

She and Andrew were given a sanitised account of Everette's attack at the printshop. Mabel was determined not to let them hear how close he'd been to succeeding. William, too, had finally been convinced that, apart from the deepening bruises on her neck and her cheek, Mabel had suffered no actual harm. She was determined she would never reveal to a living soul the terror she'd felt. She had survived, intact, and she'd done that by herself.

'It could have been so much worse, Mabel,' William murmured when they stood at the front door saying goodnight. 'If Mr Iain hadn't warned—'

'Yes, William, I know. But he did and both of you came to the rescue. I'm safe. Now you must go back to Chanynge Place, or you'll be missed.'

'I'll come and see you again tomorrow evening,' William promised.

'Will you be allowed to?'

'I think it can be organised,' he replied. He bent his head and kissed her lightly on the cheek. 'See you tomorrow evening.'

'You're too independent for your own good,' her mother said again when he'd gone. 'You need someone like William to look after you, Mabel. He's a steady lad, and you must learn to listen to people who are older and wiser than you; take advice when it's offered.'

'I know,' sighed Mabel, ' and I will, I promise, but it won't stop me from making my own decisions.'

'No, I'm sure it won't,' Alice said wryly. 'Now up to bed with you and tomorrow you must have an easy day to get over the shock.'

'I'm going up now,' Mabel said, 'but I shall go back to the workshop tomorrow, clear up the mess. And I've got to complete the spoiled order.'

'Oh, Mabel, really!' Alice exclaimed in exasperation. 'Surely one day won't hurt!'

'Sorry, Mam,' Mabel replied as she reached over to kiss her mother goodnight, 'but I've got a business to run.'

Although she was exhausted, it took a long while for Mabel to fall asleep. Her mind kept returning to her encounter with Alfred Everette. Unwanted flashes of memory: his leering grin, his vice-like grip on her neck, his questing hand around her breasts. Perhaps Mam was right. She should stay at home tomorrow and have a quiet day. She would decide in the morning.

When she awoke to find the sun streaming in through her bedroom window, she felt more hopeful. She would not let that beast stop her going back to Mr Clarke's workshop.

If I don't go back today, she thought, I might never go back.

As she pedalled past Albert's kiosk, he waved to her, staring in amazement. 'You're not going to go in to work today, are you, Miss Mabel?'

'Got to, Mr Flood. Orders to fill,' Mabel replied.

'Well, you're some girl, Mabel Oakley, that I will say.'

'Thanks for coming to help yesterday,' she said, 'and for getting the policeman.'

'Least I could do,' muttered Albert, his face turning bright red as she leant over and kissed his cheek. For a moment he watched as she began to wheel her bicycle along to the printshop. 'Some girl,' he repeated to himself. 'Old Tom would be proud as punch!'

Reaching the workshop, Mabel paused outside, looking carefully in both directions before she opened the padlock and let herself in. Pulling the door closed, she stood in the middle of the small room and surveyed her surroundings. The room looked as it always had, but she knew it wasn't the same; in some subtle way it was different. Alfred Everette had spoiled the place for her and she knew she would never be quite comfortable working here again.

She'd had an idea of what she might do, now she had her

legacy, but she had known it was early days yet. She would think further on her idea before she broached the subject with anyone else.

'Pull yourself together, Mabel,' she said to the empty room. 'You've an order to finish and deliver.'

Looking at the damp, spoiled cards, Mabel wondered for a moment how bad Alfred Everette's burns had really been.

'Serves you right!' she told him fiercely; but she knew she'd been lucky not to scald herself at the same time.

The press was still set up to print yesterday's cards and she soon replaced the water-damaged ones. Finished and packed in their brown paper wrapper, she set out on her bicycle to make her delivery. As she was riding back to the workshop, she found she was thinking about Iain McFarlane. It was he who had warned William and come to her aid. She was not normally one to bear a grudge and she had, she realised now, been unfair to him. He had been trying to protect her. So, to ease her conscience, that evening before she went home, she sat down and wrote him a short note.

Dear Mr McFarlane

Thank you for coming to warn me about Carrot-top. I'm sorry I didn't believe you. You were only trying to help. William says if you hadn't talked him into coming with you to find me, it might have ended up quite differently. I'm sorry I was so rude to you. Good luck with your exams.

Yours faithfully
Mabel Oakley

She addressed it to him at 11 Chanynge Place and dropped it into a pillar box on her way home to Cockspur Lane... and William.

Epilogue

June 1913

All three of them had been called as witnesses at Alfred Everette's trial but found they didn't have to give evidence after all. Everette had changed his plea to guilty of attempted rape and the judge had sentenced him to prison for six years.

'Nothing like enough,' muttered William when it was announced.

'It's because I was working alone,' said Mabel. 'The judge thinks it was partly my fault for setting myself up in a man's job. A woman alone in the world is considered fair game.'

'But you aren't alone in the world,' William said hotly. 'You've got us!'

'Yes, I have, and all my family, but I'm trespassing in men's domain, and they don't like it. The judge, the jury, the lawyers all believe I was the author of my own misfortune; that I should be doing the housework or cooking the dinner at home, or in someone else's home as a servant. Either way, living at someone else's bidding.'

'That's something you'll never do,' Iain said quietly. 'Live at someone else's bidding.'

Mabel smiled at him. 'No,' she agreed, 'you're right.'

When they left the court building they paused on the pavement outside.

'Croxton's waiting with the car,' Iain said. 'Would you like me to drive you home, Mabel?'

'No thank you, Iain,' said Mabel. 'Sir Keir has given Will the rest of the day off, so we'll take the bus.'

Croxton appeared with the car and, before he got in, Iain shook hands with both of them. 'Good luck,' he said, 'to both of you.'

Together they watched the Rolls disappear round a corner and then Mabel grabbed William by the hand. 'Come on, Will. Time to catch our bus. We've got some deliveries to make.'

Acknowledgements

As always, I must thank my editor, Rosie de Courcy, and all at Head of Zeus, for the unstinting time and effort they have put into the birth and production of this book. Always there when needed, always encouraging, and always ready to guide me back to the straight and narrow when I wandered off-piste.

So, thank you, Rosie, and all your team for your hard work on my behalf.

Similarly, I owe my agent, Judith Murdoch, my profound thanks for her faith in me and for all the support she has given, and continues to give. From the first inkling of an idea, through to the last page, Judith is there as a sounding board, offering confidence and reassurance.

So, many thanks, Judith, for all you do. It's much appreciated.

Thanks, too, to my go-to Medicine Man, Dr George Papworth. This is not the first time he has, with great patience, helped me out with all things medical. Thank you George.

Finally, last but certainly not least, my family: my husband Peter, my son Jeremy and my daughters Anthea and Helen.

With Covid and lockdowns and all the various restrictions, this last year has not been easy for anyone, anywhere, and we were no exception. But knowing I had you all behind me providing physical, mental and emotional support, was the encouragement I needed to write and continue to write, until I had finished the book.

Thank you, all of you, I couldn't have done it without you.

About the Author

DINEY COSTELOE is the author of 24 novels, several short stories, and many articles and poems. She has three children and seven grandchildren, so when she isn't writing, she's busy with family. She and her husband divide their time between Somerset and West Cork.